Joy Dettman was born in Echuca in Victoria and now lives in Melbourne. It was a creative writing course in 1988 which helped to turn a lifelong interest into an obsession.

Joy, a mother of four, is a full-time writer and published author of several award-winning stories. She now teaches creative writing at a community centre.

Also by Joy Dettman

Jacaranda Blue
Goose Girl

mallawindy

Joy Dettman

PAN

Pan Macmillan Australia

First published 1998 in Macmillan by Pan Macmillan Australia Pty Limited
First published 1999 in Pan by Pan Macmillan Australia Pty Limited
St Martins Tower, 31 Market Street, Sydney

Reprinted 1999 (twice), 2001

National Library of Australia
cataloguing-in-publication data:

Dettman, Joy.
Mallawindy.

ISBN 0 330 36146 5.

I. Title.

A823.3

This is a work of fiction and all characters in this book are a creation
of the author's imagination.

Printed in Australia by McPherson's Printing Group

For Cheryl,
who at the age of three became hooked on 'Once upon a time',
and who, three decades on, read this tale and demanded
a second and a third and a sixth telling.
I now give you Mallawindy *to hold in your hand.*

the birth

~

'Take the little ones around to Grandpa. Do as I tell you, Johnny.'
The words were spoken low, but the river picked them up, ampli-
fied them, carried them. Pain, mind consuming pain was controlling
Ellie Burton, making her careless. She moaned, grasped her
stomach, trying to still the unborn one with her will.

Johnny stepped away, his interest centred on the house. Only
one small light was visible at the kitchen window. Too feeble, it
couldn't compete with the full moon.

'For the love of God, will you obey me? Take Liza, and go to
Grandpa.'

'I'm not leaving you, Mum,' Johnny said.

He was her first born, and too old for his eight years. He'd
seen too much; he knew too much. He told her to run when he
saw the car slam to a halt against the fence. She should have
listened to him. Jack had been to his father's funeral at Narrawee.
It was five hundred miles south, in Victoria, with many hotels on
the long road home. Johnny knew. He could read Jack like a
book.

'Fool,' she whispered. 'I'm a fool.'

Her father called her a fool. He wanted her and the children
home, safe with him, but Ellie had made her vows in the church,

1

before God and half the town. She couldn't leave Jack, couldn't admit her marriage was a failure. Couldn't, or wouldn't.

Liza whimpered. Ellie's hand felt for the dangling dummy. She snatched it up, silencing the cry. Not yet eleven months, Liza was too young to be replaced at the breast by the one now fighting free of her womb. 'Shush,' she whispered. 'Hush, bubby. It's going to be all right.'

The house was a long paddock away, but she could hear him breaking up the kitchen, cursing his brother and father to hell. He'd wear himself out, fall down, and sleep where he fell. Ellie knew Jack's habits well. She only prayed he might fall down soon.

How long since the last pain? Time had slipped out of focus. She waited, counting seconds. This baby had been ill conceived – and too soon after Liza. From the first weeks it had been a difficult pregnancy. She almost lost it at three months, then again at five. It wasn't destined to live.

A door slammed. She turned to the house, her eyes scanning as she counted – seventy-five seconds of silence, broken only by a lone cricket chirping, the bull frogs courting, the muttering of a broody hen.

It was over. Ellie sighed, and pulled herself up to her knees.

Then a shotgun blast echoed and re-echoed along the banks of the river, and cold fear travelled through Ellie to meet head-on the contraction of her womb. The birth was close. Ready or not, this baby would be born. She crouched over the earth, Liza crushed against her.

'Mummy.' Five-year-old Ben leaned into her. 'Mummy. What did he do?'

'Leave her alone, Benjie,' Johnny said. 'You know he didn't do anything.'

They waited, crouched together – waited for the new silence to end.

It was Jack's ploy to bring her and the children out of hiding.

Ellie knew it, as Johnny did, but she was afraid of guns. She had told Jack tonight that she didn't want the gun in the house. It was the wrong thing to say. The gun had belonged to Jack's father; and it was all the old man had left him – that and the car.

To my first born, John William [Jack], I leave the Ford, my double-barrel shotgun and five hundred a year to buy ammunition and petrol, and may he use his inheritance well.

A hard, unforgiving old man, Ellie thought. She'd only met her father-in-law once. He didn't like her; didn't consider her good enough for Narrawee, and he'd taken no interest in Johnny. Poor Jack. What a father. What a family he came from. Who could blame him for what he was? She couldn't.

Yesterday he'd left with so much hope. They'd be selling up and moving to Narrawee, he'd said. They'd be going home. But his brother, Sam, had got the lot, the house, property, money, and the old man's blessing.

'Do you want me to creep back and have a look for you, Mum? I'll be really careful.'

'No! Daddy was just shooting at that old fox that's been getting my chickens.'

'I hope he got him,' Johnny said, his smile, a wry thing, shown to the moon.

The second blast was closer. They heard the scattering of shot fall to the chicken-house roof.

'Stay down.' Ellie's hand was ready to muffle Liza's cry.

'Aunty Bessy might hear it, Mummy. She might get Grandpa to come,' Ben said.

'Be still, Benjie.'

But pain would not be still. It made no concession to guns. Pain returned in red waves that grew until she was drowning in it. She rocked against the willow roots, trying to breathe under pain, think her way over it.

'Oh, God. Oh God. Oh God,' she panted between clenched teeth. 'Oh God. Oh God.' Head back, eyes wide, Ellie saw no trailing branches, saw no sky. Pain had her now. She let it take her, take her mind.

For a hundred years the willow tree had grown deep in the water, its lower branches forming their own roots as they spread out from the main trunk, so the tree had become a small forest of willows. After a dry winter and spring, the river was low, exposing large masses of fibrous roots, sculpted by the years into thick carpeted caves and hollows. There were worse places to give birth.

Slowly the pain backed away. Ellie gasped air, readying herself for the next assault. She'd have to push the baby out, or they'd both die of it. Her sister, Bessy, was a stone's throw away, just over the other side of the river; her father's house was not much further. They'd hear the gunshot, but would they recognise it? They didn't know Jack had the gun.

He didn't mean to hit me, she thought. He never meant to hurt me. He didn't know what he was doing when he'd been on the whisky. He hit, kicked out at a world that refused him his due. I just got in the way. He loves me.

Her hair hung loose to her waist. Jack loved her to wear her hair down; he called it a spill of sunshine, but Ben was leaning on it, pulling it, and the greater pain gone for the moment, Ellie became aware of the lesser pain. She tugged her hair free, coiled and knotted it high.

Pain hit. It smashed with sledgehammer blows into her spine. Small hands clutching, Liza whimpering, but Ellie was withdrawing into self, separating self. No more time now. No more time. A hush settled over her land as her limbs positioned themselves for delivery, and with the next contraction she thrust Liza from her and she pushed.

Johnny understood now. He carried Liza to a hollow, close to the large central trunk of the willow, he placed the dangling dummy in her mouth and left her there. She was barely crawling; she wouldn't climb out. Ben, he led by the hand downstream to clear water.

4

'You have to swim over to Aunty Bessy and tell her that Mum's baby is coming out. Tell her Dad's home from the funeral, that he's got a gun and he's drunk, and she has to get Grandpa.'

'The water is too dark, Johnny.'

'Then run around to the bridge. It's not far. Run as fast as you can. I bet you can be there by the time I count five hundred.'

'I'm scared of the bridge in the dark time. There might be a bad man under it.' Ben clung to his brother, but Johnny pushed him away. Tonight there was only one bad man in Mallawindy.

'You have to do it, Benjie,' he said. He drew his brother into the water, pointing to the bright light from Aunty Bessy's kitchen window, the river's breadth away. 'It's only a little way. You've swum over there hundreds of times before. See how big their light looks. It looks even bigger than ours. Go on, Benjie. I can't leave Mum and Liza here by themselves.'

Ben stepped deeper into the slow, running water. 'Do fishes bite sometimes?'

'It's night time. They're all sound asleep on the bottom. Swim. And don't cry. You'll start coughing.' The smaller boy stepped deeper. 'You can do it, Benjie. And turn on the back verandah light when you get there. Turn it on and off two times so we know you got there.' With the river at their doorstep, the brothers swam before they walked. Ellie had seen to that.

Johnny followed the progress of the darker shape cutting through moonlit water. He counted to sixty white elephants, then began again. He needed no flashed signal; the river was narrow at this point. He saw Ben scramble up the opposite bank, saw him run, then he heard Aunty Bessy's dog bark as the verandah light blinked once, twice. Only then did he return to Ellie's side.

A farm boy, he had seen many new calves born, but the thing Ellie drew from beneath her skirt was no well-grown calf. Silently he stood beside her until it was done, until she decided it was dead, made the sign of the cross, and on her knees, crawled away from it.

'What's wrong with it, Mum?'

'It's not breathing, love. Bring Liza here to me,' Ellie sobbed.

Johnny wasn't into tears. 'He killed it, and it hasn't even got its name yet. It won't even go to heaven, will it, Mum? I hate him. I hate him so bad, Mum.'

'You mustn't say hate. Bring Liza to me, then take your shirt off and cover it over.'

Johnny squatted beside the new thing; he touched its warm head, its tiny hands, its legs. 'Can I cut its cord off that stuff, Mum?'

'Cover it, Johnny, then come away.'

'If we cut it off, it might come alive.'

'It's dead. It's dead, Johnny!'

'Grandpa pulled out a dead calf once and he made it come alive. He didn't just give up, Mum.'

'It's no use. It was born too early – .' Liza's wail cut her words short. Ellie struggled to her feet and walked to the living child, leaving Johnny kneeling over the dead baby.

He knew that a task commenced must be completed. Grandpa never gave up on anything. Johnny's hand reached for his pocket and the small pocketknife Grandpa had given him for his birthday last week. From the depths of his other pocket he took a cluster of rubber bands. Grandpa saved rubber bands, so he did too.

The umbilical cord felt like the warm insides of a fresh gutted rabbit. Frowning with concentration, he made a loop with the cord, then twisted a rubber band four times around it. An extra twist for good measure, then with his knife, he cut the baby free.

It was a girl. His mother had said she was going to call it Ann Elizabeth if it was a girl. Perhaps if he gave it a name, God might let it into heaven, he thought. Hands wiped clean on the seat of his pants, he slid them beneath the baby. To Johnny, she looked as if she was sleeping. Again he thought of the dead calf dragged from the cow with a rope. He'd watched Grandpa grasp the calf by its back legs that day, and swing it around in a full circle. The calf bawled, and lived. 'Nothing ventured, nothing gained, lad,'

Grandpa always said.

Taking one small leg in each hand, he up-ended the baby, and turned in a slow circle, afraid of his daring.

There was no bleat of life.

He shrugged, licked his lips, then swallowed hard. 'Nothing ventured, nothing gained ... please, God,' he said. One bare heel for a pivot, he spun around the second time and the plaintive kitten mew sounded loud to his ears. Wide-eyed, he froze, his left hand almost losing its grasp on a stick-thin limb.

'Mum. Mum. I think she's come alive!' he whispered.

There was no reply.

Supporting the slippery being against his knee, he gathered it up to his arms, open mouthed, overawed by the miracle of her cry. He righted her, and she moved, repeated the weak mew.

No more fear of the man or the gun now. He ran to the central trunk of the willow, knowing just how God must have felt after making Adam from the dust.

'Mum? She's alive.' His mother and Liza were gone. 'Mum. Where are you? She's come alive.'

Ellie's scream came from the wrong direction. Johnny turned, saw her running, stumbling towards the house, Liza in her arms.

'No, Jack! Not the house. No. For the love of God, don't let the house burn.'

Johnny saw what she could see. The light from the kitchen was no longer a feeble thing. The curtains were burning.

Run. Get water, his brain demanded, but within that thought came another. He had made a dead baby live. Its little head was nodding against him, its little arm was moving. There was no decision to be made here. He turned his back on the house, and on his parents' game, and with one finger he touched the tiny face.

'You stay alive, little Annie Lizabeth,' he whispered. 'Johnny's got you, and Grandpa will be here soon. He'll put the fire out. He'll fix things up.' The baby held safe against his chest, Johnny Burton made his way towards the river road, and to headlights of a car now visible between the trees.

ellie's world

~

December 1969

Only nine-thirty and already the sun was a blast furnace in the sky, sucking the morning dry. Ellie wiped a wrist across her brow and it came away wet.

Too hot for ironing, but Jack's shirts had to be done. 'Three down, six to go,' she said to the toddler playing at her feet. 'Pass Mummy up another white one, Bronwyn.'

She worked efficiently, with no excess movement. The offered shirt taken, shaken, spread, her iron hissed and creases disappeared. Back, fronts, sleeves, cuffs, yoke and collar, and the shirt was draped with its mates over the back of a chair. One more and she'd be past the halfway mark.

She needed music or conversation when she ironed, but Jack was still sleeping, so the kitchen was silent. Her gaze wandered from the shirt to the back verandah where Annie was smashing mud nests, releasing the paralysed spiders placed there as host for the big hornet's egg. She was always at it, always getting stung.

Ellie shuddered. She couldn't do a thing with that girl, nor could the nuns at the deaf school. They'd sent her home after only three weeks. What was she supposed to do with her now? God can be cruel sometimes, she thought. It was as if Johnny had thwarted his plans on the night of the fire, but he was a determined God. It was obvious that Annie had not been meant to live out a normal life.

They'd saved all bar the kitchen that night. The boys' bedroom wall was scorched, but the lounge and third bedroom at the front of the house were saved by the passage. Paint and wallpaper had covered the smoke damage. It was a comfortable house, with wide verandahs, front and back. The kitchen's rough replacement spoiled it. The lining had never been put in, its cupboards were makeshift, but the little stove had survived, and the brick chimney. Ellie turned to the stove now, plied it with wood. Jack would be wanting his breakfast soon.

She was taller than average. Hard work kept her slim. Her eyes were green. Emeralds, Jack used to call them. Green fire. She was proud of her eyes, and her rich gold hair, worn plaited this morning and pinned high. At thirty-four, Ellie was still a beauty, but her complexion was fair. Mallawindy's harsh sun had already pencilled in its sad little roads around her eyes and the corners of her mouth.

She had known too much heartache in the past three years. Liza lost at seven – not knowing if she were dead or alive. And Johnny. He was on her mind this morning. He'd be seventeen today. It was fourteen months since he'd left home, and he'd never written, even though he'd promised to, care of Bessy. Seventeen was too young to be out in the world alone, she thought. Dear Johnny. She'd been seventeen when he was born. Just a baby, with a baby.

Her gaze turned to the pram, to her last born, tiny Linda, sleeping beneath mosquito net, tied down with elastic. It was the only way to keep the insects away from her. No matter what she did, no matter how often she sprayed, flies and mosquitoes used her kitchen as a thoroughfare.

Ellie's breasts were milk-full. Milk leaked, and perspiration trickled. Her blouse was ringing wet. She rested the iron on its heel and walked to the pram, peering beneath the net. 'Wake up, Linda Alice,' she said. 'Daddy will be wanting his breakfast soon, so you'd better wake up and have yours.' Linda was going to be fair, like Liza. Ellie hoped she might take Liza's place in Jack's heart. He'd never got over losing her. Nor had she. Still, Ellie had little time to dwell on yesterdays – except when she was ironing and her mind free to roam.

It was the not knowing where she was that was bad, Ellie thought. At least with the death of a child, there is a grave, and a service, the mourning, then the putting away of sadness, but to have a child stolen – . She shuddered, drew her mind away from Liza.

Ben was her mainstay. Busy packing eggs, he was wiping the stained ones with a damp cloth – more particular than she. 'How many did we get today, love?'

'Forty-three,' the youth replied, not looking up from his task. He had the build of a twelve-year-old, but he'd turn fourteen in March.

'Hardly enough for the orders. It's this heat,' Ellie sighed.

'They said on the news last night that we might get a change Tuesday.'

'I hope they're right.' Ellie picked up another garment. Ironing was a mindless, thankless task. She'd bought Jack some casual shirts that didn't need ironing, but he'd cut them up and used them to clean his gun. 'One more to go. Pass it up to Mummy, then you go and see if you can get Annie to hang them up for me.'

Three-year-old Bronwyn walked out to the verandah where she squatted beside her sister, more interested in the collection of spiders in the pickle jar than in hanging shirts. Ben stamped his foot on the wooden floor and both girls looked towards the kitchen.

'Mum wants you to put Dad's shirts away, Annie,' he said, pulling at the collar of his own shirt.

Ellie didn't attempt to communicate with her oldest daughter. She'd given up on Annie a long time ago. Jack was hard on her. It was almost as if he blamed her for being here, as if he wished it was Annie instead of Liza who had been taken.

A photograph of Liza hung on the long eastern wall of the kitchen. It was a fourteen-by-ten, head and shoulders. Ellie looked at it now. She'd been a beautiful little girl. Everyone called her the pretty one. Like dark and dawn, those two girls, they used to say in town. No-one picked the girls as sisters, Annie so long and skinny, Liza all pink and plump and gold.

Liza Jane. Born February 2nd, 1960. Stolen from Narrawee February, 1967. My golden treasure, may she bloom forever, Jack had written in the Bible. Ellie had written beneath it. *God keeps her safe.*

She hoped he was keeping her safe somewhere. She made the sign of the cross now, asking forgiveness for her doubt as Ben stamped his foot again.

'Annie! Hang up Dad's shirts.' The older girl stood. She reclaimed her pickle jar, scooped the last of her spiders into it and walked into the kitchen. 'And get rid of those spiders, too,' Ben said.

Too reliable for his years, Ellie thought. Ben worked like a man around the farm, fixing fences, milking cows. Her father had been dead for eight years now, but he lived on in his grandson. They'd named Johnny for Jack's father, and Ben for her own. Johnny was pure Burton, as tall as his father when he'd left home. Ben was all Vevers, in looks, build and ways. At five, he'd known what he wanted to be. 'I'm going to be a farmer, like Grandpa,' he used to say.

Ellie's father had built the house when she and Jack married. A footbridge joined the land on either side of the river in those days, but Jack doused it with petrol one night and burnt it, determined to keep Ellie on his side. Ben was only three at the time, but he remembered that little bridge they had used to run across to Grandpa. Two years ago, he'd planted a row of tiny saplings where the river narrowed between high clay banks. Two of his trees were doing well, and already reaching high. One day he'd build his new footbridge; Ellie knew it as surely as she knew that God was in heaven. Whether the bridge would work or not was another question, but she never expressed her doubts.

She hung the final shirt over the chairback, and took her best dress from the laundry basket. Again the iron worked hard, striving to press some life into fading cotton.

Church tomorrow. She always went to church with Bessy. When their father died, Bessy inherited the land just five minutes from town. But without the little footbridge, Ellie had a mile walk through the forest to the main bridge, then a mile back east to town. Jack refused to drive her to church.

Annie had made it as far as the sink. She stood there, washing her hands and blowing soap bubbles through cupped palms. Ben tossed a ball of newspaper at her, and Ellie watched the girl's hands make a cutting motion in the air. God only knew what she was saying – God and Ben.

'Then do as you're asked the first time,' Ben said. 'Get a move on, Annie, or Mum won't let you go to the school break-up party with me.' His wrists tapped his hips and he shook his head. 'No party,' he signed.

'Are you sure you want to take her, Benjie?' Ellie asked.

'Mr Fletcher said we could bring sisters and brothers if they're five or over. She wants to go. She never goes anywhere, Mum.'

'What's she going to do all day?'

'She'll be all right. She can sit with me.'

Ann turned to Ellie. Her uncombed cloud of dark curls pushed back from her eye with the swing of a shoulder, she thumped her breast with a fist, then made a waving motion away.

'You're going, but only if you do as Mum tells you, and if you let her comb your hair,' Ben said.

'I suppose I'll have to let down the hem of her red floral. She's growing like a weed lately.'

Watching her mother's lips, Ann nodded, and continued

nodding as she picked up a shirt and backed across the passage to the lounge room door.

The lounge room looked like her father; it smelt like him too. Clean, unused, all the nice saved to show visitors. It had an open fireplace and a polished table, it had books and stuffed chairs, and beautiful Liza. Ann wasn't allowed in the lounge room, except when she had to go through it to hang her father's shirts.

She didn't like the smell of his wardrobe when she opened the doors. It reminded her of another wardrobe. With a shake of her head, she dismissed that memory, pushing it away into the dark place, where it got mixed up in the big black of nothing.

The last shirt she hooked over the foot of the double bed. Every morning her father had to have a clean shirt, and clean socks. He liked clean. When he stood, all clean and pressed, beside the dusty Mallawindy men, she liked him being her father.

His shirts all had one big pocket. She liked pockets, but if any of her dresses had pockets, her mother sewed them up with double stitches. Pockets were for holding treasures, and one day, before Johnny went away, she found a true treasure. If her mother didn't sew up all her pockets then Johnny wouldn't –

And then nothing. The memory slid off into black. She grinned at her reflection in the wardrobe mirror, pleased with herself. She didn't have to remember anything except Johnny's birthday. She liked to remember that.

In the mirror, she could see herself from the top of her head down past her dress to her knees. Her dress was brown, to match the dirt. It wasn't a blue dress. There was no more Annie Blue Dress. Not anywhere. She was in that different mirror. Gone now. All gone now.

She tiptoed to her father's side and stood looking down at him, her hands held behind her back. One fist had pushed his mouth into a funny little Bronwyn face. He looked beautiful and so safe when he was asleep, and she knew that beneath his eyelids, his eyes were soft, and brown, and velvet. She could love him when he was asleep, she could nearly reach out a hand to pat his black head, just like she patted Mickey her dog's black head. But it might wake him, and most times she didn't even nearly love him when he was awake because he didn't love her. He only loved Liza.

A giant picture of Liza hung over the fireplace in the lounge room. Ann stole a swift glance at it. It was different to the one in the kitchen; it was a sitting down, all of Liza, picture. Her hands were clasped beneath her chin, her ankles crossed. Curls as gold as her mother's were tied on top of her head with a yellow ribbon. It matched the dress.

Ann hated that picture because it always made a whole mess of words bubble up and spew out, just like sick had spewed from her belly on the day she tasted her father's whisky.

He bought Liza's dress of shiny yellow.
Took her to Daree in his motor car.
Got a picture from the photograph fellow.
And Liza was prettiest by far.

Poems were tricky, sticky things. They remembered themselves. If you found one word, then the rest found each other. She made a lot of poems in her head. That one always made her remember about Liza winning first prize in the competition. Liza won the little photograph in the kitchen and this giant one, and a hundred pounds, which was now called two hundred dollars, and she got her picture in a magazine, and the magazine was still in the bookshelves, even though it came from November 1963. It was worn out with looking, and showing off. Liza's photograph wouldn't ever get worn out, but it was trapped behind glass, where flies liked to sit on her and leave their black stuff in her eyes, and in the winter, smoke coiled up and stuck all over her Shirley Temple curls until Liza looked just as smudged and dirty as Ann.

A smile tickled at the corners of her lips. It was a bad smile. Father Fogarty would try to get God to strike her dead for smiling about that. Quickly she trapped the smile with her tongue. Her smiling lip caught, held between her teeth, and she glanced again at the photograph.

God keeps her safe. Or so it said in the Bible.

Lots of people in Mallawindy believed in the Bible, and in the priest. On Saturdays, if her father was away, her mother cut a chook's head off with the wood-axe. She dipped it in a bucket of boiling water, ripped its feathers out and threw its heart away. On Sunday morning, she poked bread and onions inside it, put it in the oven, then she took everyone up to talk to God while the chook sizzled. The priest drove them home after church, and he stayed to help eat the poor cooked chook.

When her father was home, the priest didn't come and Ann didn't have to go to church – not since she'd learned to creep out while her mother had her head down praying.

There was a shop in the town with books in the window, and there were newspapers pasted on the blind windows of the old shoe shop, and there were packets of Weeties and tins in the grocer's window to read, and picture-show signs outside the Shire Hall. There was the cafe too, and it had a glass case full of lollies, and the cafe lady was good. She swapped Ann's church collection money, tied in the corner of a handkerchief, for a little white bag full of aniseed balls.

No-one made Ann eat the chook after church, not even when the priest was there – not since a long time. Not since she learned how to stick her finger down her throat and make the poor chook come straight back up again to her plate. And since she made the nuns send her home from the deaf school in Sydney, no-one chased her around trying to make her get in the bath either, or comb her hair. They just left her alone now – except Benjie, but sometimes Ann liked him not to leave her alone, because he talked to her, like Johnny used to, and he liked swimming too.

She was the best swimmer in the whole world. Better than Benjie. She could stay under the water until Benjie got scared and dived down to the deep hole to find her. But he only thought he found her. No-one could really find her, because she was hiding in the dark place, in the place where the words and poems lived.

She poked out her tongue at Liza's photograph, then tiptoed to the dressing table where she stood looking at her father's black briefcase. She liked it a lot. He kept things in it, locked tight and safe under its lid. She couldn't have one, so she washed out a golden syrup tin for her briefcase, and she made holes in it with a nail, and put a string handle on it, and she kept things tight under its lid.

Her hand reached out to touch the shiny black leather. When her father was home, the case lived on the top of the wardrobe where she couldn't reach, but he had come back late from Narrawee, the money tree, so today the briefcase was on the dressing table with his car keys. The point of her tongue moistening her lips, Ann picked up the car keys, careful not to let them jiggle. She found the smallest key and fitted it in the lock.

The briefcase opened easier than her syrup tin. Her eyes watching her father, she slid one hand beneath the lid to touch his treasures. A box: papers, bankbooks. Then her fingers touched something furry, and she snatched her hand out fast. It felt like a mouse. Maybe a mouse from Narrawee had got inside to make a nest, and now it was locked up in Mallawindy with nothing to eat, not even any apples.

Her father rolled over. He pouted his lips and pop-popped out some air. Quickly she lifted the lid, and gave the trapped mouse her spiders for their dinner. She was scuttling from the room when she ran headlong into Benjie.

'What you doing?' He dispensed with surplus words when he signed – as Annie did. It took too long to sign grammatical English.

'Hang shirt very good,' she replied with her hands. Unable to meet his eye, she ran out the front door and down the east side of the house where she sat on the cool earth with the dog, her back to the lounge room wall, her heels moved backwards and forwards, backwards and forwards in the dust.

malcolm fletcher

~

Malcolm Fletcher leaned over his breakfast, devouring it with small, near-sighted eyes. Six of Mrs Burton's eggs, fried in butter, were piled on four chunky slices of toast. Six rashers of bacon guarded the pile. With a shudder of anticipation that shook the man-mountain from his sagging jowls to ballooning belly, he halved one golden yolk and carried it dripping to his mouth.

Carnal things he had long forgotten. Eyes that once feasted in libraries, had given up the fight with fine print, but his taste buds compensated. Age had not wearied them. His machine-jaws working in perpetual motion, orange yolk dribbled down his chin and bacon grease painted his chubby cheeks. Rinds were stripped of their meat by small greedy teeth, toast crusts used to wipe his plate squeaky clean.

He looked at the loaf of bread on his kitchen bench. He accused the clock on his mantlepiece. 'Eight-thirty,' he snarled, and he waddled down the hall to his bathroom.

A simple equation of mass versus container had nullified the one-time pleasure of bathing in a tub, but he stood beneath the shower for the regulation five minutes.

The water in the mains was already warm. Cold was a forgotten word in this land, where heat and dust and flies ruled his life. He'd come with his family from England, seeking a better life for his son. He'd found Mallawindy, little hell hole in central New South Wales, where he was dictated to by a school bell that now pealed out its call to the tardy and the disinterested.

Malcolm dressed, slowly. He picked up a small green Thermos, slammed his back door and ambled across the gravelled playing field to the school.

He could have bought his students' approval on that final day of the school year, released them early to run from his classroom, but Malcolm chose not to. He stung with sarcasm, he whipped with his tongue, goading them, driving them.

Ben Burton returned to the classroom after lunch, his sister still in tow. An invitation for siblings to the Christmas break-up party did not extend to supplying baby-sitting services for mutes. Not in Malcolm's room.

'Will you take that child into Mrs Macy, Burton, and leave her there,' Malcolm commanded.

'I told her at lunchtime, sir, but she doesn't want to. Mum said Annie had to sit with me, or she couldn't come, sir,' Ben replied, his eyes studying his shoes. But the mute's eyes stared relentlessly into the headmaster's until he was forced to look away.

Odd little individual, Malcolm thought. He'd been watching her all morning. Inscrutable eyes, black as two smouldering coals, they were defying him now to move her from her brother's side. 'Mum says she stays, I say she goes. What do you say, Burton?' he tormented.

Ben's sunburnt face flushed a darker red and his chin dropped closer to his chest. 'She doesn't know anyone in Mrs Macy's room, sir. If I leave her there, she'll just go home.'

'So be it. Would you like to take over the chair today? You make all the decisions. Shall we finish the day with arithmetic or do you prefer English? Speak up, Burton, the class is waiting.' He continued with his own brand of wit, while studying the Burton duo. The sandy-haired boy and the dark girl. They'd rot in this filthy little town. Malcolm's mind wandered back to a better time, a kinder year. He'd tried to guide the oldest Burton boy, Johnny – named as his own son had been named. He'd offered to coach him to a full scholarship, a passport out of town. That boy had possessed one of the best minds Malcolm had come across in all his years of pounding information into thick heads.

'Pearls before the swine,' he muttered, his eyes drawn away from the dark coals to traverse the almost skeletal frame of the mute. The mark of a whipping was on her thigh, the broken skin already scabbing, but the fat man flinched away from a fact he didn't wish to know. Knowing meant involvement. He had a permanent appointment with a bottle these days, and no more time for involvement.

'Books open at page 40. Read *The Team*, note the author. I'll question you on your reading later. Take that as a warning.' He waddled back to his table and sank down to the groaning chair, his eyes turning to the eastern window.

Every Australian schoolyard seemed to have this same look of desolation, of earth worn bare of grass by little feet that came to stay for six long years. Each day they carried home a little more soil on their stinking sandshoes, until all that was left could barely support the peppercorn trees.

'Barren land. Barren life,' he murmured and reached for the Thermos beneath his table, pouring a cup of what he hoped looked like weak black tea.

Heads propped on hands, the children leaned, waiting, dreaming too of cool drinks, of raspberry cordial and of cream-puffs, pink jelly cakes and sausage rolls that the town ladies provided at the Shire Hall on the final day of the school year. The mute appeared to be reading. The two Burton heads were close together. The boy had commenced school late. He was behind his age group, but he didn't look out of place amid the twelve-year-olds. Malcolm reached again for his Thermos, shaking it to test its level. It would last him until three-thirty.

He drank fast. His cup again empty, he up-ended it to make quite certain. 'Too soon a pleasure taken, then forgotton,' he quoted, measuring out a small nip before tucking the Thermos out of reach. 'Dooley!' he bellowed.

'What, sir!' A drowsy carrot-topped teenager sprang to attention in the sixth-grade row.

'*The Team*, Dooley. The poem we have all been reading. Who was the author?' the headmaster asked. He stood and moved between the aisles, slapping a desk here and there with a chubby pink hand, his walk a pulsation, each hump and lump moving independently, sluggish and slow.

'What page, sir?'

'Dooley. Dooley. Dooley.' He rubbed at the bridge of his nose, moved his spectacles higher, then tried once more. 'Have your parents decided yet where you will be insulting the sensibilities of the teaching fraternity in the new year, or do they intend leaving you here to torture me for another year?'

'I'm goin' to high school in Daree, on the bus, if I pass this year, sir. If that's whatcha mean, sir.'

'Indeed, I do, Dooley, and indeed you have passed. It may mean that I must go down on bended knee, begging forgiveness for my gross connivance, but you have indeed passed this year,' he replied, and he pulsated on, side stepping a foot placed strategically to trip him. With a baby-fat elbow, Malcolm jabbed at a near-mature youth. 'Tell me, Mr West. Dare I contemplate the day when I have no more big, splayed West feet attempting to fell me in my grade six aisle?'

'Don't count on it, sir. The old man and lady was hard at it again last night,' Robby West cackled. The elbow nudged again, harder this time.

'Were hard at it, Mr West. The old man and lady were hard at it. They were. We were, but he was ... I was – '

'Who with, sir?' the class stirrer asked, and the elbow, with twenty-three stone behind it, slammed into the youth's rib-cage.

Unperturbed, Malcolm Fletcher moved to the next desk, stopping beside Ben Burton.

'Give me the author's name, Burton,' he said. 'On your feet, boy.'

Ben stood. He licked his dry lips. 'Henry Lawson, sir,' he said, and he sank back to his seat, his chin again on his chest. But not so the mute. Her pointed chin lifted defiantly as her eyes darted from her brother to his tormentor, then back again.

She was all points and angles, this girl-child of Jack Burton. Tense as sprung steel coiled too long in an unnatural bend, the fat man thought. The child's eyes interested him. They were the eyes of a wild thing, round, incongruous amid so many angles. Eyes without trust, without hope. A half-starved feral thing, trapped in his classroom – but only for as long as she decided to stay.

Determinedly, he lifted the hem of her faded frock. He looked at the scabbing welts crisscrossing her thigh. 'How did that happen, Burton?' he asked the boy.

'She fell out of a tree, sir,' Ben replied.

The headmaster sighed, released the fabric. 'You violate the truth, methinks, Burton. Do you know the meaning of that word?'

'They violate the graves of the dead, sir ... break into them and rob them, sir.'

'Indeed they do. Indeed they do. To break into, to disturb. You and yours violate my peace of mind,' he admitted, then he wheeled again on the class.

'Rhyme, rhythm and alliteration. A poet uses musical language to make his poem easily remembered, he uses rhyme and metre, his poem becomes a song without music. However, modern poets are leaning towards free verse. It has no metre at all. I have heard it said that the rhythm of a metrical poem can be compared to a heartbeat, but free verse is like the wind in the trees, so take up your pens and create for me a breeze, write me up a storm. Make me one worthwhile poem and you may escape this room before three-thirty.' His request was greeted by groans and the slam of desktops. His students had hoped for an easier early release this day.

Ben raised his hand. 'Please sir, can I give Annie a page out of my book?'

'I dare say you can, Burton. What you mean is, may I give Ann a page.'

'May I, sir?'

'You may, Burton. Perhaps she would prefer a slate and some chalk – to draw Christmas trees in the snow with Mrs Macy's brood. Consider for a moment her needs. You may be denying her some small pleasure by your worthy desire to protect.'

'She can use a pencil, sir,' the boy replied.

Malcolm Fletcher sat at his table watching the mute. Her hand was moving backwards and forwards across the paper. He massaged the bridge of his nose with his index finger. The heavy spectacles he wore irritated, the weather irritated, the level of his Thermos flask irritated, as did this dark-eyed brat. Her hand was still moving, mimicking her brother's.

Curiosity moved Malcolm from his chair. Approaching the girl from the rear of the classroom, he peered at the page she protected in the curve of her elbow. He frowned, leaned closer, then his hand reached out and snatched the paper from beneath her arm.

She sprang away, cowering from him, but the headmaster had lost interest in the child. He was reading.

'MY BEN Annie Burton December 1969

Grey green eyes. Hair of wheat brown dry by summer sun.

Arms thin, like Ben's bridge tree, reach for light. Face long, sad, gentle.

When he tell me things, of bridge, and secret dreams,

his grey green eyes, like fire-works that explode.

And sometime he laughs. Loud. And his face gets round and full.

Then I laugh too, because Ben is happy.'

'The child is literate!' Self-disgust at his own neglect made his voice high. 'She can write, boy.'

'Yes, sir.'

'I understood she was ineducable.'

'She is, sir. The deaf school sent her home.'

'Rubbish!' Malcolm roared. Again his eyes scanned the page of neat script. Then he noticed every eye in the classroom was focused on him and the two Burtons.

'Scat! Depart! You have been saved by a mute. Get out of my sight! Clear your desks and with any sort of luck at all, I won't set eyes on you until 1970. Go ring on that bell, Mr West. Dismissed!' he bawled, in case there may still be room for doubt, but one hand rested lightly on Ben's shoulder. 'Remain. I wish to speak to you,' he said.

Sixty seconds heard the last desktop slam shut and the last clatter of boots on the long verandah. Then silence, broken only by the tick-ticking of the wall clock.

Malcolm propped against a vacated desk. 'It is obvious that the child has had some schooling, Burton.'

'No, sir.'

'She has been taught to read and write. These things don't just happen. I, of all people, know that the human race is not born literate. Who taught her to read?'

'She was six when it happened, sir ... she could read a bit, and Johnny ... Johnny kept it going when she came home. I sort of help her with spelling.'

'You sort of help her?' His voice was disdainful, and quickly Ben corrected.

'I help her, sir. She learns stuff quickly.'

Malcolm sat watching the child. Her eyes, shielded by black lashes, were looking anywhere but at his own. Annoyed by the interest stirring in his breast, he turned back to the youth. 'This child is screaming out for education. Why hasn't she been at school before? Has she retained any speech?'

Ben shook his head. 'Mum thinks she was struck deaf and dumb, sir.'

'And by some stroke of heavenly vengeance, no doubt,' the fat man snarled.

'No, sir. It happened at Narrawee, about three years ago, when Uncle Sam and Aunty May took Annie and Liza down there. When Liza disappeared ...'

'Enough,' Malcolm interrupted, having no desire to rehash the bewildering disarray of the Burtons' private lives. 'That could explain her grasp of language. Her language skills should have been well developed by that age. How long was she at the school for the deaf?'

'Only three weeks, sir. She used to run away and the nuns said she shut down and screamed like crazy if they touched her, or tried to lock her in. They said she'd have to go into a home for retarded children.'

'Hogwash!' Malcolm pushed the thick grey thatch of hair back from his glasses, and again studied the girl. 'What age is she?'

'Nine on Christmas Eve, sir.'

'And you call her Ann.'

'Annie, usually, sir.'

'Ann!' His voice was loud in the empty room, then louder. 'Ann!' But the girl's only response was a pink tongue darting out to moisten her lips.

'Dad used to test her. He says she's not deaf. That it's just ... like shock caused it, but Mum thinks he's refusing to believe she's not ever going to be quite right.'

'I had some little experience with the deaf in England, Burton; however ... however, I refuse to believe I am capable of agreeing with your illustrious father on any given topic, so perhaps for the moment we will assume she does have a hearing loss. Is your father home at the moment?'

'Yes, sir. He got back from Narrawee last Friday night.'

'I'll give you a note, boy. I want her in this classroom when school resumes next year.' He walked to his table, and began scribbling while the children waited.

The note safe in his pocket, Ben said, 'I don't think wild horses will drag her to school if I'm not here, sir.'

'She will come, and she will learn – even if we must rely on the written word. How do you communicate with her?'

'I just talk, sir. If she wants to, she reads my lips perfectly. And we've got the signs that Johnny taught us, and she can do the deaf alphabet. Johnny sent away to the priests in Sydney when she first came home from Narrawee. They sent him a book.'

'Johnny, the paragon. Where is he, boy?'

'Mum says he's probably gone to Sydney.'

'You don't know?'

'No, sir. He never wrote. I think he – .' Ben licked his lips, silenced.

The teacher turned away, afraid of his interest. He was once a teacher, born to teach. This was a child who needed his teaching.

'Scram,' he said. 'Off with you, or you'll miss out on the gourmandising. Good afternoon, Ann,' he added as an afterthought, and for an instant he felt certain the girl was going to respond. There was a reflex lifting of her chin, a flutter of lashes exposing questioning eyes as she turned to him. Then, the chin lowered, she followed her brother from the room.

'Perhaps,' Malcolm murmured, his heart pounding, attempting to raise long-buried enthusiasm from its grave of fat. He walked to the window, watching the girl. She and the youth had stopped before the road. He saw the girl turn her head to the west, then she tugged at her brother's sleeve.

Only then did Malcolm hear the sound of a dying motor. He knew the car, knew the driver, as did the children. They ran across the road to disappear into the Shire Hall.

Malcolm remained at his window watching the battered Ford, driven by the children's father, come into view. 'Obnoxious mongrel of a man,' he said.

jack burton

~

Jack Burton's handsome mouth was turned down in a snarl as he cursed fate and his father's car while coaxing it towards the only cool place in town. The motor died twelve metres short of the school. He stepped out to the road, kicked the door shut, and the corn on his smallest toe screamed. The car left where it had stopped, Jack limped down to the garage at the edge of town.

'The bastard's died again. It's up near the school. Can you get it going?' he called to the shadowy figure beneath the bonnet of a truck.

'I'm a mechanic, not God, Jack,' the shadow replied.

Jack limped away, surveying his world through eyes half closed against the sun. His was a harsh, abrasive little world. A Post Office cum Commonwealth Bank. A butcher. A grocer. A milk bar, and Bert Norris's business, cum newsagency, cum barber, cum hardware, and timber yard. But dead in the centre of town, right where it claimed to be, stood Mallawindy's sanctuary, the Central Hotel.

'Canst thou minister to a mind diseased? Pluck from the memory a rooted sorrow? Raze out the written troubles of the brain and with some sweet oblivious antidote, cleanse the stuffed bosom of that perilous stuff, which weighs upon the heart?' he quoted as he swung the heavy door wide.

'G'day, Jack.' Mick Bourke, hotel owner was already pulling a beer. 'Not working today, Jack?'

'Bloody motor is buggered,' Jack replied, tossing his coins down.

He worked, when he felt like it, as an insurance collector for the area, going door to door, collecting a dollar here, two dollars there. He dressed well, his shoes of the softest leather, his slacks tailored to fit; he had the dark good looks that caught the eye of women from fifteen to fifty, which helped in selling policies to housewives. A policy assured them he'd return each month. Occasionally he tested an interesting bed.

In July, he played tax consultant for the town. He got a kick out of fiddling tax claims too, but these occupations brought in a pittance for one raised to expect the good life. A trust fund set up by his maternal grandfather would pay its dues each June and December until his death, and his father's five hundred pounds a year translated into twenty dollars a week. Ellie fed him when he was around, and Narrawee fed him when he wasn't. He did all right.

The first beer barely touched the sides of his throat. He halted the slide of a second glass, carried it to his mouth as his gaze moved over the other drinkers. They were a mixed lot. Malcolm Fletcher wandered in and stood alone, tossing down a fast brandy, his bottle for later swung at his side in a string bag; he made no attempt to hide his addiction.

As the afternoon wore on, others wandered in, drank in groups. The noise in the bar increased. Jack eyed the rowdies, envying them their easy friendship, their frequent laughter. He stood alone, his brain, an untamed thing, depressing him, his mood growing darker with each glass of beer.

He thought of his mother, a rotting cabbage in a back bedroom, hearing all, seeing all, saying nothing. He remembered her eyes dribbling tears as he scooped porridge into her mouth. Neglected by his father and Sam, she spent four years dying in a room few tolerated for longer than one breath of air could be held. Jack had been her favourite, and Sam, his father's boy. Bloody rotten-to-the-core bastard, Jack thought, tossing his beer down and passing his glass back for a refill. That's what loyalty got you. Nothing. Sibling loyalty. I should have dobbed the bastard in when I was sixteen. Saved myself a weight of pain.

His father was no better. Jack had flattened him the day his mother died, caught him with a lucky punch under the jaw, knocked the old bastard cold. Pure power, raw power. That was the day Jack learned that fury possessed a beauty of its own. His muscles were tingling with new power when Saint Sam came running like the cavalry to his father's defence. Jack hit him too. Then he put the boots in, broke Sam's aristocratic nose.

Jack was eighteen. His father called in the local lawman to evict him, and Jack left the white stone mansion, after ransacking it for money. He found it too. He found plenty. He stayed drunk for the three days it took to get his mother in the ground, and when the earth was heaped high on her grave, and his father was home celebrating his release, Jack went to the cemetery and held his own service.

He stayed away for four years, living the life of a gypsy – a good life, until he met Ellie, married her, and took her and their first little bastard back to meet the family. John Lawrence. He'd named him for the old man, thought it might buy him back into the family. Big chance, but Saint Sam was impressed. He married young May Hargraves that same year, but they'd produced no heir, so Jack kept breeding, just to nark them.

He'd named Liza for his mother. Eliza Jane.

'Shit on the world,' he said, tossing his last five to the beer slops.

The bar was full. His glass remained empty – as his packet of cigarettes was empty. 'Give me a pack of Marlboro.'

'Coming up, Jack,' Mick called.

The door swung wide and old Rella Eva entered. Jack smiled.

Her face always made him smile. It was a travesty of furrows she'd attempted to fill with a spatular dipped in paint. Her hair dyed a dull red, was worn long. Eyebrows plucked to extinction had been replaced by two fine black-pencilled lines. As she walked to the bar, Mick shook his head. 'Public bar's no place for a lady, Rell. I'll serve you in the lounge.'

'Watch out who you go calling a lady, Mick. Give me a beer and shut your cake hole,' she replied, then she turned to Jack. 'You look like you lost a tenner and found sixpence, Jack.'

'What's brought you to town, Rell?'

'Dave's in hospital. I'm on my way up to Warran. You've been dodging me lately, lover.'

'I've been home ... Narrawee.' Narrawee would always be home. 'Have you got a fag on you, Rell?'

She handed him a near full packet, watched him remove one, light up, inhale. 'I've missed you, lover,' she said, reclaiming her cigarettes with one hand while the other grabbed at the bulge in his groin.

'Get your hand off me, you stupid bitch,' he hissed, but his old comrade in arms was rising to the occasion. Her hands could turn him into a pleading boy. Ugly old slut. Only her eyes mirrored the girl she might have been thirty years ago. They were a fox's eyes, bright, hot with want.

Ellie never wanted him. Never had. Sex was a sin, unless it was making babies. Cold, brood-mare bitch, Jack thought as his eyes moved over old Rell. He drank his beer in one long swallow, pocketed his packet of Marlboro, then walked to the door, looked out. 'If you're heading up to see Dave, can you drop me off at the bridge, Rell? My car's buggered,' he said. 'When you're ready.'

She was ready. Ready for anything.

All tracks led to the river. There was nowhere else for them to go in Mallawindy. Each summer new paths were forged through the dust, some to remain, given names, others to fade away beneath the winter grasses. There was Milly's Track, west of town, and

Wally's Bend Road to the north, but the track they took led east. It was well used. Dead Man's Lane, they called it. It led out to the sandhills, and to an Aboriginal burial ground five kilometres from town. Until Malcolm Fletcher's son had died after finding some bones there, it had been a popular hang-out for teenagers. Now the whites left the place alone. The local blacks had always claimed it was a taboo place – but it was private.

Rella tucked her car into a bay it knew well. She spread her well-travelled blanket on the ground, and sat on it. Jack wandered, kicking sand, sifting sand between his fingers. He found a bottle top, and he smiled. It was probably one of his. He liked this place, he often came here alone to drink, and think. Miles of sand, where little grew, except rabbits and crows. On the next dune, three of the raucous black bastards were attacking a poor bugger blinded by myxo.

He watched it run in circles, trying to evade the unseen foe, then he walked to it, wrung its neck and tossed it to the birds. 'It was a woman who developed myxomatosis,' he said, wandering back to the blanket. 'Trust a bloody woman.'

Rella had the morals of a rabbit, but little interest in their diseases. She was on him. Time was awasting.

school

~

Dogs always knew the coolest places to sit. Mickey used to be Johnny's dog; he was Ann's dog now. He licked her face, trying to kiss her better, because he knew she was frightened. Dogs knew about all the bad things, but they could only lick and watch you with their worried eyes. They couldn't take the bad away. She patted his heavy coat, brushing the dust from it. Fine red dust. She liked dust and the hard earth. Nothing ever stained it. Not like the wood floor or the carpet got stained. Chicken blood, and rabbits' blood, and people's blood, just soaked into the earth or was swept away with the wind.

The fat man was making her go to school today. She didn't want to go. He came last night in his car and said he'd be back in the morning to drive her to school. She was frightened of him, and his car. Didn't like school, or cars. Didn't like . . . anything.

This morning she'd tried to pull the dark over her mind, but it was only lace curtain dark, not strong enough to hold back the memories fighting to get through. They stung her head like the wasps, stabbing their stingers through and making pin-point holes for the memory to get out. Everything was going bad, and she couldn't stop it.

Her father walked by her to the kitchen. There was a letter in

31

there that Benjie had brought home from the post office yesterday. It stunk of Narrawee, of roses and cedar wood and beeswax polish and it had money in it. There was always money when those envelopes came. Cheque money from Narrawee, the money tree.

Her father made Ann touch the letter, read it. Made her sign the words. She didn't want to, like she didn't want to look at photographs.

The letters always started with '*Dear Jack and Ellie, I hope this letter finds you and your family as it leaves me.*'

Then it talked about Sam. Ann hated Sam as much as she hated Narrawee.

Narrawee had demons. Ugly things, they came out of the ground and they stank of old earth and apples, and they laughed at her, tried to make her watch them. Light. Dark. Light. Dark. Like ... like lightning in a storm. Like something else, but she couldn't think what the something else was.

She wouldn't go to bed after her father made her touch the letter, because if she went to bed she might go to sleep, and if she did then the demons would get her, and if they got her they'd take her back there, and she'd know everything, and it was too bad to know.

Benjie worried about her when she was crazy. Last night, when everyone had gone to bed, he came from his room to sit with her and Mickey in the moonlight. He talked about school. Safe with him in the clean moonlight, she had made many words with her hands.

'Big frightened. Inside head like ... like storm. Like fast little lightning ... never make same thing two time. Never stop long time. Like that thing ... round. Pretty glass, make pattern. Twist around all time for change pattern.'

'Kaleidoscope.' He spelt the word on his fingers.

'Yes. That thing. Bad kaleidoscope. Not pretty. Make bad

picture. Get bad, then more bad, then more bad. Push, push inside head. On off, on off. Make heart say thump thump, thump. Make me big fright.'

'Do you remember the kaleidoscope we used to have, Annie? You used to look in it for hours,' he had said.

'No.'

'You must. If you remember what it looked like, you must remember it.'

'Not remember nothing.'

'What about the doll you won in the raffle that time? Remember the raffle? Number 48.'

'No. No talk in before time.'

'You have to try to remember what happened, then we might find Liza, and all of the bad stuff will go away.'

'No remember nothing. No more think, Benjie. Big hurt in think. Just think now time. Think big moon. Think cloud. We run across big cloud. Run fast over sky. Chase moon over there . . . over sunset to where Johnny live and no more demon live there.'

'I'm never going to run away, Annie. I'm going to stay here and make Mum's farm as good as Aunty Bessy's, and build my new footbridge.'

'Build bridge, then run. Find Johnny. No want fat man school. No want Narrawee. Just want here. Just want nothing.'

'Everyone's got to go to school. If you don't go to Mr Fletcher's school, then Father Fogarty will get the city people to take you away again, and you don't want that to happen, do you? I have to go to school till I'm fifteen. I don't like it either. I don't like wasting time sitting on the bus. It's not going to be like the last time, Annie. You'll go in the morning and come home at night, sleep in your own bed.'

'Big frightened. No like fat man. No like car. No like nothing.'

Today her hair was plaited, tied up with new ribbons. She had a new dress too, but her eyes were fighting to close. She looked at her new dress, and knew she shouldn't be sitting in the dirt with the dog. She stood, walked to the verandah where she could watch the yard for the fat man's car to come for her.

'I hate. I hate. I hate,' her hands signed the two words while she thumped her head against the wall, making the outside pain come so it might kill the words going around and around in her mind. She felt like Mickey trying to bite fleas on his tail.

> She had a dress that was flowers. Her purse was fat and fawn
> Full with paper money, like a lettuce picked at dawn.
> Under the leaf there is new leaf, all so crisp and new.
> That could buy anything in the whole world. Anything for you.

Narrawee. White house. Green lawns.

'No. No think. I hate. I hate. I hate.'

The baby clinging to her nipple, Ellie stood, watching Annie. She couldn't understand the hand signs, had never learned more than a couple. If the truth were told, she was afraid of her own child, afraid of her moods, afraid of her wild animal scream. 'I'm sure I don't know how that old drunk is going to do her any good, Jack,' she said. 'I don't trust him.'

'He can't do her any more bloody harm, can he?'

One handed, Ellie served Jack's scrambled eggs and sausages, she passed him two pieces of toast, then stood back. 'She was such an independent little thing, Jack. How did it happen?'

'You're the one who keeps wanting to educate her. So you're getting what you want, and you're still moaning. Pass the salt and stop your sniffling,' he said.

Ellie jumped to obey. She watched his plate clear, then as she poured his tea, the baby lost its grip and began to wail. The nipple squirted its offering into the open mouth. The baby choked, swallowed, then bellowed anew. 'Father Fogarty doesn't think it's a good idea. He said we should think about that other school. They know how to handle them. I don't know how to handle her. She's growing wild.'

'There's nothing wrong with the shamming little bitch – and shut that baby up, or put it to bed. I've got a headache.'

Ellie changed the baby over to her other arm, offering the preferred breast. 'She feels a bit feverish. Do you think she's going to be sickly like Benjie?'

'You inept wet-nurse slut. How do I know? Take her to the doctor.'

'Could you drive me to Daree, love?'

'Get your interfering bloody sister to take you.'

Ellie relied too much on Bessy and Bill to drive her around. It wouldn't hurt Jack to take the day off. Wouldn't hurt him to drive Annie to school either, as Bessy said last week when Annie refused to go to school. Ellie chewed on her lip, fighting against speaking Bessy's thoughts out loud. The sound of a car saved her. 'Here he is, Jack. You'll have to take her out. I can't get her to do anything.'

Ann was at the kitchen door, her hands signing to her father. 'No want go fat man car. No want school.'

'You'll go where I tell you to go and like it. Now, get your lunch box and get out of my sight,' he said, his hands moving to his belt buckle.

She stepped closer. 'Please, I go nowhere. I stay house. No like fat man. No like fat man school.' She wasn't afraid of his belt. She walked towards it, signing, and he understood every word.

'Talk to me and I won't make you go. Say it. Say I don't want to go. Say it.'

'For the love of God, she can't say it, Jack.'

'She can bloody well say it if she wants to,' he roared. 'Get out of my sight. Get to buggery, you crazy little bitch.'

Each morning for a week, Malcolm drove down to the Burton property and drove away with Ann in the back seat. On the first day, she sat in a corner of his classroom and went to sleep. Malcolm left her until lunchtime, then setting two sixth graders to guard her, he walked across the playing field to refill his Thermos. She was missing when he returned, and one of the guard girls had teeth marks on her arm.

At a quarter to nine the next morning he drove again to the fowl yard. Ann escaped the classroom at ten, via the open door. His back turned, he'd been writing on the blackboard.

On the third morning, she sat in her corner, and her scream continued for most of the morning. Determined to imprison her in his room, he had locked the door. Mrs Macy, the elderly mistress who taught the juniors, let her out, and thirty-five children watched with relief as Ann ran for home.

Nothing wrong with her co-ordination, or her sense of direction, Malcolm thought. He was back in the fowl yard on Thursday, as stubborn as the black-eyed child. They started the day with the blinds drawn, his old projector whirring. Ann remained in her seat, transfixed by the screen until the nature film ended.

'Stay,' Malcolm signed. 'More.' He wound the reel back and showed it again, then again.

'More,' Ann signed, when he began packing the reel into its can.

'Lunch,' he said. She picked up her bag and ran home to eat her lunch.

On Friday he gave her a seat adjacent to the open door, only fencing her in with books. Picture books, an atlas, animal books, fairytales, and anything else he could drag from the small school library. Ann sat all morning, leafing through the books. At lunchtime she took the meat from her sandwich and ate her bread and tomato sauce at the desk, and when she smudged a picture of a dog, she winced.

He wiped it away. 'All gone,' he signed.

He missed lunch that day. Missed filling his Thermos. Mid afternoon, Ann walked alone to the toilets, and Malcolm made a relieved trip himself. When he returned, she was back with her books. At three-thirty, he had to pack them away to get her out of the room.

'Holiday. Two day. I will come for you Monday, Burton,' he spoke slowly, his hands making slow signs.

'Book,' she signed, hands together, palms open.

'On Monday. Two day home, then more book.' He made the careful sign for book.

'No car,' she signed, miming the steering wheel. 'I walk. No like car.'

'Good.' Thumb up. 'Good. You walk. Walk to school on Monday,' he said.

'I walk, same like Benjie walk. I get more book.'

Ann walked to school through the heat and red dust of February and March, through gentle April, and cooler May. She walked through the clogging red mud of June, her feet shod in lace-up school shoes that she polished at night while Ellie polished Jack's.

She walked through the winds of August, and summer came again. On the day of the school break-up, she learned there was a prize for those who hadn't missed a day at school. She wanted a prize too. Mr Fletcher told her she couldn't have one, because she missed many days in the first weeks.

'No miss one day other year,' she signed.

Then Christmas came with its holidays, and New Year came, and there was no school. She went anyway. Malcolm often found her wandering there, or waiting on the verandah.

'Holiday,' he said. 'We have a long holiday.'

'No like holiday.'

He bought her a book, and told her it was her prize. She looked at the fly leaf. No words were written there. She handed it back.

'For you. You go home. Read the book. Have a holiday.'

'You keep for prize, next year. You put Ann Elizabeth name in book,' she signed.

He opened the schoolroom door, and he gave her four library books. 'You bring them back when the holiday is finished.'

She grew tall and determined the year she was ten. In August 1971, tonsillitis and Ellie tried to steal her chance for a prize, but she wouldn't stay home. Her father gave her two of his Aspros and she walked off in the wind. That year her name was called at the Christmas party. Mrs Macy handed her the prize, her name written there in dark black ink. *Awarded to Ann Elizabeth Burton for perfect attendance. 1971.*

It was a beautiful book. It was Rikki-Tikki-Tavi. She read every word, then turned back to the first page and read it again.

Measles killed her perfect record in November of 1972. She wasn't allowed to go to school. Measles was contagious.

Half the school was down with the disease, and it was a bad dose. One of the West girls ended up in hospital, and returned home partially blind. Benjie caught it and took it badly. He gave it to Bronwyn, who gave it to Annie, who gave it to Linda.

Each day, Ellie Burton grew more afraid of the measles. Bronwyn was a sturdy six-year-old. She took the spots in her stride, but Linda Alice, not yet three, had never been strong. For two nights Ellie was up with her.

The closest doctor was in Daree. She thought to ask Bessy if she could drive Linda down, but she hated troubling her sister. It was probably unnecessary. Children had to get the measles sooner or later. Everyone said it was better for them to get it while they were young.

You could have counted Annie's spots on one hand. A strange girl, she refused to give in to illness, and this morning she was champing at the bit to return to school, to the man she now called the keeper of answers. Ellie didn't like the fat old drunk, didn't trust him, but she had to admit he'd been good with Annie. Up with the roosters this morning, Annie was trying to hurry the hours along. She helped bring the cows down to the shed, helped with the milking. Since Ben had been sick, Annie had actually been a big help around the place, but both she and Bronwyn were going back to school today.

Ben, who now worked for Bert Norris, left for town at eight. Ellie cut the girls' lunches, then took a minute off for a cup of tea, thankful little Linda was finally getting some sleep.

It had been a wet spring. Everyone had coughs and colds. The rain was pelting down again, slamming against the window. It hadn't stopped for days, and the low paddocks, which Ellie relied on for summer feed, were flooded. She watched the rain as she hung nappies and cot sheets on the clothes horse before the stove. Every time she managed to get Linda started on toilet training, she had some setback. Linda looked a little like Liza, her hair was blonde, but she didn't have Liza's curls, and she was thin and sickly.

With her dark curls brushed, tied up in pigtails, Bronwyn looked so much the girl, but she was as wild as they came. She spent too much time with Annie. Ellie buttoned Bronwyn's coat, kissed her cheek, and said, 'Take your wet shoes off when you get to school and put your slippers on, Bronwyn.' No similar words were spoken to Ann, and no kiss given. The girls headed out into the rain, and Ellie tip-toed into the bedroom.

Linda was sound asleep, only her little blonde head peeping out of the blankets. With a careful hand, Ellie eased the blanket back.

And she knew. She screamed.

Bronwyn heard it. She turned, grabbed Ann's hand and they ran back to the house just as Jack came from his bed, dazed and hung-over. He pushed Ellie away from the cot where Linda lay, stone cold, her gown covered in vomit.

Shock registered slowly, belief more slowly. He felt her limbs, her brow. He picked her up, patted her back, knowing she'd been dead for hours.

'Do something, Jack. God help us. What have we done to

deserve this? What are we being punished for?'

He wiped the vomit from the tiny face. He closed the cold marble eyes, and placed Linda back in her cot. His hands covering his face, he stood there while Ellie screamed.

'God help me. God help me.'

'Shut up with that shit,' he said, and she silenced. 'Why didn't someone hear her?'

'She should have been in our room, Jack. I wanted to move her cot into our room. I would have heard her, Jack.'

'Don't pile your bloody guilt on me. I've got enough of my own. Don't you come that shit with me.' Seeking escape, but forced to stay, he turned away from the cot and away from the accusations, his eyes finding Ann, her school bag in her hand. 'Why didn't you hear her, you shamming little bitch,' he snarled.

'Don't start on her, Jack.'

But he needed a focus. Someone else had to shoulder the blame. He turned to Ellie. 'Why didn't you take her to the doctor yesterday? Haven't you got brains enough to know she needed a doctor?' He pulled the blankets from the cot, tossed them to the floor. 'Get me something. Get me something clean.'

Ann handed him a sheet, and he placed it over the tiny figure, covered it, hid it away. He hunted the children from the room and walked to the kitchen, where he snatched up his Aspros, peeled four and crunched them between white even teeth, washing them down with whisky. For minutes he stood, breathing deeply, looking out at the yard. 'Shit on this hole,' he howled to the rain, and he kicked the fly-wire door open. 'Shit on this bloody God forsaken hole.'

He drove into town, and returned with Ben and the new policeman. The ambulance came later. It took Linda Alice away.

Ann stood at the window, watching the black clouds weeping their buckets of tears. Everyone was making tears in the kitchen, but it felt empty. She walked to the girls' room, stripped the cot bare, and threw the sheets and blankets into the outdoor laundry.

Empty. No more. Gone like Liza, but not like Liza. The pusher in the corner was empty. She backed away from it, returned to the kitchen, wanting to share the tears she couldn't make.

Nappies, hung before the stove didn't need to dry now, so she moved them back to let some heat out. Nothing was the same. No-one was the same. Bessy was holding Ellie, letting her cry. Jack was smoking. The policeman left and Bessy made tea, then more people came.

It was later when the words began. Ellie sat at the stove, hugging Bronwyn to her. 'My fault. My fault. I should have checked her before I did the milking, before I did Bronwyn's hair. I should have checked her. There might have been time. She might have been – '

'It's no-one's fault, Mum,' Ben said. 'I'll have to go back to work. Dooley is there on his own.'

Ellie nodded, and kept staring at the nappies while great rivers of tears leaked away.

'The calves,' she said when Ben had gone. 'I meant to ask him to feed the calves. Poor little mites.'

Ann turned to the paddock, thought of the tiny calves taken from their mothers. Lonely. 'I feed,' she signed, but her mother didn't understand her signing, and Bronwyn was crying because her mother was crying.

Ellie stood, placed Bronwyn down on the chair. She kissed her cheek. Jack looked up, saw the kiss, and his face changed. Ann saw the change. She walked to the verandah. It would start in a moment. The people were all gone. She could see the bad brewing in her father's eyes. Something would happen, and the bad would spill over.

Ellie sniffed, wiped her face. She took her raincoat from behind the door, and walked out towards the shed where the calves were locked in. Jack ran out behind her, a skater in the red mud. 'Where do you think you're going?' he asked softly, herding her back to the house.

'The calves, Jack.' Ellie's tears and the rain, one and the same.

'The calves. You heartless cow-eyed bitch. Your baby is dead and all you can think about is your bloody calves.'

'Stop it, Jack. My heart is breaking. I'm just trying to go on.'

'Then let me see it breaking, you cold bitch.' He dragged her back to the kitchen. 'Sit down,' he said. 'Sit with me.'

Ellie sat. She reached for her black Bible, grasping its comfort in her hand, but he hated her Bible. He snatched it, tossed it through the goal post of the open door, and Ellie followed it, Bronwyn in her arms, the Bible left where it fell. She ran for the river and for Bessy. Ran from him to the safe side.

Jack walked the room, moaning, holding his head, walking, walking. Then the bad won the war, and it began.

From the verandah Ann and the dog watched him up-end the kitchen table, clear the sideboard with a sweep of his arm, toss the clothes horse and its load of Linda's things outside, kick in the cupboard doors. Like a mad bull, he raged, then he sighted Ann, leaning against the verandah post. She was wearing her raincoat, still holding her school bag, her head to one side, silently considering the chaos, the total demolition of her mother's kitchen.

She stood her ground as he came towards her, and she frowned, wondering if she was to be next on his smashing list. She never ran for the river when her mother and Bronwyn ran. Sometimes the bad got more bad, but sometimes it didn't.

He stopped before her, his hand raised, then like a stiffly starched tablecloth, placed in the laundry copper, he folded, sagged to his knees, his hand reaching palm up, open, empty, like everything else was empty. And he cried, cruel, hard tears that only he could cry.

The tears hurt a place deep inside her. She watched him for minutes, wanting to pat his back, like her mother patted Bronwyn's back. But she was too afraid to touch people. She sighed and walked by him to the stove, moved the kettle over the hot plate. Like everything else, the metal tea canister was on the floor, but its lid was firm. She measured tea into the tea pot, carefully poured in boiling water, then left it to draw while she searched the floor for the enamel mugs that always survived his rages.

The heavy table heaved back to its feet, wiped down with a dishrag, its wobbly leg kicked straight, she set it with the milk jug, and the screw-top sugar canister. 'Mmmm. Mmmm,' she said, pouring tea into two mugs. 'Mmmm.'

He lifted his head. Slowly. He climbed to his feet. 'What goes on in your crazy bloody little head?' he asked.

She shrugged, pointed to the second mug of tea, and sipped from her own.

'Crazy, like a rabid fox is crazy. You work hard at it, don't you, you shamming little bitch? Do you think you are fooling me? Do you think for one minute that you are fooling Jack Burton?' He spoke slowly, his vowels rounded, easy.

Her lip caught between her teeth, she studied his eyes, moist, and becoming soft now. Soft as the velvet cushion on the lounge. His eyes were always like that after he'd wrecked things. Like they had to get all the bad out of him before they could be good. Like his double-barrelled shotgun, after its cartridges had been fired. Even though you could still smell the hot, the gun was safe, so you could see it was beautiful. Red polished wood, shiny oiled metal, it lived behind the old wireless in the kitchen. Sometimes it tempted her hands to smooth and touch it – just like she was tempted to touch him now. But she couldn't.

He touched her. His hand reached across the table and he touched her cheek, then he took her chin, turned her face to the light, and his hand smelt of soap and cigarette. It was a beautiful hand, a gentle hand, almost too frightened to touch.

Pleasure saturated her stomach, flooded her limbs. It took some of the empty away. She sat, barely daring to breathe, to move, lest he take his touch away.

'She placed no Vevers stamp on you,' he said. 'You remember that. I saw you at the hospital the morning after you were born.

You looked like a little skun rat but I recognised the Burton in you then. They thought you were going to die. No time to get the bloody priest, so I found a parson preaching his bullshit in one of the wards and I dragged him up to christen you. ''Better your faith than no baptism,'' your mother said. But you didn't die, and you won't die. You helped me perpetrate the greatest religious coup in bloody history. Do you know that?' His fingers stroked her chin, and a sigh that was almost a sob escaped him.

'She was always whingeing about having you re-done Catholic ... ''like the other children, Jack.'' Doesn't mention it now though, does she? Doesn't think you're worth bothering about. Do you know that? To her, you're a problem that won't go away.' His hand patted her cheek, then it fell away to reach for the mug of tea, but its warmth remained.

'Can you fry eggs?' he asked.

'I no break egg,' she signed.

'Well, learn to break an egg. Make me something to eat.'

'No break egg. Never. I leave alone egg. Maybe chicken in egg.'

'Crazy little bitch,' he said, but he broke his own eggs, fried and ate them.

She stayed with him for two hours. She toasted bread on a long fork before the embers, while he told her of government departments where births and deaths were all registered. She made a fresh pot of tea, while he told her how the Russians would drop an atomic bomb on Mallawindy one day, and they'd blow it off the face of the Earth and the sooner the better as far as he was concerned. He told her about banks, invented by clever men to steal copper coins from the little man, who put aside his pleasures of today in the hope of buying more tomorrow. He said that bank accounts were sacrifices to the gods of tomorrow, and he didn't believe in tomorrow, so he spent his money today.

He spoke of his great-grandfather, old Samuel Burton, and of how he had carved his acres from a foreign wilderness, and he spoke of his father and his brother, Sam, and of his father's will. 'Vindictive old bastard, just because I wouldn't bow down and kiss his bum, he wrote me off. In this world you need to learn early how to kiss bums. Bloody Saint Sam knew how, the dirty perverted bastard. I hate his name. I hate that bastard's name.'

'I no like Sam talk,' she signed.

'That land is mine. Mine. But I'm stuck here in this shit hole.'

He spoke as he signed now, repeating words, spelling words. He spoke of his books, and he told her he had memorised the part of Macbeth when he was only sixteen years old. He told her of his mother's back room where he would take his books and read the part to her until he was word perfect. Then he recited the part, as he had to his mother. He recited for half an hour to prove he spoke no lie.

He told her he'd toured country Victoria and New South Wales with an amateur theatre company when he was nineteen, and he told her he could have been great, but he had found bloody Mallawindy. When he stopped speaking to light a cigarette, she tapped the table near his hand, and she signed, 'You talk more from that time. I like that time talk. Is good talk.'

'Talk to me,' he said. 'Use your voice. Talk to me.'

'No talk. Words talk long time all gone. Gone with blue dress. All finished. Better all finished. I like now. This way talk.'

His eyes filling with tears, he rose and walked into the yard, retrieving the Bible, opening it to the page where his children's births had been recorded. 'Get me my pen and ink,' he said.

Quickly she brought the tools of his only trade to his side, and she watched enthralled as he dipped the old pen into a bottle of black ink, then in his perfect copperplate script he wrote beneath the record of Linda Alice's birth.

Out, out brief candle. Life's but a walking shadow,
a poor player that struts and frets his hour upon the stage,
then is heard no more.

He didn't stay in Mallawindy for the funeral. He didn't see Linda's tiny white coffin sink beneath the earth. He went away, but he went often to Narrawee, so they didn't worry about him.

Summer and Christmas went, and winter came again, and Bessy bought a new electric sewing machine. She gave her old treadle to Ellie, but it was Ann who learned to thread it, and to let down the hems of Ben's trousers. He worked as a hair dresser and salesman with Bert Norris, and each week he brought his money home for Ellie.

Winter left, and still Jack didn't come home. Was he dead? He was no longer at Narrawee. Ellie had written there for news of him, but May wrote, saying she had no idea of his whereabouts.

Such a quiet year, a busy year. It had slipped away too soon.

Missing or dead, Jack was not being missed.

Bob Johnson, the policeman, came to the house. He came to discuss Jack's disappearance, but sometimes stayed for a meal or a game of cards. Father Fogarty came for Sunday dinners. Bessy and Uncle Bill came over the river often, and Linda became a pale little memory. No photograph of her hung on the wall.

a very good year

~

December 1973

12th December 1973;
Dear Ellie,
  Merry Christmas and a happy New Year to you and the
children. We were delighted to hear all of your news.
  The police constable sounds like a very able man. We
have had some of his colleagues call here. As they say, the
fact that Jack's bank accounts have not been touched since
he left Mallawindy is certainly unusual, but we must con-
tinue to hope for the best.
  Young Benjamin sounds like a great help, and Ann Eliz-
abeth, almost thirteen already. Time is indeed flying by. I
would dearly love to see her again one day. Sam and I
have been touring these last months, but Christmas and the
heat always bring me running home to Narrawee.
  I have enclosed a small gift to you and your family.
Our love and best wishes for the season.
                                        May and Sam.

'Jesus, if that's small, I wouldn't mind accepting the large gift,'
Bessy Bishop commented, handling the cheque and wishing she
had a rich relative.

Cured for forty-five years by the sun of Mallawindy, no-one, other than her mother and the registrar of births, deaths and marriages, would have named Bessy a full sister to Ellie. Bessy had trouble believing it herself lately. Ellie had about as much commonsense as a rabbit. She was still writing to Narrawee for news of Jack, when she should have been celebrating her freedom.

'I think I'll buy a ute for Ben with that cheque,' Ellie said, reclaiming it.

'You won't get much worth having for five hundred.'

'We'll sell the poddies, and we've been saving nearly every penny he makes at the shop. We should be able to get something decent for a thousand.'

Ben had been driving Bessy's tractor since he was thirteen. Bob Johnson had taken him around the block in the cop car, then given him his licence. He drove Ben and Ellie to Daree, helped them choose a good-looking Holden ute, then he drove Ellie home behind it. A divorced man, closer to fifty than forty, Bob's interest in the Burtons wasn't purely professional.

'Take it slow and careful, Ben, and you'll be jake. You got a good buy there. Old Holdens never die, they just rust away,' Bob laughed, waved a hand and drove away.

An hour later he was back, and driving anything bar slow and careful. He ran over one of Ellie's chooks. Bob had been eating a lot of dinners with Ellie and her children. He was a big man, slow moving, who in the last month had been tossing around the theory of maybe making the dinners a permanent arrangement. By the look of things today, he might have to go back to opening tins.

Ellie walked towards the squawking fowl. 'You're on its wing, Bob. Run your wheel back a bit, can you?'

He did as he was bid. He watched her stoop, pick up the chook by its legs, and with the minimum of movement behead it with the axe.

'Forget something?' she said, watching the headless chook attempting to fly.

'Yeah,' he said. 'I just had a call from Sydney. They've found him, love.'

'They've found him? Jack?'

'They've got him in hospital, in Sydney.'

'Hospital? Is he all right?

Bob looked at Ellie; he scratched his head and wished he'd been a bit faster on his feet. She was wearing a floral dress this afternoon, its soft greens highlighting her hair, which was plaited and looped at the nape of her neck – a good-looking woman. 'He wasn't alone, love. Him and his passenger had a head-on with a train at a crossing outside Sydney. The passenger died. Jack got flung clear.'

Ellie crossed herself as she stooped, picked up the fowl by its legs, and walked with it back to the house. Bob followed the blood drips to the kitchen door.

'They'd both been drinking. The driver of the car behind almost ran over Jack. He's a bit knocked around, a few cuts and bruises, but he's getting out tomorrow.'

Ellie sighed as she looked out at her land. The sun was still shining, the sky was still blue, but the warmth had somehow left the day. She didn't want Jack back. Life had been good, better than good. Even Annie was starting to act more like a normal girl.

'I don't know what I should do, Bob. Who was he with? Do they know?'

'You'll find out soon enough, I s'pose, love. Old Rella. Dave Eva's wife. They've got a place twelve miles out the Daree Road. It was Dave's car they were driving.'

Ellie's head was down. She knew Rella. Everyone in town knew about Rella and Jack. Bob placed his hand on her shoulder.

'She pissed off two weeks back, Dave said. Must have run into Jack in Sydney.'

'I should be thanking God that he's alive, Bob, but ... but I just wanted to know that he *was* alive. I don't – '

'I know, love. I know what you're saying. You're doing real good by yourself. I know exactly what you mean. We've been getting on real good too. Of course, you've got grounds for divorce. Deserted for twelve months. Proof that he was with another woman.' Ellie stepped back and Bob's hand fell to his side. By the look on her face, he might just as well have suggested murder as divorce.

Ellie studied her blood-stained shoe, wiped at it with a handkerchief. 'Maybe he won't want to come back,' she said. 'I mean ... of course, he probably won't want to come back here. He hates this town, Bob. Just because he had an accident, it doesn't mean – .' She turned to the stove where the kettle was boiling, spitting its water in skittish bubbles over the hotplates. 'Have you got time to have a cup of tea with me?'

'I'm choking for one, love. I didn't think you'd ever ask.'

Ann and Ben sat late with Ellie that night. It was a strange night, it seemed to be leaning on their shoulders, and all eyes kept straying to the yard where Ben's red ute was parked. Soon another car might pull in there. Soon their peace, their freedom to live, might be forgotten.

Ann's hands spoke quickly. Ben replied with his hands.

Ellie wanted to understand, but there was little she could pick up when these two really got going. Annie was as handy as Ben around the farm now. So different to what she was when Jack was around. Ellie was getting on so much better with her too. And the old sewing machine Bessy had given her – Annie was a magician on it, making her own dresses, and Bronwyn's. It was a rare talent that she had, and there were no two ways about it. This last year, Annie had fairly bloomed.

Each Friday afternoon, Mr Fletcher declared an hour of silence when hand signs only were used; he'd asked Ellie if she'd like to join the class for that hour, and she had thought about it. Half the children in town could talk to Annie now, but children learned things easily. She'd probably make a fool of herself. She was afraid of showing her ignorance. Jack had always called her ignorant.

Bob didn't.

Annie wanted her to learn the signs. She said Mr Fletcher didn't know how to laugh, and that he was like one of the giant peppercorn trees growing in the schoolyard. Ugly and old and smelly, but covered with delicate pink seeds that it shook off for the wind to sweep up, only his seeds were answers, and Annie was the wind. A funny girl, Ellie thought, she'd come out with some odd things lately, like Jack used to. They were two of a kind and no two ways about it.

Ben's hands spoke. Annie laughed. It was a delightful sound, and so normal. She never used to laugh out loud when Jack was around. To Ellie, the sound brought back memories of before the girls were taken to Narrawee, before Liza disappeared. Annie had been a capable, independent little thing, and she'd had that beautiful laugh. It was nice to hear it again.

She watched their hands a moment. They were so fast, but Annie didn't only use her hands. She used her eyes, her face, her entire body to lend emphasis to unspoken words. Ellie loved to watch her. She wished now she'd gone along on Friday afternoons, or had tried to learn the signing when Johnny wanted her to.

Never enough time. That and her lack of confidence in her ability to learn. She was no brain, and she knew it. Jack had picked it up easily enough. 'What's she saying, love?' she asked Ben.

'She's making up mad poems. Happy ever after no more fairytale. Maybe last for ever, they put Dad in jail. Give life for man slaughter. Make life safe for daughter,' Ben translated, his smile wide.

'Tell her she mustn't say things like that. My goodness. He could have been killed too.'

'Devil look after own man, Bessy say,' the flying hands replied as the three-way conversation continued, Ben translating for his mother. Never one to waste his own words, he enjoyed being Annie's voice now that she had found much to say.

'No more of that sort of talk,' Ellie said. 'It's a funny old night though, isn't it. It's like time has stopped. We should be in bed, but I'm not a bit tired.'

'Death of last good day. This night, very strong night. Clock tick-tock, slow. Can't wear away last good night. Tonight, heart thumping happy. Bang, bang, bang, bang. Night dodge from clock. "Yes. Yes," say night. "Go away clock. Go away time. Go away. I stay one week here. Make happy last,"' Annie signed.

'Bob said your Dad would be out of hospital tomorrow.'

'Do you think he'll come home, Mum?'

Again Ann's hands spoke. 'He come home. On bus. I think we better make early Christmas. Give him leftover. We have all thing ready. Policeman give us dead chook. Fate. Got present. Got plum pudding ready. Tomorrow we make special Christmas come. Yes. Have party?' Her eyes watched her mother's as words poured from her fingers.

Ben translated. 'We'll invite Bessy and Bill over. The bus doesn't get in until ten. We can have an early tea and a last game of cards, Mum.'

Ellie looked at her hands and the fine golden band sunk deep into the flesh of her ring finger. She twisted it, twisted it. It wouldn't come off, even if she wanted it off. It was wrong to even think such things. Jack found. Isn't that what she wanted? She shook her head. Found, but with Rella Eva. There had always been other women. Ellie knew it, whether she admitted to knowing or not. That was one thing about Jack that she never understood. Never once had she denied him his rights. Never. Not that she enjoyed it, but it was her duty, and one she hadn't missed this past year.

One wonderful year with no fear of pregnancy. She was thirty-eight, and didn't want any more babies. She looked at Annie. She's growing up, she thought, tall like Jack and Johnny, but no sign of breasts yet. Ellie was only thirteen when she matured. She'd need to talk to Annie about things – or get Bessy to. Bessy was good with her, she'd taught Annie a lot about cutting and sewing in the first months of the machine. They got on like a house on fire.

Ann's hand tapped the table close to Ellie's hand.

'What, love?'

'Yes. We ask Bessy. Play card.' Head nodding, Ann pointed to the river, miming the shuffling of cards. She made her signs painfully slow, abbreviated, repeated, willing her mother to understand.

'We will,' Ellie said. 'We'll open our presents tomorrow and tell Bronwyn Santa came early, and we'll invite Bessy and Bill over for dinner.'

'Thank you.' A nod. Fingers to the point of her chin, away.

Ellie copied the sign. 'Thank you.' She'd have to make a point of trying harder.

Annie had never been a pretty baby, not like Liza, but she was certainly going to be a fine-looking woman. Clear olive complexion and not a freckle. Good features too, strong straight teeth, and those eyes – brick walls against strangers, but tonight her eyes were speaking. Her hair was a black cloud she tried to tame in braids that swung over her shoulders. Corkscrew curls sprung free at brow, and neck, and ear. Wilful hair. She didn't inherit her curls from Jack's family. Both he and Sam had dead straight hair. Her long limbs were theirs though. The sisters at the hospital had commented on her long limbs when she was a tiny baby.

Ellie closed her eyes now and allowed her mind to wander back to the night Annie was born. Dear little Johnny. He never knew when he was beaten, so he never was beaten. That night, it was like he'd placed his claim on Annie, and years later, after she came home from Narrawee refusing to speak, Johnny had loved her, persevered with her, and finally got through to her.

And Ellie had made him run. Packed his bag and made him run.

Dear Johnny. He didn't want to go. '*I can't leave her, Mum. Don't make me leave her, Mum.*'

The silence grew long. With her index fingers, she dried two tears before they could escape, then she reached for her daughter's plait, giving it a playful tug. 'It's made of strong stuff, like you are, love. You've got a bit of me in you somewhere. I think we might both bend before we break.'

Ann smiled, and her eyes that never wept, glistened beneath the light. Ellie's own eyes grew moist again. Was a word, the touch of her hand so important to this girl? Guilt washed over her. She near drowned in guilt. Of course it was, but she'd never been able to get close to Annie. Never put her to the breast. Everything had happened too quickly after the fire. Jack disappeared for five months that time. She thought he'd gone for good, and she'd moved back home to her father's house.

How she loved that little mud-brick house on the highway.

Her eyes looked off into the distance and a smile crept across her features, erasing the outlines of Mallawindy summers. For an instant, she was her father's golden girl again. Her childhood in that house hadn't equipped her for life with Jack.

His handsome face, his smile – he was only twenty when he'd stopped to lean his bike against the split-rail fence that first day. 'Could you spare a mug of milk for a thirsty stranger, Miss?' he'd said.

She had been milking the house cow, and she'd looked up to see this handsome prince standing there. He'd sounded like a prince too. 'How old are you, Miss?' he'd asked.

She wasn't quite sixteen. Her age frightened him. He'd drunk his milk, then reached for his bike and straddled it. 'Are you going to tell me your name?'

Her blushing face turned to the old cow, she'd remembered late her father's warning. 'I'm not allowed to talk to strangers,' she'd said.

'I'm no stranger. I'm Prince Charming and by God, you're

Sleeping Beauty. I'll be back this way after your birthday, and I'll wake you with a kiss. Remember me, Beauty,' he'd called over his shoulder as he pushed off through the dust. 'I'm drunk on milk and dreams, so you'd better remember me.'

He'd returned to Mallawindy six months later. All the girls in town thought he looked like a movie star, but Jack only had eyes for her. She'd been in love with him since that first moment. His family was rich, and he was educated. He'd spent six months at university, and twelve months with a theatre company, and he was in love with her.

She could still remember his first kiss, remember drowning in his arms. He'd been so gentle, but so impatient. Ellie felt the blood creeping to her brow at the memory. She glanced quickly at her children. Their hands danced beneath the bright white electric light, their eyes on each other, only the rhythmic tap-tapping of finger against finger, the occasional slapping of a hand, broke the silence. She was safe to dream a while, remember the good times.

The upstairs bedroom of her father's farmhouse had always been her room. Bessy slept downstairs. When Jack discovered she slept alone up there, he'd climbed the oak tree and like a high-wire act, walked across the high-pitched roof to her window. She wouldn't let him in, though. He'd perched there, quoting Shakespeare for hours, his shoes tied by their laces, dangling over his shoulders, and he vowed he'd sit on her roof until he turned to stone.

For five nights he'd made that climb. It had seemed so romantic to a sixteen-year-old. She was Juliet courted by her own handsome Romeo – until the night Jack climbed through her window and romance went out the door.

Her father had built them a house on the far corner of his land, and close enough to the footbridge. 'I'm not one to hold a grudge, son,' he'd said the day they married. 'The deed is done. Now we all have to make the best of it.'

Ellie was three months pregnant, and so sick, but Jack was

good those first years. He drank a bit, and he had a temper, but he was interested in Johnny. It would have been all right if she hadn't got pregnant with Ben. Jack wanted her, not crying babies. She wanted kisses and poetry and romance, not the bed. The verbal abuse began before Ben was twelve months; by the time he was three, and she pregnant with Liza, Jack was running around with other women. He had such a wicked temper – like the night he had burnt the footbridge, which was cutting off his own nose to spite his face. He couldn't swim. Ellie could, and she made certain the children swam well.

Ellie looked up at Annie, remembering again the fragile mite in the hospital. The doctors hadn't expected her to make it through that first night, or the next day. Ellie was still in shock and too worn out to argue when Jack wanted to baptise her C of E. It had been like baptising a stranger's child; her baby had died under the willow tree. Any one of the other babies in the hospital looked more like her own than that little stick insect with legs as thin as Jack's fingers. Ellie kept turning to the other babies, looking for her own, certain the nurse had made a mistake.

Johnny knew which one was his though. 'You killed her, and I made her alive,' he'd said to Jack that day in the hospital. People heard him too. 'It's your fault she came out too soon,' he said.

Jack didn't deny it. His face had coloured up and he'd left the hospital without a word. Ellie went home to the farmhouse that night with Johnny and her father, leaving the little stick insect to God and the doctors.

The following months had been the happiest of Ellie's life. She'd put the baby out of her mind, expecting it to die. A terrible mother. Terrible. But how Liza and the boys thrived at Grandpa's house. The mud bricks seemed to keep it warm in winter, and cool in summer. Benjie's asthma even improved, and he started putting on weight. The boys loved their Grandpa, and he loved them. Annie was three months old, and still at the hospital when he died of a heart attack at the dinner table.

The house and all the land on the town side of the river had been willed to Bessy. Already well established in her own house, she sold Mr Mack the house on the highway, plus thirty acres of land, then used part of the money to rebuild Ellie's fire-damaged kitchen.

It was as if Jack had some contact in town, because two days after Ellie and the children moved back to their side of the river, he had turned up.

They picked Annie up a week later. She was still underweight. To Ellie, in those first weeks, it had been like baby-sitting someone else's child. It hadn't felt permanent – like the baby would be going back in a week or two to its own mother. She never got close to her. Independent little thing that she was. Jack had no interest in her, but he couldn't get over the change in Liza. He'd left a bald, bawling baby, and returned to a golden-haired doll. Liza was sixteen months old, and the most beautiful little girl. Jack spoiled her, wanted to dress her up like a doll. He started taking her with him when he went to Narrawee to see Sam and May. 'My little Shirley Temple,' he used to call Liza.

The Miss Tiny Tot competition came up in the newspaper when Liza was almost four and Jack knew she'd win it. He knew it before he had the photograph taken. And she did. Thousands of entries from all over Australia, and their beautiful Liza won the prize. They'd been so proud. Jack was happy for a while. It was as if he were important at last, as if he finally had something special that was his. Sam and May might own the property, but they didn't have Liza.

May couldn't have children, and Ellie knew her sister-in-law envied their fine family. She and Sam were always offering to have the boys to Narrawee for holidays. It would have been good for the boys to see how the other half lived, but Jack wouldn't let them go. Then, when they got Annie and Liza down there for that month, Liza had disappeared. For a long time after, Ellie believed May had stolen her, had her hidden away somewhere.

Perhaps she was in some school under another name.

If only, Ellie thought. If only. If only I hadn't got pregnant with Bronwyn. If only Jack had been at home when I had to go into hospital. If only Sam and May hadn't turned up and offered to take the girls. If only Johnny hadn't let them go. If only. If. If. If.

Until Liza disappeared, Sam and May used to come to Mallawindy once or twice a year. They hadn't been back since. Sam couldn't forgive himself, May wrote. Couldn't stand to be at Narrawee either. He lived in Melbourne now, in Toorak, and employed a couple to work the property at Narrawee.

It wasn't poor Sam's fault. He had nothing to feel guilty about. It was all May's fault. Ellie had never blamed Sam. He'd flown to Brisbane the day before Liza disappeared, then driven non-stop, night and day, all the way home. He was the one who'd found Annie, buried alive in the Narrawee cellar. It hadn't been Sam's fault. Poor Sam. He'd been over-generous with money since then. It probably helped ease his guilt.

Sam was the image of Jack, in looks, but so different. A true gentleman. He never touched the drink. Melbourne seemed so far away – like another country. Maybe they did have Liza. Had her in some private school down there.

Ellie shook her head and breathed deeply, attempting to still her memories, still her doubts. The police would have found out. Bob would have found out. She'd told him of her doubts. He was such a good kind man, and so handy around the farm, too. He'd helped Ben put up some new chook pens. He'd put new glass in a broken window. He'd even taken the lounge room door off and planed the bottom so it didn't stick. Such a help.

Jack never lifted a finger to help. Even in the first years he'd been worse than useless around the cows. The car accident might have frightened him. Maybe he'd changed. His hand hadn't been raised against her in the first years of their marriage. Perhaps he could change. He probably wouldn't come home anyway.

Both Johnny and Annie took after Jack's side, where Ben was pure Vevers. It had taken a long time for the blood of the two families to mix, but mix they had in Bronwyn, a wild urchin. At seven, she was an odd little mixture.

'Poor Jack,' she said, only realising she had spoken her thoughts aloud when her children turned to her. 'Just thinking out loud, loves,' she explained. 'Just thinking how much Annie is like her Dad, like he was that first time I saw him. Prince Charming on an old pushbike.'

But Ann was on her feet, her chair fallen over, her eyes angry as her hands signed, close to her mother's eyes. 'No! Not like him. You said like you. Yes, I am like you. Not like him. I will not be like him.'

'Shush, love. Shush.' Ellie's hands reached out to still the flying fingers. 'Let me just listen to the night. Do you know what it sounds like to me? Like a tired old boxer, waiting in his corner for the bell to ring for the next round.'

Two days later Jack arrived home on the midday bus. He had to walk from town and he was hot and sore. He dodged around the dog, who sniffed at his shoes, recalling with difficulty the scent of this man.

'Shit!' he screamed, stubbing his perennial corn on the splaying metal foot of the sewing machine. He hopped and he cursed and he tossed a basket of laundry into the yard. 'Shit on this bloody taxiless hole.' He pulled his shoe from his foot. It followed the laundry basket into the yard.

'Jack! For goodness sake. You've just got in the door, love.'

It was enough. Any excuse would have been enough. Tossed from the car like so much garbage. Cops treating him like shit. Stuck in a ward with the dregs of humanity and fed on hospital slops, and now he was back in this shit hole with her kids and her whining bloody voice. 'The bloody mongrel should have been put down. He's dead on his bloody feet.' He limped into the kitchen.

'Sit down, love, and I'll get you a Bandaid.'

'It's a wonder you haven't got corns on your guts. Why haven't you got the gumption to tell me to go to buggery?'

'Don't be silly, Jack. We were married in the church, and it's lovely to have you home.' She lied, and he knew she lied.

'Dishonest bitch. You wish I'd died. Freed you from your vows. Come on. Say it. Tell me to piss off. Tell me to go. Just say it. Say piss off you bad bastard. Get out of my life, and stay out of it. It's what I want to hear. Say it.'

'I didn't know if you were alive or dead for twelve months, Jack. What do you think that did to me and your children?'

'Made you all bloody happy for a while. Tell me to go. I want you to tell me to go.'

'You should have contacted us, let us know you were all right.'

'As if you cared, you gutless crawling bitch, with your little blameless face and your cold bloody bed.' His voice was tired, bored already. He needed a drink – or her.

'Not in front of the children, Jack.'

'Not in front of the children, Jack,' he mimicked. 'Why not? Let them know you keep a bloody cold bed, or did your tame copper warm it up while I was gone?'

'Bob has been a good friend to me, and that's all.'

'Then your tongue must be hanging out for it. Get down on the floor and play dead.' His right hand reached for her, black stitches half-circling his wrist like a many-legged caterpillar, but Ellie was out the door and heading for the river.

Jack stood in the centre of the room, his eyes filling with tears. He had a block of chocolate in his pocket for her. Fruit and nut. He'd thought there would be someone in town to drive him home. He didn't want to walk home, fall over the mongrel dog and kick his bloody corn. He didn't. 'Come back!' he screamed. 'Come back to me. Come back here.'

Empty house. Empty. Only a cake left to burn in the oven, only pots left to boil dry on the stove. Only the kettle spitting its ire at him, and the dog sniffing at his feet. He took a small bottle of whisky from one pocket and the melted block of chocolate from another, and he sipped his whisky, and he fed the chocolate to the dog.

'King Jack of Chook-Shit County,' he said, 'and you, you crippled bastard, my only loyal subject.'

Unannounced, Ellie and her dripping entourage entered Bessy's back door. No need for questions, nor answers. The trail of water told its own story. Bessy reached for towels first, and telephone second.

A gunshot blast cut her dialling short. It echoed and re-echoed along the river, then a long unnatural silence followed. Birds were silenced. The room was silenced. 'With a bit of luck he's shot his bloody self,' Bessy commented. She hung up the phone. 'Get your clothes off and toss them in the drier.'

They stayed at Bessy's house, wearing borrowed clothes, they stayed until the sun went down, and God took to the heavens with his paint-box. They stayed on, listening to the night birds across the river, mourning Jack's return. They stayed until their clothes were dry and Ellie's cows lowed out their message of discomfort, until the hens went to their roosts unfed. They stayed until Ellie could stay away no longer. No worthy beast should suffer because of her choice of husband.

'I'll tell him to go tomorrow, Bessy. I'll tell him it would be better for both of us to have a separation. I will.'

She left Bronwyn on the safe side of the river, and the workers rowed home in Bessy's boat. They went about their business by torchlight and moonlight, seeking Jack behind every shrub. They milked the cows, afraid the hissing machines might wake the sleeper. They fed the pigs, tossed wheat for the hens to find come morning. Ann broke eggs for the dog, mixed them with milk, then they looked for him in all his favourite places.

He was under the plum tree, and he didn't stir. Ellie reached down to pat him and her hand touched fur that was sticky, stiffening with blood. She stood in the yard and howled at the moon. Ben ran. He was too old to be seen crying.

Ann didn't cry. She stalked the fence, the yard, backwards and forwards, her eyes never turning away from the house and the murderer within the house. She walked, and her mother wept, and Ben stayed away for a long, long time.

The moon was low, a heavy gold, the night was bright with light. Strange light tonight. Ann took up the pick, walked with it to the willow where she dug at the clay, each slice of the pick cutting into her father's skull. The hole was a foot deep before Ben crept to her side with a shovel. They worked together then, knowing without need of words when it was done. Together they lifted the dog onto a bag, and carried him on his stretcher to the grave.

Ben's tears ran again. He let them trickle down his nose, drip from the point of his chin. Soundless tears of impotent rage, they gripped his throat, crushed his chest. This land had become his land. He wanted it, and the freedom he'd possessed last week, last year, to make it the way he wanted it. Now it was over. Now the old days were back again, the tiptoeing around his father, the attempts to divert his anger, the gauging of his mood before each word was spoken. He wanted to run like Johnny. But he couldn't run. He had to build his bridge. He had to stay here and scuttle around his father – a mouse in a trap. He wiped at his nose with the back of his hand, licked salt tears from his lips as Ann knelt over the dog, stroking the soft fur between its eyes. She was humming a tuneless lullaby, a primitive keening of the dead. She rarely made a murmur. It sounded strange, but somehow fitting.

'What's she doing? Is she crying, Benjie?'

'I don't know, Mum.'

'She'll bring him out here with that noise,' Ellie sobbed.

'Leave her alone. She's ... she's just ... just singing him to sleep, I think.'

Then, as suddenly as it had started, the keening ended, and Ann ran for the laundry, returning with an old sheet. They wrapped Mickey well; they tucked him into his final bed, and it was done.

'We'll have to go, loves. We'll sleep at Bessy's tonight. I'll tell him to leave tomorrow. I'll get Bob to come down and – '

'You go,' Ann signed as she walked to the overgrown plum tree and began stripping the green fruit from its limbs, dropping them down the front of her frock.

'Tell her they'll give her a belly ache. They're too green.'

'Go,' Ann signed again. 'Go. Run away.' She walked towards the house tossing plums at the bedroom roof.

'Annie! For the love of God, what are you doing? Annie! Stop that!'

Green plums, raining on the iron roof, thundered like giant hailstones, while Ann screamed, screamed, until he came, then she tossed her plums at him.

Through the chicken-wire gate, across the paddock to the river's bend she led him, Ben behind them, jumping stumps, skirting clumps of timber, adding his own scream to the night.

'Swim, Annie! Swim!'

But Ann had stopped dead at the river bank. Her father braked, almost fell on her. She tossed her last handful of plums in his face, and laughed at him.

No sound. No movement. A night fly settled on a gum leaf, creating thunder. Somewhere in another dimension of time a leather belt whirred in the warm night air, guided by a master's hand. Whirr, thwak! whirr, thwak! Too clear, crystal clear.

Bessy was screaming abuse from the opposite side of the river.

Whirr, thwak! Whirr, thwak! Whirr, thwak! Only that and Ann's laughter, old as her eyes that had stared too long, old as memory, old as time.

Ben, immobile figure carved from stone, howled for his lack of height, of breadth, for his inadequacy, while the belt whistled in the air, thunked on flesh. 'I'll break you yet. I'll break you, you crazy bitch,' Jack screamed.

He didn't know he was wearing himself out on a lost looking-glass.

Ann could feel the belt as if it were landing on glass, see the shimmer of glass. She was the girl dressed in blue, laughing behind the looking-glass. And she could hear the words, hollow words.

'Break you. Break you.'

Only diamonds can cut glass.

Her laugh and the words mingling. She couldn't stop the words, or her laughter. Didn't want to. Laughter cut him more deeply than his belt could cut her.

You're just a reflection, an opaque rejection, you won't pass inspection.

'You're mad, you black-headed little bitch. I'll kill it in you.'

She heard those words, too. And she laughed louder because she heard them. He gave up before she did. He ran from her laughter, and she lay on the sand laughing and counting the silver stars circling in the sky. Strange sky. Strange light tonight. Everything looked strange. Crystal clear. The world was a flea beneath a magnifying glass. She could see every dust speck, every hair.

Ben squatted beside her, his eyes brimming with tears, and she watched one lone teardrop glistening like a diamond beneath the light of the grieving moon. It moved too slowly. She watched it, until it moved not at all. 'Are you all right, Annie? Talk to me.'

Dear Ben, of so few words, now needed her words. They were there, too, and she knew it, but they were too hard to find yet.

'Stop it, Annie. Stop laughing. You're frightening me,' he pleaded, carefully straightening her skirt, modestly covering her pants and bleeding thigh, all the while weeping. An excess of tears, diamonds to spare.

Ann reached up her hand to make him some words, but her index finger found Ben's diamonds and she stole one for her own eye, placing it carefully there, trying to blink it into the place that made the salty water flow.

'One tear,' her hands said. 'Annie Blue Dress, only find one borrowed tear for our Mickey.'

the test

~

December 1973

Dear Mr Fletcher,
Ann will not be attending school today, due to a sore throat.

Yours faithfully,
Mrs J W Burton.

Ellie didn't like writing lies; the sore throat eased her conscience. She'd slept in Jack's bed last night, and they'd made up. He'd said he was sorry. He'd been gentle, like he used to be and she'd been feeling very hopeful, until she saw Annie.

'No school today.' Eyes down, Ellie pushed the note across the table, attempting not to see what Ann's wild hair did little to camouflage. She was marked from throat to calf. Thank God he hadn't marked her face. Ellie looked at the skirt hem, hurriedly lengthened. 'Note. Bronwyn will take it to school. You stay home today.'

'I wear high neck cardigan. Pull sock high,' Ann signed and mimed.

Ellie shook her head. 'Write it down for goodness sake.'

Ann gritted her teeth, tossed her hair back and went to the door, signalling Bronwyn to her side. 'Tell her I wear cardigan. Pull sock up high.'

66

'Tell her she can't go out of the house like that, Bronwyn. I've written a note to Mr Fletcher.'

'Tell her, so sorry she waste good paper on note. I must go today. Stupid priest, long nose in everything. Now got Daree high school headmaster big frightened. Don't want dumb girl. Think dumb mean stupid. Must do test. Must do good, Mr Fletcher say.'

Backwards and forwards the argument continued, Bronwyn translating as easily as Ben, and like him, adding her own comments. 'She has to go today, Mum. Old Fletch said so.' Again the hands flew. 'A big nose from Sydney is coming to see how dumb she is – to see if she has to go to the deaf school again.'

'She can't leave the house looking like that. Tell her she'll be the death of me with her wilful ways. She always did bring the worst out in her father. He was asleep. He would have been all right if she'd left him to sleep it off. Tell her she's getting too big for her boots, lately.'

'Tell her sorry. Better buy bigger boots for Annie. I will not be same like her. Last night, she very strong lady, say, "Yes, I tell him must go. We not want him here." Today she say, "Yes Jack, No Jack, three bag full Jack".' Ann thumped the table with a closed fist and the cups jumped high. 'He kill my dog. I hate him. I want him go away.'

'Tell her we would have had to have Mickey put down soon. He was fourteen.'

'Tell her, I don't care. Maybe he live seventeen year. Maybe twenty. Yesterday, she person. Like Bessy. Like my mother. Today she got ant brain. Got worm heart back.' Ann pivoted on her heel, and left the room, leaving her small translator giggling.

'Annie! You come back here at once! Annie!'

Bronwyn shook her head. 'She's going to go, Mum, and we're late already. You know it's no good yelling.'

* *

Ann's acceptance at the Daree High School was important to Mr Fletcher. She wouldn't let him down. The Burton girls arrived in the school yard in time to join the march into classroom. Bronwyn joined the tail end of Mrs Macy's group. Ann marched behind Marlene Dooley, her seat mate. She was older by ten months than Marlene, and a foot taller, taller than most of the boys. Yesterday it hadn't mattered. Today she was conscious of her height.

She slid down to her seat, stealing a glance at a seated stranger. He was as thin as Malcolm Fletcher was fat, his pinched features non-giving, like shoes saved for church and funerals. His rat-eyes stared at the dark faces scattered amongst the white.

Mr Fletcher looked uncommonly dry. His well loved Thermos wasn't on the table.

'Would you like me to light the fire, Burton?' he snarled. 'Go to the cloak room and remove that sweater.' Her cardigan today was like a red rag waved at a sweating bull.

'Sore throat.' Ann signed. 'Mum say, must keep warm.'

The inspector sniffed twice, a habit he repeated every minute, on the minute. Too mean to give up bodily fluids, he sniffed as he handed the test paper to the sixth graders. He sniffed as he stopped beside Ann's desk. She looked up, caught an eye that skidded away like fat on a hot frypan. He sniffed again, and sat, made a note in his black book.

'Time,' Malcolm bawled at a quarter to twelve. 'Scoot. Go run your heads under a tap and clear the brains. Scat, and allow me to clear mine. And get that confounded sweater off your back before you re-enter my classroom, Burton. The temperature is forty in the shade and ten more in here.' He waddled across the playing field to his house, faster than he had moved in many a day, his lips moistened in anticipation.

Ann had no cut lunch. She could have borrowed a sandwich from Bronwyn or Marlene, instead she spent the hour in the tiny cubby hole library, looking up words in the dictionary.

Malcolm and the stranger returned together to the classroom. They ignored her.

'To continue educating her within the normal school system would be detrimental to her well-being. My report will be to that effect, Mr Fletcher.'

'Look at the girl. She reads that dictionary as some read the Bible.'

'My argument is not with her ability to handle the work. I speak of her psychological well-being. Is she out in the playing field with the others? No. She will be better off with her own kind. I'd also like to discuss your handling of the Aboriginal students. You must find the parents of the white – '

'The Burton child is my primary concern at this time. To place her in an institution, at this stage of her development, would be criminal.'

'You have heard my opinion, Mr Fletcher. Now, the Aboriginal problem. Whites sit with whites, the blacks sit with other blacks,' and he sniffed. The droplet was saved.

'I have no Aboriginal problem. In my school, students sit where I sit them. They like it or lump it,' the fat man snapped. 'To get back to the Burton child.'

'The subject is closed, Mr Fletcher. I can only agree with the departmental heads on this matter.'

'Brain like a steel trap. You're incapable of seeing the obvious. The girl's lip-reading skills are outstanding. Too outstanding. We make few allowances for her. Her classmates understand her. They will be with her next year. You are treading on dangerous ground recommending she be sent away from her family again. I explained in my report her response when she was placed in a school for the deaf some years ago. You did read the report, I assume.'

'At length, Mr Fletcher, and the department is the first to admit that you have achieved admirable results, however – '

'And knowing the girl's history, you still recommend removing her from her familiar environment – '

'It has been proven that these children are better off with their own kind.'

'These children? You can't pin a label on this particular child. Pack her off to an institution, steal her freedom, and I for one would not wish to be responsible for the psychological damage it will do to her.'

'Which only proves that you have failed in your duty, Mr Fletcher. The break should have been made years ago. Why was she not brought to our attention back in – ' he leafed through his papers. 'Why was it left to the family's priest to bring her to our attention now? The longer we leave it, the harder it will become for her. Why did you not, at the very least, see that she was fitted with a hearing aid?'

'I don't believe she needs one,' he replied, peering at the girl in the tiny library.

The inspector followed his gaze, then clapped dry hands. The girl neither flinched nor turned her head. The visitor sniffed, his mouth lifted in a sneer. 'Her parents will be receiving a letter in the coming weeks. I know I can rely on you to assist the Department and the parents with the transition, Mr Fletcher.'

'Strangled, hog-tied by your own red tape ... red tape that cannot allow for the one child who does not fit into the Education Department's pigeonholing system – ' Malcolm's tongue, eager to strip shreds from this little man, stopped short. He was bashing his head against a wall of bureaucratic red tape, a wall which he had to admit shielded his own peccadilloes. Amused by this flash of insight, he smiled and turned away, peering at his watch. 'As always, the Department can rely on me, sir. I believe Mrs Macy would like to have a word with you before you leave. One of her Aboriginal students has a definite hearing loss.' At a near run, Malcolm crossed the playing field to his Thermos. Only four minutes remained to the bell.

The inspector packed up his notes and left.

Malcolm was reeling when he returned a quarter of an hour

late for the afternoon session. 'Get that sweater off your back, Burton,' he demanded. Ann shook her head. 'Shall we give her a choice, class? The sweater or the blackboard? Which will it be, Burton?'

'The board. The board.' The class played to him, urging him on, enjoying the games he only indulged in after a long session with the brandy bottle.

'Then, indeed you shall clean the board, Burton. Your peers have decided. Peers are important in this world. Obedience is also important; however, the choice is now yours. The sweater or the duster. The money or the box.'

Ann pulled her sagging socks high and walked to the front of the class, holding her skirt down with one hand while reaching for the top of the blackboard.

Big as an elephant and silent as a mouse, Malcolm's finger was on the pulse of his classroom. Nothing got past those eyes, blurred, magnified by the thick lens glasses he wore. He saw the thin line of calf visible between socks and hem.

'You shall be elected permanent blackboard cleaner. You no longer need a chair to reach the top. Someone has been putting fertiliser in your shoes lately, Burton,' he quipped.

'Chook manure,' she signed. 'We got plenty for free.'

The class laughed and the fat man smiled, well pleased with himself. He had put this girl together, bit by bit, built her out of a discarded confusion of skin and bone and wild hair. Less than four years ago, he had considered the day a success if she remained inside the room for half a day. Now she was making her own jokes. He was still smiling when he handed out an arithmetic test to grade six. 'Not a whisper, not a groan. Don't even breathe until I say you can,' he warned, then taking up his Thermos and tea cup, he propped his feet on the table and relaxed.

Ann sat, elbow on the paper, chin rested on the palm of her hand, scribbling her answers, then she pushed the page away. Finished. Everything was finished. Happy home. Happy school. Other heads were still down. The blank paper, handed to her with the test, lay unused. It tempted her pen.

'*Inspector*,' she wrote. '*Person who inspects – school. Little big man. Closed eyes. Closed mind. Closed heart.*

A weed unearthed by city mind, a noxious thing of certain kind,
   ripped from the earth then left to die in different soil, neath
      different sky.
Weak grows the weed no longer tall, its leaves all young will
      wilt and fall
pining for familiar sand. Strange wild weed of arid land.
Annie Burton, December 1973

He did it every time. Without a sound he materialised behind her, snatching the paper from beneath her hand. 'You will remain after class, Burton.'

Her sigh said it all. The red cardigan, pricking, she sat on in his classroom at three-thirty while the room cleared. She watched him place her test papers in an envelope. He glanced up, caught her eye.

'Do I note a spark of defiance in those inscrutable eyes, Burton?' he asked. Her reply a shrug, his attention returned to his table and to his pencils. He sharpened each one to a fine point, testing each point with a chubby index finger. 'Will you remove that sweater now?' he said minutes later.

'No.' A shake of a head.

'You will sit there until you do.'

She shrugged. Looked at the clock. It ticked away another five minutes before he rose, and waddled down to her desk, took her wrist in one hand, then with the other pushed her left sleeve high.

The bruising was vivid. Welts cut her forearm in a cross. He nodded, satisfied, then repeated the action with the other sleeve. 'I heard that your illustrious parent had risen from the dead,' he commented, returning to his seat where he sat again in silence while she removed the cardigan, tossing it over the back of her seat. His baby lips pursed and he shook his head at the deep purple mark on her throat. 'So,' he said. 'So, what is a weed, Burton?'

'Weed?' she spelt, eyebrows raised in question.

'Yes, a weed. Give me the definition of *"weed"*.'

'Plant. Grow with no cultivate. No care, just grow. Accident,' she signed.

'And despite adversaries, Burton. Very apt. An apt analogy. A weed, Burton, is the last plant to die in a drought and the first to show its head after the rain. A weed is a survivor. Australia is full of weeds. They are the sustainers of life.' He sharpened two more pencils and she watched him, remembering the first day he attempted to imprison her in this same room. He had given her a new book and a sharp pencil that day. She had thrown the book at his head, and stabbed his wrist with the pencil.

'You have sat in my classroom for the best part of four years, Burton. Watching you, teaching you, became a challenge to me. I wanted to find out what went on behind those inscrutable eyes. I never did. Give me the definition of inscrutable.'

'Mysterious,' she spelt with her fingers.

'Mysterious,' he nodded. 'You have made good use of our classroom dictionary. I have never taken you for a fool, Burton, so answer me a question and please don't take me for a fool. How did you come by that ... that bruising?'

'Fell from tree. Very high tree.'

'You insult me, insult my intelligence. However, let us see if we can do any better with this one. You were in the library when the sniffer and I returned to the classroom after lunch. We were for the most part hidden from your view. Given the optimum conditions, I would consider him to be virtually impossible to lip read, yet you knew his decision.'

'No,' her head denied.

'Then explain yourself,' he bawled, and she sprang upright in her seat. 'I warned you of the importance of today's tests. I told you that your admittance to the high school next year may depend on your results. Your morning's work was neat, exemplary. This afternoon's is a protest in blots.'

'Answers still right,' she defended.

'Answers scrawled by a spider after a swim in an inkwell. You knew the sniffer's decision. Deny it you may until you are blue in the face, you frustrating, damnable child.'

Ann slid to the side of her desk, one eye on the open door while the fat man poured himself a drink. He knew her too well, had spent too much time watching her.

There was little she remembered of the years before this classroom, but the years since were clear. He had made them clear, refusing to allow her to let her yesterdays disappear into the dark place in her head.

'Why do you write your poems in my arithmetic classes, Burton? Why not in English or history?'

'Don't know.'

'Do know. Open your mind to me. It's a brilliant mind, locked inside a concrete cage. Set it free. Let it live. Why in arithmetic?'

'Word come. Head full with talk word. No good English. I must find right talk word for English. No good history. Same thing. Number different, different side. No think with talk word, only number. So words come from other one ... other side. I write down. So.'

'Words come from the other side and she writes them down amid the equations. A tall weed with its roots in the sand will one day bloom with a brilliance to eclipse the hothouse flowers.' He slid the drawer of his desk open and started rummaging there, while she waited for the next burst. It was long in coming. 'Do you have a dictionary at home?'

'Benjie have one time for high school. Mum tell him sell all book when he leave high school.'

'But you'd have open access to a Bible.'

She nodded, her elbows on the desk, her chin resting on her palm.

'Have you read your Bible?'

'Big bit.' A gesture, her right finger and thumb, measured the approximate thickness of pages read.

'Did you enjoy it?'

'Read for ... for promise,' she said with a shrug. 'Stupid. Got no story. Got no showing of how man live before ... just rules, rules, rules ... all same. Ten, twenty, hundred time, same rule. Song of Solomon, I like. Little bit like Shakespeare.'

'So the tall weed of Mallawindy has read a little bit of Shakespeare.'

'Little bit. My father, he have book. I must not touch. When he not come back, long time, I touch a lot.' She gnawed on her lip, then she looked the fat man in the eye. 'I take one for me. Put my name on.'

'Which book?'

'Just poem. I love poem. Honey Breath special. Love middle bit.'

'Oh how shall summer's honey breath hold out against the wreck full siege of battering days. When rocks impregnable are not so stout, nor gates of steel so strong, but time decays. Oh, fearful meditation, where alack shall time's best jewel from time's chest lie hid, Or what strong arm can hold his swift foot back or who his spoil of beauty can forbid,' Malcolm quoted.

She sat barely breathing until he was done.

'What age are you now, child?'

'Thirteen.' Five fingers shown twice and then three, finger spelling, 'Soon.'

'The high school headmaster has the final word, you know. He may be approachable. If he is prepared to accept you then we have a chance.' He sighed and looked out the window. 'If I had started earlier perhaps? But it's too late now. That has been the story of my life. I have always been a little too late.' Though he appeared to be speaking more to himself than Ann, she dared not look away.

'Headmaster of a two-roomed school in a one-horse town. Headmaster with a drinking problem, I might add,' and he sipped from his tea cup to prove he spoke no lie. 'I hate this town, Burton. When I landed here, I had a wife and son. I had dreams. I despise this town. Its dust, its flies, but mainly its people. My wife and son are buried in the cemetery and I can never leave them. Never return to old England. If they put me out to pasture, I have no place to go, so what do I do? Doctors tell me that alcohol kills, and I say, but slowly, too slowly. What do you think of that, Miss Burton?'

'I know. Your wife, your son dead. Your son get encephalitis. He was friend for my Johnny. Same name, same year. When your Johnny die. My Johnny go.'

'Your Johnny. My Johnny. All gone, Miss Burton. All gone. It's a fly trap, Mallawindy. One of those filthy, sticky, pink things you used to see years ago. When they were new, they held a strange fascination, but as the months passed they built up a covering of flies and dust. I looked up at Mallawindy one day, Burton, and I saw myself dangling there. Stuck fast. Not even struggling. The fly trap was no longer sticky, yet still so hard to break away from.'

He removed his glasses, placing them on the table. Ann saw his eyes for the first time, free of their magnification. They were blue, so misty blue, like an autumn sky when it knows a long, cold winter is coming. 'I understand your talk,' she signed. 'I understand. Like fly trap, become habit. Better stay stuck, you think. Oh yes, better stuck in the old fly trap, Mallawindy. New trap maybe worse, but sometime maybe new fly trap not worse, but better.'

'You may be right, Burton. You may be right,' he said softly, rubbing his eyes with fingertips before replacing his spectacles. 'Off you go, child, or I'll have your arisen parent on my doorstep, accusing me of foul play. Take this with you.' From his table he picked up a small blue dictionary, offering it to her as she replaced her sweater. 'It was my John's,' he said. 'It still has his name on it.'

He opened the book, touching the script on the flyleaf with a fat finger. 'Tell me Burton, is it fair that disease should steal into this town, pass by the Aborigines' camp, skip over the Wests and the Dooleys with their uncountable hoards, who probably wouldn't have missed an offspring or two, then take my boy?' He fondled the tiny book for a moment more, then he tossed it to her and watched her sure hands catch and hold it. 'Perhaps there is a good lesson to be learned there. Man must never place all of his eggs in one basket.'

'No. Maybe fall over, spill all eggs. Two basket carry more eggs, make better balance, but sometimes fall with two basket, break more egg. Sometime better be careful, only take one basket, I think.'

'You speak from a wealth of experience with eggs, child,' he smiled.

Ann smiled with him. 'Yes,' she nodded. 'Thank you for your Johnny book,' she signed. 'Wish I have bigger word for say thank you. Not say what I feel. I will treasure your Johnny book forever.'

'Forever is too long, Burton. Far too long, and too far away.'

'Yes, forever. Sorry for messy test paper.' Signing, she backed away, the book clasped to her breast.

'Don't give up hope of high school. Other avenues are open to us. Good afternoon, child. Put your name in that book.'

the books

~

On the final day of the school year, Malcolm declared a half day holiday and the ladies at the Shire Hall cursed him. He didn't care. His Thermos was empty. He'd promised himself an early appointment at the hotel.

It was after seven before he left the hotel to drive to the Burton's property. It had been a long afternoon, but well spent. He was barely able to stand.

'What do you want here, you bloody old drunk?' Jack Burton opened the front door, found Malcolm gaining support from the wall.

'A slight case of the pot and the kettle, Mr Burton. However, I am here tonight to see the child, Ann,' Malcolm said, eyeing the man who had it all, while he had nothing.

He led Ann back to his car and opened the boot, steadying himself a moment before hauling a heavy case to the dust at her feet.

She could smell the strong scent of brandy. Wide-eyed, she stood before him, her head shaking, denying the gift, but he placed a hand on her shoulder. 'My only treasures,' he said. 'Into your hands I commend them. Fare thee well, child. You prevented my life being a total fiasco.' His bulk squeezed into the small vehicle, he drove away.

The case was old, heavy. Ann couldn't lift it. She squatted beside it, opened its clips, then peered at its contents. Benjie came and together they struggled with it to the verandah, then Jack took charge, lifting it easily to the kitchen table.

Open mouthed, the children grouped around the treasure trove of books, old books, expensive books. Jack handled them, selected, rejected, until he found Macbeth. An unfamiliar smile on his lips, he walked to the lounge room where he sat close to the light, reading. It was almost ten before he handed the book to Ann. 'Treasure them,' he said. 'I envy the bastard's guts.'

As Ann took the book, a sheet of paper fluttered to the floor. She stooped, picked it up.

Miss Ann Elizabeth Burton,
I defer to our good friend Mr Shakespeare, in an attempt to explain my actions.

> *'When to the session of sweet silent thought,*
> *I summon up remembrances of things passed,*
> *I sigh the lack of many things I sought*
> *and with old woes, new wail my dear times waste.*
> *Then can I drown an eye unused to flow,*
> *for precious friend hid in deaths dateless night,*
> *And weep afresh loves long since cancelled woe*
> *and moan expense of many a vanished sight.*
> *Then can I grieve at grievances forgone*
> *and heavily from woe to woe tell ore,*
> *The sad account of for bemoaned moan,*
> *which I now pay as if not paid before.'*

Words that build a bridge across the centuries, child, and relevant to me tonight. I am pleased you finally found Macbeth. Devour him, and may he whet your appetite for more, and if on reading my words, you summon up

remembrances of a fat old fool whom you once knew, then
let them be kind.

> *God bless,*
> *Malcolm Fletcher.*

Ann understood – as her father had. She ran for the river. Her shoes left on the bank, she dived cleanly into the water, emerging on Bessy's bank. Through the paddock she ran, dodging cows, and the mad bull. Across the lucern paddock, treading where she would, and under a split-rail fence, built by her great-grandfather.

No time to catch her breath, to consider the stitch in her side, she sprinted down the road. There was no thought of what she'd do when she got there, but just to get there. Then she was in the dark of the school yard, sprinting across the playing field and in through the headmaster's side gate.

Only one light showed in the weatherboard house. She ran to the window, great gasps of air replenishing muscles as she cupped her hands to her eyes and peered through.

And he was there. He was on his knees convulsed in pain.

Get someone. Have to get help. Only now she thought of the 'what', but within the thought came another.

Can't run any more. No time now.

What can we do?

Something.

She ran to the back door, pushed it wide, entered the strange kitchen and looked down at her teacher.

'Ahhh,' she yelled, her hands flying. He heard her. One hand signalled her away. She turned to the table, where a small brown bottle stood beside a taller relative. Empty. Ann recognised the small bottle. Her mother used weedkiller. She reached for it, held it beneath the light, looking for she knew not what.

And she saw it.

Induce vomiting. Then the hand holding the small bottle flung it at the wall where it smashed, spraying its glass to the sink, to the floor, and to her one God, the old God of knowledge, now grovelling on the floor like a grey slug.

Salt. Soap. Have to prop him. First have to prop him. Can't let him get on his back. He'll choke like Linda Alice choked on vomit.

Still sucking air, Ann up-ended the kitchen table as professionally as her father. Dragging it behind the convulsing hulk, she propped it on its side, its four legs jammed against a kitchen bench. Perhaps it would hold him. She knew she'd never move him should he roll onto his back. The salt shaker, fallen to the floor, was snatched up, emptied into the milk jug, then half filled with water, a finger used to stir it.

He wouldn't take it. His hand tried to wipe her presence away. His mouth gaped open, his face contorted as his stomach attempted to refuse its last supper.

Ann stamped her bare foot, her eyes wide, angry. 'Mmmm,' she demanded. 'Mmmm.' Again she stamped her foot.

'Go,' he signed.

She pushed the jug at him. His hand hit it, spilled the saline water, and she jumped away.

Have to hold his head still. Have to grab his hair. Have to pour it down his throat.

She couldn't touch him. An internal scream of desperation seized her throat as she stood back from the dying man. Her heart was racing, her mind numb with fear and too much air. Have to leave him. Run for Constable Johnson.

Too late.

I can't do anything.

He gave us everything. Him. Only him. He wouldn't give up. You are the strong one, Annie Blue Dress. Remember. Aunty May said only diamonds can cut a looking-glass. Remember. Do what must be done, Annie Blue Dress.

She screamed then. Her hand grasped at his thick grey hair. She dragged his head pack, poured the salt water over his nose, his mouth. Wasted it, but she found more salt beside the stove, mixed more.

There was so much body and too little space. She had to lean on his body. Again she dragged his head back, forcing him to see her. His lips parted and she poured liquid into his mouth. He spat it back at her, clamped his jaws, wept.

And she hit him. She punched his shoulder, slapped his fat face, pounded his heaving flabby chest, refusing to admit to failure. Her lips were mouthing one word, over and over. 'Drink. Drink. Drink. Drink.'

He saw no word. His eyes had closed, as she had closed her eyes to his words so many years ago. His body heaved and his heavy legs pounded the floor.

She moved to the side, knowing there was only one way. There had only ever been one way. Perhaps it was too late. 'Du wa,' she whispered, the word tested and found wanting. 'Dur-igh.'

She coughed and tried again. 'Dur-wingk,' she said. It was deep. It rasped against vocal cords unused for too many years, but the word sounded near enough in her ears. 'Der-wingk,' she scolded. Loud. Loud enough.

And his eyes opened. He looked at her.

'Du-wink, darm-oo,' she demanded, emphasising her word with the stamp of her foot.

His eyes misted. The child, who held his life in her hands, blurred, faded as he felt the jug again pressed to his lips. And his hand reached out for life, and to the slim hand that held it, and he drank the salty brew down like nectar.

Vileness gushed from him in unending stream. She sought a receptacle and found a bucket too late; still her face was pleased as the room filled with the stench of her victory.

'Derwink,' she said, when the gush had slowed. 'Dewink,' she said gently.

And he drank again from the new cup she held to his lips, and again his abused stomach expelled its contents while she guided his head with her hands.

Three times in the long night she thought him lost, and three times he vomited himself into awareness. At 5 a.m. he coughed, stirred, and the girl, anticipating, held a towel to his lips, protecting the floor she'd cleaned too many times. But the night was over, the roosters were signalling dawn and for Malcolm Fletcher, the worst was over.

Helpless, weak, sick, he slumped against the table, watching her worried face, waiting for her voice again, knowing, as her father had known, that she could hear.

'You m-ore derwink?' she asked, her voice deep and husky, but her pitch was good and her consonants were clear. He closed his eyes, too weak to control the tears blinding them.

Not deaf. Never deaf.

'Too much,' he whispered. It was all too much, the emotion, the pain, the overwhelming joy, and the nausea. He wanted to lie on his back and die, and he wanted to sit all night and listen to the words he, the drunk, the fat old failure had forced from her. For too long no-one had cared if he lived or died. But she cared. A thirteen-year-old child had cared enough to break free of her cage of silence to give him back his life.

Feeling the warm cloth on his face again, he opened his eyes to her, wanting to pour out his words, words he knew would make her run from him. His own weakness saved him.

'You sur-leep. On su-sum-mig. No on ba-ag.'

'Not on back,' he agreed. 'On stomach.'

She was still creating the words with her hands but her tongue was also making the words, determined words, and making its own slow corrections.

'Mm-my ba-bee, oolin-da, on ba-ag. Die on ba-ack.'

'Baby Linda. Yes, child. Yes, child.'

He looked at her eyes, twin fires beneath the naked light globe, and he saw each small success imprinted there. He did as she bid him. It took him forever. His arms were heavy sacks of grain, each leg the trunk of a gum tree. It took him forever and only when she was satisfied did she cover him with a blanket.

'I go,' she said. 'I come. B-b-ber-wing m-mil-g. You dewing milg.'

'Milk,' he whispered. 'Yes, child. You come back to me.'

Only when the door had closed behind her did he allow his emotions free rein. Howling aloud, his bulk convulsed with the weight of his tears. He bawled for the son he had lost, and for the girl he had found, and because she was Jack Burton's daughter. He blubbered like a baby because she looked like Jack Burton. She had his features, his height, his hands and his colouring, but it was not Jack Burton she had spoken to.

He tried to laugh, but bawled again into his pillow. He wanted to live, to live forever.

Comical, bloated, blubbering mass of man, waiting for a child to come with the milk, a child whose first stumbling words in seven years had been given with trust to her teacher.

the bankbook

~

The river wore a dusty reptilian skin; it matched the sky and the land. The wind had started before dawn; now it howled across the paddocks, stripping them of their top soil and flinging it arrogantly to the water. Cows, heavy with calf, prowled the Burton property, lowing their discomfort, while hens with ruffled feathers grouped in corners, clucking over the predicament of tomorrow's eggs.

Ellie Burton's mind was on eggs and hatchlings. There would be a new baby in January.

'Are you sure you want to walk to town, Annie? The boat will hold three,' she said, stepping from land into Bessy's rowboat. Ann shook her head. 'Then don't forget to bring Mrs Crocker's cream.'

'I've got it,' Ann replied. Her voice was deep, as if the patina of rust had etched and burred too deep on her vocal cords. Three years of speech, or thirty, would not alter its tone. She was close to her sixteenth birthday, five foot nine and still growing. Nature had lately imposed a tracing of womanhood on her, then moved off to more satisfying tasks.

One oar each, the sisters pulled away from the bank, while Ann stood watching, her back against one of Ben's bridge trees. They had long outstripped their planter, their futures planned, assured. Ben tended them well. He flooded them with water, plied them

85

with cow manure, trimmed the lower branches off, which forced the trees to reach high. He would cut them down one day, build his footbridge, and maybe give Ellie a more stable shortcut to town.

She hadn't withdrawn her child allowance for twelve months. It was little enough with just the two girls, but it grew if she left it alone. The farm was doing well, and with Ben and Annie bringing in their own money, she had no need to touch her account. Still, it would all come out this morning. Bessy was driving her to Daree to buy a few things for the baby.

Annie had already made six gowns and hemmed new nappies. She'd made the most beautiful christening gown too; it would have sold for a fortune in the shop. Dressmaking was a wonderful trade for a woman and Annie was a wonder with a needle and thread, but still wasting her time at school. 'Good dressmakers are as scarce as hens' teeth,' Ellie frequently said.

Ben had been working for Bert Norris since he left school. He sold newspapers and toys, pots and pans; he was the town barber, but in his heart, still a farmer. Up at five and in bed at twelve, he worked around Jack's presence. Ellie didn't know how she would have coped without Ben.

Each year Jack spent more time with Sam and May, then made up for his months of sobriety by drinking more when he came home. Perhaps the seventies were a time of more in Mallawindy. There were more cows, more pigs, there was more money, and more abuse too. God only knew how Sam and May tolerated Jack. Ellie had to. He was her husband.

Bronwyn was becoming a worry. She had Jack's temper, and his unforgiving nature. Ellie didn't know what to do with Bronwyn, or Annie, for that matter. Since the night Jack shot the dog, Annie had spent her life goading her father, tossing insults, plus anything else she could get her hands on, at him. What with her and Bronwyn and Jack in the house, it was like living with three time bombs. Boys were easier to raise than girls. Ben and Johnny hadn't ever talked back to her, hadn't given her a minute's trouble in their lives. She hoped the new baby would be a boy. She'd suggested to Jack that they call it Samuel Patrick, if it was a boy, but Jack refused to name it after his brother. His attitude towards Sam was difficult to understand; to hear him speak, it seemed as if he hated his brother, but he never refused his money, or his invitations.

Ann watched the sisters until the boat was tied to the makeshift dock on the opposite bank, then she picked up the basket and walked away. She had a bike, but bikes and Mallawindy's August wind didn't agree. She enjoyed walking, enjoyed the neither here nor there of it. Walking gave her open space and time to be alone.

Her eyes near closed against the stinging dust and the whip-like slap of her hair, she skirted around the potholes and dry chis-elled ridges on a path that followed a cow's morning ramble through the western paddock to the unmade road. Here the wind swept up new gritty ammunition to fling at her. As she swung into the full face of the blow, a howling gust dragged her hair back, exposing features that sat well together. Large eyes, high cheek bones, a determined jaw accentuated her wide mouth and her father's strong even teeth. She was lucky to have inherited his teeth, Ellie often said. Like Jack, Ann hardly had a filling. Ellie wore top dentures.

Ann hadn't inherited her father's eyes. They were large like Ellie's, but dark enough to look black in some lights. There had always been an agelessness about her eyes, now age draped her core. She could have been twenty. Many thought she was older than fifteen. Perhaps her height lent her age. The town women trusted her with their fine fabrics, stripping to their corsets in the fitting room behind Bert Norris's business, while Ann tacked and pinned. Male eyes followed her when she walked by. The boys she went to school with, who had to find a new name for her when she was no longer Dummy, had lately stopped calling her Lank-the-crank and tried to chat her up.

She wasn't interested in the Mallawindy boys, didn't think about any boys – not much. She studied, and she worked the farm at Ben's side. She drove Bessy's tractor when they borrowed it to cut hay, and she could drive Ben's ute. She started up the pump that sucked water from the river to fill the house tanks and flood the lower paddocks. She dug trenches with Ben, milked cows, collected and packed eggs, and she sewed. Like Ben, she worked long hours. They were mates, best mates, she and Ben. They still spoke with their hands too – Ben more than she, these days.

When her voice had been accepted as a permanent thing, her father and Bob Johnson questioned her about her time spent in Narrawee. For weeks after, both separately and together, they asked her what she remembered about Liza's disappearance. People from the city drove up to speak to her too. She even got her name in the Melbourne papers when they rehashed the old story. Bronny read it, but she didn't.

'I remember nothing before I was nine,' she said to everyone. It was no lie, but as the months continued to pass, some memories began filtering through. Disconnected scraps of conversations, and pictures that moved before her eyes like slides in a slide viewer, rushed at her.

She told Mr Fletcher about them, and he tried to place the memories in chronological order. There was a bond between Ann and her old teacher that Ben and Bronwyn couldn't understand. They didn't know about the night she spent at the schoolhouse. No-one knew about that. Mr Fletcher had been sick for months after his attempted suicide. He'd even lost weight – then made up for it double when he was well again.

Ann had always had dreams about a white house and green lawns, now she knew they would be found at Narrawee. Mr Fletcher telephoned Sam and May, and they sent him a pile of photographs. There was a recent one of them taken at Narawee. It gave Ann goose bumps to look at her uncle.

In the photograph, Sam's hair was grey, and worn long. It fell to his collar. His moustache was bushy. It grew down the sides of his mouth to his chin, and he wore tinted glasses, and long shorts.

He looked even taller than her father. May was small, slim, also wearing shorts. Perhaps her lack of height made the man at her side appear taller. He looked older than her father too, with his grey hair and moustache.

The house was a palace, a double-storey, white stone mansion; it seemed to shimmer in the sunlight. It was hard to believe her father had grown up in it, but she could understand now why he loved it, and fled there each time the invitation came in the mail.

There were old photographs of Ann and Liza, also taken at Narawee. Liza always posing, Ann's own eyes wide, as if she'd been looking at magic. Ann could find no memory of that magic, or of her sister, or even who the photographer had been, be it May, Sam, or a stranger.

The people, who came from the city to speak to her about Liza's disappearance, said she had probably seen the man who they believed kidnapped her sister. Why couldn't she remember him? She tried, tried to force memory. Only a week back, she'd taken the small portrait of Liza from the kitchen wall and stared at it, both right side up and upside down, straining to see beyond the glass, to know the older Liza. There was nothing. It was like a blank sheet of paper. Nothing.

Her father caught her with the photograph. 'Get your bloody hands off her,' he said.

'I hated her,' Ann told him, and when she said it, she knew it was true. She hated a blank sheet of paper. That's all Liza was to her. That old fake photograph, and blank white paper.

He came at her, unbuckling his belt, but she dodged around the table and tossed the photograph at his head. He caught it, as she knew he would. He couldn't let his precious treasure smash to the floor, but he screamed after Ann, and she screamed his own words back.

It had taken eighteen months for her to regain her fluency with speech. She liked practising on her father. Once, long ago, she had felt sorry for him, even thought she'd loved him when he used to talk to her, and teach her things about the world. But what was love? She'd loved old Mickey, and Johnny. She loved Ben and Bronny, but that love was a two-way thing, and mixed in with respect. How could she respect her father?

But still, she could, and sometimes did. Like when the city people came to talk to her, he had stayed with her, sat on the couch beside her, protected her. He'd been so sane and sober, sounded so educated, like a father she could be proud of. The city people respected him, and when he said that they were upsetting her, and that they'd asked enough questions, they left her alone and drove away.

Ann respected Aunty Bessy, but she didn't love her. She respected Bessy's fluency, and her vocabulary which could match any truckie's. Ann would have liked to add some of Bessy's words to her vocabulary, but she couldn't yet. One day. One fine day she would.

For twelve months after that night of his suicide attempt, Mr Fletcher had worked with Ann, developing his own brand of tutelage and speech therapy. She trusted him, totally, yet she didn't quite trust him enough to tell him about the voice.

Maybe everyone had a second voice inside their heads. Maybe it was what people called conscience, she thought. She used to call the voice her conscience until Marlene Dooley started talking about her sister who worked for two weeks at a psychiatric hospital as part of her nurses training. Marlene talked for weeks about her sister's experiences, entertaining travellers on the school bus with her stories. She spoke of little rooms with padded walls, and the straight-jackets her sister had to help put on one lady who believed she had God living in her head, talking to her, telling her to drown her babies.

Ann learned a lot about life on the school bus, and the God voice sounded too familiar. She had nightmares about it for weeks, and panic ate her mind each time she heard the voice. Maybe she was stark raving mad too, just like the lady who tried to explain the voice in her head as God's. There were weeks, months, when it didn't happen, months when Ann could convince herself the voice was imagination. Then it would come back. And the words were strange. They were not her words, nor were they spoken the way she might speak, and when it happened, the words seemed to separate her from wherever she was, place her behind the glass mirror where her own words bounced back at her. Some months ago, she had identified the voice tossing instructions against her inner ear. It belonged to the little Annie she used to be before Narrawee.

For six weeks after that night with Mr Fletcher, Ann had hidden her new ability, but there was no way Malcolm would allow her to be sent away to the deaf school. He said she had to speak to her mother, or to Ben. It was too embarrassing – like she'd been shamming all along, just as her father had always said.

In the end Mr Fletcher worked out a plan, and it was the first time she'd ever heard him laugh, the first time she ever saw a glimpse of the devious mind he hid from the world.

He said that in Mallawindy it was a well known fact that she had been struck dumb by some stroke of heavenly vengeance, so who better than the interfering Father Fogarty to take credit for the cure. It was in church that Ann spoke her first public words, and only the week before she was due to pack her bags for the deaf school.

Poor old Father Fogarty, ever since that day he'd preached about God's hand reaching out through him to make the miracle. But though he tried reaching out to others in the community, arthritis didn't disappear like magic for more than a week or two, and Jenny West, almost blind, still couldn't see.

The mud-brick farmhouse, built by Ann's great grandfather Vevers, was on the edge of town. From its fence, part of the Burton's tin roof was visible. So near and yet so far.

Ann turned her head to glance at her mother's childhood home as she walked by. She always looked at it with her head to one side, attempting to set it straight on its foundations; its chimney had a definite lean towards the setting sun. The bricks had been up so long, they now appeared to have grown out of the earth. Jasmine and ivy, honeysuckle and ornamental vines covered the walls, and probably held them together, Ann thought. If the plants ever died, the house would tumble down in a heap of dust.

She hadn't seen inside the house, hadn't walked its hallowed floors, or wandered its sprawling garden. Although Ben remembered it as Grandpa's place, Ann only knew it as Mr Mack's; thus it was his prerogative what he did or didn't do to it, even if Bessy and Ellie looked on him as a caretaker not taking proper care. They never passed it by without a halt to see if the fig tree had enough fruit on it to warrant pinching for jam, or if the scented lilies had survived Mr Mack's latest attack.

Ann came on the sisters outside the butcher's shop. They were talking to two women from the church. 'I won't be late, Annie, but if I am, get some vegies on for Dad's dinner, and heat up the stew,' Ellie said.

Ann nodded, her concentration on her mother's waist – or lack of it. Each day now the baby was more obvious. Baby brother, baby sister. To Father Fogarty, it was proof of love. Babies were created out of married love, but as much love had gone into this one's conception as the making of a pumpkin. Petals had opened and been accidentally pollinated by a wandering bee.

The world moved in cycles. The land, the seasons, dancing to some master's plan. When her mother's cycles stopped four months ago, Ann's began, as if the big computer in the sky had been waiting for that exact time to hit a switch.

Lunar cycles. Women and the moon must have been the old timekeepers, Ann thought. Each month now, when the blood began, it reminded her of something, somewhere. The voice in her head was bad at those times, and the picture memories kept piling, one on top of the other, until her head crawled with them.

Her father had his cycles too, but she couldn't blame the moon for that. His bouts of drinking, his trips away, his wild returns. And any wonder, leaving that mansion to return to this place. He had arrived home from Narrawee in a new car two weeks back, and he hadn't been sober since. Every night he screamed and kicked and cursed his brother's name.

His car was parked in front of the hotel again today. Poor old Sam would be in for it tonight.

They must have pitied him in Narrawee to put up with him. They always sent him home with new things. New television, new cap on a front tooth, broken in a fight at the hotel with some woman's husband. Although in pain for days, he didn't go to Daree to have it fixed. The Daree dentist might be good enough for Ben and her mother, but he wasn't good enough for Jack Burton. He drove to Melbourne, hours away, had his tooth fixed by a Collins Street dentist.

Grey Melbourne, where Ann had been taken once. Place of tall buildings and small white beds and a boy, and − . 'Don't think,' she said, and hurried on.

Mallawindy's shopping centre was busy today. Farm trucks and utes lined the street. It would be a good day for business. There was a crowd in front of the Shire Hall, where a draper from Daree set up shop once a month. With no competition closer than Daree, he had the monopoly before Ann started frequenting his stall. Each month now, she ransacked his rolls of fabric for bargains, which she transformed into blatant copies of his children's wear. She sold them at Bert Norris's shop.

Ben suggested it. He had a good head for making and saving money. Twelve months ago, Ann had made up six small dresses. Ben sold two on that first day. Now she had a small rack of children's and babies' wear in the far corner of the shop. When her business began to expand into orders, Bert had offered the use of his barber room for fittings. 'Half a dozen for you, young Annie, and six for me,' Bert said.

She hadn't understood what he'd meant, not until she'd noticed her customers browsing in his giftware section, where his signs, LAY-BY NOW FOR CHRISTMAS, hung all year round. Even her rack of clothing was drawing young mothers into his store. Few left without buying a magazine or a packet of gum.

Deadeye Dooley was Ben's age. He worked in the hardware side of Bert's shop. She saw his head pop up from behind a stack of paint tins.

'How are ya, Annie?' he said, his good eye looking directly at her, his grey blob looking at the ceiling. He was in church for a brother's baptism on the day of the miracle, when Father Fogarty announced Ann's re-baptism. 'I don't want to,' she said. Four little words that created a stir that took months to settle. It would never settle for Deadeye. Each time she spoke, he expected bolts of lightning to strike his bad eye and make it whole.

Ann waved a hand to him as she turned to her rack. No lightning bolts, but since yesterday, two frocks and a baby's dress had sold, and a lay-by note was pinned to the shepherd suit. She searched her stock for a mini skirt she'd flung together in ten minutes flat. It was gone too, and the little girl's frilly blouse. Mentally she tallied her week's takings, adding this morning's sales and the ten percent lay-by deposit. Money. Money. Lovely money for her bank account. Money for her escape. One day. One fine day she'd take her bankbook and go to Melbourne and Sydney and everywhere until she found Johnny.

'A good week, ah, young Annie,' Bert Norris's voice cut into her thoughts.

She smiled, nodded, walked to the counter waiting for Norris to pay her, eager for the feel of notes in her hand, notes made by her hand, money gleaned from women's desire for pretty things that would buy her a future.

'Benny's cutting old Fraser.' Bert pointed a thumb towards his back room. 'Mrs Fraser was talking about a wedding dress for young Janey, and in a hell of a hurry too. Wants to know if you can do it by Saturday week, and how much.'

'About fifteen dollars,' Ann said. Eager to win work, she kept her quotes too low. But this would be her first wedding dress and she wanted it. She knew Janey, had been through school with her. All the kids on the school bus knew of the pregnancy, long before her parents. Janey had mentioned the dress to Ann a week back.

With a finger to his lips and his head close to hers, Bert said, 'Thirty, more like it, young Annie. Dick Fraser's worth thousands and you've got him over a barrel. Ya gotta learn when to twist the knife if ya gunna do any good in business. Fraser'll be willing to pay a fortune for a dress in a hurry. Don't sell ya merchandise too cheap or they'll reckon it's no good.' He laughed while Ann stood nodding, allowing his advice to stick. Finally his till sprung open and he counted the notes into her hand. 'Where ya going to now?'

'The Post Office, then the Shire Hall.'

'I'll tell Dick to tell his missus she can meet you there, and it'll cost her twenty-five. Hoo Roo, young Annie. Don't work too hard; makes ya old before ya time. An' no more flirting with Deadeye. He's no good to me for a week after you've smiled at him.' The old rascal was chuckling as she hurried out to the street and across the road to the Post Office cum Commonwealth Bank, where each week she added to her account, her own small sacrifices to the gods of tomorrow.

Mr Ponsford, the postmaster, had been rushed to hospital at the weekend. Today a stranger stood behind the counter. He was young, average height, average build, brown hair. His suit was modern, city.

'Good morning,' he said, instead of 'G'day, young Annie.'

'Twenty dollars, thanks.' Ann passed over her bankbook and a roll of crumpled notes, suddenly wishing she had a fine leather purse and her notes were lettuce crisp. The stranger sorted and counted, he wrote the new figure in her book, then looked up and caught her eye.

'You should invest some of this,' he said.

'Where?' She was always interested in learning more about money.

For ten minutes he spoke of interest and short-term deposits while she watched him speak. Her habit of watching lips, watching faces, would never change, and when he was done with talking, and the book and forms were in her hand, he smiled a different smile, and she wished she had never learned to read faces, read eyes. 'Anything to do in town, Ann?' he said.

She shook her head and looked quickly away. She'd have to learn to look at people's belts when they spoke to her. They probably thought she was eyeing them. Like Jimmy Willis last week on the school bus. 'You've got come-hither eyes, Annie,' he'd said, then he'd asked her if she'd go to the pictures with him on Wednesday, and she'd almost said yes, because he looked like Robert Redford, and all the girls wanted to go out with him.

Half the girls her age had boyfriends. Half of them were on the pill too, even some of the Catholic girls, who swore they only took it for pimples and periods. Ann wanted to be like everyone else, she tried hard to be like them, but Mallawindy was too small. People didn't forget. Jimmy had been at school with her for years. There was no way she was going to sit with him, let him think he could tell his mates all about it the next day.

The stranger spoke again. 'Do you have a dance, a picture show up here?'

'Not tonight,' she said to his pen.

'I'm here until Friday. I'm staying at the Central.'

She shrugged. 'There's a picture show on Wednesday at the Shire Hall. A travelling picture show guy comes up here.'

'Are you going?' he asked.

'Probably not.' She never went to the pictures when her father was home.

'Have you seen it?'

Her eyes had returned to watching his mouth again, his eyes. 'No,' she said.

He smiled at her, and his smile made his face look more than average. Again she looked at his pen. 'Could I talk you into going?'

She shook her head, and he said his name, but she didn't hear it. Her mind was working over-time. He didn't know her. Didn't know anything about her. Wouldn't it give the kids on the bus something to talk about.

'What's showing?' he asked.

She told him, her concentration on her book, and her basket. Then she licked her lips, and added, 'I thought about seeing it, but it depends on how much work I've got to do.'

'Where do you work?'

'I . . . I've got my . . . my own business.' The words spoken to her shoes.

'Lucky you. Do me a favour and give yourself a night off.'

'You've probably seen it. By the time we get the pictures up here, they're years old.'

'I don't mind watching a good show twice, particularly if the company is good.'

She placed the forms in her basket, nodded, backed away. 'Thanks. I might invest a bit in that term deposit,' and she turned, walked to the door. There were people waiting, people listening.

'You can let me know what you decided on Wednesday. I might come up with some other options,' he called after her.

She felt her face grow hot as she walked across the street, but her mind was darting from Jack Burton's briefcase and his investments, to the picture show, and what she might wear if she went, and why shouldn't she go. She was almost sixteen. Bronny had sneaked out to go to a slumber party at Becky Martin's place and had gotten away with it. If Bronny could, so could she – if she wanted to. But she didn't want to. Why should she want to?

Her mother liked her to go out. She pushed her to go to church socials, even wanted her to go to Marlene Dooley's birthday party.

Nothing to wear, so I can't, she thought. She spent her life sewing for other people, but rarely made anything nice for herself. But she could, if she wanted to.

'Why waste money?'

Last month the draper had some blue woollen material, midnight blue. She'd looked at it, almost bought it, then changed her mind. Maybe he'd have it with him today. If he did, she'd buy it, and go to the pictures. If he didn't have it, she'd forget about the bank man. Let fate decide. He was probably just making conversation anyway. He'd probably said the same thing to every girl in town. God help him if he had, because every girl in town would turn up and want to sit with him. He had the bluest eyes, ocean blue. They sort of picked up his smile, sort of twinkled like the sun on the ocean when Sam and May took her and Liza to –

'Don't think,' she said. 'Stop thinking about her.' With a shake of her head, she walked into the Shire Hall.

The midnight blue material was there, and it had been reduced. She bought two metres, then helped Mrs Fraser and Janey pick material and a waist-skimming pattern for the wedding dress. It was close to two before she left the town centre.

At three-thirty, when Malcolm entered his study, Ann was seated there, typing up an assignment on his ancient Royal. 'Burton,' he said, watching the fingers fly.

'Good afternoon, sir.' Her rhythm broken momentarily, she turned, smiled.

And he smiled. He had a scholarship earmarked for Ann. Had she been his own flesh and blood, he doubted that he could have cared for her more, but he censored every word, he shielded every glance, and he stayed far away from his bottle while she was in his house.

They sat at the kitchen table and drank tea while he read her work, adding a comma here, a question mark there, then the papers pushed back, he began his questions. And she replied.

'I got that old smell of apples back again last week. Everything I ate smelt of apples. And maybe a bit of a memory about Liza ... maybe going to the beach, but I couldn't see her, just knew she was there.'

'It will happen, child, but you must allow it to come.'

'I remember a lot of silly things, but it's like ... sort of like waking up from a dream and trying to bring it with you to your conscious mind. The more I try to remember, the faster it fades. I remember the house, the big gate, the green paddocks with all the horses leaning against white fences.'

'Keep talking.'

'Sam riding a horse. He always gives me goosebumps, sir.'

'Forget your goosebumps. Concentrate on the house, the white stone house, the garden. What do you remember of the garden?'

'Uncle Sam's roses. May was never allowed to cut them, only him. And the apples. A worm. A crazy big bloody worm – . I don't want to do this today, sir.'

'It was your past, child, and until you know your past, there can be no real future for you.'

'I remember the taste of big red apples and the juice running down my chin. I think I ate about a million apples one day. It might be imagination, but sometimes I think if I could bite into one it might jog my memory. I can't. I smell them and ... and I switch off.' She stopped short, the point of her tongue moistened her lips.

'Continue, Burton. Each segment you grasp is a gain.'

'That face I told you about ages ago. I dreamed it two nights back and woke Bronny up with my screaming.'

'The face?'

'I used to call it the demon's face. It's ... it's pulsations of light, of shadow ... light shadow. It's like a kaleidoscope, made of melting fat. It keeps changing as I turn it, then it forms a face, and just as I'm about to grasp it, suddenly it melts into two, breaks up, and sizzles away in black smoke.'

'Your Aunt and I spoke at length on the telephone. Apparently they found you beneath a window that looked out on the rose garden. Try if you will to think of that window. Was it a large window? A small window? Were the roses in bloom?'

'Nothing. I don't know. Thinking about it makes me feel as if the inside of me is going to implode. Like all of the outside of me will be sucked into the inside – like a deflated balloon. When the last of the air is gone, I'll just shrivel up and blow away.'

They talked an hour away, both keeping one eye on the clock.

'I'd better go,' she said at four-thirty. 'I have to sew tonight, sir. I might be going to the pictures on Wednesday.' She walked with him back to the room he had set up as a study for her. He watched her stack her books, place them on a shelf, while he played with the old typewriter.

'I did a little typing when I was in the army. They say it is like riding a bicycle, once learned never forgotten. I have not put the theory to the test in some time ... bicycle or typewriter.'

'I'm off then, sir. Thank you.'

'Any time, Burton. The door is always open.'

When she had gone, he poured a small brandy, tossed it down and sagged to the chair before the desk, his mind on Jack Burton. He hated the man, and though Ann never admitted it, he knew her father still abused her. He began poking at keys with two index fingers. *Fell out of tree*, he typed. *Very tall tree.*

He was still there at nine o'clock, his out of practice fingers growing faster at finding the right keys. Only the empty bottle forced him from his absorbing occupation. He stood, his bones grown stiff with sitting. He picked up a small sheaf of papers, leafing through them as he wandered into the passage, flicking on light switches as he went.

A half a dozen chops tossed into a frying pan, he stood close to the stove, reading, then re-reading his evening's work as fat sizzled and flew.

Publishers hadn't wanted the lyrical prose of his youth. They'd returned his manuscripts without comment. Now, chuckling and jiggling beside his frying pan, Malcolm read the type-written words aloud. The first page was discarded, and the second, but by the time he got to the third, he began mentally editing.

She allowed the blouse to slide from her rounded shoulder and her heavy breasts sprang free of their restriction. Backing away, she taunted him as he reached eagerly for his prize.

In all his life Malcolm had never seen a heavy breast spring free, but it looked good on paper, as the names of his characters looked good on paper. He read two more pages.

Mack Curtan and Bell Reva were a fiendish pair. They were reaching out from the paper, ensnaring his imagination. For years, while his liver soaked up alcohol, his subconscious had soaked up a thousand scenarios. Mallawindy, tiny hell on earth, might yet pay for what it had stolen from Malcolm Fletcher.

david taylor

~

Ann's scissors were sharp and confident. Each stitch she placed in the blue woollen fabric was a positive stitch. She finished the hem on Wednesday evening, and when she modelled the frock for Bronwyn, the ten-year-old told her she looked like a fashion model in a magazine, and all she needed was some lipstick.

Ann didn't own any lipstick, so Bronwyn crept into her parents' bedroom, and returned with her mother's. 'Put a bit on,' she said, supervising as Ann outlined her lips with the Burnished Spice. 'More. A bit more,' then she palmed the lipstick. 'Who are you going to sit with?'

'No-one. Probably no-one. I just want to see the picture.' Her lips felt greasy, she blotted half of it off.

'Why the new dress then?' Bronny scoffed. She sounded like Aunty Bessy.

Jack and Ellie were watching the seven o'clock news when Ann left. Bronwyn stood at the lounge room door, playing watch-dog. Ben was in the paddocks.

'Want a ride?' he called.

Ann waved a hand, shook her head. She wanted the walk, wanted the time alone to think. She didn't even know the bank man's name, and by the time she got to town, she'd convinced herself that he wouldn't be there, and if he was, Mallawindy girls would be a metre deep around him. She'd just walk past as if she didn't see him and she'd sit with Jimmy Willis and his mob.

But the bank man was waiting alone on the corner – as if he were waiting for her. Her heart began to beat against her ribs like a jackhammer. If he hadn't seen her first, she would have turned and run for home. But he had seen her. He walked across the road.

'I hoped you'd come,' he said.

'Hi.' That one word was enough to choke her. She licked her lips, tasted Burnished Spice, and walked ahead of him to the hall.

He wouldn't let her buy her ticket. She stood back, praying for the lights to go out before she had to enter. It wasn't to be. The picture-show man only turned off the lights when he was sure he'd get no more customers.

People stared at her. Eyes turned to watch her take a seat in the second back row. Then the lights went out and she breathed an audible sigh of relief.

He bought her a bottle of Coke at interval. They stood outside, and he took a packet of cigarettes from his pocket, offered it.

'No thanks,' she said. 'I don't – '

'I'm glad you don't. I don't much either,' and he put the cigarettes away. 'How old are you, Ann?'

She couldn't say fifteen. She tried, but she couldn't say it. Couldn't even say nearly sixteen. 'How old are you?' she asked.

'Twenty-four.'

Johnny would be twenty-four. Johnny grown up, not sitting with a fifteen-year-old at the pictures. 'How old did you think I was?' she asked.

'Twenty?'

She shook her head.

'Eighteen?'

'My birthday is on December twenty-fourth.' She hadn't lied, just hadn't told the truth. Just for tonight she could be nearly eighteen. He'd be gone on Saturday.

'I thought you'd be older. You're only a baby.' He took the hand fiddling with the empty Coke bottle, held it.

Jimmy Willis walked past, saw her holding hands. 'G'day, Annie,' he said.

'Hello,' she replied, surprised she had breath enough to reply. Her heart was trying to ram an extra airhole in her throat. She was going to die if he didn't let go of her hand. But he didn't, and she didn't die. They walked inside holding hands, and the whole of Mallawindy stared.

Two older girls, who never spoke to her, walked over. 'Hello Annie,' they said. Their eyes were on the bank man. She didn't know his name, and the longer the night went on, the harder it was becoming to ask.

'This is Greta and Lyn,' she introduced.

'David. David Taylor,' the bank man said. Then he led Ann to her seat.

There was magic in his hand. Everyone was smiling at her. She started smiling too, and her smile suited her well. Tonight she was someone else in lipstick. Cinderella at the ball. Scarlet O'Hara. Miss Ann Blue Dress from Narrawee –

David held her hand for the next two hours, and when the film ended with a passionate kiss, Ann's intestines ached like nothing she'd ever felt before. For the first time in her life, she wondered what it was like to be kissed. Her face grew hot. She didn't want the lights to come on, and when they did, she made a great show of looking at her watch. It was just after eleven. Midnight, with its pumpkins, was an hour away. If she could play Cinderella for just one more hour, just one more hour of magic, then she'd die happy.

Outside the hall, his arm crept around her waist. He walked her to a car she thought was her father's, but he opened it with his own key, then expected her to get in. She was fifteen going on eighteen tonight, so she got in.

Never get into a stranger's car, her mother always said to her and Bronny. Never, never get into a car with a stranger. Now she was in his car, and the doors closed.

The night was cold, light rain was falling. How was she going to explain not getting wet? Maybe they'd all be in bed. Please God let them be. What's on television tonight? she thought. Nothing much. Please God let Dad get bored and go to bed, and I'll go to church on Sunday. I'll go every Sunday for a month.

David said something. She hadn't been listening. 'Pardon?'

'Have you got any brothers and sisters?'

'Two brothers and one sister.' She told him her mother had a small mixed farm. It was becoming easier, like speaking to Bessy's Mick, like getting a lift home from the town with a cousin. He wasn't like a stranger.

'I'll walk from here,' she said, when the car stopped before the old wooden gate.

'Do you have to go in straight away?' His hand was on her shoulder, burning a hole through to her bones. She was going to die of pleasure tonight. No-one ever touched her, held her. Only Johnny. Johnny used to hold her hand, and give her a hug, and lift her over fences. Her father had held her once, and he'd touched her face the day Linda Alice died, but this was something different. She was drowning. Waves of delicious warmth washed over her as his arm drew her closer. Her shoulder was against his shoulder; it was like with Johnny, like warm, like a place to lean when she was tired, or shy. She wanted to lean against him, let these new warm waves crash over her, wipe out the old her and wash up someone better.

Then his face was close, like he was going to – . Quickly she pulled away, sat back, ram-rod straight, grabbed at the door handle.

The lights were still glowing from verandah and kitchen. They'd be off if her father was in bed. Maybe she should sit a bit longer. How long did other girls sit? Perhaps if she sat for ten minutes. If her father knew she'd gone out, he wouldn't expect her home for half an hour, not if she had to walk from town. Her eyes scanned the land, seeking his tall shadow. He liked to lurk in shadows, creep up and spy, listen at doorways.

'How many cows are you milking, Ann?' David wasn't trying to touch her. He probably wanted her to go. Probably thought she'd do it, and now he was bored.

She swallowed, released the door handle and folded her arms. 'We've got ten at the moment. Eight more should calve soon. We've got a few pigs, and half a million chooks. We sell eggs to the egg ... egg board.'

'Got a bull too,' he said, sighting Bessy's bull at the gate, rampaging, wanting to get out and kill.

'That's my Aunt's, from over the river. He's a problem, swims over and gets at Mum's – ' She stopped. Perhaps it wasn't the right thing to say. 'I'd better go around to the top paddock tonight. He's as mad as a hornet,' she said.

The verandah light went off, but the kitchen light still burned bright. Her father must know she'd gone out. He'd be waiting for her, another bull, but madder than a hornet.

Then the kitchen light went out, and the house became lost in the shrubbery.

Thank you God. Thank you God. 'I'd better go now,' she said.

He left the car too, so he wasn't that eager to get rid of her. He walked with her down the road, and he held her hand again. He held the fence wires apart while she climbed through, careful of her new dress. Safe from him on the other side, she took the magic hand he offered. She shook it, and he laughed, drew her back.

'Watch the barbedwire,' she warned.

'Sensible parents,' he said. 'Barbedwire entanglements around you. I enjoyed tonight, Ann. Can I see you again?'

'Again? I thought you were leaving on Saturday.'

'I don't live too far away. Would you like to see me again?'

She had thought no further than this night. Just one night, just to see what it was like being with a boy, holding his hand. There could be no more. David would find out about her, and her father would find out about him, and − . But her mouth was wearing lipstick, and it said, 'If . . . if you really want to.'

'Oh, I definitely want to. Saturday?'

'There's no picture show on Saturday.'

'We'll find something to do. Do you dance?'

'No. Just church social stuff.'

'Do you fish?'

'Yes.'

'Well, if it's a nice day we'll go fishing and have a picnic on the river.' He leaned across the wire, brushed a place between mouth and cheek with his lips. Her intestines twisted around her heart and threw her lungs into turmoil.

'Okay. I'll call for you around two.'

'No. No,' she said. 'I'll . . . I'll meet you at the bridge,' and she ran across the paddock, sucking air, her hand touching the place of her first kiss.

She met him the next Saturday and they caught a sack of fish. 'You take them,' she said at the canoe tree. 'We get plenty.' Then he kissed her. Kissed her properly. On the lips, and she ran.

He came each Saturday through September, and she met him at the bridge, and drove away with him to somewhere. He kissed her often, not only when he was leaving, and she loved it, loved his mouth, loved his arms, loved him − and she went to church with her mother each Sunday.

David took her to Daree one week to look in fabric shops. She spent twenty dollars and wished she'd brought more money with her. He wanted to lend her twenty. She shook her head, but let him carry her parcels. She felt eighteen, so totally old and grown up, and happy as she'd never been before. Then she left him at the canoe tree, and she was fifteen, and home. She was mad Annie until next Saturday, when she was catching a bus to Warran. He would meet her at the bus, at ten, and take her to the market. A whole day. One whole day with him, and in another town where she could be anyone she wanted to be.

Warran was an old city, its shopping centre huge. David knew every street. He lived there, owned a block of land there. His parents had bought it for him, for his twenty-first birthday. He drove her to the estate in Mahoneys Lane, and she looked at the fine houses on each side, and she walked with him on his land while he spoke of the house he planned to build there one day. At one, he took her home to meet his parents.

His mother, a big, loud woman, dominated the conversation, her voice accusing when she spoke of a girl called Melissa, a girl David had dated off and on for four years. Ann wanted to run, didn't want to know of the other girl with a prior claim to him. She asked for the bathroom, and sat on the edge of the bath for fifteen minutes, listening to his mother through the thin wall.

'How old is she?'

'Almost eighteen.'

'Eighteen? You're twenty-four years old. Wake up to yourself and apologise to Melissa. I was speaking to her mother yesterday. The girl is broken hearted.'

'Crap. She's been going out with other blokes,' David said.

'Who is this Ann, anyway? What do her parents do?'

'They're farmers. They've got a place just out of Mallawindy.'

'Watch out for her, my lad, or you'll end up with more trouble than you want to handle. Steer clear of the quiet ones. They're hiding something. You mark my words.'

They didn't stay for lunch. David knocked on the bathroom door, and when Ann emerged, he took her hand and led her away. They went to a take-away shop.

She wasn't hungry. She was trembling, internally. The woman's words kept running around in her brain. Hiding something. Hiding something. In his car, the windows up, their breath, the hot chips

108

and hamburgers, created fog on the windows. She tried to hide in it. She didn't want to talk. She nibbled chips and thought of the other girl. Someone else had kissed him, probably slept with him. Someone. His mother liked her. He'd go back to her and the magic Saturdays would be over.

'Eat up,' David said. 'Nothing better than hot chips out of paper.' His words sounded hollow, muffled, and she remembered another voice speaking the same words. Her father's voice. Her father's car. Stopping at a shop. Foggy windows. Eating chips. Hot, crisp, salty chips. Going home. Going home to Johnny. Safe. Safe Johnny.

'Nothing better than chips out of paper.' Her father? When had she shared chips with him? Before Narrawee? When had she ever been alone with him before Narrawee? Liza, yes, he'd taken her often in the old car, but not Ann. Still, she could see that day, she could see her father's head, see the old car, and hear him –

She was staring at David, her eyes wide. Staring at him but seeing others. Memories were rushing her. Hospital. White beds. Ladies in white uniforms, and the boy. Thin yellow hair. Who was that boy?

A girl in a yellow sweater saved her. She came to the foggy window and knocked. David rolled it down and the fog began to melt away.

'Hello, Hon,' the girl said.

'Hello, Liss,' David replied.

'How have you been?'

'Great.' Then he introduced the girls.

Melissa turned to look at Ann, hiding in the fog. Without comment, she walked away, and David closed the window.

'You are very quiet, Ann,' he said.

'I'd better get home.'

'I thought we were going to the market.'

'I – ' She shook her head.

'It's finished with Melissa. It was over months before I met you. Our mothers are friends. We kept being thrown together. Don't take any notice of what Mum says. I'm an only child, and she doesn't want to hand me over to anyone, you or Melissa.'

'I wasn't – . I didn't mean – .'

'You are the one I want to be with,' he said, drawing her to him, kissing her in the middle of the main street. He tasted of chips and she loved the taste, wanted his mouth to move against her own until all the hell in her head went away. He pulled away. 'What are you doing to me?' he said and he took a bite of his hamburger.

They were back in Mallawindy just before six. He parked his car beside the old canoe tree, south of the Burton track – as she liked him to. He helped her gather her purchases. 'Wednesday. We'll go to the pictures.'

'Saturday. At the bridge.' She was in a hurry.

He didn't argue. 'Okay, my love. Make it early. I'll be here around ten.' He kissed her again, and she ran, loaded down with plastic bags.

Bessy knew about David. Ann had given him her aunt's phone number. Her mother knew about him. Perhaps her father did. Mallawindy was no place to keep a secret.

Mr Fletcher even knew. Ann spoke of eating chips with a friend when she told him she'd remembered a car ride with her father, and of eating chips out of paper, of knowing she was going home to Johnny.

'Don't allow your social life to interfere with your school work, Burton,' he said, then added. 'Your father drove you home from the Melbourne hospital. No doubt you stopped to eat on the way.'

'But I remembered his voice. It must have been before that.'

'Was it your uncle's voice?'

'No. Never. No.'

He was silent for minutes, his eyes watching her. There were questions he wanted to ask about Sam and May, but in the end he said, 'You say you remembered the hospital, and a boy. Try to recall his name. Work your way through the alphabet. Try to find the boy's name.'

He started with the A's. 'Adam. Alan.'

She shook her head. Shook it at the B's, the C's, at the X Y Z's. 'It's a short name, starts with a vowel, I think. I can almost see it written in red. Maybe it's got an E in it.'

'Edward. Eric,' he said.

And she sprang to her feet. 'It's Eric, and his other name was ... was ... Eric ... His surname started with a J-o-n. The same letters as Johnny. I know it. I know it, sir. I can see it written, and it is red.'

And it wasn't all she knew. She remembered a colouring book. Eric had a colouring book. He gave her a red crayon. But though they spoke of the boy and the book for an hour, she could take the memory no further.

David came each Saturday through October, and his lips became more demanding, and his hands strayed from hand, and waist, to her shirt buttons, to her breasts.

'No more,' she said.

'No more?' he asked.

Her eyes down, she shook her head.

He came in November and the heat was intense. It drove them to the river. For hours they fished, and frolicked in the water. Ann dived deep, and deeper still, striving to reach the river's floor.

'You're a nut,' David accused, after one dive found him looking for her, concern on his face. 'I thought you were stuck under a log. I thought you'd drowned.'

A water nymph in her natural element, she laughed at him, and dived again, grasping his ankle this time and dragging him with her to deep water, just as she did with Ben, or Bron. But he caught her to him underwater, trapped her there, kissed her

111

underwater, near lost in her mermaid hair. They surfaced, both gasping for air.

'Does Melissa swim?' she asked.

'No. And forget Melissa. I have, a long time ago.'

'Why doesn't she swim?'

'Because her legs are like turnips. Yours are like slim silky eels,' he said, pouncing again, dragging her back into the silent world of opaque green, his arms locked around her hips. Her back arched, and her small breasts were close to his mouth. His mouth sought them, but she grasped his head, pushing him away, while bubbles laughed out through lips turned up in play.

Tumbling rolling bodies entwined in a liquid land where his hands dared too much and she wanted too much. So close, she could feel him hard against her. Something she had feared no longer seemed frightening – not with him. She wanted to hold him, to close her eyes and her mind and be closer to him, closer than this.

Let him slip her strap from her shoulder, let his mouth seek, find. Let his lips make the world go away. But it wouldn't stay away. It would just end the magic and she knew it. She pushed him away, dived deep and swam strong, underwater.

'Are you ready for some lunch?' she yelled, emerging near the bank.

'No. I'm ready for you,' he replied. Two deep breaths and he was after her, swimming into uncharted waters.

'Lunch or nothing,' she said.

He walked with her through the trees to the gate. ' I don't want to let you go, Ann. Half of me is being drawn away, lost to me for a week. I want you. I want to sleep with you. Stay with me tonight. Please stay with me tonight.'

'I can't,' she said.

He locked her in his arms, kissed her until she wanted to stay. 'I'm going to buy you an engagement ring for your birthday.'

Then she pulled away, covered her mouth with her hand, safe from him. 'I'm too young. You'll get bored with me soon, David.'

'Idiot girl. I can't remember a day I've enjoyed more than today. I want to be with you tonight, tomorrow. I want to be with you for the rest of my life. I love you.'

'I'll have to go. It's almost six.'

'Saturday is not enough for me any more. Can I come down and meet your parents?'

'No.'

'No. Just like that. What about me, what I want?'

She stood before him, shaking her head. Saturdays were all she had. Her father spent his at the hotel. When would he go to Narrawee again? 'Maybe after Christmas,' she said, closing the gate between them.

David watched her walk barefoot down the track. The ground was rough; she had feet like a native. He'd dated a few girls, slept with a few, but this one had managed to get under his skin. Her face attracted him, her voice held him, now he was in over his head.

He wanted her tonight. Didn't want to drive away. He wished her older, but he liked her innocence too, and the clean uncluttered lines of her. She was as tall as he, but pencil slim. And her eyes – one minute wide, laughing, the next like a frightened faun's, pleading for one last chance from a hunter's gun. She walked well, easy, her head high. He knew so little about her. She dressed well, spent her money wisely, spoke with the trace of an accent, as if English might have been a second language. She was dark enough to be Greek, or Italian, but not with the name of Burton.

Since the night of the picture show, she had refused to go near the town, and she always seemed to breathe easier once out on the road. She'd introduced him to no member of her family; he'd caught a glimpse of a young girl spying on them from behind a tree, and he guessed it was her sister. He'd sighted her brother in a paddock one day, but that was it. Most girls dragged him home to meet their parents whether he wanted to or not, but she never spoke about them.

An enigma, he thought. I've stumbled on some Brigadoon, stumbled on some once-a-week town, and I want to move into it with her.

'Marry her,' he said to the gate. 'Marry her.'

As he walked towards his car, its twin sped by, turned down the Burton track. The driver had to be her father. Big, dark as Ann, he drove like a maniac. David watched him out of sight.

Maybe she knows what she's doing, he thought. Wait for her birthday. Only six weeks away. 'A short engagement, and a fast wedding,' he told his car.

David didn't come to Mallawindy over Christmas. Ann telephoned him from Bessy's place, told him she couldn't get away. Ellie was huge with the baby, and Jack, a whisky-drinking bull the family dodged around. The farm could afford to buy a new kitchen suite and new cupboards, but what was the use? The old table was solid and the tubular metal chairs stood up to Jack's rages. Most of the doors on the old cupboards had been replaced with curtains on elastic. Elastic gave. Thank God he never attacked the lounge room, Ellie frequently said.

He couldn't. That was his room. Liza's memorial. His books, his good furniture was in there. It was his oasis in the place he named Chook-Shit County.

Ann never used the lounge room. She sewed in her room, and she dreamed, and she wished Christmas and her father gone. She thought of David, and his kiss, and his hands, and her blood trickled around her body like honey through honeycomb. She thought of the day at the river, and knew that she couldn't allow any more such days or she'd end up trapped like her mother was trapped, like Janey Fraser was trapped. But with David, it would be a very fine trap to be caught in. With him, nothing could ever be bad. He was gentle and funny and . . . and his body was . . . beautiful. And he had said he loved her. Somebody loved her. He had a block of land where he might build her a sane house.

The days continued to drag by.

Then the letter and the cheque came from Narrawee.

Dear Jack, Ellie and family –

Sam and May would be at Narrawee until mid January. Sam wished to speak to Jack – *if he could spare the time.*

Two days later, Jack picked up his briefcase and he drove away.

Peace. Laughter. Cards at night with Bessy and Bill. Pure, delightful peace, and David on New Year's Eve.

the baby

~

Ellie's baby was due in a week. She wanted it out and in her arms.
She wanted her old energy back. All the farm work fell to Ben and
Annie now, but at least with Jack away, everyone could relax and
get on with it.

It would be a different birth, this one. She'd have time for the
new baby, be able to give it more too. She was sitting in the
kitchen, doing a crossword, and willing a small nagging ache into
the familiar pain when Ann entered with a boy she introduced as
David.

'Nice to meet you, David,' Ellie said.

Such a nice looking boy, and well spoken too. So, he was the
one responsible for the change in Annie. Ellie was delighted. Her
daughter hadn't missed a Sunday at church for months. It was a
miracle and there was no doubt about it. After all the years of
worry, to look at Annie now, standing there, like a normal girl,
holding her boyfriend's hand; it was more than Ellie had ever dared
to pray for. She crossed herself, thanked God and Father Fogarty –
and this David, and she wished her back would stop aching and
her stomach start.

'Could I take Ann to a New Year's party in Warran, Mrs
Burton?'

'If you don't have her home too late,' Ellie replied.

They stayed for dinner. Annie wasn't much use in the kitchen, but she and Bronwyn tossed a salad together, and they ate it with cold boiled eggs and leftover lamb. It was a relief not having to cook for Jack. With any sort of luck, she'd be back home with the baby by the time he returned. She'd have her energy back.

Annie had made another new dress. It was short and red, definitely her colour. It looked well with her dark hair and eyes. She'd bought a pair of platform shoes too. They made her look even taller. Ellie watched the couple as they left at eight for the party. Such a handsome couple. Annie looked twenty, she thought.

'He must be of our faith,' she said to Ben. 'That would explain Annie's new interest in the church ... not that she's old enough to be thinking weddings for a few years.'

'She seems very natural with him, doesn't she?' Ben said.

'She kisses him too,' Bronwyn added her own piece of information. 'How do people get the air in when they kiss, Mum?'

'Bronwyn!' Ellie said.

They were on the road to Warran when David handed Ann a small blue velvet box. 'Happy birthday, Merry Christmas, and marry me soon, all rolled into one.'

Wide-eyed, Ann looked at him and at the box. She didn't take it.

'Open it,' he said, and when she wouldn't, he opened it himself. A small lone diamond stood proud on a slim golden band. 'I love you, Ann, and I believe the feeling is mutual. Take it. Put it on for me. I'd like to introduce you tonight as my fiancée.'

'I'm ... too young. I can't.'

'You can. You're eighteen, and now in control of your own life.' She shook her head, turned her face to the window. 'It's got to the stage where I can't imagine a life without you. I've got a block of land, and I want to build a house and plant a garden. I've already looked into getting a loan from the bank.'

She took the box, closed it and placed it in the glove box.

'Don't spoil tonight,' she said. 'I'm free. I'm out of that place and I'm going to a party. Don't spoil it.'

His concentration returned to the road. He hadn't expected this response, but he usually got what he wanted, and he wanted her. Okay, so he'd gone the wrong way about it. He'd ask her father for her hand. Do it the old way. Do it slow. But he would marry her.

The party was at a property two kilometres south of Warran. There were hordes inside and out, and more continued to arrive. Ann stayed close to David. She watched, surprised, as he tossed down a glass of beer. She drank fruit punch. She watched his glass refilled, emptied, as the voices grew louder. After the third refill, she walked away from him, and he didn't see her go.

The fruit punch was spicy and cold, and the night was hot. Her own glass refilled, she looked for a corner, out of sight of a tall guy in blue who kept following her. Maybe it was her fault; twice he caught her staring at him, but only because he looked a bit like Johnny. Tall and dark – even his nose, and his jaw. His eyes weren't Johnny's eyes, and his voice was . . . was slimy.

Two minutes later he found her in her corner and he put his hand on her bare shoulder.

'Where have you been hiding all my life, Brown-eyes?'

'Excuse me,' she said, sliding out from beneath his arm and hurrying outside to the garden.

The stars were bright tonight. She stood, her back to the warm brick wall. She'd expected there would be young people here, but of course they wouldn't all be. Some looked about forty. David was probably the youngest. Twenty-four. Johnny's age. And the ring he'd bought. It was an engagement ring.

'Stupid,' she said. 'I shouldn't have let him think I was eighteen.' She walked down to the road, looked towards the city.

Warran was like the hub of a buckled wheel, with spokes leading off in six different directions. Her new shoes weren't made for walking, and there was no bus tonight. She was stuck here until midnight. Sucked into a vortex that had begun to spin. Where would it spin her out?

She shouldn't have let it all start, but she didn't know it would end up with him wasting his money on a ring. The kids on the bus changed their girl and boyfriends like her father changed his socks. There was no such thing as love at first sight, except in books. But she had loved David at first sight, and she knew it.

'That's where you're hiding. Come back in, Ann.' David found her in the drive. He put his arms around her, kissed an ear he found amid the curls.

'You smell of beer.'

'And you smell of spice and kitten's breath,' he said. Unable to claim her mouth, his lips traced a path to her throat. She pulled away, but he caught her hand and drew her back inside where he introduced her to two married women who must have been at least thirty.

Penny was from Melbourne. She asked what Ann was drinking, and brought her another glass of punch.

'One of my brothers lives in Melbourne,' Ann said, just for something to say.

'What suburb, Ann?'

'I'm not sure. He's just moved.' Her tongue was loosening. She was feeling better, safe on a couch between two women.

'Where does he work, Ann?'

'Teacher,' Ann said. Maybe Johnny was in Melbourne. Maybe he was a teacher. He had been her teacher, and she couldn't admit that she hadn't seen her brother for nine years. She looked at the rings on Penny's hand. Three rings. Engagement, wedding and eternity. Her mother only had the one ring. No time to get engaged.

Rings. Everywhere she looked tonight she saw them, big ones, little ones.

The memory came at her hard, jarred her, and she spilled her drink to her frock, but she didn't notice it.

119

Walking with Johnny in the sandhills, treading on his footprints, safe in Johnny's footprints. Following him and ... and ... and a flower. It was growing on a reed. A reed flower, but reeds didn't have flowers. Her hand picked it, locked it in her palm. And Johnny wanted to see –

Her eyes closed and she conjured up a clear mental image of her brother. His hair had been as black as her own, but straight, his eyes a lighter brown, his father's eyes, but they held a different expression. Tall. Tall as his father, but his hands were Ellie's, his fingers shorter, his palms and wrists broad. 'Remember,' that hand said. Fist to temple, tapping the temple. She had made the same sign, then her fingers opened, blew the thought away. 'Forget.'

Chill of liquid through her frock. She looked down at it, brushed at it. Penny offered a tissue, and Ann looked at the offering hand, but she was away again. Just for a flicker of a second she was standing with Johnny on the sand. His face was sad, his eyes beautiful, worried. 'Tell me, Annie love. You have to tell me.'

Then Johnny went away. Went down the road and the big truck came and it took him away, and all the safe was gone. And ... and ... and ... nothing. Slam. Bang. Head first into a wall of opaque glass.

Slowly she took the offered tissue, blotted the spill. Gone. Gone into nothing.

David had returned some of that safe time to her. Maybe she should sleep with him. Get pregnant. Make her own wedding dress and get away, get far away from Mallawindy, and everything. Start new again. Be a new person. Mrs Taylor. Safe Mrs Ann Taylor.

She looked at David. He was standing with the host. He caught her eye. 'Okay?' he asked. She blushed at her thoughts, and turned her face away to the group of women immersed in babies and motherhood. She could be one of them if she had a baby. She'd have something to talk to them about. Maybe tonight when they got back in the car, she'd take the ring out of its box and put it on, and he'd kiss her and she'd just let his hands do what they wanted, what she wanted. She'd let it happen. Just be close to him, then closer, and after the first time it would be easy. That's what Janey Fraser said.

The thought of it made her stomach feel weird. Nice weird. Lots of the girls on the school bus did it. Janey Fraser was only twelve months older than Ann, and she already had her baby, born three months after the wedding. Ann drained her glass. She felt weird, giddy, throbbing. She looked at her watch. Still an hour to midnight. She looked at David, then the tall guy in the blue shirt winked at her, as if he knew what she was thinking. She tossed her hair back and looked at the wallpaper. The women were laughing at something, so Ann laughed too, then she stood and walked to the bar.

It was close to midnight when David joined the group of males surrounding her. There was no way out of the tight circle, no way she could shake off the hand of the guy in blue, so she stood there, laughing with the rest, and saying anything that popped into her head. It was easy. Melissa had attached herself to the group. Blonde. Dressed in yellow – a plump canary, who wanted to get David in her cage.

'I'm missing you,' David said, close to her ear.

Ann turned to him, smiled, then continued her conversation about London. 'I flew over with Dad when I was sixteen,' she said to Melissa, but her new friend had lost interest in London.

'How are you, Hon?' Melissa's arm slipped around David's waist.

'Great. And you?' He stepped away.

'Just great.' Melissa left for the bathroom and David's hand was around Ann's waist. She leaned against him, needing his support. The guy in blue walked away and the other males dispersed.

'So, you've been to London? You didn't tell me you were a world traveller,' David said. 'Tell me about yourself. Tell me where else you've been.'

'Not to London.' She laughed. 'He who enjoys a good novel is never in need of fast fiction.' Her head rested against his, her free hand replaced Melissa's around his waist. He didn't step away from her. He drew her closer, so close.

It would be so easy. Tonight she was a different person, a whole person. She found out why when he stopped kissing her.

'What have they been giving you to drink?' he asked.

'Fruit punch. And I've been giving it to myself. It's got watermelon in it. See.'

He took the glass of pink juice from her hand, tasted it. 'It's spiked,' he said. 'It's full of vermouth. No more, Ann.'

'What's vermouth?' The glass reclaimed, she tested it too.

'I can't take you home drunk. Don't drink any more.'

'What about you? Anyway, I don't ever want to go home again. I like it here. I like me here. See that guy over there, in the blue,' and when David looked where her glass was pointing, she added, 'Well, he keeps following me around and calling me Brown-eyes. Every time I look up, he's staring at me, or leaning on me.'

'The whole world is staring at you, but you are mine, and if you were not staring at him with your big brown eyes, then you wouldn't know that he was staring at you.'

Her head felt wobbly. All the tension had left her muscles. She felt free, and so happy. The noise, the voices and music were playing directly against her eardrums. She wanted to dance, wanted a reason to hold David close. She wanted to swim with him, swim beneath the moon, and be a boneless puppet and let him play her strings.

But the blue shirt was back, his hand on her shoulder, so sure of its right of possession. She slid away, stepping around David's feet.

'Where's your wife, Tony?' David asked.

'Home in bed where all good wives should be, barefoot and pregnant,' Tony Blue Shirt replied. 'Where's Melissa, Dave?'

'Melissa who? What are you doing for a crust, these days, Tone?'

'I sell cars. Want to buy a good used car?'

They laughed. Ann stepped back, and leaned against the wall, dissecting the conversation. Totally unfunny, she decided. Drunks at a party laughing at unfunny jokes. 'I sell cars. Want to buy one, Davey?' Utterly without humour, she decided, and she tossed her head back and laughed with the other drunks. For minutes she leaned there, a part of the group, waiting each time for the laughter, performing well until she grew bored with the game and laughed in the wrong place.

Their group expression gave her excuse to return to the punch-bowl. They were still laughing when she wandered back. Perhaps having left the clique, they now laughed at her. Maybe someone here knew she used to be Dummy Burton, or perhaps she looked as drunk as she felt. Apart from the woozy nausea, drunk was a delicious feeling. Never before had she seen people with such clarity. From the outer circle, she studied Tony.

He looked more like her father than Johnny. She laughed alone then, giggling for minutes while wondering who her father might have been sleeping with twenty-odd years ago. Everyone in Mallawindy knew he slept around. Had he passed on that noble brow, that straight aristocratic nose, hair as black as a raven's wing . . . or a crow's wing.

'Old Ted Crow, where did he go? Gone in the trees, like the birds and the bees,' she said. No-one took any notice. 'Who is Ted Crow, little Annie? Who cares who he is tonight,' she said, and she giggled again.

Tony turned to her. Again his hand reached out to claim. A hand like her father's. Long fingers, clean well-shaped nails. 'By the way Tony, did your mother happen to know your father's name?' she asked.

The question seemed innocent enough, but like well-oiled, wind-up toys, jaws dropped all around her, telling her plainly that she'd hit a nail directly on its head, if she could only concentrate long enough to recall what nail she'd hit – . Maybe she should stop saying whatever came into her head. Try to concentrate. Johnny used to always keep telling her, 'Concentrate. Concentrate, Annie love.'

She tried to concentrate as she watched the people take fast mechanical steps backwards, but Tony didn't step back. His fingers tightened their grip on her arm and he hissed, close to her face, 'You smart-arsed, bitch. Give me a night or two with you and I'd make you crawl for it.' And he pinched her breast.

She wasn't concentrating when her glass of pink couldn't-give-a-damn juice hit the self-satisfied face. She was as surprised as he was. Just a reflex reaction. She didn't mean it to happen, but she giggled as she watched a ball of watermelon land on black hair, slide slowly down, hit the floor.

No-one else was giggling. The host was beside Tony. David took Ann's arm, but she'd been dodging this man all night, and she wasn't going to run any more. Couldn't, anyhow. Her legs weren't quite right. She giggled as the room silenced. Glasses froze, half raised to lips; even the crooner on the record-player stopped crooning and started to hiccup. Some comment was necessary. Ann looked around her at the plastic people dissolving in alcohol.

'Aunty Bessy always says that the next best thing to a knee in the right place is a glass of water in the face,' she said.

The crooner gave a heart-stopping hiccup, an amazing trill, jumped a few tracks, then crooned on, and glasses continued their pathway to lips.

David drew her into the kitchen. He sat her down on the tiled floor, sat beside her. 'Did you know him before tonight?'

'Not personally.'

'Then who told you about his mother?'

Her head was at peace on his shoulder, and she yawned. 'He looks like my father – acts like him too. I just thought he might have known Tony's mother . . . in the biblical sense.' She yawned again.

'Who are you? I picked up a girl at a bridge in Mallawindy this afternoon, a shy kid I planned to spend my life with. You are like a stranger. I don't know you, Ann.'

'I like you not knowing me. But he knows me. Look at him, David.' Tony had followed them to the kitchen. He stood at the door, his eyes shooting daggers.

'I'd better get you out of here. He's a bad drunk, and so are you.'

'I bet he is, but I'm just a happy drunk. It's turned my worry knob to the off position, so everything looks just fine, except him. Ever since I got here, he's been after me. Every time I take my eyes off the floor or the ceiling, he's staring, like he knows every- thing about me.'

She looked at the door to prove a point. Tony caught her eye. Quickly she dropped her chin to concentrate again on the tiled floor. Minutes later, when she knew how many tiles it had taken to cover this floor, she looked up again and his lips mouthed two little words she had seen many times before.

'See. I'm right. How does he know I can lip read unless there's some ancestral brain-cell link?'

'What?'

'Jung.' She scrambled to her feet, pushing herself off from the wall, negotiating the space between her and the door. David wasn't as fast to his feet.

'Please repeat your last words after I find a full glass,' she said.

'Fuck you, you smart-arsed bitch.' Tony spat the words at her. 'I'll get you.'

'Would you know what to do with me? I've heard it . . . on the best authority, that your other appendages are as limp as your wrists. They tell me that your wife has an annual . . . an annual stud booking with the local bull – '

David was between them. He tossed Ann over his shoulder and

carried her through to the laundry and out to his car, then he poured her into the back seat and drove towards Mallawindy, his laughter non-containable. At the halfway mark, he pulled off to the side of the road, and climbed into the rear seat with her.

'Your mother says I'm dangerous.'

'I thought you were asleep, and I wouldn't touch you tonight with a ten-foot pole,' he said, drawing her head to his lap.

'Melissa told Penny something like that.'

'Shut up, Ann, and sleep it off. I can't take you home like this. Your father will castrate me.'

'More likely to shoot you, if he was home. But thank God, he's not home,' she said. 'Hey, is the world spinning or is it me, David?'

'It's you. Close your eyes and count sheep.'

'Bessy took some pigs down to the Daree show last year and Bronny and I went with her. We went on one ride where they put you in this little room like a barrel, then it spins around and around until you can walk up the walls like a fly. We did. I bet I could walk up the walls of the world tonight. I'm spinning, spinning, spinning.'

'Close your eyes.'

'I'll fall off if I close my eyes.' She giggled and lay watching the world turn. 'Annie,' she whispered. 'Little Annie, give me a hiccup to let me know you're still alive. Yoo-hoo, Annie. Come out, come out wherever you are and meet Ann of inebriation.'

A smile twitched his lips, but he held his silence, hoping the lack of an interested audience might put her to sleep. Better to arrive home late than to take her back like this.

'Melissa hates me, you know, David. All the time she was charming me with London this, and London that, her eyes were slicing off bits of my flesh and feeding it to the goldfish.'

'I hate you too. Turn your brain to the off position and go to sleep.'

'Is it safe?'

'You're safe. I don't make love to drunks.'

'But you ride penny-farthings. That's what Tony called Melissa. He didn't know we were distantly related. He said she was a pneumatic penny-farthing. A bit more class, a little older, well pumped-up tyres, but basically the town bike – anyone could get a ride since you parked her back on the street.'

'Ann. This is not you, and certainly not the you I love. Watch your mouth.'

'He said I was a red racing car and – '

There was only one way to shut her up. He kissed the mouth, relaxed by spiked fruit punch, and she spoke against his lips. 'You said you wouldn't touch me with a ten-foot pole.'

'My anatomy has been much exaggerated.' He kissed her again while his hand traced a pathway from face, to throat, to breast. 'God, I love you. I've been seduced by you, Ann, ensnared by you. Who are you?'

'Love me?' she said. 'Even when I'm drunk? Even when I insult your friends?'

'Even more when you insult my enemies.' Again he kissed her and his fingers worked their way beneath her shoulder strap.

'David.'

'That word will be your downfall. Call me Dave, or Davey. Learn to say it with a nasal twang. I love you. I want you.'

'What if I don't love you, don't want you?'

'You do, and you talk too much.' His lips stopping further protest.

Hang the consequences. The ring was in his glove box. Perhaps this was the way to get it on her finger tonight. He slid the zip of her frock down. He unhooked her bra, and she lay in his arms like a rag doll, her lips opening to him. It had been a long time since his last back-seat lovemaking, and the last time he'd had a little assistance. His hand found the silky slip of stockinged thigh, crept higher.

She was eighteen, old enough to make her own rules. Let her

stop it if it must be stopped. He'd had too much to drink too. Blame the beer. Blame the moonlight and the lonely road. His hand slid up to the elastic of her briefs.

'I think the world's stopped spinning because I'm falling off it.' She rolled to the floor, and he gave up on the back seat.

'Will you come to a motel with me, Ann?'

'No motels in Mallawindy. Anyway, I'm sober now. Maybe next time.'

'A life of celibacy doesn't suit me.'

'You could go back to the party and get Melissa. I'll walk from here.'

'Jesus. Jesus. What have I done to deserve this?'

'Mum's always saying that. She doesn't know that Jesus never listens.' She opened the door and tumbled out to the road. 'You know, I once asked him to do one tiny little thing for me. I made a bargain with him, and he tricked me into reading all but thirty-seven pages of the Bible, then behold, Jack Burton arose from the dead and shot Mickey ... and Father Fogarty still had the stinking audacity to expect to re-do me Catholic. Can you believe that?'

'Get in the car, Ann, and who was Mickey? Some other poor fool who fell for you?'

'He was my dog. He was fourteen, and he would have lived to seventeen, because I looked after him. We buried him near the willow tree,' she said, heading off into the moonlight, straightening her dress as she went.

'Get back in the car, Ann.' He walked to the front seat and started the motor. 'Get back in this car, Ann.'

For half a kilometre he followed her before she agreed to get back in. On the remainder of the trip, he learned more about her than he had in five months. She told him her brother had run away when he was nearly sixteen, and one day she'd have to find him because he remembered all the things she'd forgotten, and she told him her father was away in Narrawee, so she probably wouldn't get murdered tonight. She told him her mother owned the farm, and her father just boarded there, part time.

'Do you love, me?' he said when they were at the gate.

'I'm too young.'

'You're eighteen, allowed to vote, allowed to love, even allowed to drink.'

'I'm sixteen,' she said.

'What?'

'Sorry. Sixteen.'

'You're not. You said you'd turn eighteen in December.'

'No,' she corrected. 'You said you thought I was eighteen or twenty, so I took the eighteen. I knew you'd run a mile if I told you the truth.'

'Oh, Christ.'

'What's it matter? Some people know all about life when they're six and some are still spoilt kids when they're forty. Life gets handed out like bunches of grapes, and we have to eat the bunch we're given, and keep eating them until we're dead, so it doesn't matter if a few of us get little sour bunches, and some get big sweet ones. When they're gone, they're gone and there is no more.'

'Is that so?'

'Yes.'

'Can you walk a straight line yet?'

'I can do what I have to do, when I have to do it.'

'If you want to do it,' he said meaningfully. 'Hop out and walk around for a while. Get your head straight before you go in.' Guilt was riding him now. He could see the lights still burning in the Burton house. Her mother was probably worried sick.

'Hop in. Hop out. Sit down. Roll over. Woof. Woof.'

She was only a kid and it was almost two o'clock. He'd picked himself up some half-grown thing from the Mallawindy forest and got her drunk. 'I wish you'd told me the truth months back, Ann.'

'Then you wouldn't have come back.' She was out of the car and not walking well, the rough ground not so stable beneath her platform soles. She walked to the gate, flung it wide, then rode it to a bone-jolting crash against the post.

He stood watching her. She was more the child tonight than he had ever seen her, and he loved her more. 'Do you still want me to come back, Ann?'

The gate closed. She was in, and he was out, locked on the other side by a rusty loop of wire. He hated that bloody gate . . . he wanted in, wanted her. Wanted to rape her on the grass in the moonlight.

'I don't feel any different at sixteen to what I felt at eighteen five minutes ago.'

'Saturday?' he said, kissing her across the top rail.

'At the bridge,' she sighed, and she ran.

miscast

~

Ellie had been leisurely packing her hospital case when Jack arrived home two hours ago. She was tossing the last items in. The birth was near. Maybe she'd left it too late to get to the hospital.

She saw the car lights at the gate as she closed the case, fixed its strap in place. It must be Annie and David. Jack saw the lights too. He'd been cursing his brother's name since he walked in the door, determined to start something too, but Ellie had aborted it so far. And now Annie was home, and God help her. Jack was waiting in the yard, priming his belt.

'Where have you been, you little slut?' he yelled as she wandered through the chicken-wire gate.

'Celebrating New Year.' Ann, dodging around him, ran for the rear of the house.

'Who drove you home?' he roared.

There was no reply, but Ellie heard the bedroom door close. She sighed, relieved. At least Annie had decided against taking him on tonight. He never went into the girls' bedroom. If Annie stayed in there. If she just stayed in there.

Ellie lifted her hospital case to the floor, then grasping her stomach, crouched over the table, riding down a contraction. They were coming fast. She'd have to go.

'Who was she with?' Jack was at the passage door. 'I asked you, who was she with?'

The pain eased. Ellie took two short breaths. 'She's sixteen, Jack. He's a nice boy. It's good for her to mix with people.' She picked up her case. 'Can you get me up to the hospital, love? I think I'm running out of time.'

'A nice bloody boy. You wouldn't know nice from shit. Get in here, you black-headed little slut,' he roared. 'Get back in this room now.'

Shoes off, Ann came to the eastern door, stood leaning there, the length of the room between herself and her father. Ben was up too. Bronwyn followed Ann from the bedroom, stood behind her in her nightie.

'I'll have to go, Jack,' Ellie said. 'The baby is coming.'

'Bloody baby-bearing bitch. A poor bloody man drives all night and gets home to this.'

'Yes. You're probably worn out, love. I wasn't thinking. You go to bed. Benjie can take me.'

'Don't tell me to go to bed like your bloody kids. I'm God here. No-one tells me what to do here.' He picked up a chair, threw it. It hit the case, which hit Ellie's knee. She tripped over it, grabbed for the table, but fell heavily. Ben ran into the room. He stood between his parents. 'I'll take her up to the hospital, Dad. Go out to the ute, Mum. I'll just get dressed.'

'You'll take her. You bloody mummy's boy, mealy-mouthed little bastard. Get out of my bloody sight.'

'Yeah. Yeah. Well, you get out of our sight too. If you're going to be like this every time you come home, then don't bother coming home. Stay at your stupid Narrawee and just leave us alone here.'

Jack stepped forward, his closed fist aimed at Ben, who ducked beneath the blow and picked up the fallen chair, using it as a barrier as he tried to go around his father. Jack snatched it, tossed it into the passage, then flung Ben after it.

Ellie was grasping the table, trying to regain her feet when he hit her. She went down again. She lay on her side, protecting her stomach with hands and drawn-up knees. 'Don't, Jack. For the love of God. I've got to get to the hospital.'

But he was out of control now. It had begun and wouldn't end until it ended.

Ann edged inside, edged along the wall to the wireless corner. She watched Ben run at the mad man, try to hold him. Jack caught him by the collar of his pyjamas, ripping the garment from him, exposing Ben's too thin chest.

Ben was the wrong build to play hero, all heart and guts, but no killer instinct. Blood streaming from a gash below his hairline, he sprang to his feet, dived at his father's shoulders, locking his arms around his neck. Jack swung around, slamming him against the wall.

'Get up, Mum. Run,' Ben screamed, but Ellie lay where she had fallen. Too late to run. She'd done it again. Waited too long. She lay on the floor and wept.

Noise was everywhere. Screaming. Bronwyn's scream disappeared into the night. 'I'm going for Bessy. I'll ring up Bob Johnson . . .'

'Get back here, you little bitch. Get back in here now.'

Separate, Ann watched the players from her corner. She was away from it, in that other place. Reality, life, was out there with David. Life was parties. Life was love and arms to hold. Not this. Not this. This wasn't real. Just a picture of a pregnant woman, moaning on the floor. Just a mad bull, rampaging. Bellowing.

Bronwyn was miscast. Much too young for the role she had to play. They were all miscast. What is my role here? she thought. Do I have a role here? I should be in a motel bed with David, holding him inside me, loving him. Living life. Not here. Not in this place.

'Annie,' Ben screamed. 'Annie, help me, for God's sake. Help me. He'll kill her.'

Help? How? How do you fight a bull-man who has kicked out

a wall and tossed the table at the door? Don't get in his way. That's how. You stay out of his way.

The baby got in the way of his shoe. A worn wedding band, two hands, drawn-up knees couldn't protect it, and Ellie's scream wouldn't die.

Ann moved fast as Ben picked up a broom, tossing it between the mad bull's legs as he jumped on his back. The bull's feet entangled in the broom, he overbalanced, and went down, Ben riding him triumphant to the floor.

Ann picked up the gun that had lived for all her life behind the old wireless that no longer sang. Its weight surprised her. She looked at the red polished butt, at the barrel of gleaming metal. It was a thing of beauty, with a god-like power over life and death. Now her hands held it. They held the power of life, of death.

Slowly she raised the barrel until it pointed at her father's back. He scrambled awkwardly to his feet. 'Bang,' she said. 'You're dead.'

Slowly he turned to her, saw the gun pointed at him. 'Put that down, you crazy-eyed bitch.' His smooth, dark-chocolate voice was confident, but his three fast steps back gave lie to that.

The barrel of the gun followed him. Her eyes followed him.

Ben's twisted face followed him. She saw her brother's hand go to his jaw. One hand, his other, was trying to lift Ellie.

'It's not loaded,' Jack said, watching the hammers being lifted back.

'It's always loaded,' she said.

Jack had loved this gun, his father's gun. He'd lavished care on it. His hands had cleaned it, oiled it, smoothed the polished wood that now felt warm and secure against Ann's shoulder. She loved it too. Always had. So now she held it, and her finger was on the trigger.

'Put it down, you stupid bitch of a girl. Put it down.' But she laughed at his fear. Two drunks in the kitchen, and only one held the gun. It seemed very funny.

Do it, she thought. Do it. Squeeze. Blast him away forever. Make life possible.

But would the life it made be possible, or would it start a different cycle, a cycle without David? A cycle with barred windows. She remembered a barred window.

'Annie. Help me. Jack. Help me.'

Poor Ellie. Ben was trying to get her up. He couldn't. He fell to her side, defeated, as she rolled to her back. 'The baby. Help me!' Ben on his knees now, was holding his jaw with his hand.

Jack took two more paces backwards, glancing quickly from his wife to the gun.

'Get me to the hospital, Jack. For the love of God. I'm bleeding. Help me.'

Ann watched her father's mouth snap shut, and panic race down the dark corridors of his mind to end in his eyes ... in his brown, soft as velvet eyes, his bewildered eyes. Panic brought sanity with it. His hand went to his mouth, to his pocket, to his car keys. He took two steps towards his wife, but the barrel followed him.

'My nemesis,' he said. 'My bloody nemesis.'

Ellie's mouth was open, ugly. 'Put that gun down, Annie.'

Ann looked at her mother, saw the bloody pool staining the floor. A flowing river of gore, black red beneath the bright white light. Too much blood.

Blood. Liza. Blood. Liza.

And the world stilled. It slipped out of focus, slowed down to stop.

Open mouths screamed soundless words, while she stared at pictures. Pictures from Grimm's fairytales. Too harsh. Too cruel.

Close your eyes Annie Blue Dress. You don't want to look any more.

Ben slumped against the wall. Bronwyn, shivering, wet curls slicked around her face. Bessy. Bill.

No card game in the lounge room tonight, Annie Blue Dress.

The policeman.

Quick march. Quick march, through the door
Drag a tiny boy from a river of gore,
And place it down on the kitchen floor.

The policeman can't make it breathe. Bessy can't make it breathe. What a clever baby, it even defies Jack Burton. No Johnny here to force life into this one, so it stays dead. Clever baby. Give it a pat on the back.

The policeman breaks the gun, removes the cartridges while he listens to the lies, believes the lies. He saw Bessy's bull in the fowl yard. He dodged Bessy's bull.

'She got it to shoot the bloody bull. It's your fault. Keep the mongrel thing on your side of the river.'

Cast off blame, Jack. Give it to another. Stay blameless, Jack Burton. You must stay blameless. Not your fault. You didn't mean it. You never mean it. You always say you're sorry.

Benjie tries to place the blame where it belongs, but his jaw is broken. He can't talk. Bob told him not to talk. He sits, two hands now hold his face together, while his eyes turn to the mute in her corner, near the old wireless that was also struck dumb by a fall. Ben's eyes overflow as he tries to drag Dummy Burton back from that foggy, misty place where she is safe, that place where she went to before, where she wants to go again. Better there. Much better there.

Hear no evil. Speak no evil. Just file it away,
to polish up at leisure, use on another day.

The gun is leaning against the wall. The cartridges are on the table. The policeman doesn't know about this gun. It is a magic gun. Like Annie Blue Dress, it came from Narrawee.

Everything bad came from Narrawee.

Don't think, Annie Blue Dress. Don't think of that place.

We waited, little Annie. We waited, eating apples. We kept saying, Aunty May will open the door. We waited until there was no light to hope in. Remember.

Push me Johnny, push me high.
I'm a bird and I can fly
High up to the clear blue sky.
I made Liza Burton –
I made Liza Burton –
I made Liza Burton –

Hole in that piece of paper. Hole rubbed by a moistened finger. What did it rub away, little Annie? Lie? Cry? Sigh? Or was it Die? I made Liza Burton die. I made her die?

No! No.

I made her die? I remember the blood.

Shush. Don't think. Don't think, Annie Blue Dress. Hush now. Be still.

A face flew into semi-focus amid the mist clouding her brain. Bronny's face. Her fists were punching, pounding a passage through the fog, her mouth screaming words.

'You wake up Annie. Tell them, Annie. Tell them. Don't you go trying to pull your deaf and dumb act again. You wake up and talk to me.'

Ann stared at the younger girl's mouth. Remembered. Lipstick. David.

Bronny. Strong little Bronny. Let me be safe, Bronny. It's safe here. I don't want to know. I can't live if I know.

'Talk, Annie. Tell them what happened. Tell Mr Johnson that it's lies.' Bronwyn's small fists, pounding Ann's stomach, forced the air and one word out.

'Yes.' Ann's voice was hoarse with tension, but free. 'Yes. Lies. Everything he says. Lies.'

Bob Johnson knew. He knew, but he did nothing. He patted Ann's arm. 'You get me some more towels, Annie. The ambulance will be here soon. They'll look after your mum. She's made of strong stuff. She'll make it.'

Ann looked from him to Bessy and Ellie, to the baby boy on

the table. She walked to it, touched it, spoke to it. 'I made you a beautiful dress for the christening, then I went to a party, and I killed you too,' she said, and she walked from the room.

The night was black as pitch, the road deserted. Distant headlights gave ample warning of a vehicle's approach. She had time to hide. She was under the five-mile bridge when she heard the ambulance screaming towards Mallawindy, then she watched it scream back to Daree while she cowered with her bike in a water-filled ditch. She saw the police car cruise by twice, her only cover the tall dry grass, and from behind a tree, she gripped the handlebars while she watched Bessy's truck slow, turn back, its spotlight scouring the sides of the road.

She would have to be off the road before dawn. Go bush. Leave her bike and follow the river.

She had her schoolbag, and her bankbook, her scissors and the midnight blue dress. She had her purse, and a battered golden syrup tin. She had her good shoes, and her old shoes. Her load wasn't heavy.

When the road was dark again, she mounted the bike and rode on.

Maybe she'd make it. Dawn was only hours away now, but Daree was not too far ahead.

novel lovers

~

She knew what he wanted, what they all wanted. Slowly she slid the zip open, shrugging off her skirt and stepping away from it. The buttons on her prim blouse, slowly, tantalisingly undone, it slipped from her rounded shoulders, and as her heavy breasts sprang free of their restriction. She smiled knowingly, backing away as he reached eagerly for his prize.

Mack was sweating with desire as he approached her, his mouth open, sucking air deep into aching lungs.

She laughed at him, allowing her hands to slide seductively from her firm ripe breasts, down to her hips, stripping her hips and buttocks of their sheer covering, before kicking the flimsy panties to his feet.

'Come to Mommy, baby boy,' she crooned. 'Come to Mommy.' Her dark triangle tantalised with knowledge of the silken place it hid, her nipples were pink crumpled petals of a dusty rose. His mouth sought the twin flowers, and Mack sucked.

THE END

Malcolm Fletcher closed the novel with a snap then used it to flatten two flies making love on his kitchen table. Lust was barely a memory, but the novel had stirred places that hadn't been stirred for years! He stood, took too-fast breaths, eased his trousers around the crutch, and eyed the cover picture as Eve might have eyed an overripe apple in the garden of Eden.

An earthy beauty bared her left breast there, the name of the author emblazoned across it. *Coll M Chef-Marlet*, the letters read. The letters could as easily have spelt Malcolm Fletcher!

He mouthed the name. 'You black-hearted old sinner, Chef-Marlet,' he said.

In the Burton house, near hidden by overgrown shrubs, Bronwyn Burton had her nose buried in one of the hottest passages of an identical copy of the novel. She closed the book as Ben walked into the kitchen.

'You shouldn't be wasting your money on that smut, Bron.'

'Everybody is reading it.' Weak-kneed with second-hand desire, Bronwyn stood, tossing her long hair back; it was a sleek, rich brown. She was almost eighteen, old enough to read what she liked. And she liked Chef-Marlet – as did half of Australia. 'Anyhow, where's your patriotism? At least he's Australian.'

Ben picked up the book, looked at the photograph of a moon-faced youthful author. 'He looks as if he should be writing obscure history, not this smut,' he said. He tossed the book back to the table and watched his sister light a cigarette. She held it as her father held a cigarette, and her mouth, when she sucked on the weed, was shaped like her father's. The final mixture of Burton and Vevers, Bronwyn had her mother's green eyes and her father's nose, her mother's build and her father's temper.

'You shouldn't be wasting money on cigarettes, either,' he said.

'I don't. You know me, Ben. Money well spent is never wasted.'

Ben saved two-thirds of his wage each week. He didn't understand this sister. She'd developed young, and had half the town louts chasing her since she turned thirteen. She was average height, and not a lot like Annie, except her hands. Every time he looked at Bron's hands, he thought of Annie's.

He had his mother's hands, or his grandfather's, as Ellie always said. He had his grandfather's build too, five foot six when he stopped growing. He'd expected to make five-ten at least. Ben still lived at home when Jack was out of town, but he was in residence at the moment, so Ben slept on a camp stretcher in a junk room behind Bert Norris's shop. He hadn't spoken to his father since the night Annie left, and he'd sworn to Ellie that he never would again.

On that New Year's Eve, Ellie had lost the last of her fight, her baby, and her womb. She'd lost a lot of blood too. It was months before she was back to her old self. Jack had remained sober for twelve months after. He'd even taken a job with the stock agent. Two years passed before Jack got back to his old self, but he rarely hit Ellie, or so she said, and when he did, it was usually brought on by outside influences, Ellie stressed. If people didn't stir him up, everything was fine. They had a good relationship. Both Ben and Bronwyn stayed out of his way now.

It was almost six. Jack always ate at six. Ben helped himself to some boiled pumpkin and potatoes and a bit of stew. He helped himself to a few eggs for breakfast, a couple of slices of bread and a thick wedge of cake. He was packing it carefully into his Esky as Ellie came from the shower, hair brush in hand.

'Got your dinner, love?'

'Yes thanks, Mum.'

Head down, Ellie stood before the stove, brushing the yard of wet silk. Ben watched her for minutes, then his gaze wandered the room, resting a moment on the portrait of Liza, almost forgotten, as Linda Alice had been forgotten, as Annie would never be forgotten.

They'd found her bike near Daree, but no-one had sighted her there. She'd disappeared as completely as Johnny.

Never much good at putting his thoughts into words, always nervous and shy in his youth, Ben attempted to get through life unnoticed. Annie was the one he'd spoken his dreams to. Far easier to sign a dream than to give it voice. Her leaving created a gap in his life that eight years, eighty years, would do little to fill.

'Sunshine shower, fall from sky,' he signed the words. He could still do it.

'That's what Annie used to call Mum's hair,' Bronwyn said.

'What love?' Ellie tossed back the wet mane and began plaiting it.

'Nothing, Mum. I'd better get going, I suppose, before my dinner gets cold. Anything you need from the shops tomorrow?'

'Just the bread, love. Oh, and you can get me some baking powder, and a couple of light globes. And get onto Jim Bourke about that fence too. We can claim it on our tax, and you really haven't got the time.'

Bronwyn walked with her brother to his ute. He still had the old HR, but he'd had the rust cut out a couple of years back, and a new paint job, so it still looked good, and got him as far as he wanted to go, which wasn't far. 'You can give me a lift up the town, Ben.'

'You don't want to go hanging around there all night.'

'I don't want to go hanging around here all night, either. He likes her hair when it's been shampooed. The old bed springs will be rattling tonight.'

'Bron!' Ben slid into the ute, swung the passenger door open.

'Do you think much about Annie these days, Ben?'

'She'll come back one day.'

'Like you always reckoned Johnny would. How old would he be now?'

'Thirty-one. Three years older than me. He was eight when Annie was born.'

'I don't even remember him. I must have been at least two when he left. What was he like? Who was he like?'

'You've seen photos. He was the image of Dad.'

'Like as in, wild? Quiet?'

'Oh, he wasn't anything like him in ways.' Ben scratched at the scar at his hairline. 'Mum wanted him to be a priest.'

'That would have made Jack happy.'

'It did. He called him Jesus. They hated each other.' Ben started the motor, backed the ute around and headed slowly up the track. 'Johnny and old Fletch's son were good mates. They were together the day they found the bones down Dead Man's Lane.'

'Fletch's son died young, didn't he?'

'Yeah. He was sixteen. From encephalitis. But his old woman blamed the blacks for putting a hex on him – pointing the bone. She drowned herself when he died.'

'Tied three flat irons to her belt, the kids reckon,' Bronwyn laughed and sprayed smoke.

'It's not funny.'

'Not funny, but original, you've got to admit that much. Can't say I blame her either. Imagine doing it with that fat old toad.'

She left the car, opened the gate, and Ben drove through. He waited as she closed it behind him, looping the circle of wire over the leaning gatepost. He'd have to get onto that fence, or get onto Bourkey. It was almost down. He loved this piece of land, always hated leaving it behind him. The town meant nothing to him.

'What made Johnny take off?'

'I don't really know. I was only twelve when he left.'

'Only twelve, my goodness? Just a child. Can you imagine me saying one day, Oh I can't remember much about Annie. I was only ten when she left home.'

'Of course, I remember him. I remember he dropped out of school; he was always stirring up Dad – and big enough to do it too. They used to have stand up fights at the end.'

'This was after Annie came back from Narrawee?'

'Yeah, but they never got on. After Annie was born, I think Johnny thought he'd turned into God. He was eight, Bron, and he used to treat Dad like dirt. If Dad started getting into Mum, Johnny would go for him. It got worse as he grew, then after John Fletcher died, Johnny sort of flipped his lid.'

'The bone pointers did him in too.'

'The old man didn't notice Annie much until after she came

back from Narrawee, and his Liza didn't. He seemed to hate her when she came back. He'd belt her when he was drunk, try to make her talk. Johnny used to keep her out of his way, take her everywhere with him. That's when he started missing school. If he went to school, he'd take Annie to Bessy, and leave her there until he got home.

'Mum was pleased to get rid of her. Until the Narrawee thing, Johnny used to be Mum's slave, but I suppose he started seeing her for what she was or something. She was worse than useless with Annie. Scared of her. You'd remember that.' Bronwyn nodded. 'I dunno what you want to know, Bron.'

'Everything. Give me all the dirt, Ben. Why did he run? If he was so protective of Annie, how come he left her? I mean, wouldn't you think that he would have come back for her when he got older?'

'I always thought he'd come back.'

'He was fifteen?'

'Going on sixteen. All I know, Bron, is that in the weeks after John Fletcher died, the house was bedlam. Dad was blind blotto all the time, and it was like Johnny was taunting him. Then that afternoon, Dad had been getting into Annie for hours. Johnny picked up Mum's poker, and he belted Dad over the back of the head with it. He knocked him down and hit into him with the poker while he had him down. Mum had to fight him off or he would have killed him, I think.' The utility drew to a halt on the forest side of the bridge while a herd of sheep was driven across. Ben's voice raised to compete with the bleating, and the dogs barking.

'Anyway, Mum packed Johnny's bag and told him to go. He was howling, saying, "Don't make me leave her, Mum. Don't make me leave her. I'll kill him, Mum. I'll come back and kill him." He was screaming in the end, and Annie was screaming after him, and I went after both of them, and – .'

Ben turned his face to the window, silenced. He sucked in a deep breath, and let it out slowly before continuing his story.

'Johnny would turn around and make his hand signs to Annie, and she'd run towards him screaming. In the end, he flagged down a truck and left Annie standing in the middle of the road. That was the last time I ever saw her howl.'

'I've never seen her howl. I can remember Dad belting her and yelling, talk to me, talk to me, and she'd just scream at him or laugh.'

'Yeah.' Ben rubbed at his eye, then at the scar near his brow. 'He always knew she could hear. I used to think she could too, so did Johnny. She knew exactly what was going on. When you were out in the paddocks with her, you knew she heard stuff. Like when the dog barked, she seemed to hear it, and Dad's old car. She used to hear that.'

'How much do you know about Narrawee?'

'Not much. Dad's old man left it to Sam and May, then to their kids, but they haven't got any. I think it's supposed to revert back to Dad, if Sam dies.'

'So, we could eventually get it?'

'I suppose so. I don't know what happens if Dad dies first. May has got cousins. It might go to them.'

'I could take to being rich, Ben. Did you know them, May and Sam? Ever meet them?'

'Dozens of times. Dozens – when I was a kid. They used to come up here a couple of times a year. Sam's the living image of Dad, but he had a moustache. I remember him as a real snob, and as tame as Dad was wild. Like he was under May's thumb. Sort of crawly tame he was, but his eyes didn't look tame. Like one of those blue-heeler dogs that cringe at your feet, but you know they'll go for your ankles as soon as you turn your back. Patronising to Mum, he was, but she couldn't see it. They wanted to educate Johnny, send him to a private Melbourne school. Dad wouldn't have a bar of it. He hated Sam back then. Jealous of him, I suppose. He got stuck into him one day. Called him everything but a gentleman, and Sam just walked off and got in the car. "There but for the grace of a fool, go I ..." Dad says to May, "I could have had it all. I could have turned that old bastard against him back then, but I kept my bloody mouth shut." Sam was beeping the horn, so May just sort of shook her head and backed away.'

'Maybe they've got Johnny. Maybe they sent him to school. Mum still believes they've got Liza hidden away somewhere. Maybe they got both of them. Their hidden family.'

'No way, Bron. Johnny didn't like Sam much either.'

'How come Liza and Annie went down there that time?'

'Mum went into hospital to have you while Dad was off on one of his drunk trips, so she sent a telegram to Narrawee, thinking Dad was down there. She never knew where he was, never cared much either, as long as he stayed away. Anyway, May turned up. Me and Johnny were doing okay, but we couldn't cope with Liza. Johnny used to try to pull her into line when Dad was away, but she'd save up all her tales to tell when he came home. She was a posing, spoiled-rotten brat of a kid, Bron. "I'm Miss Tiny Tot," she used to say. Dad ruined her. She could do anything, get away with anything, when he was around. Me or Annie always copped the blame. We used to try to stay away from her, but then we'd cop it because she'd dob on us, say we wouldn't play with her. Anyway, I'm getting carried away. I haven't thought of her for years, you know.'

'It's interesting. Go on.'

'That's another story, Bron. May turned up that day and offered to take the girls back with her until Mum came home, and me and Johnny jumped at the chance to get rid of the brat. Annie wanted to go. Liza had been to Narrawee a dozen times, and she'd come home lording it over all of us. Annie was different back then, Bron. She was never a baby. You would have sworn she was the older one of the two girls, and May really liked her. You could see it sticking out a mile. I think Johnny just wanted Annie to have something.

'Anyhow, the old man finally came home and Johnny copped

it. He'd never just shut up and run. He was yelling at Dad that day. "Well if you'd stay home like a normal father and helped us, I wouldn't have let them go with Aunty May." Dad was belting hell out of him when Mr Ponsford comes down with the telegram. The two girls were missing, and so was the bloke who worked there. The gardener.'

'Crazy. As Mum says, what has she done to deserve it?'

'I dunno. That last baby would be eight now. Johnny's age, the night he made Annie breathe.'

The sheep had long since cleared the bridge. Ben started his motor and drove on. They were close to town before they spoke again.

'I'll be doing the old Burton run soon, Ben. I've applied for two jobs in Daree. I've got an interview on Monday.'

'What about the supermarket?'

'I can't live on twenty hours a week.'

'Mum won't want you to go. She'll have no-one, Bron.'

'Christ, Ben. She made her own bed. We don't have to lie in it with her. Come away with me. We'll get a flat, get a life.'

'I can't. He won't make me run.'

jack's party

~

Jack's hand was feeling for the familiar bottle he'd left on the sideboard. A light might have simplified his search, but he never turned the lights on when he wandered the house in the night. He and the night had a covenant. They kept each other's secrets.

'Blind as a fowl-yard rat, you poor bastard,' he muttered, as his hand found, snatched up the bottle. He'd slept like one of the dead until 3 a.m., but his bloody tooth woke him.

'Pain. A man is dying of pain, and she's lying there snoring, in the arms of Jesus.'

He found the Aspros. Cursing softly, he ripped the small tablets free of their wrapping, working by feel alone. Everything was wrapped up these bloody days. What was wrong with bottles? He liked bottles. As he freed each tablet, he tossed it in his mouth, crunched it, then washed it down with whisky.

He'd have to get down to Melbourne, get his tooth root-filled. He hated dentists, hated sitting in a chair while they poked their bloody fingers in his mouth and drilled him. Hated the bastards.

His lips compressed, his tongue massaging, he felt his way back to the door and to the miserly light from the moon. An odd figure, his white T-shirt his only garb, it barely covered his backside. Still, he'd discovered a new freedom since the last wild little bitch ran baying from the shack two weeks ago.

His bare feet dancing on the cold lino, Jack saluted the empty rooms with his bottle. He'd never wanted kids. He'd hoped the breed might die with him and Sam.

His face was on fire with pain, but his feet were cold. One foot, investigating its surrounds, stumbled on the mat Ellie placed near the kitchen door. He picked it up and positioned it on the floor, then he sat, knees up, enough mat left over to offer his feet protection. The wall for a back rest, he lifted the bottle to his mouth and a groan of near content escaped, as whisky settled in the warm swamp of his gut. He could feel it sending out its feelers, feel it relax his neck muscles, singing the nest of bull ants gnawing at his gum.

'Die you little bastards, die,' he said.

The bottle at home in his large hand, he could sense the level of whisky left. Carefully, he placed it on the floor and shook a cigarette from the packet.

'Oh, God,' he prayed to his weed, blowing smoke into the dark. 'Give him a fag and a bottle, and a man's a king. Give him a fag and a bottle, and he wouldn't trade Chook-Shit County for Sam's silk pyjamas or his warm bed.' Again the bottle was lifted to his mouth.

He felt old tonight. He was fifty-four. He'd always believed old age was for others, but it was creeping up on him like a malignant bloody disease. 'Cruel slayer of vanity,' he said. 'The ugly bastard is the lucky bastard. The ugly bastard who loses his teeth when he's sixteen, and his hair at twenty, he's the lucky bastard,' he mused, manipulating the aching eye-tooth, considering taking to it with a pair of pliers. 'He's never had anything to lose, has he? But the poor bastard who's had it all can see it dropping away with his teeth.

'Look at her,' he said to his friend, the bottle, pointing it towards the room where Ellie lay snoring. 'Take her as a prime example.' His head, lifting in sudden anger, jarred the bull ants into life. He flinched, whimpered, sucked cold air, while his tooth screamed, but the shock of cold air momentarily killed the other pain. 'I planned to take her home to Narrawee once and flaunt my prize – bloody booby prize,' he sneered.

'Bloody Saint Sam. Bloody mongrel bastard. That's my land. My house, and a man isn't allowed to take a bottle there. It's mine. Mine.' His fist slammed into his chest, Ann's sign for right of ownership, but it knocked the glowing ember from his cigarette to the mat.

'Burn, you bastard,' he said, sniffing in the rank stink of dusty wool, willing it to set the floor alight, to burn this hell hole down, and Ellie with it.

Sitting, sucking smoke, sipping whisky, slowly the pain wandered from his tooth to his shoulder, pressed against the upright. He straightened. His chin lifting, he stretched his jaws, stretched the sagging skin of his throat, testing for pain while his thoughts wandered back to Narrawee, to his youth, to a time when dreams had hope of substance.

He, and May, and Sam. A threesome. They'd shared a boundary fence as kids. May's old man and his were two of a kind, money coming out of their ears. Hard old bastards, both. *To my first born, John William [Jack], I leave the Ford, my double-barrel shotgun and five hundred a year to buy ammunition and petrol.* The words were imprinted on his brain. His father used his will to get in the last hit below the belt, but Jack had got in a few good ones of his own.

'I was the one who carried your bloody name, you old bastard,' he said, but he kept his voice low, guarding his stolen hours. Chin cupped in the palm of his hand, his gaze turned towards the moon, floating free at the window. 'If a man had enough guts sometimes, he'd shoot himself. Make the old bastard happy in hell,' he told the moon. 'Fifty-four. He was only sixty-six when he died. Died. Dead. Mum was forty-two. I thought she was old then.'

His bottle was feeling light. He lifted it again to his mouth, allowing the whisky to wash around his aching tooth, anaesthetise it. 'Peace,' he commented. 'Some nights a man would sell his soul for peace. I wonder if there's anything in her Jesus. I wonder if the bloody bastard is up there, guarding his pearly gates, holding up a big freeway sign. "Wrong way, Jack. Go back." A bloody big red arrow, pointing down. Old Nick, waiting to sink his pitchfork into my bare bum. A man ought to put his pants on if he's going to shoot himself.'

He smiled, and placed the bottle back on the sideboard. There was a sip or two left. He always left a bit in his bottle, and one smoke in his pack to greet his new day. In Mallawindy, this was his only self control. Mornings he held at bay as long as he could. Ellie's witless, 'Jack love! Breakfast's ready, love,' was like a death-knoll in his ear every day of his life. Only the knowledge of his bottle and cigarette could move him from bed in the mornings.

He hated her at the breakfast table. He hated the sight of the crepe throat, and her dried-out breasts that flapped around her waist like a pair of empty shoulder bags. Still, with the choice of four beds in the empty shack, he continued to use her bed at night – and her, when he could get her to roll over and play dead. And he still woke screaming in the night too, his face buried in the silk of her hair.

He'd loved her once, loved her hair, and her green fire eyes. Bloody loyal, baby-bearing bitch. 'A poor bloody man's dreams were defeated by her fertility,' he said, but the memory of her sunshine hair teased at his loins. His old colleague in crime was awakening.

'Go back to sleep, you rapacious bastard. Be like a blind worm seeking pay dirt in a hummock of dry grass tonight,' he muttered. 'A man should have been a monk, sworn off women, locked himself up in his monastery with his books and bought himself points in the hereafter. A man might have been happy with his books.'

He'd taken four Aspros. Mixed with the whisky, they were making his ears ring, and the wind, threatening all day, had finally arrived to wail around the roof. Unable to find an easy pathway through the hills and valleys, it turned, howled around the twin chimneys like the hounds of hell.

Jack straightened. His chin lifting, he sat erect. He didn't like the wind, or the creaking doors and rattling windows. The house was surrounded by trees. Branches moaned, groaned. At times, you'd swear there were voices out there, riding the wind. Bloody spirits, haunting him.

'Bloody old bastard,' he said, hearing his father in the wind. 'Piss off. I'm doing all right without you. Jack bloody Burton is doing all right, and no thanks to you.'

Other noises began to unite with the wind. Walls murmured, floors moved, like footsteps in the empty bedrooms. Head up, his ears strained to hear the plaintive plea on the wind. *'Daddy! Daddy! I'm your good girl, aren't I, Daddy?'*

'Stop haunting me,' he moaned. 'Piss off, all of you, or I'll blow my bloody brains out and leave you nothing to haunt.'

His gun still lived in the corner of the kitchen. He laughed softly as he walked to it, picked it up. 'I ought to do it. If I shoved it in my mouth, one of the first pieces of tissue to be blown to hell would be my tooth. Slight case of over-kill, but what the hell,' he said.

Then he stubbed his toe, right on the corn. He danced, grabbed his foot, dropped his gun, and it went off. Its blast and his scream reverberated through the sleeping house.

A torch peered out from the lounge room doorway, the ghostly shape of its bearer behind it. He'd taught Ellie better than to flood the night house with electric light.

'Jack! Jack! What in heaven's name are you doing out here?'

'Blowing my bloody brains out. What's it look like? I got my toe instead.' He'd got her crates of eggs too. They'd been piled near the door for collection on the morrow.

'I've warned you to be careful with that gun.' Her torchlight searching, Ellie sought evidence of damage and found it. 'Oh, Jack,' both voice and torch slid low. 'Oh, Jack! Look what you've done to my eggs, love.'

But Jack was looking at her. She was draped from neck to ankle in a washed-out rag of a nightgown; her hair plaited loose for sleep, fell long across her shoulder. In the shadowed kitchen, and to a man with failing vision, she could have been sixteen, her gown the white of her bridal night.

'What he can't possess, man will ever crave, and on the outside of a half a pint of whisky, he is prone to self delusion. Come here, Beauty,' he said.

'There's egg everywhere, Jack. Don't walk in it, love. You'll slip over.'

'Bloody eggs. You're more concerned about your eggs than you ever were about me. If it had been my blood leaking all over this floor, you would have danced on me, celebrating your bloody release.'

'Don't be silly, love. Go back to bed while I clean up this mess.'

'You never cared about me. A poor bloody man is dying of toothache and you're lying in bed snoring. You don't care if all my teeth fall out.'

'I got Bessy to make you an appointment with my dentist in Daree, but you wouldn't go. Put some oil of cloves on it, then go back to bed. It's freezing out here. You'll catch a chill in the kidneys wandering around with nothing on.'

'And die of bloody frostbite in your bed.'

'Hush, Jack!' she whispered, as if the night had ears.

'Hush, Jack,' he mimicked. 'Hush Jack, the children will hear you! Don't, Jack, the children will see you! Well, there's no bloody kids left here now, so get down on the floor and play dead, you cold bitch.'

'Jack.' Reproach in her voice, Ellie turned her torchlight to the lounge room door and she hurried after it.

'Get the oil of cloves for me,' he demanded.

'It's in the top cupboard,' she replied from behind a wall.

'I know it's in the bloody top cupboard. Get it, I said.'

Slowly she made her way back to the kitchen, lifting her gown to step over the pool of seeping egg. He caught hold of her night-gown, pulled her to him.

'You know I've got a bad back, Jack.'

'You've got a bloody worse front,' he commented. A palm on her breast, he tried to force her down. She evaded him. He stuck out a foot, hooked her ankle, and Ellie sprawled headlong into the door with him on top, and he laughed and mounted her in the doorway, wasting no time on preliminaries. She didn't fight him. She lay like a length of unrisen dough beneath him, attempting to ease first one hip then the other away from the floor and sticky egg.

'Hail Mary full of grace, the Lord is with . . . ' He chuckled in time to his exertions, building slowly, excited by the night and the white-gowned one who had materialised in the passage. She'd prayed in the early days when he made love to her. Now it was his game. He prayed and she kept her mouth shut.

'Blessed art thou . . . amongst women . . . and blessed . . . '

She felt more alive with the floorboards prodding her into action than she ever felt on a mattress with only his prodding. He sucked air around his tooth, pain driving him as he drove again and again into the deeper warmth of her, the only warmth her church couldn't kill.

It was a sport he'd excelled at in his youth. It was a sport of control. His knees were being punished on the floor, but it excited him – this ability to override pain, push it down and grow stronger for it. 'Blessed art thou . . . '

He could go all night. He'd needed this, needed to prove tonight that he wasn't old, to prove to himself he wasn't old. He drove ruthlessly into Ellie, enduring passionless altar of his lust.

154

Other women wanted him. Couldn't get enough of him. He'd make her bloody want him too before he died. He sucked on her dry nipple, he used his hands well.

'Jack. That's enough. Get finished, love.'

He didn't need her words to steal away his magic, so he slapped her face. She whimpered, and he kissed the whimpering mouth, and entwined his long fingers in the silk of her hair, buried his face there.

It smelt of egg, and of countryside, of still waters. There was a time when she used to condition her hair with egg yolk. He remembered it, remembered being young with her, in love again. He was king, and Ellie his golden queen. No kids. No bloody kids. Sam might have got May and Narrawee, but he had his Ellie.

If he could only stay in this place, hide from age and memory in this place, driving deeper and deeper into her. If he could only – .

She was pleading now, her thighs pushing against him as her feet slapped and strained against the floor.

'Yes. Yes. Yes! Blessed art thou . . . Yes! Blessed ah . . . Jesus!' He screamed as his strength flowed out of him.

She took it, took his strength, and his youth. She took it, and absorbed it, and gave him back to pain and memory. He pushed her from him, took two more Aspros and returned to bed, fifty-bloody-four, going on ninety, hating her again, hating her for defrauding him of his youth. But he slept well enough.

It was close to five. Ellie cleaned up the broken eggs, and washed the ones she could save. She tossed her nightgown in the wash, had a shower, and went out to start the milking. When Ben arrived, he didn't bother asking why she was wearing her sunglasses. He shook his head and helped her finish off the cows.

All morning she went about her work with the sunglasses in her pocket, just in case someone came to buy eggs, or Bessy rowed over. But no-one came.

She changed the sheets on Bronwyn's bed, just in case her job didn't work out and she came home. Then at nine, the magpie she had taught to whistle came for his breakfast.

At ten she woke Jack for his. She was wearing her sunglasses. Over the years, those big dark glasses had hidden a multitude of his sins.

'It's ten, love. Brekky is ready.'

'Have you got any cash in the house?' he said. He didn't look at her glasses, or her sagging breasts.

Ben returned late in the afternoon. They looked at the kitchen, spoke of a ceiling, of getting someone in to plaster the walls. The need for new fences was more important. He fixed the fly-wire door so the snib caught. He unblocked the sink, and put a new washer in the dripping bathroom tap. Ellie followed him around while he worked. Like a child starved of toys who had fallen head first into a toy box, though somewhat bruised, Ellie was now happy. Jack had probably gone to Narrawee, so Ben could move back home. Her Ben would never leave her like the others did. His trees had grown so tall too. One day he'd build his bridge. One day he would.

Jack always ate at six, so when he hadn't arrived home by seven, Ellie knew he'd gone. The vegetables were drying out in the saucepans. She served her meal and placed the left-overs into bowls to put in the fridge. She was about to sit down in front of the television when she saw the lights of a car jiggle down the track. It wasn't Jack's car. She put her sunglasses on.

'Hello, love,' she greeted the young man in blue. Jeff Rowan was the new town constable who'd replaced Bob Johnson. He was only a boy, no older than Benjie.

'Good evening, Mrs Burton. Jack about?'

'No, love. He didn't come home for his tea,' she said, swinging the door wide as she spoke. 'Will you come in?'

'Any idea how long he might be, Mrs Burton?'

'He's probably gone to Narrawee. He's had a bad toothache

and he goes to a dentist in Melbourne. I was just about to have my tea. Will you have some with me?'

'I ate with Ben at the hotel. Take your glasses off for me will you, Mrs Burton,' the young constable said, following her into the room, and when she didn't, he removed her glasses, touched the swelling, and stood waiting for an explanation.

'I fell against the wall in the dark this morning. Broke a pile of eggs too. I should have put the light on,' she said.

'That's not what Ben tells me, Mrs Burton.'

'Ben wasn't here at the time, Officer, but he did see the broken eggs.' The sunglasses reclaimed, Ellie placed them determinedly on her nose.

'Ben asked me to come down and have a talk to you and Jack, but my hands are tied unless you're prepared to charge him. No woman has to put up with abuse. Not these days.'

'I don't know what you are talking about, love.'

'You're a fool, Mrs Burton.'

'Yes, I am, but I've learned my lesson. Next time I go wandering in the night, I'll put the light on. Have a slice of cake with your tea. I made it this afternoon.'

the gold coast

~

'Hon. Come here, quick.'

'I won't be a minute,' the other half of the couple replied from the motel bathroom, where he was scraping a safety razor over a face sacrificed to Queensland's sun. Red as a boiled yabby, only the eyes peering back from bathroom mirror held colour other than red. They were bloodshot, but they were blue.

David Taylor loathed the ocean, and had no liking for the Queensland Gold Coast. Rivers were what he liked, rivers with their shading trees to creep beneath when the sun grew too hot.

'You're too late. You missed it.'

'What did I miss?' he asked, running a comb through his hair, peering closely at the temples for the grey hairs, not too bothered by what he had missed.

'That girl. You remember that girl you took to Paul's New Year's party. She was on television.'

David walked from the bathroom. He stood beside the bed, close to the small screen where Romans were spilling blood. With a shake of his head, he turned away. 'Hardly likely, Melissa. She wasn't born when that one was made.'

'Not the picture, you fool. It was a commercial for something,' she said, one foot held high while she painted her toenails a vibrant red to match the rest of her.

'You'll have to stay out of the sun tomorrow, Liss.'

'I'll be brown by tomorrow. When you come up here for a holiday, you have to go back with a tan or people think you haven't had a good time. A bit of sunburn isn't going to kill you.'

'Neither will it help prolong my life,' he replied and sat gingerly on the bed, stacking his pillows and easing his parboiled back down, his eyes on the Roman chariots, his mind far away.

'What happened to her anyway?'

'I have no idea.'

'Did you know she was into this sort of thing?'

'I knew her eight years ago. She was only a kid.'

'She had the shape to be a model, I suppose. They like them dumb, with that half-starved look; which you were obviously pretty keen on yourself for a while,' his bed-mate said, finishing with one foot and starting on the other.

'No-one could possibly accuse you of having that half-starved look, Melissa, and you are the one I am here with,' he said, his concentration on the foot with its many sunburnt faces.

'But I'm dumb enough. Is that what you're saying?'

'We came up here for a holiday, not to wage war.'

'Sorry Hon. She was with a little girl, the absolute image of her. It had to be her own. Don't shake the bed. You'll make me smudge.'

The couple sat through two blocks of commercials before being rewarded. Both sprung upright as a wild-haired nymph rose from out of the waves to the thunder of a full orchestral backing. In slow motion, she glided up the sand to a sewing-machine, then stood lonely there. Frowning, shaking her head at the camera, she appeared puzzled. A mermaid, beached.

David swung his legs over the side of the bed, crowding the television as the screen filled with Ann's face. There was time enough to see puzzlement exchanged for mischief. He knew that expression well. She lifted a seashell to her ear. And he knew that hand, had held that hand, had chosen a ring for that hand. In the other, she held a scrap of fabric, edged with embroidery. She studied it, comparing it to the seashell; then she began speaking, her voice near lost against the background of waves.

'She sews seashells by the seashore. The shells she sews are seashells, I'm sure, but does she sew seashells by the seashore? No ... ' Her eyes sought the camera, and with a shrug, she turned to the ocean. 'No,' she repeated, the puzzle solved. 'Her mermaid machine sews the shells.' The fabric dropped to the sand, the orchestra built to a crescendo as the mermaid dived back into a wave and was last seen swimming out to sea.

His sunburn forgotten, David sat over the box, willing the Romans and their chariots gone, willing the box to spit out the next commercial.

'It's different to the one I saw. She had her hair up – looked a bit more normal. How long since you've seen her, Hon?'

'David, Dave, or Davey, please, Melissa, call me anything but Hon. I loathe that term, and I last saw her on the night of the party. I've told you a thousand times. She disappeared. Go to the library and read the old papers.'

'I remember it. Her mother and brother were attacked by a bull.' Her eyes slitted, she looked at him. 'If she hadn't disappeared, then you wouldn't be here with me now, would you?' She turned the television off.

His finger recalled the Romans to war. 'How old was the child?'

'About five, but she's so tall; she might have made the little girl look younger. Why the interest? You didn't get her pregnant, did you?'

He turned away as the screen filled with a labrador pup and a little girl, falling out of her frock. Her hair was thick and black, her wide eyes dark. Baby fat still clung to her chubby limbs. Five, maybe, or less. She looked like Ann – could have been hers.

David laughed outright when a scatterbrain version of the one he had known came on screen. She was doing all but stand on her head as she struggled with an antiquated machine. He remembered too much. He remembered the party girl, high on spiked punch. He remembered the silk of long limbs that day at the river.

In silence the couple watched the last frame. The mother and child were together, a modern machine between them.

'If that's not her child, Hon, then I'll eat my hat.'

'Yes,' he said, hitting the on/off switch before crawling into the double bed with his wife. 'It's certainly a very clever match.'

melbourne

~

For three years now, Ann had been using the office box number as her postal address, ever since the cheque from the bridalwear shop had gone astray. It was safer for a wanderer. The office was the only permanence in her life. She was a fictional character in a play on the grand stage of Melbourne; the rooms she slept in were props in the temporary roles she lived until she found Johnny and the play ended, then the costume trunks could be locked away, and she could take Johnny home.

Jan dropped a letter on her desk as she walked through, and Ann looked at the handwritten address, turned it over. No return address. She received little mail that didn't have windows. The handwriting looked familiar. It was like her mother's, large, not well formed. Had Ellie seen the ads, tracked her to this box number? Had Johnny gone home?

It was possible. Eagerly she ripped it open, wanting it to be from her mother, wanting her to have cared enough to write.

Dear Ann Burton, It wasn't from Ellie.

In reply to your advertisement for information regarding John Lawrence Burton, born 1952. I work with John at

Box Hill Sales and Service. I have heard him speak of family members in Mallawindy, and in particular, about his sister, Ann. I hope this information may be of value to you.

Best of luck, Dave Jones.

'Jesus,' she said. 'Jesus.' No contact number. Nothing, but the letter sounded genuine. She picked up the phone book. Practised fingers found the used-car listings, and it was there. Box Hill Sales and Service, Maroondah Highway, Box Hill. 'Let it be,' she whispered as she dialled the number, tapping her pen on her desk while the phone rang. Rang. Rang. 'Please. Please. Please answer it, Johnny. I will know your voice. Please God, let it be.'

'Box Hill Sales and Service. Tony speaking.'

'Good morning. Could I speak to John Burton, please?'

'John? No, I'm sorry. John is at lunch. Can I give him a message?'

'Yes . . . No. No. Thank you. I'll call back,' she said.

'He should be back by two.'

Her hand now shaking out of control, Ann placed the phone down. So easy. Too easy? She looked at her watch. One thirty-five. Box Hill was only half an hour away on the train. The letter tossed in the black hole of her bag, she stood and walked to the office next door. 'I have to go out, Michael. I'll take a long lunch.'

'Did you get onto Roger the Red?'

'Yes. He's flying over in two weeks.'

'Okay. Don't forget we've got Davis coming at four.'

'I'll be back by three,' she said, and she ran for the stairs.

Five flights to the ground. Running up and down them kept her slim, she said. They kept her too slim. She was all legs and arms and hair. At fifteen, many had believed her to be twenty; at twenty-four, she sometimes looked fifteen.

She didn't like lifts – refused to use them – got the blind unreasonable panics every time she looked at a lift door. Michael thought she was mad. She knew she was, but apart from the lifts, she hid it well. She played the city girl now; at home in this hub of noise and movement.

She jumped a tram to Flinders Street, and raked at her hair with a wide-toothed comb before catching the Box Hill train. The station was only a block from Maroondah Highway. She had a Melway Street Directory with her, the city man's bible; few Melburnians moved without their directory. Now her finger tracked Maroondah Highway through its pages until she found Box Hill. She circled it with red.

'Let it be,' she prayed to her new bible. 'Let it be.'

How many phone calls had she made in the past years? Countless. Systematically, she'd worked her way through the Burtons in the telephone book, then she'd started calling large companies, giving her spiel. She'd called the Education Department. Since the night of the party in Warran, she'd often imagined Johnny as a school teacher – but a used-car salesman. Never. Hundreds of phone calls, and none had borne fruit until today. Apart from her call to Sam. She'd come across her uncle's Melbourne number on a wet Sunday afternoon.

'John Lawrence?' the familiar voice replied. 'You don't mean brother John William, do you? Jack Burton? What has he done? Won the lottery? Robbed a bank?'

Ann broke the connection fast, knowing the voice had to be Sam's. So like her father's voice. She'd checked the address. Toorak. Sandon Grove, Toorak. M A Burton. May Alice Burton, of course. She'd have the phone in her name. May had always been the boss. She'd carried the money, signed cheques, paid the bills – a liberated woman before it became fashionable.

Memory had come at her hard as she walked away from the phone box that day. Memory of May, driving into a small garage. It had a lift-up door that crashed to the concrete in a wind. May holding small hands on a tram. Little trains that were not trains, running down the middle of the road making sparks. May pulling on a wire overhead when they wanted to get off. Noisy. Maybe she and Liza had been to the Toorak flat.

Many memories had returned in the past eight years, but they were floating things, colourful bubbles on the wind, that burst as she grasped them.

Ann checked her watch, then turned to the window as the train slowed. Camberwell Station. Not far now. Johnny would be back from lunch by the time she got there. Her heartbeat was rapid, and her lungs kept asking for more air. She breathed deeply, held the breath, tried to calm the frantic heartbeat.

What does he look like? Will he want to see me? I should have waited, should have rung him first. He must have seen my ads. He probably doesn't want to be found.

Slow train, stopping at every station. Too slow, but not slow enough either. Hope was in the finding of him. What would be in the meeting? The end of hope?

Perspiration beaded her lip, but her mouth was dry. 'Stupid,' she said, searching her handbag for gum, or sweets, something that might make saliva. Nothing there – or nothing she could find. Again she read the letter. He'd be there. At two, she would see him. 'Relax. Just relax. You're an adult. He's an adult. If he doesn't want to see me, then at least I'll know where he is, that he is alive. At least I'll be able to stop wasting money on phone calls and ads.'

She found the car yard at the northern edge of the centre, and she stood scanning the lines of cars, seeking a tall dark head. No movement, apart from a youth with a blue bucket. 'Where might I find John Burton?' she called to him.

'Dunno. Ask at the office.' He pointed with his cleaning rag.

And she saw a tall man walk from the office. Dark, as she expected him to be, dressed impeccably, as his father always dressed. Her hand went to still her heart. His back was turned, and she watched his back, her own borrowing support from a powder blue Holden stationwagon, a few years younger than Ben's ute.

He was with a male customer, and appeared to be doing a hard sell. She smiled, shook her head. She swallowed, licked her lips. Be calm, she warned. Take it slowly, just in case he doesn't want to be found. What did people say to a brother, unseen in too many years? Hello stranger. Or, got any bargains today, mate? Or, Johnny hold me. Take all the hell out of my head. Make it go away.

Her eyes were misting when his buyer left without buying, but her smile was wide. She watched him turn, sight her from a distance and walk quickly towards her.

He was laughing. 'God is kind,' he said. 'What can I do for you, Brown-eyes?'

He wasn't Johnny.

Brown-eyes?

The smile left her face. Her head grew cold, colder.

He wasn't Johnny.

The world leaned, she swayed to the side, attempting to level the ground.

He wasn't Johnny.

'I'm looking for John Burton – '

'And you found me instead. Isn't this your lucky day?'

Mad. Blood roared like the ocean in her ears. Then she recognised him. He was the mauler in the blue shirt at the New Year party she'd gone to with David. Tony. Tony George. He was the man who looked like her father, who had her father's hands.

'By the way Tony, did your mother happen to know your father's name?'

'What do you do for a crust, Tone?'

'I sell cars.'

Die on the spot. Drop dead.

She cringed from him. Away. Get away. Reflexes swung the blue car door open, and she crawled inside it, needing to hide from his eyes, needing the dark place of her childhood. Disappointment sucked the air from her lungs, embarrassment leached the marrow from her bones. Crawl into a hole and die. Fool. Fool. Bloody fool.

But ... but John Burton was here somewhere. The letter said

so. The man said so, on the phone. Said he was at lunch. She looked at her watch, and Tony opened the passenger side door. He was in the car, filling the car, using up all of the air. 'John Burton,' she said, her mouth too dry to say more.

'I knew it was you, you bitch. We have some unfinished business.'

It made no sense. She stared at him. Nothing to say. Got to get away. Hide. Can't let him make me run from Johnny. Can't let him see me dying. Johnny is here. She had the letter. Who wrote the letter? Tony's was the voice on the phone. And she knew, but she didn't want to know.

'Dave married Melissa, six months after that party. You didn't leave a very lasting impression on him, Brown-eyes, but you impressed me. I swore I'd get you one day.'

'John Burton.' She sounded like a parrot, with a two-word vocabulary. She added two more. 'I rang.' Too many hopes had been placed on this meeting. She couldn't let go of hope. She grasped her handbag, took the letter from it, pushed it at him, and watched the paper shiver there while a pulse in her stomach flopped around like a dying fish. She sucked in used-up air, sucked in the heavy male scent of his sweat, breathed it out too fast, as she offered him the letter.

He didn't look at it. Didn't need to. He wrote it. 'Good old Davey Jones been up to his old tricks again. Tut, tut tut,' he said, and he laughed. 'I got you a beauty, you smart-arsed bitch. I've seen those ads in the missing column for years, then last week I went to Mallawindy. Did some research. That's the day I decided you'd get your just desserts.'

Then the parrot learned new words. 'Bastard. Vicious bastard.' She opened the door, sprang from the car, the contents of her open bag spilling to seat to earth.

He sat there, laughed at her fumbling attempt to sweep up the scattered junk. 'No use running, Brown-eyes. I've only just begun.'

An older male wandered over to lend a hand. He knelt,

retrieved her wallet from beneath the car, handed it to her with a small box of tissues and a Burnished Spice lipstick, two pens and a roll of Butterscotch.

'I'll take that wagon,' she said. 'That's if I can drive it away in half an hour, and you can get his stink out of it. Someone ought to buy him a can of deodorant. Trying to test drive with him in the car would put off a lot of prospective buyers.'

She had killed two birds with the one stone, bought a long promised set of wheels and re-wounded an old enemy. But she hadn't found Johnny, and she'd had to give a home address where the car would be parked. She didn't think fast enough to lie, which meant Tony George knew where she lived. He was in the office when she ran back with her bank cheque, and by the look in his eye, he'd come knocking on her door with a cocked pistol in his pocket. She'd have to move again.

At five past four, she returned to the office – a car owner. Big car owner, and she couldn't parallel park the thing for love nor money. She told Michael, while they waited for their late four o'clock appointment to arrive.

She'd known him for five years, had worked with him once in a larger space, and when he decided to form his own company, he'd hijacked her. He liked her madness, used it. They were a good team.

'You bought a ten-year-old Holden,' he said.

'A twelve-year-old stationwagon, would you believe. It sort of . . . sort of seemed like the right thing to do at the time.'

'You're mad,' he said.

'I thought we'd already agreed on that.' They laughed, and they drank bitter coffee, and they waited until five, but the man didn't show.

It was after six before Ann and the wagon found their way home to Collingwood, to the house she shared. Four girls in three bedrooms, a shambles of who owned what, and a bathroom no-one cleaned. The stink of age ruled each day and hung over into night.

The tiny backyard smelt of age; no sun could find its way there to renew the earth, allow it to breathe. A hundred years of living and dying had gone on in this street of narrow houses, packed together like out-of-date cartons on a supermarket shelf.

Her possessions were few; by seven most had been transferred to the street. It wasn't until she opened the wagon's tailgate that she realised she'd bought more rust than metal, the rust hastily covered by plastic filler. Still, the loading area took her kitchen table, her cases, boxes and blankets. She considered tying her bed on the roof, but with no roof-rack, knew she'd probably lose it at the first traffic lights. 'Live without it,' she said, eyeing each end of the street for a prowling vehicle. 'Just cut and run.' The office box number was safe. If the mauler wrote again, she wouldn't open his letters. 'Go.'

The last box of books hurriedly tossed to passenger side floor, she drove away from Collingwood and slept the night at a motel in Parkville. The next week she spent at a hotel in St Kilda, her loaded vehicle parked all week in the street. What she needed was a flat, with a carpark. She was ready for a bathroom and a front door she could call her own, and maybe a beach not too far away, and she found what she wanted in St Kilda, a short walk from the hotel.

It was her twelfth city address, and there would be no thirteenth. Thirteen was unlucky. Thirteen was when the questions began. Thirteen was when she placed Mickey's blood-stained collar in her golden syrup tin and found the mouse nest of papers hidden there. Thirteen was when she first read those scraps of paper. She didn't like thirteen.

A tiny kitchen off the lounge room, tiny bedroom, miniature bathroom. A carpet near new, fresh painted walls and a private letter box. It was a rear flat, on the second floor, its lounge room window looked down on the parking bays, where one neglected tree had managed to survive. Tenacious thing, it clung to its small circle of earth, and in the week since she'd first seen the flat, and named the tree some sort of plum, its dirty limbs had become a haze of pink. Nature was erupting even in Melbourne, eroding the concrete and allowing the grey earth to produce.

She wound her window wide and popped her head out, attempting to catch a brief scent of the plum tree in Mallawindy, but the breeze was from the wrong direction. Car fumes, and the slight scent of the sea. A heady mixture, but no Mallawindy.

Today she'd buy a bed, bookshelves, a couple of chairs, get some food in, then go down and claim the beach. Almost out the door when the phone rang, she cursed it. Only one person had her new number.

'It's Saturday, Michael. You may own me body and soul all week, but today is Saturday.'

'I've just been speaking to Roger the Red. He flew in last night and saw the ads. He's rapt.'

'I'm glad someone is.' There was a long silence that she waited for him to fill.

'He wants you to fly up to Sydney tonight.'

She changed the phone to her left hand, and drew her hair back from her face. 'I'm not going. I've done enough.'

'He's our bread and butter. Appease him. It's just for two nights, you can fly home on Monday night. He's picking up the tab. He's got some big party on tonight and a meeting on Monday afternoon, and he wants you there.'

'Tell him to hire a call girl.'

'His parents are over. He just wants to introduce his Mermaid girl.'

'I'm not his Mermaid girl. It's Saturday. I have to buy myself some furniture. All I've got is a television, a table and a telephone. I haven't even unpacked my cases.'

'It's fate. Just pick up a case and go.'

'I've been sleeping on the floor since Wednesday, and my back is killing me. Today is mine, and I'm going shopping for a bed.'

'I'll get one for you.'

'I'll get my own. Tell him I've got a slipped disc.'

'Do it for me. This is the last time I'll ask.'

'I did his stupid ads for you. Now everywhere I go, little old ladies smile at me.'

Michael laughed, but Ann wasn't laughing. 'I thought you got on well with him.'

'I'd probably get on well with a rabid corgi too, but it wouldn't mean I wanted to sleep with it.'

'I'd say that's the last thing on his particular mind. I think he prefers guys.'

She looked at her cases, stacked against the wall, and to the kitchen bench, buried beneath boxes. For eight years she'd lived by impulse, moving on when the spirit took her, packing her cases and running to another suburb. Free. No strings. No-one making demands. That was before the crazy Yank walked through the office door.

She was good with words, legacy of Malcolm Fletcher, and a life spent in books. She wrote jingles for television commercials, and catchy ads for magazines, and it had all been a glorious game she was paid to play, until Roger bloody Wilkenson the Third.

He was forty if he was a day, and ugly as a red-headed bag of monkeys. He'd breezed in that day with an idea for a TV commercial. A vision, he'd called it, and he wanted them to make his vision live.

'Picture a cute kid, coming apart at the seams. Picture a gorgeous Mommy, struggling with an antiquated sewing-machine.' He spoke to her, ignoring Michael, and for the next hour his eyes had been on her every time she lifted her head, so she kept her head down, picked up a pen and began doodling.

It came, as Annie's poems always came, complete. It came while her concentration was far, far away. Then, like Malcolm before him, Roger snatched the paper from beneath her hand, and he read the silly little ditty aloud, in an infant voice.

'My Mummy can't make button holes, she press-studs all my dresses,
but press-studs are embarrassing. I get in lots of messes.
If she had a Mermaid sewing machine, that button holes so fast.
I wouldn't show my knickers to the neighbours walking past.'

'Faster than a speeding bullet, more powerful than a locomo-
tive, able to make quantum leaps in a single bound,' spouted Roger
bloody Wilkenson the Third. 'Is this a girl? Is this a gem? Is she
married?'

Michael had put aside the afternoon for him, prepared to court
him, prostitute himself to get the account. The company had been
struggling to hang on in '83. The Wilkenson empire was huge in
America and growing daily in Australia, and the weird little guy
who controlled it had a reputation for demanding perfection. Now
he thought he'd found it.

'Where did you come from? Did someone give birth to you,
or did you evolve from the ocean waves and the night wind, my
lovely?'

'My name is Ann.'

'Too plain Jane and no nonsense. I like nonsense.' He spoke
then of a second vision – a mermaid rising from out of the waves.
He was like a little boy who still believed in magic, and if the
world refused him his magic, then he was prepared to make his
own. And he had the money to buy the right ingredients.

He took them out for dinner that night, and he plied them with
wine. Ann saw its price on the wine list. She was drinking liquid
gold. 'You were my inspiration for the mermaid. You have her
eyes. Dragged from the ocean, overawed by the enormity of the
vast city. I want you for it,' he said.

'I'll write your ditties, and drink your wine, but that's it.'

He started talking money and he ordered more liquid gold.

'I'm not a member of Actors Equity,' she said.

'I'll get around those details, my lovely.'

'My name is Ann.'

'We've been through that,' he said.

The next day Michael began twisting her arm. 'We need him, Ann, or we're both going to be out of a job. Give him what he wants.'

Two days and two dinners later, she gave in, proving once more to the little maniac that his money could buy him anything. He'd flown over again when they shot the ad, and he'd bought her a watch for Christmas. 'It's got your name on it, pretty lady, and I don't know any other Ann.'

She wouldn't accept it.

'They are only zircons. I picked it up in Bangkok.' He'd lied.

And now he was back in Australia, trying to buy a date for a party.

'He's booked you on the six o'clock flight. He said he'd pick you up at the airport.'

'And what did you say?'

'I said you'd be there.'

'Then ring him back,' she said.

'I can't. I don't know where he's staying.'

She hung up, but the phone rang immediately.

'I'll buy you a bed. I'll get it delivered before you get back. I'll get Jan to fill your fridge. Do it for me, Ann, and I promise I won't ask you again.'

'Promise. Spit your death and hope to die.' She heard him spitting on the other end of the phone. 'I spat,' he said, and she laughed. 'What sort of a bed do you want? Think I should buy a queen size?'

'Manipulating swine,' she said, and she placed the phone down. But why knock it. A weekend in Sydney. There were things she wanted to do in Sydney. She'd been planning to take a week off and go there. Fate.

A small red case unzipped, revealed a small black briefcase, identical to her father's. It was tossed to the floor while she unpacked a larger case, transferring items to the red.

Crazy. Crazy world, crazy life, but it left her little time to think. The weekend wouldn't cost a cent; she'd have her own room, with a bed, and a telephone. She probably wouldn't have to spend more than a few hours with the Wilkensons, so she could hole up with a telephone book, and work her way through the Sydney Burtons.

Jeans. Shirts. A frock to wear to the dinner, a suit for the meeting. A few pieces for emergencies, and shoes, all with heels. She liked high heels and made no concession to her height.

The red case closed, placed beside the door, she took up the briefcase she'd found seven years ago in the window of an opportunity shop. Like Mary's lamb, it followed her wherever she went. Its key was on her keyring, now she turned it in the lock and up-ended the briefcase on the table. The litter of many years tumbled free.

A yellowing handkerchief, the initials AEB were embroidered on its corner. A tiny white comb, on its handle were two blue birds in flight. A wind-up mouse that one time had danced, she held in her palm a while, turning the key. Its spring was broken. Long broken. A dog collar, still stained with old Mickey's blood. A bubble pipe, made by Johnny's hands from a reed and a large gumnut. The staring eyes of a broken doll. Blue eyes. Liza's eyes. And beneath these things, and amongst these things, were scraps of paper – pages and pages of randomly folded paper, each one covered by script that had altered through the years.

She read some and refolded them. Others were placed to one side. A yellowing scrap, she smoothed and worried over, its faded, pencilled words, written by a childish hand, were almost gone. *The Crow swi* – ... *tomato* ... *fishes fl* – ... *wing* – There were many in similar condition. *Daddy went* ... *ar* – *we* ... – *Liza and* ... Impossible. Tatters carried through time from a previous life. Some were typewritten pages, their ink new.

Dear Miss Burton,
  Further to your inquiry re John Lawrence Burton. We have no record of a marriage.

Dear Madam,
  Enclosed, a cheque for the sale of the size ten, beaded wedding gown. We have a customer eager to order the same style in a size sixteen, in the cream silk.

She was an accomplished seamstress, but these days she named her creations, therapy. It was something to do with her hands when her mind refused to lie down and rest. Sewing was a mindless occupation, but lucrative. She received more for one wedding dress than she'd paid for her car. Some good lessons had been learned in Mallawindy. Sell your merchandise too cheap and people think it's no good, Bert Norris once said. It was true. Put two thousand dollars on the price tag, and a dress caught the eye of exclusive buyers who had no idea the fabric was picked up cheap at the markets.

The bridalwear shop in Chapel Street took thirty percent, and sent her the cheques when the frock sold. She'd seen one of her creations in a women's magazine. Some footballer's bride had bought it. That photograph was also squirrelled away in her briefcase.

Her hands continued to search the litter, for what, she was unsure. A trigger that might force a memory. Something. Maybe she'd find something.

Dear Madam, We are unable to supply a copy of death certificate, as requested. John Lawrence Burton – .

She knew Johnny wasn't dead, but it had taken her a long time to raise sufficient nerve to write that particular letter. A small square of white butcher's paper almost fell apart in her hands. She spread it on the table, carefully.

– Sam was a – a very – ad – call for – wife – and he –
1- 2- 3

That one was almost gone too. Maybe it was better to bury the past. Bury Johnny with his secrets. Maybe he ran away because he knew the secret. Had to stay away so she couldn't find out.

Push me Johnny, push me high. I'm a bird and I can fly.

High up to the clear blue sky. I made Liza Burton – .

Had he seen that one? It was still strong, written on a page ripped from a colouring book, the paper stiff, the words clear. Red crayon did not fade. Had the word she had written last been die? Had he tried to protect her, rubbed at the word until his finger wore that hole, wore the word away, or had she rubbed it out?

She didn't know, and it haunted her. She knew Liza was dead. She knew it. Did Johnny know too? She had to find him, and she would find him. Even two grains of sand moving through a giant sandpit must eventually come together in the same sandcastle. It was only a matter of time before the letter came, or the voice on the end of the line replied, 'Just a moment. I'll put you through.' But eight years of time had gone. Disappeared into the big anonymous Melbourne. Big sandpit, growing bigger every year.

Carefully she returned the papers to the case, placing Mickey's collar on top. The handkerchief she held to her nose, expecting it to have retained some scent of Narrawee. Nothing. Old. Stale. She placed it with the dog collar, and closed the lid, locked it.

The sun was coming out, the light breeze had blown the early cloud away. Today the world outside the city would be green with spring. She didn't need to be holed up here. No use ordering a bed if she wouldn't be here to take delivery. Next week.

She had a car now. Her petrol tank was full, and her engine sound. 'Old Holdens never die, they just rust away,' she said, and for a moment saw the face of the man who had said it. Sergeant Johnson. The words spoken during that year of laughter. Year of happiness. Ben's new second-hand utility. Ellie? Almost a mother, that year. A person, not his punching bag.

She shook her head, tried to shake all of their names from her head, shake the face of the dead baby from her head. Little blue boy. Thick black hair. Little hands, crumpled.

'Get out in the sun,' she said, and she picked up her red case, and her briefcase, she locked her door, ran downstairs to the carpark and drove away, her street directory on the passenger seat.

Michael needed her to have a licence when he started the company. She'd done a little city driving, but his car was an automatic. It was taking her time to get used to the gears, and the car was too big. Pity she hadn't crawled into a smaller car that day. A modern automatic Toyota. That's what she'd been planning to buy. 'Something a little more racy,' she said. 'Idiot.'

With a few deviations, she found her way onto the Tullamarine freeway, busy today, and she followed the signs towards the airport. They had a long term carpark, where she'd leave her car. No self-respecting thief would bother to steal it. It was a rattle trap, rust bucket. Too early to book in yet, she drove past the airport and continued on, looking at green paddocks, seeking a forest floor where she might sit and smell the earth, and the scent of rotting leaves. For an hour she drove and dreamed, turning down roads at will. Her mind was far away when the pictures began flashing, like family slide nights in fast motion. Flash of sewing machine. Flash of purple fabric. Flash of pale blonde bowed head, and with the pictures came the scattering of disjointed words.

Hollow words. She shook her head, trying to ignore them. *'Uncle Sam. Uncle Sam.'* High. Discordant, like the needle jammed in a cracked record. *'Royal dress for a princess.'*

'Shut up, Annie.'

'Ann Elizabeth. Ann Elizabeth.'

'Shut up, Annie.' Her foot tapping the brake, she steered the car around a long curve and down into a valley where the trees ahead grew close to the road, meeting overhead like a tunnel of green.

WELCOME TO NARRAWEE. The signpost sprang from behind a

curve and the world darkened and the car filled with the primal scream of her childhood. Reflexes hit the brake too hard and her tyres screamed as her brakes attempted to obey her foot's command. The car slewed in a half circle. She was flung against the side window, then sideways across the bench seat, but her belt held her.

Hissing of huge wheels, the long high moan of brakes, and a transport halted two metres behind her. 'Bloody stupid moron. What do you bloody think you're doing?' The driver was out, at her window. Big, heavy.

Her key turned. Petrol pumped. Her starting motor growled. The truckie's mouth was working overtime, but she didn't hear his words. She kept pumping petrol, turning the key.

'She's flooded. Stop pumping in more bloody juice. Keep your foot flat to the boards.' And she tried to follow his advice. Shaking, shaking cold, the signpost over her shoulder. Other cars beeping their horns now, other people emerging. 'You're just flattening your battery. Shove over. I know these old buggers.'

Ann scrambled from the car, her back to the sign, and he took her seat, held the accelerator down and kept the key turning until the motor coughed, caught, flooding the world with the sweet stench of petrol.

'I'm sorry,' she said. 'Thank you.'

'You could've caused a bloody ten-car pile up.'

'A dog,' she lied. 'A little dog.'

'You don't brake for a dog. If I'd been a bit closer, you wouldn't be talking to me now.' He looked at her then, stared at her face. 'Don't I know you from some place?'

'No,' she said.

'I'll stake my life on it. Ever lived in Ballarat?'

She shook her head. 'Thanks. I'll move it. I'm sorry.'

'No harm done. And no more braking for bloody dogs, love,' and he returned to his truck.

She pulled over to the side of the road and sat for a few

minutes, sat until her hands steadied and strength returned to her legs.

'*Go home.*'

'Sydney,' she said. 'I'm going to Sydney,' and she turned the car around, away from Narrawee, following road signs pointing back to Melbourne. Dear old grey Melbourne; it may invent its own nightmares, but they were preferable nightmares.

It was after three when she came on a beach on the western side. She parked, and walked barefoot to the water. It wasn't the river at Mallawindy, safe and known, but it was free. She loved the ocean. Wonderful wild thing, untamed by this grey metropolis, no red and green lights told it when to stop and go.

An old dog chasing waves, came to sniff at her bare feet. She reached out a hand, patted his unkempt fur. 'Good dog,' she whispered. 'Good dog. What are you doing here by yourself? Where's your person?' He licked her hand, and she stroked his head. 'Did you know I needed someone to talk to? Do you read minds, doggy? I had a dog once who could read my mind. He knew everything.'

The dog murmured, sniffed her knee. Smelt her fear.

'I hate that place, doggy. Hate it. Hate it. Why do I hate it?'

Stranger dog, he didn't know that answer. She scratched behind his right ear, finding the exact place he hadn't been able to reach since arthritis had crept into his bones, and he pushed against her, asking for more. 'Ever met a split personality in your travels, doggy? Ever had a conversation with a reflection?'

He twitched an ear, definitely interested.

'Good boy,' she said. 'Good old dog. You're a bit like my old Mickey. Who owns you? Tell your person he should brush you. If you were mine, I'd brush you.'

In ecstasy, the dog watched her sit in the sand at his level. He lay his head in gentlemanly fashion against her knee, and she took her comb from her bag, and combed his coat gently, tossing fur to the wind, and when he'd had enough and he told her so with a prodding nose, she wrapped her arms around him, and told him many things.

They sat together while the wind tangled her hair and her watch nagged her to leave, but the slap, slap, slap, of waves on the sand, the warmth of holding a living thing, soothed the ache in her. She didn't want to leave. Didn't want to fly.

'I have to though,' she said.

The dog kissed her hand, and rose to his feet, again peering out to sea. The waves were moving in again. 'Back. Back,' he yelped.

'You sound like Annie. She wants me to go back home.'

'Go back and start at the beginning. Find the place of the mistake, trace it to its source. Erase it, sad lady.'

'I think I already erased it, doggy, rubbed it out until there was only a hole.' She stood and brushed the sand from her jeans, watching him warn the waves back. 'You can't go back to a hole, can you, so you keep on walking around it, around, and around, and around it, until you get giddy and you fall down the hole and someone tosses the dirt in.'

She made the flight. No comb to tame her hair, no time to pin it high. It was a cloud of shoulder-length curls that she tried to flatten with her hand as she was hurried through. Maybe she'd hoped fate would make her miss the plane, but Roger Wilkenson the Third had fate in his pocket, and he probably owned Ansett.

She'd flown before. She'd been up to Darwin two years ago, because Johnny had once spoken about going to Darwin. She'd phoned all the Burtons in the Darwin telephone book, but he wasn't there either. She didn't like flying, tried to think of it as a bus, but the drag of the craft sucked air from her lungs as effectively as any lift. Black holes in hell. Melbourne was full of lifts. She never used them, not after the first time. They took her back to some place. Choked her. Took her back to ... to – . She closed her eyes. Saw the signpost.

WELCOME TO NARRAWEE.

Shouldn't have gone there. Should have looked at a map, she thought. Should have known Narrawee was out that way. For minutes she kept her eyes closed, breathing in, breathing out. Then the plane was up. And she opened her eyes and thought she'd died and gone to hell – or the Russians had dropped their bomb on Mallawindy and set the world on fire.

Red, below her. Ocean of red. 'My God,' she breathed, and the woman in the seat beside her turned to the window.

'I love these sunset flights,' she said.

'I'm riding a sunset,' Ann replied, and her hands began signing. ''We run across big cloud, my Benjie. Run fast over sky. Chase moon over there ... over sunset to where Johnny live and no more demon live there.'' I'm riding the clouds home to where he is,' she said.

'Beautiful, isn't it?' the woman said, and she talked all the way to Sydney.

Roger was waiting at the airport. 'I've been riding a sunset. It was unbelievable. Unbelievable, Roger. Did you order Jesus to turn it on for me?'

'Just for you. I've ordered a full moon for tonight too, and a cloudless sky.' He reached up, kissed her quickly on the lips.

She laughed, laughed because his kiss was the dry-lipped kiss of a boy, and it meant nothing, and she laughed because she had been in a sunset, and she had to tell someone all about it, and he was there and he hung on every word she ever uttered, because her utterings were rare. And when he took her hand and led her away, she clung to his small dry hand and she laughed again, because she knew she was going to find Johnny this weekend. She knew it. Her mother used to tell people that Johnny was in Sydney. And she laughed because people everywhere were stopping to stare at her, and it wasn't because she was six inches taller than the man at her side. She laughed because Roger didn't know she had once been Dummy Burton. Nobody knew, and nobody need ever know. She was anyone she wanted to be. David of the magic kiss, on those magic Saturdays, was married to Melissa. No more dreams of David and what might have been. And she laughed because Roger always made her laugh, and because Mallawindy was a horror story she had once read. Banned now, taken from the bookshelves, and all copies burnt. And Ben, dear gentle Ben? He was a boy from that cruel story, a memorable character she would never read about again. Her past was dead. Dead and gone, and she had a life to lead. Business woman, off to a grand party, and a long date tomorrow with a telephone. And answers, all of the answers. Then she could put the last of her past away.

'Marry me.'

'Just because you ordered me a sunset?' she said.

'I'm all there is to breed the new generation of Wilkensons, and you're the only one I want to breed with, my lovely.'

'Why breed little fish for all the big fish to gobble up?'

'I'm one of the big fish. I will guard our spawn well.'

That night while his elderly parents snored, Roger plied her with potent drinks in a suite on top of the world. Five bedrooms, a wall of windows overlooking the moonlit harbour, and too many stairs to climb. She'd wanted to book in downstairs, but he wouldn't hear of it.

'These lifts don't jam,' he said. 'I won't let them jam. Just close your eyes, and hold my hand, and when you open them, we'll be in fairyland.' And she did, she gripped his hand, and somehow knew his will could override any threatening power failure.

Too much drinking tonight, too much laughter; alcohol always made her happy, turned her worry knob to the off position. It made her believe in the impossible too.

As the hour grew later, he returned to the subject of marriage. 'The oldies like the look of you. "A bit thin in the hips, but she's healthy enough," Pops said. "We'll fatten her up".'

'Give it up, Roger.'

'Long genes,' Mom said. 'We could do with some long genes, Roger.'

'I'm going to bed. There are things I want to do in the morning.'

'You're getting old. Women should breed before they're thirty.'

'My race is doomed,' she said, and she drained her glass.

He brought her another drink and stood behind her chair, his arms lightly around her, his chin resting on top of her head. 'Couldn't you love me?'

'I love dogs.'

'Pretend I'm a poodle.'

'I'm not into pedigrees,' she said, and she tried to change the subject, spoke about the dog at the beach, but he cut her short. 'I'm flying home on Thursday and I want to take you with me.'

'A true Made-in-Australia souvenir. Not great workmanship. Rough around the edges, but an unusual piece.'

'I'm obsessed by your indifference, pretty lady. There are a thousand women out there, ready to fall in love with my millions.'

'Make one of them happy.'

'I want to make you happy. I want to take that sad little girl out of your eyes and make them laugh every day.'

'I can't understand how people can get married, live day, after day, after day with a stranger. "But I love him," I hear women say, and that excuses everything. What is that sort of love, Roger?'

'It's wanting to kill anyone who chats up your love at a party. It's wanting to brand your name on a forehead, and wake up each day in one bed – '

'But I haven't got a bed. I'm supposed to be in Melbourne buying one, but I'm up here in the clouds, and I can't get down to the earth without you.' She walked to the window and looked out across the harbour, and at the lights across the harbour. It was the fairyland he'd promised it would be.

This weekend wasn't real. The party, the people, everyone

knew him, everyone respected him, and he had been at her side all night.

It was nice to be so cared for.

'Is there another man in your life?'

'Not at the moment.'

'Has there ever been a man in your life?'

She shrugged. 'One, but he got married six months after I left. I don't leave a very lasting impression on people, Roger. I pass by, and for a moment I become visible. I leave, and memory of me disappears.'

'Then stay, my lovely.'

'I'm going to bed.'

'Can I come with you?'

'No.'

'This is the eighties, pretty lady. Everybody is doing it with everybody else.'

'Good night.'

'Night. Dream of me,' he said.

He'd been in his own bed an hour when he heard her scream. Up, and through the door, he hit the light, flooding her room, but the dreamer saw nothing. She screamed and thrashed at the air with her arms, fighting off old demons, her back against the bed-head.

He grasped her arms. 'Ann. Wake up. Ann!'

'Jesus.' She screamed at him, wrenched her arms from his grasp. 'Get out of my room. Get out.'

'Tell me what you were dreaming and you'll never dream it again. I've been where you are. I've dreamed those dreams.'

'Get out of my room, Roger.'

'What were you dreaming?' He was on the bed, his arm around her, strong, and he pulled her to him.

'Nothing. Let me go.'

'Trust me, my lovely.'

She closed her eyes, but it was there still. She shook her head.

It was Narrawee. It was the road, the trees. It was the crow's head with the fish tail. One for sorrow, two for joy, he sang. Just in case, he sang. She stared beyond Roger, her eyes wide, then she let her head fall to rest against his.

'Talk to me. Tell me your dream, and I'll take it all away.'

'It was nothing. I don't need this – '

'Nothing does not evoke that scream.' Both arms were around her, and she leaned against him while the terror slowly seeped away.

Let it all seep away. Let it all go. Open your mouth and drive it away.

'I'm driving the car,' she said. 'It's just a road. It's . . . I know the road, the church, the house on the corner. I go around the curve and . . . and . . . and it goes back to the same as I've had forever. It's always the same. I'm walking then. It's narrow . . . dark. I open a door. Huge room. Beautiful magic room, but while I look at it, it changes. It's old. It's falling down. And crows. Crows everywhere. Black crows in the rafters, then they turn blood red, and I see they aren't crows – .' Her hands began to reach for the words. 'All face turn. Got no eyes. Blood come from eyes. Crow face all go. All get same face. Same face. Not crow face.'

'You sign?' he said. 'You said face.'

'No.' She snatched her hands to her sides, pushed him away, and she locked her tell-tale hands beneath the blanket.

'Yes, you did. Yes, you did, my lovely. I've got a deaf cousin.'

'Leave me alone,' she said. 'You're screwing up my brain.'

'Look at the face. Who does it belong to?'

'I don't want this. I don't want you in here, either.'

'Look at the face, Ann.' She covered her face with her hands, sat head down, and he took one hand, and he lifted her chin. 'Look at the face. Who do you see?'

'The kaleidoscope man,' she said to his eyes. 'The demon face. Flesh disintegrates, reconstructs. It's coloured. Orange glow, purple dust. No more. Don't make me think about it, Roger.'

'Recognise him. Spit in the bastard's eye and tell him you are not afraid.'

'No more,' she pleaded. 'I stopped. For years I stopped dreaming. You are bringing them back. You are filling my head with magic again, and there is no bloody magic. There never was.'

He found her dressing-gown, and she became conscious of her brief nightie, that hid little from his eyes. She slipped quickly into her gown and he buttoned her up, when her own hands couldn't find the buttonholes. He took her hand again, and led her to a well-equipped kitchenette where he heated milk and mixed two mugs of Milo.

'Where do your parents live?'

'Mallawindy,' Ann said.

She sat with him for an hour. It was like it had been with Malcolm Fletcher. He asked questions, and she replied. So good to talk again. So good to open her mouth and let words pour out uncensored. She couldn't lie to him, and she knew there was no need to lie. She told him she had lost her speech at the age of six when her sister disappeared, and how for seven years she had been mute. She said she remembered a name. Ted Crow. That she remembered blood, then she spoke of her accidental trip to Narrawee and how she almost blacked out while driving.

'I ran from a signpost,' she said.

'Go back there, lay the old ghosts, my lovely.' She sat before him, shaking her head. 'We all have to confront our demons sooner or later. Once we face them, we can come to terms with old nightmares.'

'I'll die if I go back there. I'll shrivel up and die. I'll blow away.'

'I'll come with you, hold your hand, and the wind won't dare to blow you away.'

the opalescent gem

~

The young copper had a mother fixation and a bloody long nose. Jack had always made an effort to steer clear of confrontations with the law, but the copper and Ben were thick as thieves and out to get him. Since the night of the toothache, the officious little bastard had taken to dropping in at the house at odd times, so Jack had started staying away, trying out a few new beds.

He would have gone to Narrawee, but May had banned him after his last visit. He'd gone on a bender, spent his days drinking and planning a slow and painful death for teetotaller Sam. May was a wild cat with claws when things didn't go her way, a bloody-minded manipulating bitch. She'd got too used to thinking she could have things her own way.

He could live without her. He'd show her, and he'd been doing all right too, until yesterday. Women today were into stuff they wouldn't have thought of in his youth. Vera Owen didn't live too far out of town, and though she wasn't much in the looks department, she was a bloody contortionist in bed. Jack had been feeling twenty years younger – until yesterday.

He had seven stitches standing to attention on his scalp; his hair, kept short and always lightly oiled, was usually worn brushed back from his brow. Today it stood on end. Vera's husband, a truckie, home ahead of schedule, crept into his house at dawn, eager to surprise his wife. He caught her napping, Jack at her side.

Bloody big-mouth Bessy passed the news on to Ellie. He couldn't go home to rest up, like the Daree doctor told him to do; he was in no mood for Ellie's cow-eyed accusations, so he was resting up in the pub, head propped on his hand, one eye on the window, watching for the truckie and his tyre lever. Instead, he saw a maroon Ford brake sharply and thunk to a stop against the deep gutter. The driver got out and lit a cigarette, while his woman snapped a fast photograph of King Billy and his bottle.

The male was familiar. Jack knew he'd met him, but he couldn't remember where. His brain was functioning on the level of a bowl of mashed pumpkin today. Then the woman stepped out, and Jack knew he knew her too. His past was coming home to roost today. He rubbed his head and watched the door where they would enter. Who was she? One of the Daree farmers' wives he'd sold a policy to. He started mentally ticking off names, forcing his brain to work. Bleached hair, a fat and frumpish fifty, her husband a lanky, bald, bean pole.

The couple walked into the main bar, scanned it, then sighted Jack. 'You're Sam Burton's twin brother, or I'll go eat my hat,' the male said. 'Harper, Bill and Edna Harper from Narrawee.'

Jack shook their hands, he straightened his shoulders and dug out the old bullshit artist from his boots. He could do it well when he was sober, but even drunk he could still charm the pants off a virgin if it was worth the effort. It might be worth it today. His arm around Edna, he guided her through the maze of narrow corridors into the ladies lounge, a ten by ten dark hole, opening onto the rear of the bar. It gave the illusion of privacy.

'The bar is no place for a lady,' he smiled, and his jaws ached with the effort.

'What will you drink, Jack?'

Jack considered a free whisky, but settled for a beer. He'd need all of his remaining wits intact.

'Three beers,' the traveller called to the barman, busy wiping the backside of his bar, priming it with his beer wet cloth. Bill tossed twenty dollars down. 'You live around here, Jack? I knew you were up the mulga some place.'

Jack nodded, and it hurt his head. He looked through the gap to the main bar, sighted the bull-necked truckie. Shit, he was big. He hadn't looked so big sitting in his truck. Have to get out of town, Jack thought. He was in no fit state to drive. His concentration was shit, everything he looked at, lopsided and back-to-front.

'We've been checking out motels up through Dubbo. Supposed to be back home yesterday, but Edna decided to run into a post. Had to wait for a new radiator.' Bill Harper's laugh raised a small echo from his woman.

'You used to be on the land, Edna?' Jack's eyes flitted over her. She had bloomed once, for a season.

'My father worked on the property next door to yours, Jack.'

'Oh, not likely I'd forget you, Edna,' he said, and she had the decency to blush. Her old man used to work for May's father. Jack had given her a few tumbles in the hay shed when he was sixteen. He nodded, and sipped his beer. She was another Ellie. Bloomed early, faded fast. Christ only knew where she'd picked up the coot she was with. The ugly bastard's B. O. was turning Jack's stomach.

'Motels. That's where the money is, Jack. We've just built a nice little place in Narrawee. Though your sister-in-law might not agree with my adjective.'

'Her great-grandfather and old Samuel Burton cut the town up between them. May still thinks she owns the deeds,' Jack said with feeling, and Edna, eager for some character assassination, opened her mouth. She closed it abruptly when a shoe beneath the table caught her ankle. Her beer spilled.

Mick Bourke lifted the side of his back bar and wandered out, rag in hand. 'Same again, folks?' The cash was still on his bar; he could be relied on to keep filling the glasses while it remained there.

'It's a small world, Bill,' Jack said, viewing his back-to-front, too-small bloody world through the side of a beer glass. He could see the truckie through it. He looked lopsided, but magnified behind glass. 'What time are you leaving for home?'

'We'll go through in the cool of the evening. This bloody heat is only fit for the Abos.'

'You'll think I've got the hide of a rhino, but I was supposed to be in Narrawee today. I hit a roo on the way home yesterday.' Jack pointed to his stitches. 'If I were to offer to put in the petrol, Bill, could I beg a lift?'

'Christ, it will be my pleasure, Jack.'

'You're most welcome, I'm sure,' Edna drivelled. 'If we can't do a neighbourly service for an old friend, then what's the world coming to, I always say.'

'Ready when you are. I keep a few things at Narrawee. Backwards and forwards so often, it saves a man the burden of packing and unpacking.'

Fate or the devil still looked after Jack Burton.

The tourists off-loaded their passenger at the gates of the old Burton property seven hours later. 'Thanks,' Jack's voice was weary, his cast-iron stomach ready to give up its contents. He grasped his bottle, his only luggage, and walked away sucking in fresh air to replace the B.O.

'A pleasure,' Bill Harper said. 'Give our regards to your family.' They drove off as Jack flung the big gate open and started on his long walk up the drive to the house.

It never failed to please him. By moonlight, the white stone glowed like a pale opalescent gem against the velvet backdrop of night. He'd known the house since birth, but his first visual memory of it was by moonlight, his hand held firmly in his father's. The trees had been smaller then, the lawns, uncut grass; it had seduced his four-year-old heart that night, and held him captive still. His uncle was dead. Now the house was his. His father had said so.

'*That's ours, boys. That's our land now. One day it will belong to both of you, and to your children, and to your children's children.*'

'*Yes, Father.*'

'Yes, Father. Mean old bastard.' The four-year-old boy, still locked inside Jack Burton, cried for his land.

The house was sleeping, or deserted, but he knew where the spare key was kept. He found it with the help of his cigarette lighter and a singed finger, then silent as any robber, he crept inside.

Tonight the kitchen door wasn't where it ought to be, but he was becoming accustomed to his twisted state. He found his way to the downstairs bathroom, felt for the cupboard over the basin, found painkillers. A generous dose popped to his palm, he washed them down with the whisky, warm after its long drive from Mallawindy. Bugger May, and her house rules. He needed its hard teat tonight. No woman was going to lay the law down to him. She could take him as he was or go to buggery. Anyhow, she probably wasn't here. He hoped.

With inordinate concentration, the bottle held to his breast, he felt his way through the long passage to Sam's den and the big recliner chair. No gain in taking his bottle upstairs, in finding a bed. If she was up there, she'd smell his whisky a mile off.

He sipped and he nodded until the nodding head became too heavy. The bottle still three-quarters full, Jack placed it tenderly on the floor, and his head sank down into the sweet oblivion of sleep.

'Jack! Jack? What are you doing here like this? And what is this doing here?'

He woke with a start that jarred his brain into orbit. He blinked, slowly focused on May and the bottle she held high.

'What on earth were you thinking of? How dare you come here like this after that last time.'

'For Christ's sake, keep your voice down and have a bit of compassion. Give me back my bottle.'

May was still slim as a girl. Her blonde hair, kept that way by her hairdresser, was worn short. She walked purposely to the kitchen, and Jack tried to rise, to follow. Too hard. He sank back to his chair and listened to his money glug-glugging down the sink. 'Mean bitch,' he moaned.

'You know better than to bring drink here. If you don't like the rules I set, then you stay away, Jack. It's your decision. But I will not have you here in this state.' She was back in the den, her eyes roving over him.

His hand went to the stitches on his scalp, then flinched away. 'I needed it, May. I broke out of hospital last night,' he said. 'Took a taxi home. I've got a brain tumour. It's inoperable.' It was the tale he'd intended for Ellie, until bloody Bessie got in first. Tilting his head forward, he displayed his many stitches to May. She gasped, stepped forward, looking closely at his stitches, and at the shaved scalp.

'Not a very clean cut, dear. I'd change my surgeon if I were you.'

'Emergency operation, May.'

'Obviously, dear. You're going to have another terrible scar. How did that happen?'

'It won't worry me too long. I've got three months at the most.'

'Yes, dear. Now tell me the truth. Did you smash that car up? You're getting beyond a joke, Jack.'

'I told you. I'm dying.'

'I don't have time this morning for your games. What happened to your head?'

'Irrational behaviour? The old man said it all my life, May. Headaches. I've had them since I was a kid. They've been getting worse. You'd remember those headaches.'

'I remember your youth well. Now what happened to your head, and I want no more nonsense?'

'Everyone remembers my youth, and bloody Sam's too – .'

'If you are staying, Jack, then we cut that conversation here. What happened to your head?'

'I've crawled home to die, May. The quack in Daree sent me down to Melbourne for tests and that's the truth, and may Jesus strike me dead if I tell you a lie.'

'I believe you, dear, but thousands wouldn't. Now go to the shower, and fix yourself up. Where did you put your case?'

'Sorry. It's just me today.'

'Oh, Jack. What am I going to do with you? This cannot go on.'

'But it will, May. It will go on and on until my name is on that bloody Narrawee title. It's my land, May. Mine.'

May sighed and looked towards the ceiling. 'I've got the cleaning ladies coming in at nine. Come upstairs and I'll see what I can find for you.'

narrawee

~

'Narrawee. Green place. White house, green lawns.' Like an incan-
tation, Ann chanted the words, willing more information to come.
'Narrawee. A town like any other town. Houses, ordinary people
living out their ordinary lives.' Old Samuel Burton had named his
property Narrawee before there was a town. Jack had been proud
of Samuel, but he hated the straight-laced little town that didn't
even have a hotel. Her hand reached for the windscreen wiper
switch as the clouds split open to drop their load on her car.

'Narrawee, green place. Narrawee, green place.' Again she
picked up the chant, creating a rhythm that kept time with the
wiper-blades. Visibility was cut to nil. She slowed, navigating by
the white posts alone. It was eerie. Locked in.

'There is nothing to fear except fear itself. I was six when it
happened, now I'm twenty-four. What am I afraid of? Of you, little
Annie? Fear of one's self is irrational. Look at me. I'm an adult. I
hold down a responsible job. But I'm the mermaid too, and they
are an endangered species. They scream in the night.'

Since the night in Sydney, she had planned this day. Roger
called her often from America, and each time he asked if she'd
been back there. He was flying over next week, and he said they
were going there together, but she didn't want him there, didn't

194

know what she'd find there, so she had to do it alone.

Roger Wilkenson. She liked him. She'd been out with other men. Younger men, boys. None had ever got close to her. A few kisses, a few who expected more, and got annoyed when they didn't get it, but none of their kisses had been like that other mouth, that asking, laughing, David mouth.

'Go away. Get out of my head, David Taylor. You only waited six months. What if I'd gone back? All I thought about that first year was going back to you. Have ring, will wed,' she said. 'And to a penny-farthing.' Not that she was surprised that he'd married, but to Melissa. Maybe he'd got her pregnant. They probably had kids. I should have slept with him that night. Stayed out all night. Mum would have had her baby. Everything would have been different.

David had been back in her mind since Sydney. They were all back in her mind again. Benjie and his ute. Every time she drove her car now, she thought of Ben's ute. Malcolm Fletcher was back too – because of Roger. They were two of a kind. Questions, always questions.

How old would Malcolm be now? Was he still alive? How had she been able to leave them all behind? Easy. Good enough for Johnny to run, then it was good enough for her. She wasn't fit to stay with them, wasn't fit for David to love.

But she'd changed. She'd grown up.

'I should be driving up to Mallawindy. I've got one precious week off and I'm tossing it away, pursuing nightmares.' She braked, looked for a place to turn around. The car was crawling when she broached the last hill of brown before the green, and the gods in their heavens turned off the rain and cleared a pathway between the clouds. Bright sun shafted through. Her eyes, slitted against the instant glare, the assault of green. Too green. It shocked the senses, it woke little Annie.

No prickles grow in happy ever after land. I can run bare foot anywhere I want to go, Aunty May.

Goosebumps grew thick on her arms; she rubbed them, shivered. 'Turn me 'round Annie Burton, with danger I'm flirtin,' she screamed to the trees and the land. It eased the tension building in her throat but didn't slow her breathing.

Her head felt light. Ice crystals crawled on her scalp. She drew in a deep breath, held it long as her foot touched the brake. A stream of traffic was crawling behind her – excuse enough to stop, but no safe place to do it. The road curved down, narrowing as it approached the tunnel of green. Then too suddenly she was lost in a camouflage net of dappled light, caught in a crossfire of hollow words and moving pictures.

I hate her Aunty May. She's bad and I hate her.

She halted the car on the edge of the bitumen, allowing the traffic to pass, irate drivers beeped their horns. She didn't hear them. Scents, sounds from another lifetime flooded her. Lavender pillows in the tidy drawers. Soap bubbles. Blowing bubbles through cupped hands.

Look Aunty May, I made one with a rainbow. It's full up with colours like a rainbow. It's got purple in it and green and – .

Petite woman on her knees beside a big white bath, a bath large enough for two little girls, but only one could make a rainbow in her hands. Not Liza. Only Ann Elizabeth. Ann Elizabeth, Aunty May's little girl. Blue dress, white lace collar, long sausage curls, tied up with a big blue ribbon.

The old black cat had her kittens in the cellar.

Odour of apples. Earth and apples.

'Stupid. Stupid. I don't need this.' And she started the motor and turned the car towards Melbourne.

'But I do need it. I came here for answers and I'm not going back until I get the answers.' Carelessly, she swung the steering wheel again, making a screaming U-turn, and heading again into the valley.

The old black cat had her kittens in the cellar.

'Repeat, Annie,' she taunted the companion of her mind.

'Repeat. Been there, done that.' The car entered the tunnel of green, and she increased her speed. 'Hang on, because I'm going through.'

Someone with great foresight had planted the Avenue of Honour. The twin wall of trees made an interesting entrance into the place of twisted dreams. Her foot heavy on the accelerator, her hands gripping the wheel, she fled through the trees, bursting out into sunlight and a brand new motel, advertising 'Vacancy'.

It looked so normal, no different to a hundred other motels. She booked bed and breakfast for two nights, knowing that at least she would have a sanctuary to escape to if things went bad.

The room was stuffy. Even with the door open, there was little breeze to stir the air. It lay heavy, like time long spent, used up. There was an odour of newness too, of fresh paint and unworn carpet. The smell was cloying, like a place somewhere before. Her hand went to her temple in an attempt to massage away the feeling of displacement.

'You're the girl on those machine ads, dear,' the motel owner said, presenting her with fresh milk.

'I'm also a – ' What did it matter? Five years of writing ads and no-one knew her. Thirty seconds on the box, and strangers spoke to her in the street. She attempted to close the door, but the woman was determined to stay.

'My husband saw your name. He said to ask you if you were related to Sam Burton.'

'Niece,' Ann said.

'Then you'd have to be his brother's girl. Jack's daughter.'

The name startled Ann. Jarred her back to the moment. She frowned at the motel owner. 'Yes,' she said. 'Do you ... do you know him?'

'Oh, my word yes. I grew up with both boys. I saw your father just days ago. We gave him a lift home, from Mallawindy.'

Ann looked at her case. This woman was talking herself out of a customer. If her father was in town, then that would be a good enough reason to run, and she wanted a reason. She'd come back next week with Roger – or not come back at all.

'You'd be the little one who was here that time before. With your sister – '

Ann walked to her case. Reached for it. She didn't need this. Then she looked out to the town. Just a town like any other town. She filled the jug, set it to boil, while Edna spoke on. Ten minutes passed before the raucous ringing of a phone called her interrogator away.

'Have a nice visit. There's a lot to see in town, dear.' Edna left the door open.

The town was breathing. Birds in the trees, breathing. Cars on the road, breathing. Strange, hollow silence. Narrawee was closing in on her, ready to gobble her up. She and Liza had probably placed it on the map. Everyone here would know her, or know of her. They'd stare as she walked by, whisper about her behind hands. She shivered, shook her head, scratched at her crawling scalp.

'Shouldn't have come. Shouldn't have come.' She turned away from the door, poured water over a tea-bag. The smell of new carpet was in her nostrils, she could taste it in her throat.

Slippers, Liza. We don't wear shoes inside, do we?

'Shut up. I don't need this today. Get out of my head, Annie.'

Come with Uncle Sam, and we'll get your slippers, Darling.

Leave her be, Sam. She knows where she hid them. Get your own slippers Liza. No television until you do.

'Shut up. Shut up.'

She saw a moving light on the edge of vision, and as she turned towards it, the world closed down to black.

Curled in the foetal position on the floor, the motel's Gideon Bible held in her hand, she woke when the day was gone. Someone had closed the door, turned on the light, pulled the curtains. Someone had made the cup of tea, drunk it. Someone had moved the coffee table, taken a bite from a motel biscuit, discarded it. As Ann lifted her face from the carpet, her eyes saw these things and she grew cold. Colder. Deathly cold.

She held her wrist before her eyes, straining to see the hands on her watch face. Almost seven. Not four when she booked in. Three hours had disappeared. Gone. Gone where?

Her heartbeat frantic, she uncoiled, attempted to gain her feet. She swayed, crouched there on hands and knees, waiting for strength to return. The Bible was still in her hand, her thumb holding it open.

Cold sweating fear was in her. What had happened? Where had she been in those three hours? What had she been doing?

She didn't know. Maybe someone had been in the room, hit her. She felt her head for bump or bruise, but no-one had been hiding there. No-one.

'Oh Christ,' she whispered, rocking backwards and forwards, clinging to the Bible, as if it were an amulet against some hidden foe. 'Please God, please God, help me. Someone help me,' she moaned, licking her dry lips, attempting to raise sufficient saliva to swallow. Minutes passed as she knelt there, looking at the Bible, looking at the words, then her eye was drawn to a passage underlined by a pen.

I will not leave you comfortless; I will come with you

Yet a little while, and the world seeth me no more; but ye see me: because I live.

'Mad,' she said. 'I'm stark raving bloody mad.' She tossed the Bible from her, tossed it across the room. She stood, stumbled to the bathroom, stripping as she went. 'Mad. Nuts, raving lunatic, nuts.'

For half an hour she stood beneath the shower, allowing the hot water to wash over her, afraid to turn the tap off, to still the noise of the rushing water. Safe. Safe within tiled walls. Safe in the fog behind the glass screen. Safe. Her eyes darting, watching for shadows, she began soaping herself. She washed her hair with soap. No conditioner to tame it. Just wash, wash, wash fear away, wash her away.

'Better not to be alone. Better out of there, amongst people. Concentrate on doing. I'll be okay. I'll be fine. I am fine. I fainted. Okay. People faint every day.' And the water was off.

She dressed quickly, picked up her keys and ran, her wet hair cold on her neck.

Unlike Mallawindy, the town of Narrawee had been planned. Built solely to service the rich pastoralists, it had gained no personality, but lived its life in rigid bluestone lines, in rigid bluestone squares – until the advent of the brazen motel.

There was little Ann remembered of the town, until she saw the Anglican church. She'd dreamed that church.

She pulled into its drive, turned, and drove slowly west. She made a right-hand turn after the second street, because there was a tall red brick house on the corner. Dream house. Functioning on automatic now, she drove on.

At the second crossroad, she saw the railway line. No dream train racing her to the crossing, but the crossing was there – as she knew it would be.

Her heart beat in her stomach, in her throat; still she continued on, playing some mystery board game she had to play out to the end. Over the crossing. A halt at an intersection. She didn't know which way to go. There should have been a wide dirt road, stretched between green paddocks. The road was wide but a narrow black bitumen strip paved its crown, and the paddocks were not so green. She took the road, drove slowly.

The stand of trees beside a stream. The narrow stone bridge. A fork in the road. She took the right fork because it led up a steep incline. And she knew, she knew what was around the next curve.

And it was. It was there. White palace on the hill.

'Oh God!' she cried. 'God!' A prayer, a litany. 'Oh God. There stands a dream I've lived. Oh, God, what have they done to me?

What have you done to me? I've loved this place forever.'

Memories fought for their freedom now. She let them spill. Spill over, flood her senses. Pretty pictures. Little girl in blue, trailing Sam, the snipper of perfumed rosebuds. Dew drops on petals, her tongue tasting.

'Oh, God. God help me.'

And the dolls. Emma for Ann. Louise for Liza.

'Oh, God.' She could remember. She could remember.

'Oh God.' Emma? Black shiny hair. Brown eyes.

May, money in her purse. Leaf after leaf of money. Taking the leaves out, giving them to the man, and the man giving Ann Elizabeth the big beautiful doll. Her pick. She got first pick. Her own. All for her. All for her. Liza got the leftover doll. Got the blue-eyed doll in the pink dress.

'Oh, God. Oh God, Annie. We're in there, in that house. Something of us got lost in there. We have to find it, to stick us back together. I've got to get in there. I have to, Annie. But not now. Tomorrow. Tomorrow in daylight when the sun is too bright for demons. We'll come back tomorrow, Annie.'

She followed the road back to town. She bought chips at a take-away and returned to her motel bed late, too afraid to sleep. Daylight was filtering beneath the heavy curtain before she closed her eyes, and her subconscious tried to sort out the day's litter in dreams.

It took her to a room with a heavy door. It took her to a golden syrup tin filled with bloody worms. It took her to red fishes, swimming in a sea of blood, then it took her to the demons, and when she screamed, her subconscious tossed its hands in the air and said, 'I wash my hands of this matter,' and it left her to scream her way through a labyrinth of nightmares until Edna Harper and her rattling breakfast tray woke her at eight.

At two that afternoon, Ann drove back to the property. If her father was there, she'd leave. If Sam and May were home, she'd play the role of successful city girl. Perhaps no-one would be home, and she'd be free to wander the grounds and peer in windows. Maybe that would be enough. Maybe it would be more than enough.

The house was set well back from the road. Feeling for the gate latch she had known as a child, her hand reached too high. She watched her hand slide down, down, down to waist height. It was the same latch. Only the child had grown. Defiantly she drove her car through, leaving the gate swinging wide. If their demons were on her heels on the way out, she'd need no gate to slow her flight. She parked in front of the house, and sat a moment, breathing deeply. No sound. No movement. Nobody home?

The lion-head brass knocker was still on the front door. She rattled the lion's jaw, and snarling teeth gnashed. Then the door opened and a tiny woman stood before her.

'Aunty May?'

May's hand rose to cover her mouth. 'Ann Elizabeth? Oh my dear, dear child. It is you.' Her arms reached out, drew Ann into the wide hall, and the door closed behind her.

Cold. Ice cold, cold to death, but May's arms were warm, and her tears were wet. For minutes she stood in the hall, holding her niece to her and weeping, repeating words, silly words. 'It has been so long. I'm sorry, darling. I'm sorry. Forgive me.'

Then there was a drawing back, a gathering of herself. 'What a foolish woman I am. Come. Come through to the lounge. Whatever will you think of me, Ann Elizabeth?'

On robot's feet, Ann followed where she was led. She swallowed, striving for control as May urged her to sit, then sat beside her, hugged her.

'I ... I – ' It was all wrong. Long-rehearsed words died on her tongue. 'I ... I'm ... I'm sort of – ' Ann grasped for words now. 'I'm here. I can't believe I'm here. I can't think, Aunty May.'

'So pleased. I am so pleased you came back to me. So pleased you wanted to come back. So very pleased, my dear, dear girl.'

She released Ann and wiped at her eyes. 'Let me look at you. Let me feast my eyes on you, you darling child.' She sat back. 'My goodness. You're the girl in that advertisement.'

Ann shrugged, but the words shifted her from the old reality into an easier new. 'That's me,' she said. 'And it was the biggest mistake I've made yet.'

'Every time I see it, I feel that I know the girl, and I do. Oh, Ann Elizabeth. If you only knew how much I've wanted to see you. How many times in the past I've set out to drive to Malla-windy, then turned back. I had so many fears for you, my dear, and to think ... just to think of what a success you've made of your life. Forgive me. I'll be fine in a moment.'

It took more than a moment. Five minutes of tears and laughter followed, before she asked, 'What has brought you back to me today?'

'I should have phoned. I didn't mean to come in. Not really. Well, maybe I didn't think you'd be here. Is Dad down here?'

'Were you expecting to see him?'

'No. Just the woman at the motel said – . I haven't seen him for years. I'm living in Melbourne now. I ... I just came to see you,' she lied. But it was the right thing to say. May hugged her again.

'Jack was here, but he's gone now. You are lucky to catch me home. Sam and I spend little time in Narrawee. We've still got the Thomas's in my old home. You'd remember the Thomas's from when you were here, Ann Elizabeth. They run both properties for us now, and do a wonderful job.' She sprang to her feet. 'My pasties.' She hurried through to the rear of the house and Ann followed her, her eyes roving, taking in the old rooms, barely changed in the eighteen years since she had been here, her fingers running along the wallpapered passage. Flock wallpaper. Blue and gold. Then down two steps and into the kitchen, where the odour of yesterday was strong.

'I remember that smell, Aunty May. Cornish pasties. I used to help you make them. I remember folding them, fluting the edge with a little wheel.'

'You loved my pasties. Do you know, dear, I was sitting here, wondering what to fix for dinner tonight, and I felt this craving for Cornish pasties. I must have known you were near to me. I made four. Will you stay tonight?'

'I've got a room at the motel,' Ann admitted.

'Ann Elizabeth! You didn't. You go around there at once and get your belongings. Good Lord, if it was learned that one of my relatives was staying at Bill Harper's "Eye-sore Motel", I'd never hold my head up here again.'

'She knows who I am. She's a talker.'

'A talker is putting it mildly. That woman! I fought her and her husband tooth and nail, trying to prevent them building there. It's an ugly hideous thing and right at the entrance to our town. You run along now, and I'll have a shower and fix up my face, and we'll start our visit again.'

memories

~

Your hostess sheaths her claws neath velvet glove
While cool blue eyes conceal a thousand lies.
Her honeyed tongue, that speaks sweet words of love
gives no replies . . .
She'll twist, she'll dodge with many an artful quip,
she'll parry with claw, and turn you from recall.
So tip-toe. Take great care you do not slip,
or down you'll fall.
Then eyes will fire with gleeful enmity
Her tongue, a rasping thing will sear, will burr,
As you cower down before my enemy,
You'll hear her purr.

Annie E. Burton

Two o'clock and alone in the one room she'd never wished to
enter, Ann's light still burned bright. The novel May had loaned
her hadn't been able to claim her mind. When she finally placed
it down, she saw Annie's message on the inside flyleaf.

Annoyed, she removed the page, folded it, tucked it into her
briefcase. Her obligation to keep these messages, that turned up in
odd places, was never questioned. She made no attempt now to

analyse them, but she cherished each one. Past experience had proved them to be the name calling of a coward as little Annie ran for cover.

To her knowledge, she had not fainted before – and certainly not since she was nine. Prior to nine, she had little recall. Maybe she'd blacked out often back then. That part of her life was like a permanent black-out. Something strange had happened the night Mickey died, but it had been a ... a non black-out ... a walking from black-out into light. An awakening.

She lay on her back, thinking, while her eyes searched the walls, the ceiling of this room, once called the girls' room. It was the room she and Liza shared. The walls were old, cracked. She followed a crack down to a wardrobe, and remembered it. Her small frocks once hung there. Small shoes had been placed neatly side by side on its floor. Were they still there? The urge to look grew strong. On tiptoe she crept from her bed, opening the squeaking door. The wardrobe was bare, containing only the scent of age.

Back between the sheets, she pulled up a blanket and slid low in the bed. Dawn was near with its accompanying chill. 'Sleep,' she said. 'Sleep and please God, no dreams, no screaming,' and she reached for the light switch, plunging the room into darkness that closed in like a black void.

She lay stiffly there, waiting for Annie or the demons to pounce. She searched corners for them, knowing they would come, and that her screams would send May's ghosts scuttling for cover.

'Uncle Sam,' she whispered. A horse rider. Slim shadow, with her father's shadowy features. Her memory of the younger May was clearer. She'd probably spent more time with May. Sam, like everyone else, would have preferred Liza. Pretty golden Liza. Ann attempted to conjure up the face of her sister. She couldn't. All that came to mind was the chocolate box photograph on the kitchen wall.

Her muscles tensed in this bed. For a moment, she felt the heat of Liza beside her. They had shared this same bed. She sat, pulled up the second blanket, wondering if her father had slept in this bed. Almost incestuous. A smile became a yawn. She snuggled down, allowing her mind to map the layout of the rooms.

The total darkness was a blanket. Heavy. Inviting. The total silence after the noise of St Kilda, too complete. She rolled to her side, hearing the crisp rustle of sheets.

'Ann dear. Ann Elizabeth. Are you awake?'

Springing upright, her eyes only closed for a second, Ann was near blinded by white light. She caught a glimpse of movement against the white light from the window.

'It's nine-thirty, you old sleepy-head.' May, already dressed for town, kissed Ann's brow. 'I'm off to do some shopping this morning. I thought you might like to come with me, otherwise I'm afraid it's a morning with the painters. I'm having the external woodwork done today. It's been some time.'

'I slept like a log. I didn't even dream. Ten minutes for a quick shower and I'll be with you, Aunty May.'

She shopped with May, all the while remembering, and in the afternoon, she wandered alone through musty rooms. Few were furnished for use. Each hour was like the page of a book opening readily, then closing with the knowledge that the book was here to be reopened at will.

May asked no questions, and Ann preferred it that way. She wasn't ready yet. Again she spent the night in the comfortable bed. No Annie. No dreams. Roger had been right. Perhaps she should marry him, go to America, let his will send all the demons away.

The following morning, May found her in the rose garden, her nose buried in lost perfumes. She was tasting dewdrops, and she laughed, caught out being a child.

'Uncle Sam used to know all the names of these roses,' she said. 'I used to know some of them, Aunty May. This big one is the Peace rose, isn't it?'

'It is, dear.' May named a few more beauties. They touched the blooms, smelled buds and wandered.

The painters were back. Their scaffolding on the west side. May spoke to them for a few minutes then came to stand with Ann at the overgrown lily pond.

'Do you remember the day Liza fell in the pond, Ann?' she said.

Ann shook her head. 'I can't get a picture of Liza being here. For some reason, I have blocked her out of my mind.'

'Do you remember the big bushfire up in the hills?'

Again Ann shook her head, then she turned to the hills. 'Yes,' she said. 'Yes. I can. Yes. The big wind. The wall of flame and the smoke ... and the fire leaves all blowing down here, and – '

'Yes, dear. And all the cleaning up the next day. Ash and leaves everywhere. The house smelt of smoke for weeks.'

'That wasn't long after we came, was it?'

'Only days. Remember the blue dress I made you to wear to church that first week? I made it from one of my own frocks.'

'I remember that dress. I've always remembered it. And the mirror. The long oval mirror. Do you remember the day we came, Aunty May, and you sat at the sewing-machine and made twelve pair of bloomers out of a sheet?'

'I certainly do. The shops were closed and Liza kept wetting her pants.'

'I thought you were magic. I thought you were the magic lady. Mum couldn't sew. I'd never seen anyone just cutting into material and turning it into something. It was magic. Aunty Bessy gave me her old machine when I was about eleven. I wanted to be magic too, so I did it. Just cut and sewed.'

'Liza loved my dress-making scissors. Can you remember the day she cut up a frock I was sewing for you?'

'Purple. I remember the dress. Purple with white smocking.' Ann's hands moved to her breast. 'White smocking down the front, and on the tops of the pockets. I loved pockets. Did she set fire to the sewing-room curtains one day? Did I empty a vase of flowers over them?'

'Oh, my word, yes.' They walked and they laughed and they remembered. It was easy, so easy. May was the magic lady again and she held the secret key. She was unlocking all the doors as they walked and talked an hour away.

'And the doll I bought Liza. Remember the day she threw it in the incinerator because she wanted yours?'

'I remember my doll. She had real hair I could comb. You bought me a tiny comb with blue birds on the handle.'

'Did I, dear?'

'Yes, you did. I've still got it. The doll was Emma. Emma's comb. I've always kept it.'

'I still have Emma. She slept on the bed in the girls' room for many years before I finally packed her in a box with your books. She's in the cellar.'

'Cellar?' Ann turned away from May's eyes, her own half closed, searching a garden suddenly grown cold.

May stepped back. She'd allowed herself to be carried away by remember games, but the cellar was forbidden territory. She looked at her watch, looked at the house. 'The painters will be expecting morning tea soon, and I have nothing in the house. Come inside and we'll mix up a batch of scones.'

Ann turned towards the cellar as her aunt walked away. 'Did I ... did I push Liza down some stairs one day, Aunty May?'

'Quite the contrary, darling. She was the bully.'

'Did we go to school down here?'

'For a few weeks, dear.'

'I sort of remember it. A book. It smelt ... shiny. Is the school close?'

'A block east of the church, Ann.' May led the way to the kitchen and busied herself with flour and eggs. 'You used to read to me from your reader every night. You loved the little poems, and you learned them so quickly.'

'And Liza?'

'Oh, she wasn't ... wasn't interested. She liked the television.

Do you remember the teacher? Miss Simons? She's still here.'

'I can't even remember Liza, Aunty May. It's like she's been cut out of all the pictures of my years, and placed in a photograph frame on the wall. I can't remember what she looked like down here, what she wore. I know we slept together in that bedroom, but all I can bring back is the heat of her beside me in the bed. Maybe I don't want to remember her?'

'She was a little minx, hopelessly spoiled. A head of golden curls, and sweet small features. All pink and plump and gold was Liza, but she bit, she scratched, she screamed. Everything you owned, she wanted. It is no wonder you don't like to remember her. When you first arrived here, you shrank from her, gave her your toys, even your slippers when she screamed for them. I attempted to alter that and Liza wasn't pleased. She wouldn't have a bar of me. She preferred Sam. He ... he pandered to her every want. She was a greedy little girl – '

'Dad used to take her away with him in the car. I know that, and she'd come home with beautiful shoes, and dresses. They all fitted me, even the shoes.'

'Your father brought her here. He loved showing off his treasure. With no children of my own, I envied your parents.'

'Mum put one of the dresses on me one day, and the shiny red shoes. Dad, he ... he – '

'Would you like to look at the photographs? I have some delightful ones of you.'

'I have to know it all, Aunty May. That's why I came back here. I've got to know what went before, or I ... I can't move forward. I feel as if I'm only half of me.'

'It will come. Don't try to force it, sweetheart.'

'The doll. Emma. Could you – '

'I'll pop down and find her for you. Would you like to give the painters a call for me? Tea in the kitchen in fifteen minutes.'

The doll was as Ann had left it, a little faded, a little dusty. She straightened a small white sock, wiped dust from the shiny black shoe. 'Ted Crow,' she said, when the painters had climbed back to their scaffolding. 'That name has been inside my head forever, Aunty May. Why do I know it? Who was Ted Crow?'

May shook her head.

'Who was he, Aunty May?'

'He ... he helped out in the garden. He ... he disappeared on the same afternoon as Liza. How much do you remember of that last day?' She waited long for the reply. Ann was staring out the window at the cellar door.

'Nothing. Just his name and the smell of apples.'

May took the doll. Studied it long, then she said, 'Ted Crow arrived at our back door one morning, looking for a free meal. We ... needed help at the time, dear. What do you remember about him?'

'It's weird. It's like Liza. He's been cut out of the picture too. Just a blank white shape, but I can describe him to you. English. About forty. Sandy hair.'

'Good Lord. You remember that?'

'It's mad. How do I know what he looked like, but not remember the man?' Her face was pale, her eyes had grown darker. 'Was he English, around forty?' May nodded. 'Tell me why I know him? Why I've remembered him. What did he have to do with that day? What happened to me, Aunty May? I have to know.'

'It is a day I have tried to forget, to put behind me.' May stopped.

'Please.'

When further words came from May, they were cold, emotionless. 'Three children in town had been struck down by meningitis. My dearest friend's son was left deaf by the disease. He was only two. You and Liza were in my care. I became paranoid, darling. That last week I didn't send you to school, I was afraid to take you into town. Foolish, foolish woman. Then something so much worse happened.

'Sam had to go to Queensland, you see. He was considering

buying a property in Queensland. The flight was booked. He had to go. He left late on the Wednesday. The next day ... The next day, I ran out of bread. I ... I left you and Liza watching a movie on television. I told you not to move. "Don't leave this room," I said.'

'The gardener was here?'

'Yes. He was here ... in the rose garden. He was fond of Liza. He let her follow him around. A man of many strange moods, but he loved beautiful things, loved the garden, and how he made it bloom. I had no reason to distrust him with you and Liza, and I was gone for less than half an hour.' May shook her head. 'He ... he wasted no time that day.' She stood before the window, breathing deeply. 'No time at all. I ... I was told later, by a reliable source, that he had previously shown an unhealthy interest in ... in small children. I ... I should have known. I should have known, but I didn't know.

'I was frantic, out of my mind. Out of my mind when I couldn't find you. I called the police, then contacted your father. We called Sam's hotel a dozen times or more, but he'd driven out to look at some properties. To this day, darling, I honestly don't know what happened in those hours before Sam returned.' She covered her mouth and wept.

'Don't cry. It's all right, Aunty May. Shush. Someone told me that Sam found me.'

'He found you. He got here on the Friday, in the late afternoon. He had hired a car when he arrived in Brisbane and he drove night and day to get here. He ripped that cellar apart with his bare hands until he found you.'

'The police hadn't looked in the cellar?'

'They were looking for an adult and two little girls. Ted Crow had a motorbike, with a side-car. The search was concentrated on the roads and up in the hills.' May looked to the hills, then she shook her head. 'I'd already looked in the cellar. I'd called for you in there. There was no sign of you ... or Liza. It was a junk filled storeroom in those days, and the door was still locked.'

Ann sat willing memory of those last days to return. What she was hearing had no reality. 'Did you store apples down there?'

'Everything. Wine, old furniture, old carpets.' May stared at the hills and her eyes filled again. 'The police were down here when Sam arrived. He found you, you poor wee mite. You must have climbed up to the window, climbed on the apple crates. An old oak wardrobe had somehow fallen over you. How you were not crushed, I don't know. It was your hair he saw first. You were unconscious. I thought you were dead. I thought ... I thought I'd – .

'One of the wardrobe doors was missing. Had the other side hit you. Oh God.' She wiped at her tears, then her handkerchief balled in her hand, she took a deep breath. 'But your little heartbeat was strong. May God forgive me, Ann Elizabeth. May he one day forgive me for what I did. I will never forgive myself, I promise you. I shouldn't have left you with him. I should have found you sooner.' She was sobbing now, and her face looked old, eye make-up washed away by tears.

'It's over. I'm alive. You'll make me stop asking questions if you cry, and I have to ask them.'

'Forgive me.'

'There is nothing to forgive. I was so happy here with you. I know that. I was special here. I was at Daddy's Narrawee and I was so special. I got first pick of the dolls. You didn't give me leftovers.'

'I always wanted a little girl. God, how I envied your mother. She had it all, Ann, while I had ... I had only Sam.' She sighed deeply, and lifted her chin. 'And Narrawee,' she said. 'I had Narrawee.'

Ann stared again at the cellar door. It was open, hooked back on the stone wall. Maybe she should walk from this room now, go to the cellar, look inside. The door wouldn't, couldn't shut.

May dried her eyes, blew her nose. 'Do you want to ... to go down there, dear?'

'You used to have a kerosene lantern down there, didn't you?'

'In those days, yes.'

'I ate apples in there one day. It must have been that day. In the dark. I ate apples, feeling out the biggest ones with my hands.' She looked at her hands, half expecting to see an apple there. 'Nothing. Just a black nothing. Apples and then nothing. Until the boy. The boy at the hospital. He picked up the dark and put it back on top of the sky but he didn't get the core. It's still in there.' She tapped her forehead. 'It's still in my head.'

May took her hand. 'Perhaps we've spoken enough today?'

'Did I . . . kill Liza?'

'Don't you ever think that. Whatever happened was no fault of yours. Don't, don't you ever blame yourself for that day. I am the one at fault. I left you here with him.'

'They didn't find him.'

'There was a country-wide search. The newspaper cuttings are all here. I kept them. God alone knows why. If you'd like to read – .'

'Maybe later.' Ann turned her back to the cellar door.

'Your father came down the day you were found. He stayed in Toorak. We visited you daily in that hospital. Your terrified eyes stared at us, but you didn't see us. There was a young lad in the ward next to you. His legs had been crushed in a riding accident. He used to scoot around the corridors in his wheelchair. To keep him out of mischief, the sisters gave him a stethoscope and a white coat. They told him he was an apprentice doctor, that his job was to talk to you. And he took it so seriously. He read you stories, drew pictures, spent hours with you. He was showing you a colouring book one afternoon . . . a picture of a small child on a swing.'

'Push me, Johnny, push me high. That's the boy,' Ann said. 'He gave me a red crayon.'

'Terrible weeks. We were backwards and forwards to the hospital. Narrawee was never to be out of the news, it seemed. ''NO

RANSOM NOTE," the newspapers reported. "CHILD STILL IN COMA."
Oh Ann, those headlines are still imprinted in my mind. Jack spoke
to the reporters at the hospital, and didn't they have a field day.
"FATHER TELLS REPORTER. I TRUSTED MY MOST PRECIOUS POSSES-
SION TO A PROTECTOR OF PERVERTS."

'Oh, God, darling. I should never have left you with him.' She
was weeping again.

Ann took her hand. 'Shush. I'm sorry. Shush. I didn't come up
here to upset you. I'm sorry. We'll give it a rest now.'

'I wish I didn't have to leave tomorrow. I'll cancel the
tour.'

'No. I've got to get back to work.'

'You'll come again, Ann Elizabeth?'

'If you'll have me.'

'My dear, dear girl, how can you ask me that? Lord, if you
only knew what it means to me to have you here. I loved you,
darling. I did, so much. You were my own little girl for that month.
It was the happiest of my life.'

'I loved being here with you.'

'I'll contact you as soon as I get back to Melbourne, Ann.
You leave me a phone number, and I'll call you the minute I
get in.'

'Does Uncle Sam spend much time at Narrawee?'

'He's happier at Toorak, but he'll be here in June. We have an
open day in June, and a party in the evening. It may be good for
both of you to meet again.'

Ann went to the cellar before she left the next morning. She
went only as far as the landing, where she stood looking down
at the place where it had all begun. Nothing. No scent of apples,
no scent of earthen floor. Just another dusty storeroom, its floor
cemented now, a bright white globe hanging overhead. She
glanced at the steep steps. Wooden. Old. She shivered, and turned
away.

At ten, she left May at the airport and waved her away, then she drove back to the city where she searched the skyline for the tallest building. She had no business in its foyer but walked confidently to the wall of lifts. A door opened. Nonchalantly she stepped inside, hitting the top floor button and waiting for the doors to close.

'I'm cured,' she said. 'I was locked in a cellar and I got out. I was cut and bruised, but I healed. I am healed. I went back for you, little Annie, and I let you out. You're safe now. It's over. There will be no more voices in my head. We are one. We are whole again, and now it is time to get on with life.'

But the sliding, sickening, sucking shut of doors siphoned the air from her lungs as she spoke. 'The light is on,' she said, staring at it. 'It is not black. There is no more black place. I am not afraid of lifts. I was locked for a day in a cellar. So what. I got out.' Then there was no more air to make words and no conscious mind to form words. The black void was coming for her.

Lungs empty, muscles in arms and legs, weak with need of air, blood screamed in her ears while staring eyes watched figures move above a door. Illusory door. Meaningless figures, changing. Each second was a year, each minute a decade, until all movement stopped and her knees gave way. Only her hands, gripping the hand rail, prevented her falling to the floor.

And eons passed while new suns were born and died and a gap opened, then widened. Two businessmen stood talking. Smiling. 'Going down?' one said.

Ann sprang from her steel tomb, almost knocking a briefcase-bearing male from his feet. Instinct guided her to the stairwell and down, down. Sandals tap-tapping on the concrete steps, her eyes not focusing, she ran blind, ran scared, ran in circles of never-ending steps.

Doors confronted her at each level.

Seventeen. Sixteen. Fifteen.

None would open. Doors never opened.

Twelve. Eleven. Ten.

Apples. Red juicy apples. Eating apples while the sun went down, and the sun went down.

Eight. Seven.

She might run in circles until the flesh was gone, but her bones would continue their mad flight down, down, forever down.

Red overalls.

Three.

Two.

Heart-shaped bib.

Blood on the golden curls.

Blank eyes staring.

Long bloody-red worms.

And then there was no door. Free exit to the milling crowd.

Scatter the milling crowd. Run for freedom. Run for air.

Black bitumen. High heels drove deep into melting tar, and the black city smell seeped into her nostrils and down to her lungs.

Deep gasping breaths. Fill the black. Kill the black. Too many breaths. Too fast. Light-headed now. Too much fear. Too much oxygen.

'Oh, Jesus. Oh, Jesus Christ. Too long. Too long. I can't cure it in a day.'

Or in a week, or in a year, or in one hundred years. We are lost between fairyland and the demons den, Annie Blue Dress. You search for answers and gather in lies. Cinderella dressed in yella played with the worms in a musty cellar. Fly away Annie Blue Dress. Fly away home.

america calling

~

June 1985

Roger rang her twice a week from America. Easy to talk on the telephone. No eyes to meet. Easy to get away. Just hang up the phone.

'Mom's knitting baby clothes,' he opened the conversation.

'Any grandchild she ever had would be certified at birth.'

'But what a grandchild. Roger Wilkenson grown longer in his son. Annie Wilkenson, long self-willed daughter.'

'There is a girl in the flat downstairs who is over six foot. Would you like an introduction? Oh, and before I forget. You said you'd be here in June, didn't you?'

'Planning a June wedding, my lovely?'

'I've got an invitation to a party in Narrawee, for Ann and friend. Want to see it?'

'You're a master at the alteration of subject matter, but yes, I would be interested to see your Narrawee.'

'I'm hanging up, Roge. It's very late.'

'Not here, it isn't.'

Ann had been back to Narrawee twice and she'd visited May once at the Toorak flat. They talked for hours at night on the phone, and Ann learned much of her father, much about his youth. May, Sam and Jack, had been childhood friends, May said. Her father and old John Burton always planned that their properties would be joined by marriage. Just a matter of which son she wed. The boys knew it too.

'I told the boys I wanted to marry both of them. I was around ten at the time, and they said I couldn't marry two people, so I'd have to decide which one I liked best. They blindfolded me, then took it in turns to kiss me. "Okay, which one of us is the best kisser? First or second," they said. I couldn't decide, or wouldn't. I think I liked the game too well.

'They were a pair of pranksters as boys. Jack, always the daredevil. Ride like a demon, he could. His mother adored him, but she was an invalid for years, and her husband was a womanising old coot. The boys always knew about his women. Towards the end, he used to bring them home, entertain them in his room while his poor wife was dying downstairs.

'They were older then, and changing. Sam attempted to hide from his mother's illness, but Jack denied it. He'd force her to eat, he'd carry her outside, sit her on the balcony in the sun. He adored her, and grew to hate his father.

'Sam withdrew. He hid his feelings. Few ever knew what Sam was thinking in those days, but Jack could hide nothing, and he had such a temper.'

'He hasn't altered much,' Ann commented.

May laughed. 'Always a villain was my Jack, but a lovable villain. His mother died when he was eighteen, and he left home. I didn't see him again until after he'd married your mother and had a son. So, the decision was made for me. I married Sam. We knew there would be no child to pass the land to,' May said.

The couple they'd employed to manage the two properties were now past retirement age. May said she doubted she would be able to replace them when they decided to leave. 'I'll be too old soon to continue this nomadic life. Perhaps I'll move back to Narrawee permanently in a year or two, Ann. I loved it. Always wanted to own it. I had a nice comfortable home as a girl, but Narrawee was always my Camelot.'

So much history. So much Ann had never known, and May knew it all.

The house had been built by the first Samuel Burton, back in 1857; it was huge, but not functional. Ann's grandfather had been a second son, and a Melbourne lawyer until his older brother died without issue, so the younger son inherited. He and Eliza had renovated it, but that was fifty years ago. Everything was antiquated. The bathrooms were mouldy. Narrawee was a time warp – in more ways than one. The only place to sit in the winter was in the kitchen with the old wood fire tossing out its heat.

It was the third Saturday in June, one of those bitter days when the clouds refused to lift and the chill of the earth crept through the soles of shoes. The garden was at its worst, the roses stiff with thorns.

'Why have their open day in June?' Roger asked. He had flown from summer to the depths of winter, and he wanted his summer back.

'I asked the same question. It was Eliza's birthday – my grandmother's birthday. May says it's a chance to light all the fires and turn all the lights on. Bring the old place to life for a day.'

'So your father inherits if he outlives his brother. How old is Sam?'

'Fifty-four I think, going on fifty-five.'

'And they live away from Narrawee?'

'For most of the year. May travels a lot. But she's been in Melbourne for months now, at the Toorak flat. It's old too, but it's been renovated recently. It's very classy.'

Maybe that's the way to go, Ann thought. Two houses, on opposite sides of the world. Marry him, make his mother happy.

Buy a flat in Melbourne and flit backwards and forwards across the ocean.

She'd been pleased to see him when he flew in yesterday. He had become a good friend. Perhaps friendship might be a safer foundation for marriage than love.

She glanced at him as they stepped from the warm car to the cold earth.

'You, when seen against your natural backdrop, are the fabric from which my most fantastic dreams are woven. We could make it work. Fly home with me.'

She shrugged. Maybe they could make it work. She'd make the rules. Spend time with May, leave Roger to do whatever he did when he wasn't with her.

Ann's first sight of her uncle was from a distance. He was waving away a bus load of tourists. She took the opportunity to study him without being studied, and to grow accustomed to the idea of being near him, to ride down the panic his name always brought with it. He looked so much like her father. His stance, his walk. She grasped Roger's hand as her uncle came towards them, but his first welcome was brief.

'I won't shake your hand,' he said, showing a bandaged wrist and a hand held high in a sling. 'Came off a nag yesterday.'

There was still a crowd at the property. May called him away.

Roger and Ann wandered the grounds alone until the last car was gone. 'So, that's over for another year,' May said. 'There were more than last year, dear.'

'What about these two? Did you get their money?'

'Oh, they looked so poverty stricken. I thought we'd give them a complimentary pass,' May said. 'Let's get inside. I'm freezing.' May linked arms with Ann and they walked up the front steps behind the men.

Roger was at home in any company. Ann listened to their voices. Sam's held her father's tone, but it was softer, more cultured. His moustache was grey/white now, and his hair, completely grey, was thick; it fell over brow and collar. He wore tinted, gold-rimmed glasses, and a heavy gold chain at his throat. In his denim jacket and jeans, he had the appearance of an ageing bohemian. Maybe the years hadn't been as kind to him as they had to Jack; still she hadn't seen her father for eight years. He may have aged too, put on weight, allowed his hair to go grey.

Sam held the front door wide, and as Ann stepped in, he said, 'So, have you decided yet which one of us is the better looking, Ann Elizabeth?'

'Oh, you, of course, Uncle Sam,' she replied.

'You've got thirty minutes in which to give Roger the grand tour, Sam,' May said, then she turned to Ann. 'You come with me, Ann. I must show you old Samuel's portrait. We had it restored, and they did a wonderful job.'

Their guests were due, the old house was alive with light and caterers. May wandered from room to room, touching a flower here, straightening a chair there, supervising the workers.

'I love June in this place,' she said. 'How I love to see all the lights burning again and the noise of people. This is where I want to grow old. I was envious of this house when I was a young girl. Why don't we live here all the time?'

He shook his head. 'Where are our visitors?'

'Out there. Look at her.' They stood together before long glass doors that opened out onto a courtyard. Roger was smoking. Ann had a cigarette in her hand. She looked relaxed, at peace with the funny little man.

'She's her father's daughter, May.'

'Oh, yes. When I saw her at the door that day, I recognised her immediately. I loved her, you know. How I loved the strength and the independence of that little one.'

'Has she remembered anything new?'

'No, but she's still obsessed by Ted Crow. She keeps coming

back to him all the time. She says she has no mental image of him, that he's like a character she's read about in an old story book without pictures.'

'Selective memory.'

'Possibly,' May said. 'Look at those long Burton limbs. She reminds me of that photograph of your grandmother as a bride.'

'The wild black Celtic strain.'

'She belongs here, in this house with all of the lights burning. I feel so much better since she returned. I can see her and her children in these rooms when we are gone.'

'You're disregarding Jack.'

'I never disregard Jack, but he is not long for this world, my dear. I'm convinced that the day is fast approaching when we will see no more of Jack.'

'Don't bet on it. He's a determined bastard, May,' he replied, turning to snatch a savoury as one of the workers walked by with a tray.

'Better for us if he wasn't so determined. We cannot continue this way.'

'Poor old Jack. Life didn't deal him much of a hand – '

'Poor old May too. When is it her turn for some peace of mind? Sooner or later we have to stop this ridiculous life we lead. I want to live here, and with a full-time husband. It's just a case of making the decision, and carrying it through.'

'It gets to me. I can take it for a while, then it starts eating at my gut. Small town people never forget. They remember, May. They look at me, and they remember, and my guts turn to water and I have to get out.'

They were silent then, and stood looking out the window at the odd couple.

'He seems pleasant enough, but not at all what I expected. She speaks about him quite fondly. I had this image of some fine tall American boy with a crew cut. But he's old. He's far too old for her, and so horribly plain.'

'He's a fairy. I'll give you ten to one odds, May.'

'I hope for her sake you are wrong. He told me he was going to marry her.'

'What did she say?'

'She didn't comment. How is that bandage?'

'It's okay. Stop fussing.'

'What did you do with the sling? Go and get it. I wish you'd be more careful of yourself.'

'You just don't want Jack to get the property.' He laughed.

May and Sam were a handsome, well-matched pair. May's hand constantly touched, smoothed his hair, slipped around his waist. His hand was on her shoulder, claiming her. Jack and Ellie never touched.

'They seem such good friends, don't they? They've been married for over thirty years, and they still like each other.' Ann spoke her thought aloud.

'And they are still lovers,' Roger replied. 'She can't keep her hands off him.'

'I dare say it's because they don't have to live day after day together. Every meeting is a honeymoon.'

The guests were mainly local and fifty-plus, the party was a dry affair in more ways than one. Ann sat on the couch, watching faces, watching people, and remembering the party she'd gone to with David, remembering the ring he'd bought for her.

All so long ago. No chance of May's punch being spiked with vermouth. Sam and May didn't drink. Ann looked at her uncle's left hand. He wore no wedding ring. He used to wear a ring.

Rings and parties seemed to go together. She couldn't get her brain away from rings tonight. Something spoken of often, had a way of creeping up on you, becoming reality. This house, its history, had given her substance, given her identity. Niece of Narrawee. Great-great-granddaughter of old Samuel. Pride?

224

Ann Wilkenson, diamonds dripping off her ears. Maybe she could do it. This morning she stood with Roger in front of a jewellers, actually looking at diamonds, actually considering the possibility – until she sighted the black onyx ring and went cold on the idea.

Her eyes refused to leave her uncle tonight. It wasn't a conscious thing. Perhaps she was attempting to over-write old memories with the new. She stared at his back while he spoke to one of the local men. She heard his laugh. It was a pleasant laugh. She hadn't been looking forward to re-meeting Sam, but he'd surprised her. Ellie always said he had beautiful manners.

Like visiting royalty, everyone wanted his ear tonight, and he was in his element, moving from group to group, neglecting no-one. A wonderful host.

It would be nice to be so confident, to have it all, she thought; and she would have it all at Roger's side. Hold his hand and be brave. Tell him all her secrets. Get them all out of her head. He wouldn't flinch. Maybe he had some secrets of his own.

Through half-closed eyes, she stared at Sam's back, trying to bring to mind the younger Sam of twenty years ago. He'd possessed an uncontrolled energy then, couldn't sit still. And his eyes. She remembered his eyes. Now he wore pink-tinted glasses that disguised their chill. His hair had always been worn long, though dark as her father's then, but he'd been slimmer than her father.

Roger returned to her side. 'Where is your mind wandering to, pretty lady?'

'He came off a nag,' she said. 'I can remember him trotting a horse around the paddock, Liza sitting in front of him. I had a Shetland pony. Liza wouldn't ride it. Tiny.' Her brow creased and her hand rose, massaging her brow. 'And his roses. The garden was his thing. He lived in the garden. He won prizes with his roses at the Melbourne Show.' She paused, catching the edge of Roger's yawn. 'Am I boring you?'

'No, but you're the only one here who isn't. You know me. I'm not into dry affairs, lovely.'

'I'm ready to go. Let's quietly disappear?'

'If you put it like that.'

It was after midnight before they reached the city and stopped off at a bar.

'Can't you love me a little, as a mermaid might love a sardine?'

'Your mother loves you.'

'Sam doesn't.'

'What did he say to you?'

'It wasn't what he said, but how he said it.'

'What did you think of him?'

'Old money. A superior bastard, but he comes across as a fake. May is a fine lady. What you see is what you get.'

'I'm a fake, Roger. What you see with me isn't what you'd end up with. Underneath this facade of up-country gentility, lurks a heap of bullshit, and if you had fifty years to spend shovelling it out, the facade could collapse in on you like a deflated balloon.'

'I'll take the fifty years shovelling bullshit.'

They sat on until two, drinking a little, talking a lot.

'Say yes.'

'I rode a lift up to the top floor a while back, did I tell you? It didn't kill me.'

'Are you drawing a parallel?' They laughed. 'A baby a year for two years, then if you decide you want out, a quickie divorce, a good pay-out, and no recriminations. I'll put it in writing.'

'Okay.'

'You'll marry me?'

'Why not?'

'Monday?'

'I have to work.'

'I'll tell Michael to give you the day off.'

'January. If you haven't come to your senses by January, then we'll do it. At Narrawee.'

going home

~

Summer almost come. In Narrawee, May was supervising the installation of three new bathrooms. Sam would be there for the wedding, and stand in for his brother, give Ann away. That was what May wanted, so that was the way it would be done.

Ann went with the flow. It would happen. She'd started thinking of the first Saturday in January as a TV commercial for wedding dresses, and she'd be the star. She'd learn the part in time, or get the giggles and run at the altar.

Roger's parents were ecstatic. They had flown over, and were spending a week with May – God help her. Roger's mother never stopped talking, and his father never stopped walking. Ann was on her way there to lend some moral support, just as soon as she picked up the ring.

Go home.

'Shut up, Annie,' she said. 'I'm going to Narrawee.'

The voice had been screaming at her for days – so much for the new identity. Little Annie refused to move on.

Annie Burton has bare board floors, and sticking doors, she has willow trees and dogs with fleas. Shake your head Annie Blue Dress. Shake it hard. Get away from him. Go home. Home. Home.

'Shut up,' Ann repeated and a passer-by gave her a look

reserved for people you don't want as neighbours.

January – too close for comfort. The honeymoon in Europe booked. The Anglican church in Narrawee, booked. The wedding rings, chosen. Cake on order. Her bouquet would be rosebuds from Narrawee.

Ann was sleeping badly, dreaming again. Perhaps she needed a bedmate to wake her up, as Bronny had. She hadn't slept with Roger yet. In this day and age, no-one took on a partner for life without some sort of trial marriage. But they spent so little time together, and most of that with a table and a bottle of wine between them. She couldn't imagine sleeping with him. The mental vision of the two of them in their marriage bed reduced her to near hysteria. He never touched her as David had, just made jokes about saving himself for his wedding night.

It would be all right. She'd get drunk and tune out.

A bride wasn't supposed to feel this way. A bride was supposed to be wandering around on cloud nine, not wandering the early city streets working out how much she'd need to drink before she might consummate her marriage.

The fabric she'd chosen for her gown was cream satin to match the heavy hand-made lace May had dug out of an old trunk. Three months ago, Ann had intended sprinkling the panels with seed pearls, but she was running out of time. Each time she spread the fabric, considering the first cut, she held back ... couldn't decide on a style. Didn't feel like sewing. Didn't want to marry Roger, or sleep with him.

Maybe she'd buy a dress, or hire one. Maybe she'd get married in jeans and T-shirt.

She stopped in front of a bridalwear shop in Bourke Street, taking mental notes of a dress displayed there. She liked the bodice, but not the skirt. With a shrug, she turned away and walked towards the jewellers. The shops weren't open yet, nor would they be open for another half an hour or more but when little Annie was nagging it was safer to be out of the flat and amongst people.

Melbourne, city of extremes, she thought. City of cities within a city, offspring of the rattling towering hub, each successive offshoot becoming braver, moving further away from the mother hub, creating the suburban sprawl. A strange conglomeration, a strange mixture of people. She was ready to leave Melbourne behind. Johnny wasn't here. Maybe he was in America. London.

She watched Lady X alight from a chauffeur-driven Rolls. She was wearing a leather and fur-trimmed coat. Three metres away an Aborigine, more grey man than black, looked cold. He, who should have been wearing animal skins, wore only a navy singlet and drill trousers. The bottle of wine at his side was as empty as his eyes. Bleeding fists were beating out some near forgotten rhythm on the concrete pavement. Old alien amid the jostling crowd who had come from all parts of the globe to blend here. Old alien in his own land.

What was Melbourne before the European came, she thought. Where were this old one's forefathers buried? Below the concrete that he is trying to smash with his fists. Or in Mallawindy? Or in the sand dunes of Dead Man's Lane? Where do I belong? Ann thought. In Mallawindy, or New York?

'In a looking-glass,' she said.

It only ever took one body to form the nucleus of a crowd. Around her, the cells were still splitting, multiplying, but she was not a part of the splitting cells. She turned again to the broken man, now clutching his broken wine bottle, threatening the onlookers. Just another play being played on the big stage of Melbourne. Just fodder for the printing press. Newspapers tomorrow might read ABORIGINE HOLDS CROWD AT BAY WITH BROKEN BOTTLE HEROIC SALVATION ARMY CAPTAIN DISARMS HIM

I have to get out, or I'll sit down on that pavement and smash my head into the concrete, and a Salvation Army captain will carry me off to an insane asylum and stick me in a straight-jacket. 'Got her,' they'll say. 'We've finally got her.' I've got to run. But where to? Not to Narrawee. Not today.

She walked on, thinking of the ring she was in town to collect. Roger's mother wanted to see it, and though Roger might not want to sleep with her, he wanted everyone to see his great lump of rock on her finger. His brand, if not stamped on her rump, would be on her finger.

Ann thought of her mother's wedding ring. It had been sized for a slim finger, and if it hadn't totally cut off the blood supply like the rings they used to cut off lambs' tails, it had kept her mother's finger narrow at that point. All the growth had been in the knuckle, and around the knuckle.

She looked at her own ring finger, unmarked yet. In the months since Roger bought the ring it had only spent a few days out of its box. It was too big, so she'd had it made smaller, then it was too small, so now it was being made bigger. It got in the way. Laddered her pantihose. Scratched her. She didn't want it.

She liked him, sure, but she didn't miss him when he wasn't around.

'It's a done deal,' she said. 'Go with the flow. Learn the part and say I do.'

But she didn't want to say I do, and she definitely didn't want to do, because once upon another time she had known what love was. Once upon a time, she had known what it felt like to want to be close to a man, sleep with a man. What she felt for Roger wasn't love and never would be. He was just the dripping tap that wore the rock away.

The jeweller in Swanson Street hadn't opened his door when she arrived. She tried it, then looked at her watch. Still twenty minutes to fill. 'Damn it, and damn him,' she said, turning to the window.

The onyx ring glared at her. Its one great black eye on its heavy band of gold, its diamond shoulders glittering. She knew it, and she hated it, and she didn't know why she hated it. Her hand went to the pocket of her jacket, surprised that the pocket was there. She rubbed her fingers against the lining.

'*Home*,' little Annie said.

'Yes,' she said. 'Yes.'

Seven hours of driving behind her and she was almost there. A signpost pointed to the last road. **Mallawindy 22**. She made a right-hand turn, and drove on, stiff with sitting. Those last kilometres were the longest.

Mallawindy slunk out of the landscape. Undignified clusters of corrugated iron-roofed shacks waited beside the road to nowhere, their window eyes small, hooded, ashamed of their dust and their flies and their lethargy. Dusty trees, they sprinkled dusty shade to dusty walls.

Ann slowed the car to a crawl, her head turning from side to side, absorbing changes that were few. A fibro garage had been built where a tin shed once stood. A leaning verandah had disappeared from the grocer's. A modern car was parked in front of the hotel. It would be her father's. For a moment, she considered pulling into the kerb, sharing the shade, fronting up to the bar, and slamming her money down. 'I'm as mad as you, Dad, so let's drink to it.' She said the words aloud, and the car crept onwards.

A new roadhouse had been built in a paddock where cows once roamed. An unfenced lot across the road from her grandfather's home now boasted a house. Bessy's house looked as it always had – like Bessy, plain and down to earth. She turned down the road to the bridge. No bitumen crown for it. Dust and gravel were still heaped high on its sides, its corrugations deep, its potholes well known.

Her heart beat quickened. 'Strange to return,' she said. 'Somehow the years had altered my image of Mallawindy, dusted it, turned it into something it never was.'

She was down to second gear by the time she crossed the bridge. It looked smaller, older than she remembered, its timber floor death-rattling beneath the weight of her car as she crossed over. The river was low, slow, but it turned its head and fish plopped up to spy, and write with ripples on the water, 'Annie's home, Annie's home.' The forest hummed, and the working bees stopped their labour a while to stare. Their scent of honey was strong in her nostrils.

This forest track had known her well, known her bare feet. Now her feet were shod as her father's feet were always shod, in only the best of leather. Money was in her matching handbag. The small case, packed for Narrawee, jiggled around in the trunk of the car. Was it fit for her mother's property? Was she fit?

She sighted the old canoe tree, slowed, turned right down the track that led to her mother's land. 'Oh my God, look at the willow. And Ben's trees! We've been away too long, little Annie.'

A new boundary fence, but no new gate between its posts. The old wooden thing still earned its keep. She swung it wide, drove through, then returned to it to ride it to a bone-crunching stop against the post, as she had since Johnny taught her how to ride it.

Maybe he'd come home while she'd been away. Maybe they'd heard from him. Maybe he was married with six babies. Then again she was in the car, and creeping forward.

Chickens squawked in ill humour, making way for her unfamiliar wheels. A brindle cow peering over a fence, eyed her, distrustful of a stranger. So tense. Her stomach was tied in knots. 'I belong here too,' she told the cow and the hens. 'I knew your mothers.' Then she saw the old straw hat in the middle of the pumpkin field, shielding the one playing bee, pollinating pumpkin flowers with a feather as she had every spring of every year. 'Do I know my own mother?'

No. She shook her head. She had learned more of May after one day spent at her side than all the years of her life had taught her of Ellie. A mist for a moment blurring her vision, she watched Ellie look up at the approaching car then down to her house dress, unfit for entertaining guests. The straw hat quickly removed, hands went to her fading golden topknot, straightening a pin.

Ann pulled on the handbrake and swung the door wide, inviting in the scent of the fowl yard; the scent of home. Shy, nervous, she wanted to run to Ellie, say, look at me, see me, see what I have become. Love me like you loved Johnny and Ben. Kiss me like you used to kiss Bronny. Hold me, Mum. Let me cry on your shoulder, while you pat my back and say, it will be all right, love. Make me whole, Mum. Make me into the one I should have been. 'Hi, Mum,' she called through the chicken-wire gate.

Ellie's hand shaded her eyes as Ann walked into the home paddock, covering the ground between them, her arms reaching tentatively towards the one still standing amid her vines.

'Annie?' One step away. One step back. 'Well, my goodness. You look just like you do on the television, love.' After eight years, this was to be her only greeting? No, not quite. 'You're looking well.'

Slowly Ann's arms fell to her sides. The script long writ was not open to editing. Ann smiled, held the smile long while her heart wept. But ... But, she thought, I have done the right thing in coming home, if only to discover there is nothing to come home to. As each option is cancelled, I'll be more prepared to accept my last option. Right? Mrs Roger Wilkenson the Third. Not a bad last option.

Ellie made tea and spoke of the unseasonably warm weather, then she poured the tea and cut the cake and the conversation progressed to the heat's effect on the hens. They had gone off the lay. She touched on who had died, and how they had died, but this was not what Ann had come home for. With half an ear she listened, while she thought of her father, and of his frequent returns. It had always been like this, the old 'Come in, love. Nice to see you. The kettle is boiling. By the way the brindle cow had twin calves this morning, and old Mrs Crocker died in her bed.' Cold Ellie. Would Jack have been different ... could he have been different if he'd married May? A villain, but controlled.

Her head, a seething, burning ache of questions and disappointment, Ann sat until five, then she left Ellie peeling pumpkin, drove back to town and walked into the newsagent's, slapping the counter for service.

'Do you get the Melbourne *Sun* up in this neck of the woods, mate?' she yelled.

'Annie?' Ben's head emerged from behind a stand of magazines.

'In the flesh.'

'Annie?'

He walked towards her, his smile too wide, his hands full. Then he dropped the magazines, reached out a hand, but changed his mind and pushed it into his pocket. 'Well, you're about the last person I expected to see today.' He was behind the counter. He reached beneath it and picked up a women's magazine. 'I saw your photograph in it, Annie, and I wrote to them,' he said. 'Did they get in contact – ?'

Ann took his hand away from the papers, and she squeezed his hand, then signed. 'I miss you. Little Annie miss you too much. Think this morning, better go home, see Ben. Make him come my wedding.'

He shook his head and his green eyes threatened to overflow. 'Course I'll come.' He coughed, turned away, looking for something to do. 'I'll telephone Bron,' he signed. Signs were safer than words right now. Ann watched him escape to the back room.

She heard him blow his nose. She heard the dialling, and the, 'I told you so. Guess who's just walked in the door?' He was smiling his gentle Ben smile when he came back to his counter. 'She said, don't go away. She'll get one of her boyfriends to drive her up. Should be here in half an hour. She's in Daree. Who are you marrying?' He leaned there, smiling, shaking his head.

'The red-headed Yank in the – ' Deadeye Dooley wandered in the side door, and she stopped. His hair was the same carrot red.

'Look who's just turned up,' Ben called, and Deadeye stared

at Ann with his two matching pale blue eyes. The white blob had been replaced by glass. No thunderbolts, but a modern-day miracle. He was better looking than Roger. She laughed.

'How a ya doing?' he said. 'I seen you on the television.'

Then Jimmy Willis arrived, booked in for a late haircut – but it wouldn't take long to cut what he had left on his head. 'G'day, Annie. Bloody famous now, Ah?'

Did he really think that one lousy television commercial had nullified all her years as Dummy Burton? Didn't they know that little Dummy was still cowering in the dark place, wanting someone to talk for her?

'Hello, Jimmy,' she said, then she commented on the weather, offered them a topic to pursue. She'd have to get away. She wanted Ben, not them. She wanted – .

'They say it's going to be another hot one tomorrow.'

'All the old blokes are forecasting a long hot summer.'

'Is Mr Fletcher still here?' she said.

'Yeah, the bloody old soak. Dunno how,' Jimmy said. 'I've got my oldest starting school next year. I was hoping the stupid old fool would be dead.'

'Tell Bron I'll be at the school, Ben.' Ann left them with their forecasts and their haircuts.

The old schoolhouse looked smaller. Everything in Mallawindy looked smaller. Would he look smaller? She walked to his front door, a door she had never entered. Always the back door had been left open for her, but she knocked at his front door. Knocked twice. Waited.

He flung it wide. Bigger, older, his face belligerent, then his features collapsed and he cried. He grasped her, held her to his bulk and he cried.

She drew him inside his house, safe from prying eyes. She closed the front door and he disappeared into his bathroom. She walked to his kitchen, filled the jug, at peace here, finally at peace. He, who still smelt of brandy, he, of all the ones she had left behind, had given her what she needed this day. Peace in those old arms. God that he had been my father, what a life could have been mine, she thought.

The tea was made and poured when he joined her at the table. 'No ghost,' he said. 'No ghost.' His podgy old hand grasped her own, and he held it long, patting it. Patting it.

They talked, talked of many things, of work and cars and Melbourne, and of Narrawee, and when she looked at her watch, he hurried to his den and returned, his chubby old cheeks unable to hold back a smile as he slapped two paperback books on his kitchen table, unashamed of the voluptuous near-naked women featured there in high colour. Like a guilty boy, he waited expectantly for her reaction, his eyes watching her expression as she frowned over first one, then the other.

'I've read these, sir.'

'Have you, indeed. You read this trash, Burton?' His smile was wide.

Her mouth fell open. She lifted her eyes to his, holding his with an unspoken question, which he replied to anyhow.

'I cut down the cherry tree. I am the rogue, the unscrupulous capitalistic abortionist.' They laughed together, their laughter real. They bellowed with laughter, until the windows rattled in their frames, and the table shook, and the chairs squealed on aching legs. Then they drank more tea and controlled their laughter while he signed the flyleaf of the two novels, signed them with his real name, and he placed them in her hand.

'When I am dead, you may give up my secret.' She allowed him the floor, knowing he had been starved of an ear in which to pour his secret. She listened and she laughed and it was so good.

It was almost six when she told him she was to be married in January, that she'd be living in America. She spoke of May, and Sam. She looked him in the eye then, and said, 'I don't want Sam to walk me down the aisle, sir. Would you? I'd prefer to have someone of my own – make it mean something to me.'

He hurried from the room again, his face crumpling. He stayed away a long time. When he returned, she was sitting relaxed where he had left her, and he sat beside her, taking her hand in his, seeking words that wouldn't come.

'Proud. Proud and honoured, Burton. You do an old fool the greatest honour. The greatest honour, Burton. Proud,' he repeated. 'I am so proud of you, child. Seeing you this day, seeing what you have become. Knowing that I played some small part in ... Ah.' His sigh shook his massive frame. 'Proud,' he said. But the old man of words was lost for more words. Head shaking, mouth trembling, he turned away.

Ann left soon after. Bronny was banging down his front door.

Eyes flashing a language of their own, Bronwyn sent her friend and his motor-bike on their way. 'See you at Ben's after ten. Don't forget me,' she yelled and she ran to Ann, hugged her, danced her up and down the footpath.

Little Bron, all grown up. A dry wit, her cigarette packet offered to Ann before she lit up and sucked life from the weed, as her father did. As if resentful of its escape, Bronwyn attempted to possess the smoke to the end.

'I'm getting married, Bron,' Ann said, studying her sister's hand, its shape around the cigarette. It was her hand, but smaller. Strange. Bron, so vital, so alive – and she? 'I thought you might be my bridesmaid. Ben said he'd come. He'll be best man. Mr Fletcher will be there. I hoped maybe ... I'm going to ask Mum, but I don't want – '

Bronwyn laughed, spraying smoke, wasting smoke. 'Mum? Invite Mum and not her Prince Charming? Do you really think she'd leave her cows and Jack just to go to a wedding? Big joke, Annie, but I'll be there with bells on. I'm dying to see Narrawee. Can I bring a friend?'

'Bring as many as you like. Most of the guests will belong to Roger's parents and to May.'

Bronwyn was an explosion of nervous energy, limbs tossed to the passenger seat, mouth erupting in chatter, she puffed smoke as Ann drove again over the bridge.

'Will he be home?'

'You've been away too long. Don't you remember? He always eats at six,' she mimicked his voice, and did it well. 'Get the bloody food on the table. It's six.'

'Is he safe these days?'

'Ah. He's weak as shit. Ben has got the young cop dogging his footsteps. He's scared of cops. He hasn't hit Mum for six months. Not that we can see, anyway. And if he ever placed as much as one finger on me, I'd kill him, and I've told him so. Told him I'd blast him to hell with his own gun while he slept, then I'd scream long-term child abuse from the roof tops. Everybody is doing it these days – and getting away with it.'

Jack's eyes were watching the fly-wire door; he was ready for Ann, but he hadn't expected Bronwyn, who walked to the corner where his gun was kept. He watched her pick it up, break it professionally, and remove the cartridges, her eyes daring him to comment. She took out her cigarettes, lit one, then tossed him the packet. He caught it, lit his own and pocketed the rest. Tame.

Ellie left her stove to kiss Bronwyn's cheek, but Jack's eyes were on Ann.

'What are you doing home, you crawling Narrawee bitch?' he commented.

'I thought crawling home to Narrawee was a Burton neurosis I inherited from you.' She watched Ellie return to her stove, to her pumpkin. Two hours ago she was forced from her pumpkin patch; at five she was peeling pumpkin, now she was mashing it. She hadn't kissed Ann's cheek, hadn't touched her, wouldn't look at her. 'At least they were pleased to see me down there,' Ann said.

'Good old Sam, and how was he?'

'Bought you a new car, I see, or did you win the lottery? Rob a bank?' He laughed cynically and emptied his glass. 'I don't get you. I would have crawled for that place. I would have developed calluses on my belly, licked the old coot's boots, and backside, if Narrawee had been the prize.'

'You don't know what you're talking about.' He pushed Ellie away from her plates, picked up his bottle and refilled his glass, while Ellie stood, spoon raised, pumpkin pot in her hand. 'You don't know the half of it, you stupid bitch.'

'Don't drink any more, Jack. Annie! Don't go making trouble as soon as you walk in the door,' Ellie said. 'Sit down, Jack love. Don't let her upset you.'

Jack tossed the whisky down, while Ann stood smiling. 'You come back here thinking you can lord it over me, you smiling bitch. Thinking you can tell me what I should have done. This is my bloody castle, and I'm God here, and never you forget it. No-one tells me what to do in Chook-Shit County. Get out. Get back to Narrawee. A poor bloody man had his life stolen from under his nose by his bastard of a brother, and you come here and laugh about it.'

Ann had walked to the door. She stood there, looking at the two oddities in the kitchen. A love match. A marriage, made in hell. She shook her head, no longer able to raise energy enough to tolerate one meal. 'Well, it's been lovely seeing both of you, as always.' She held her plastic smile as she stepped down into the passage, and the wire door slammed behind her.

'I've cooked enough dinner, Annie. You're welcome to stay if you just behave yourself,' Ellie called after her.

'I'll take a raincheck, Mum.'

'Don't stay away so long then, and good luck with your career.'

Ann turned, looked at her mother through the fly-wire. Stared at her. She'd driven here with so much hope. Driven eight hours, almost got a speeding fine for this. For this? 'Crap,' she said. 'Good luck with my career? You don't know what my career is. You didn't even ask. I can take your disinterest, Mum, but don't insult me with pretence. I've been a problem to you all my life. I know it and you know it. I'm trouble you prefer not to have around.'

'That's not true, love. It's lovely to see you looking so well.'

'But more lovely to watch me making a fool of myself on television. That's my daughter, Annie. Electronic tube that you don't have to touch. Don't understand how it works, of course, but I don't try too hard either. Well, now trouble has gone away for good. I'm off to America. I'll do a real Johnny this time – '

'Don't you mention that disloyal little bastard's name around me,' Jack yelled. 'Don't you bring his name back here. Get out. Get off my land. Stay away from me, you wild-eyed bitch.'

'You can bank on that,' Ann called back, she was already halfway to her car. Bronwyn came at a run through the eastern door.

'Get!' he bellowed through the window as the car took off, eager to be gone, to return to bitumen and sanity. 'Get out of my bloody life.'

Ann drove wildly along the rutted track, Bronwyn bouncing, laughing, spraying smoke at her side. The old gate closed behind them, Ann drove again. Her brain was on fire. Migraine? Stroke? She wasn't sure. She only knew she had to get out of this town and fast. 'What was I thinking of, Bron? What did I come back here for? Her approval? Her blessing?'

'Self approval is all that counts for me, Annie, and I'm pretty good at it. Where are you staying tonight?'

'Where are you living?'

'Daree.'

'I'll take you home, then head back to Melbourne. I'm supposed to be in Narrawee entertaining my future in-laws. It's the last place I want to be, but it's the only place I've got to go. Funny, but not funny.'

'I'll have to hang around until Mark comes back. I didn't know your plans, Annie. I told him to pick me up at ten, and there's no way I can contact him. Do you drink? Let's go to the pub. Show the town what Jack's daughters are made of.'

'Stuff the bloody town – and him, and Mum. I've got to get out of it, Bron.'

'You just got here, for Christ's sake. What about Bessy? What about Ben?'

'I didn't come back to visit with Bessy. I thought Mum would be finally pleased to see me. I talked myself into thinking she'd give me a kiss, Bron. She always gives you a kiss. But she gave me a rundown on who died. ''Oh, and by the way, love, old Mrs McDonald had a stroke. Oh, and by the way, old Dave Eva finally passed away. They opened up Rella's grave and put him on top, love''.'

Bronwyn giggled. 'Poor old bastard. So he finally got on top, did he? I wonder how many he had to push off to get there?' Ann couldn't even raise a smile. 'Mum can't help what she is, Annie. Any normal responses she might have had were gone long before we knew her. She's his punch-drunk puppet and she's learned to love it. It'll buy her points in the hereafter.'

Ann left Bronwyn in town and she drove away from Malla-windy. She wanted a long straight road, where no cops prowled, wanted to flatten the accelerator to the floor and let the farm land, and farmhouses, farm fences become a grey blur. It was over. Finished.

The city of Warran looked like an advertisement for the wealth of this land when given rain and sun in the right proportions. Only twice had she been there. She drove in circles, cruising the unfamiliar streets, looking for a signpost that may point her south. Her headache left somewhere on the road, her stomach now demanded to be fed. She saw the take-away on the corner.

'Chips,' she said. 'Chips out of paper.'

There was a crowd already waiting, all younger than she, or older. Her generation was at home, cooking mush for babies.

That's what I need, she thought. A baby, to raise in love, and with love. Roger's baby. Roger Wilkenson the Fourth, and he'll look like Deadeye Dooley. Oh shit. What am I going to do?

Have a kid a year for two years, then a quickie divorce and no recriminations. That's if I'm not in a nut house after the first week, or an alcoholic after the second.

For five minutes she stood waiting while bodies packed in behind. Slowly she was pressed to the front of the queue.

'Two hamburgers with the lot.'

She heard the voice behind her and ignored it. A queue jumper. Then the words were repeated, close to her ear, in her ear.

'Two hamburgers with the lot, and toss in a few chips.'

She swung around, and their noses near brushed in the crowd. 'David?' Her heart was swimming, drowning in her own gastric juices. 'David Taylor. What are you doing here?'

'I live here. More to the point, what are you doing here?'

She looked at his mouth and his eyes above his mouth, and she knew every curve, every line. Her heart beat too wildly. It filled her with its beat, dismembering words before they were spoken.

He filled the silence. 'Been down at Mallawindy?'

'Just to say goodbye. I'm off to America.' Tongue tied, she sought for words, then the woman called above sizzling fat, 'Next. Next.'

'Two hamburgers with the lot and a serve of chips,' David said.

'We don't like queue jumpers in Melbourne. I was here before you.'

'I can't eat two. I presume you're still addicted to chips,' he replied.

'I live on them.'

'They suit you.'

'How is Melissa?' she said. Eyebrows raised, he looked at her, his head to one side. She explained. 'I ran into Tony George in Melbourne.'

'Ah, ah. What's he doing these days?'

'Selling cars,' she said, and she laughed, and he laughed, and the crowd stared, not in on the joke. But laughter ended and an embarrassed silence grew. Ann dived into the centre, needing to fill the silence. 'I'm getting married. Five weeks away and I haven't started my dress yet. Each week I leave it, the style becomes less complicated.'

It didn't help, as the crowd of people in the confined area didn't help. Arms brushed arms, drew away. Ann concentrated her attention on the woman behind the counter; a one man army, she cooked, wrapped and made change.

'So, who are you marrying?'

'A Yank. His mother actually approves of me, apart from my slim hips,' she said, and it was the wrong thing to say. It brought back memories of disapproval and created another silence. What more was there to say unless she dredged up memories from the past? When in doubt, do as her mother did. Speak of the weather. 'Wasn't it a hot one today? They reckon in Mallawindy that it's going to be a long hot summer.'

'When the conversation deteriorates to discussing the weather, it's time to bring it to an end,' he said.

'You're probably right.' She shrugged and tried again, knowing it would be easier if his eyes would turn away from her. 'How are your Mum and Dad, anyhow?'

'The same could be said of feigned interest in family members, but to answer your question, they sold up, retired to New Zealand. Dad is a New Zealander. He's got family there.'

'Oh!' Nodding, nodding, she prayed for the hamburgers to cook in a hurry.

'Two hamburgers with the lot, and chips,' the one woman army called.

David paid. He handed the parcel to Ann. 'Do you get to eat

the lot or can old friends sit in a car in the middle of the main street and share them?' His lips wore that same smile, but his eyes had lost their laughter. He looked sad, older somehow and the reply on her lips altered mid sentence.

'It's your town. I don't have to live here.'

'While they are gossiping about me, they are leaving some other poor sod alone.' He led the way to his car, held the door open, watched her seated, then walked to the driver's door and slid in beside her.

Together they unwrapped the food and together they attacked it as they had in the days of old. They spoke with mouths full, while tomato sauce and hamburger juice dripped onto Ann's T-shirt. David opened a glove box, neater, smaller than her own, and he handed her a box of tissues.

'You've obviously got a tribe of kids,' she said, wiping at the stain.

'No.' End of subject. 'Tell me what you've been up to.'

'Nothing to tell. I've been in Melbourne for eight years, and it gets bigger every year. I think I'll be pleased to leave it.'

'No ring yet?' He took the hand seeking a chip.

'It's at the jewellers.' She looked at him, shrugged. 'It was too big, then it was too small, and now it's probably too big again. I think I'm just petrified of the thing – scared I'll lose it down a plughole. And it's a great, ugly block. He's not very tall and he's got this idea that big is beautiful. He only wants me so I can inject some long genes into the Wilkenson clan. They're all about five foot nothing.' Determinedly she removed her hand from his grasp, and when it was free, she tucked both hands beneath her knees, safe from his touch.

'Where did you get to that night?'

She shrugged. 'I rode my bike to Daree, then caught a bus to Melbourne. I've lived in a dozen or so suburbs. It's the way to get to know the place. Every time I moved, I thought I'd find Johnny living next door, but I doubt he's even in Australia. If he is, he doesn't want to be found. Maybe I'll find him in America. I found an aunt and uncle,' she finished lamely.

'And a fiance.'

'And a grey hair the other day.'

'It still looks as black and wild as I remember it.' His hand brushed the woolly mane over her shoulder, an old habit, but she swung the car door wide, the hamburger laying heavy, somewhere in her chest.

'I must keep going. It's getting late,' she smiled. 'Nice to see you, David. Remember me to Melissa.'

'Where must you go?'

'Somewhere.'

'Stay a while. Talk to me.'

'Melissa will have a search party out.'

'She's holidaying with her parents in America – won't be home until January.'

'America and January seem to go together. But I do have to go. I'm pleased I ran into you, David. Have a good life.' She picked up her bag and walked away without a backward glance.

David watched her go as he disposed of the litter. He was in his car when he heard her call. 'Wait! My keys. I must have left them in your car.'

Their search was unsuccessful. Fingers slid between the seats. They emptied the glove box, checked the floor. 'I hate keys. I loathe keys! Where in the name of hell did I leave them this time?'

'Maybe in the shop.'

When she returned empty handed, David was rummaging through hamburger wrappings he'd tossed in the bin. She stood beside him, her eyes hopeful.

'Are you sure you didn't lock them in your car?'

'I might have, but I haven't done that for months. Have you got a screwdriver or a knife?'

'What are you going to do with a screwdriver, hot wire it, take the door off?' His anger was sudden, and for no rational reason.

He wanted to be gone, wished fervently he'd opened a can of beans and not obeyed the call of his stomach.

'I've got a spare key behind the number plate. If you haven't got a knife, I'll borrow one from the shop.'

'I'll have something in the boot.'

She waited while he opened the boot and found his tool-box, but instead of a screwdriver or knife, he handed her a plastic bag, dusty, sticky, full of bits and pieces. 'Yours,' he said. 'I cleaned out the glove box before I traded the old car in. For the small amount of time you spent with me, it is amazing how much of your life you managed to leave behind you.'

'I shed things. You ought to see my car,' she said, her hand delving into the plastic bag in search of better days. She found a woollen glove, three combs, a photograph, a cancelled bankbook, a nest of hairpins, a reel of white thread and the blue velvet box. 'That's not mine, you nut.'

'I gave it to you and you tossed it in the glove box with your bobby pins.'

'Don't be stupid.'

'Throw it in the rubbish if you don't want it. Sell it, pawn it, stick it on your key ring if you ever find it. It's yours. I'd forgotten about it until a minute ago.'

She flipped the box open. The ring sat in a blue satin pillow. One diamond.

'Old fashioned now,' he said.

'I prefer a single rose bud to a vase of gladioli. I thought you'd given it to Melissa.' She locked it away from the light, handed it to him as she took the screwdriver from his hand. He aimed the tiny box at the rubbish-bin.

'Bullseye,' he said, and he was back in the car, the motor running.

'You can't do that,' she moaned. 'David! You can't do that. What's happened to you? You can't throw away something precious.'

'No? You're a great one to talk, aren't you? You invented the bloody game. Why didn't you phone me that night, or ride to Warran, to me?'

Head down, she ransacked the bin until she found the velvet box sitting on a half-eaten pie. Her eyes accusing him, she took a handkerchief from her purse, wiped the velvet clean, and walked to his window. 'Please take it. Where is the banker I used to know, the cash coach, guardian of ten thousand postponed dreams? Take it, David.'

'Try it on,' he said. 'Put it on. Take it out of the box and try it on your finger – just once. Prove or disprove a point for me. Let me see if I knew you, knew your hand as well as I thought I did back then.'

'Stop it. Stop that. The world has moved on.'

'Not for me. Try it on. Prove me wrong. I want to be proven wrong tonight.'

Slowly she did as he asked. She tried the ring on her right ring finger, twisting the small band, attempting to force it over the knuckle, because he wanted her to. But the ring wouldn't fit. She shook her hair back from her face, her eyes huge, hurting in the near dark street, and she handed him the ring. He took it, and the hand that extended it. He slipped it easily onto her engagement finger.

'I chose it for your left hand,' he said. 'Right hands are always larger than the left.' His grip on her hand was strong. She stood dumbly there, her head down until the pressure relaxed. Then she turned and ran for her car, his ring on her finger, his screwdriver grasped in her hand.

She found her keys taunting her from the ignition. By the time she started the motor and swung around the corner, David was gone.

There were six roads leading out of Warran, but directly opposite the signposts, she sighted a licensed hotel-motel, its light blinking vacancy. She drove in, booked a room, then walked next door to the hotel where she purchased a bottle of cherry brandy.

A fast glass, a faster shower to wash the dust away, then a second glass of cherry brandy and she was brave enough to dare all. The exchange gave her his telephone number.

'David Taylor speaking,' he said.

'Good evening, Mr Taylor,' she said. 'You are one of the lucky Warran residents to be offered a night at your local motel, with the – '

'I love you,' he said.

' – with the Mermaid girl. This is an obligation free, once in a lifetime offer, and not likely to be repeated – '

'I love you. I have loved you from the day I first saw you and I'll die loving you. Where are you, Ann?'

'Please present yourself at the Motor Inn, near the Dorby highway, opposite the signpost. Unit six – ' But the connection was broken.

She greeted him at the door, a glass in hand, and it was so easy to slip into his arms where she belonged, and so good. So good to feel the strength of his arms crushing her to him, and his mouth on her own, to taste his breath again, and smell the scent of him. So easy and so right.

'Oh God,' he breathed against her lips. 'What have we done to each other?'

'I'm sorry. I'm sorry. I'm sorry,' she said, and he kissed each word away while the drink in her hand tilted, releasing the pink stuff to trickle down his shirt. 'Now we're both stained,' she said, reaching for a tissue. 'Perhaps it's fitting,' and they were kissing again, her mouth as hungry as his.

Later, so much later, when the world was back in focus, he kissed her and tucked the twisted pillow beneath both heads and he pulled a blanket over their cooling flesh. She hadn't spoken, nor had he.

He wanted to cry. His throat ached with tears, and love, and guilt, and questions he wanted to ask, but he didn't want the answers, so he held her and kept his silence.

Caught up in a marriage that was no marriage, he had built his memories of Ann into a shrine. And now she was here with him, in this bed, but getting married in January.

Why? Brides might still dress in white, but only one in a thousand made it to the altar with virginity intact. She'd almost been that one in a thousand. He didn't understand. He couldn't understand. Why? Why had she called him? 'Why?' he finally said. 'Why in God's name did you do it?'

'Was it that bad?'

'I thought . . . I thought you'd be experienced.'

'You sound like a character from a Jane Austen novel.'

'I feel like one. Some rakish cad. Why did you call me, Ann?'

'Your number came up on the computer.' He didn't reply. 'I think the man I'm marrying is gay, and I know I'm going to run at the altar – or if I don't, I'll damage him for life when he tries it,' she said.

'You think he's gay and you're still going to marry him!'

'His mother had a heart attack two years ago. He wants to give her a grandchild. Two actually.'

'Do you love him?'

'I don't know. He's a good friend.' She breathed deeply, and turned to face this beautiful man. 'Everything I ever do is wrong, David. Every plan I ever make is wrong. I came home today to see Mum. That was a very bad move. I don't know why I drove up to Warran. Probably because I wanted to be close to where you were. I don't know. Was it so wrong?'

'What do I say? What can I say?'

She slid from the bed. 'It didn't feel wrong. It felt like the least wrong thing I have ever done in my life,' she said, and she walked to the shower.

He heard the shower's hiss, and waited, unsure of her next

move. Would she steal away while he was sleeping? His limbs spread in the tumbled bed while he waited for the water to be turned off. His eyes closed.

It was just before dawn when he woke and knew the bed he was in was not his own. Memory filtered back. He felt for her beside him, but he was alone. He sprang up, found the light switch, stared into white light. Her case was on the bench. He looked through the window, saw her car was there.

He found her in the bathroom, sitting on the floor, scribbling on the back of a motel breakfast menu, the bottle of cherry brandy at her side.

'So you're still here,' he said.

'You too.'

'What are you doing?'

'Making a shopping list.'

She was wearing a towel, and he reached out a hand, exploring the painfully thin shoulder, the child-like curve of neck. He wanted to gather her back into his arms, but he stood, turned to the mirror. She was making the rules. 'It's almost dawn,' he said. 'Warran still has a small town mentality. Our reputations will be in shreds.'

'I didn't like mine much anyhow.' She stood then, holding her towel close and brushing the damp strands of hair from her face. He watched her fold the menu and place it in a briefcase, lock the briefcase. 'You go if you want to, David. What do you want to do?'

'What a silly, silly question.' And he reached for her, gathered her to him, and he kissed a mouth, fresh with toothpaste. 'What a silly, silly question, you idiot girl.'

lost innocence

~

It was with some cynicism that Malcolm Fletcher watched the building of a new brick school. For twenty years he'd pleaded for improvements, but his plea had been ignored. Still, he goaded his students, he drove them with sarcasm, and he whipped them with his tongue, his voice overriding the hammer and the drill. He taught the unteachable, and he sipped his brandy from a teacup until the final bell.

On that last day, the bell rang non-stop for six hours, and when townspeople complained, and the rope was removed, Robby West's youngest son shimmied up the pole and the bell continued to peal.

Malcolm now at retirement age, was given six weeks to get out of the schoolhouse. No-one cared that he had no place to go. They bought him a cheap gold watch, allowed him to declare the new school open, then the solid citizens hurried away, eager to indulge the new man who was promising to inject some enthusiasm into the dust.

Malcolm bought a new Falcon stationwagon, suitable to his stature. He bought a caravan and a five-hectare paddock from Bluey Fraser. He chose it because it faced the Burton property, gave him a perfect view of Jack Burton's bedroom window.

It took two days to load his caravan, and one more and a bottle to raise nerve enough to tow it away. His new car aimed in the direction of the river road, Malcolm hoped his caravan would follow. It jibbed at the bridge, so he stopped, halting a truckload of beef one side and the town clerk's new Toyota on the other. While they cursed him, he walked around his van and edged sideways through its door, exiting with the gold watch. He studied it a moment, nodded to the town clerk, and the farmer, then he flung the watch high, watching the sunlight catch it and glide with it into deep water. It shimmered as it sank. He stood at the railing until the watch disappeared from view. Chubby cheeks trembling with suppressed amusement, Malcolm drove on to commence the next phase of his life.

The year came in wild, intent on leaving its mark on Mallawindy. Bert Norris died two hours into New Year's Day. He left his house, business, and bank accounts to Ben Burton and Deadeye Dooley. Then on the 4th of January, Ethel Dooley, long-term cook at the Central, dropped dead at the stove, throwing the counter meals into chaos, and leaving a husband, fifteen children and umpteen grand-children to welfare.

'Two down, one to go,' the old ones whispered, eyeing each other for signs of imminent demise. Death always came in threes.

Deadeye, still in a daze over his good fortune, couldn't wipe the dollar signs from his glass eye. It dazzled as his mother's coffin was lowered, it tallied when his father over-balanced and almost followed his wife to her rest. It subtracted as he dragged his father back to the brand new car he'd bought on account of he was going to be able to afford it as soon as probate went through.

Unchanged by the years, untouched by the sun of Mallawindy, protected in the cool dark cavern of his bar room, Mick Bourke, owner/barman of the Central Hotel poured beer into glasses while drinkers poured cash into his pocket. He was stressed out. He needed a new cook. His wife was giving everyone indigestion, and

Jack Burton was giving him indigestion by asking for credit again.

The heat of that last January day was threatening everyone's sanity.

'You've got a few bob on it from before Christmas, Jack,' Mick said.

'You'll get your money. You always get your money.' The price of whisky was high. Inflation had reduced Jack's annual income to a pittance. There was money to be had at Narrawee, but he had to crawl to get it and May was turning the screws. There had been no cheque for three months, and he was stony motherless broke.

'It's your liver,' Mick said. He reached for his top shelf and passed a full bottle across the bar. He took his red account book from beneath the bar, licked his pencil, coughed, grabbed his heart, and that was the last move he made.

Jack walked away with a free bottle and the old ones in town breathed deep sighs of relief and gossiped on, safe again now the third pin had fallen.

For years now, Ellie Burton had been hearing rumours about women's liberation, but she'd learned early to close her ears to gossip. She ironed Jack's shirts and cooked his meals. She didn't miss him when he wasn't around, and she dodged his bad moods when he was. She collected her eggs for the egg board, she milked her cows and fed her pigs, while her golden hair paled to white at the temples.

In the evenings, when she sat alone doing the crosswords, the old house seemed to ache with silence, and the iron roof groaned, as if it too mourned her lost children. The blackened rafters in the kitchen trapped no more childish laughter, hid no more children's tears. The beds were still made up in the empty rooms, though cobwebs hung grey in dark corners. Rusty hinges creaked, windows rattled, doors slammed on still evenings. And sometimes ...

sometimes on the darkest night when the air was still, Ellie swore she heard the plaintive cry of a child trembling on the air, and from the yard, bright eyes watched and seemed to follow her.

Only an owl. Only a feral cat, or some wild thing of the forest.

the baby

~

Ann wasn't in the private ward. David found her sitting alone in the sunroom.

'Get me out of here,' she said.

'Doctor Williams wants you to stay in for a few days. Dad and Mum are flying over from New Zealand at the weekend. They said they'd stay as long as necessary.'

'Just what the doctor ordered.' Ann turned, walked to the door.

'You're not supposed to be walking around. Sit down, or better still, go back to your room and lie down.'

'Heel, Mickey,' she said. 'Come to heel, boy. Sit. Roll over, and play dead.'

'Do you want to lose the baby, Ann? Williams warned you that it wasn't going to be an easy pregnancy, and yet you go racing up to your bloody old school teacher's death-bed instead of looking after yourself. Is he more important to you than our baby?'

'They told me he was going to die, and I sat with him for two days and I wouldn't let him die. He lived because I made him live.'

'And in the process you almost lost the baby.'

'If it is determined not to survive, then no doubt it will succeed. Far better we lose it before we know it.'

'You won't lose it if you do as you are told.'

'But I don't. I never did. Don't try to control me, David.'

Control her? That was surely a witticism. She was still the girl he'd known and loved at sixteen, but so much more. She was a businesswoman, a supervisor of builders, and something else, some indefinable quantity he couldn't fathom.

He'd railroaded her to the altar. When his freedom papers were in his hand, she didn't want marriage. They'd had a wonderful year. The best of his life. The best of her life, she said. 'Don't try to cage me, David. Leave me free to come and go at will. I'll never leave you again, but sometimes I need to be by myself.'

How many times had she repeated those words? But too afraid of losing her again, he'd forced the issue and tried to tie her to him with a wedding ring. The pregnancy so soon had been a mistake. The house in Mahoneys Lane was barely finished, their plans placed on hold because of the baby, but for a while she'd seemed pleased. Then, for no apparent reason, she'd begun disappearing for the day. 'Just felt like a trip to Melbourne. Just wanted to be by myself.' She'd creep from his bed in the middle of the night, and he'd find her walking the yard, or seated at the table scribbling stuff she locked in her briefcase.

The briefcase was kept beneath her side of the bed. She caught him as he was about to open it one night, and she snatched it from his hand, snatched the key. 'Private. It's clearly marked private, David. Can you read, or will I add, Keep Out Snoopers?'

The key went missing from her key ring that day. Now she wore it like a charm on her watch band. For days after, she'd barely spoken to him. He couldn't touch her. She slept in a spare room.

'Hormones,' Williams diagnosed, when David went to him seeking advice. 'Hormones and the fear of miscarriage.'

It was more than hormones, and David knew it. He wanted this baby, and he hated the fat old slug of a teacher Ann treated like some god.

'Right from the first weeks, you made no concessions to the baby, Ann. Climbing up and down ladders like a monkey, sewing curtains at all hours of the night. You didn't want to become pregnant, did you?'

'No, I didn't. Not so soon – but I don't want it to die, either, so don't go trying to heap any more guilt at my door. There's mullock-heap enough there already.' She turned to face him, her eyes searching his face. 'You were the one who wanted marriage. Not me. I told you it wouldn't work. We're together, day in, day out. I need space, and I don't need someone trying to tell me how to live my life.'

She walked from the room and he followed her to her private ward where he sat with her case on her bed. Her briefcase was beside it. She never moved without the thing – and he didn't know what she kept in it. Two weeks of marriage to Melissa and there had been no more surprises left, but each week with Ann only made the puzzle more intricate. There was no working her out. The pieces didn't fit into any recognisable pattern.

He watched her slam wardrobe doors and open locker drawers, her jaw tense but determined. Aware that he'd said more than he should, he waited until the case was packed, closed.

'Why won't you stay here? Just for a few days. Pop back into bed, please. You're worrying me. You're as white as a ghost.'

She picked up the case. He took it from her.

'Leave me here for another night and I'll be a ghost, or in a nut house. Hospitals are for the dead and dying. I'm going to live, David, and with a bit of luck this baby will too – if you get me out of here. I hate hospitals and poking, prying doctors. I hate them. They make my head crawl.'

'Have you spoken to Doctor Williams today?'

'Get me out of here! Now! I'm falling into a black pit, and there's a tonne of dirt pressing on my lungs. I can't think about it or I can't breathe. I'm suffocating in here.'

'Sit down while I telephone him.'

'You pick up that phone and I start walking, and when I get home, I start driving.'

'Oh, Jesus,' he moaned. 'What am I going to do with you?'

'I can't change what I am. I wish I could. I don't want to lose the baby, and I didn't do anything wrong. I sat with a lonely old man who has no-one else to sit at his side, and he held my hand as if it were a precious thing. If you find something in me to love, then know that he alone planted it there. He is part of my life, David, and apart from you, the major part. He can become a part of our life, or you can continue to see his bloated old exterior and hate him each time I run to his side – but know, know now, if he needs me, run I will.'

David's mother thought her new daughter-in-law was intolerable. She said it often. Said it loudly. She and her husband arrived in Warran on the Saturday, having packed for the duration. She had decided to tolerate the intolerable because of the pregnancy. Beggars with an only son couldn't afford to be too choosy.

Three days after the senior Taylors moved into the second bedroom, Ann moved Bronwyn and her cigarettes into the third. Marge Taylor couldn't tolerate smoke. Within days of Bronwyn's arrival, Ann began stealing the occasional cigarette, as she had when she was with Roger.

It was too much for Marge. The bomb had been fizzing since she arrived. Now it went off with a bang. Ann took off in her car and David drove his parents to Sydney and put them on a plane back to New Zealand.

Bronwyn remained. She was twenty, temporally unattached and unemployed, and Ann loved having her around.

'Get off your feet, Annie,' she'd demand. 'You think I want to see another baby born on a kitchen floor?'

It was working. For free board and lodging, Bronwyn became David's built-in watchdog. Ann was resting, but her hands were busy beading the gown she'd once intended sewing for her own wedding. Some bride in Melbourne would wear it now, but they wouldn't wear the old lace. Ann had posted it back to May.

If it wasn't quite the life David had imagined for himself, he made few complaints, and he got on well with Bronwyn. The sisters had some physical similarities, but Bronwyn was an open book, where there was a wall of glass beneath the façade Ann showed to the world. He couldn't break through it.

'That girl is hiding something,' his mother said, when he left her at the airport. 'You mark my words, son.'

Maybe she was right.

In late June, Mallawindy was hit by another spate of deaths. It was an old town, where aged pensioners ruled. Bessy's husband was the first pin to fall, and Mr Mack the third. Ellie Burton's childhood home went to auction, and Ben bought it for a song. The house was a wreck, the property run down.

Ellie came with Bessy to look at the house; they wept as they walked neglected rooms, then Bessy went home to the no-frills farmhouse she'd shared with Bill for almost forty years. Ellie stayed on. Jack was in Narrawee again, so she came each day with her scrubbing brush and bucket. She ordered wallpaper and paint, and she scrubbed and pruned. Ben worked at her side, a half smile on his lips. He had played the last ace in his hand and he'd finally won the game.

Ellie shed ten years in as many weeks. She climbed ladders, hanging wallpaper as she had with her father so many years ago. She hadn't forgotten how it was done, how to cut and trim like a professional. She polished windows and watered dying creepers, and she drove with Ben to Daree where they ordered linoleum for the floors and a new rug for the lounge room.

When it was fit again to inhabit, and Ben bought his small case of possessions to stay, he asked which room had been Ellie's.

'I always had the little attic room, love,' she said, then she saw his expression. 'Oh no. I won't be moving. I could never have your Dad here. He hates this house and all it ever stood for.'

'I bought the house for you, Mum.'

'I know why you bought it, and you're the best son any mother could ever wish to have, but I can't leave your Dad. He needs me, love. I'm the only one in the world who accepts him as he is.'

'What about when you need him? He leaves you, Mum. Every time a letter comes from that rotten place, he goes off and leaves you for months.'

'I know, love. I know. But he's not happy here. His roots are in that land, like mine and yours are here. Now I've got my old home cleaned up for you, it will be like having my Dad living here again. You're so much like him. Just think, love, when you get your bridge built, I'll be able to run across and cook your dinner, just like I used to do for my Dad. I'll sit in your front parlour, have the church ladies down for afternoon tea. You're such a good boy, Benjie. You've made me so happy, knowing I can walk straight in that front door again. I don't know what I would have done without you all these years.'

Ben moved into the house alone, and he stocked his thirty acres with heifer calves bought cheap, and he measured the height of the gums trees he'd planted half a lifetime ago.

'We wait hundred year for tree will grow tall.' Annie had signed.

'When I'm thirty they'll be tall enough. I'll chop them down and they'll land on Aunty Bessy's side and I'll hammer a few planks on them, that's all.' A small boy's dream. It had seemed so simple back then.

Each year he trimmed his trees, only allowing the top canopy to grow. His care and cow manure had paid dividends. The trees were tall enough to reach his side of the river. He'd chosen his site well back then. The banks were high, the river narrow. They'd reach. But – . 'Give them year,' he said. 'Another year and I'll give it a go.'

Jack sat in May's parlour, drinking coffee. May wouldn't give an inch on her house rules and she could sniff out smuggled bottles with the perspicacity of a bloodhound on the scent of a decomposing bone. Through the years too much money had been emptied down her sink; he even stopped hiding them in the sheds. His mother still lingered here in odd places. Maybe she helped to keep him sober here; maybe he didn't want her ghost to see him drunk.

He was looking at her photograph now. Tall, and too fine, she was already sick when the photograph was taken. He placed the picture to one side and sorted through an old box of photographs. May leaned over his shoulder as he reached for a professional study of Ann and Liza. He turned to her. 'Is there any more of that shit in the pot?'

'Try calling it coffee, dear, and you'll never sleep tonight.' She refilled his coffee cup, handed it to him.

'Thanks.' He took up a sepia photograph of his grandmother. 'That's who she takes after,' he said. 'She's breeding, they tell me.'

'Is she happy? What is David like?'

'Who's happy?' Jack's hand reached for a professional shot of twin toddlers. Even at that early age, he could recognise himself. Identical in feature and dress, Sam was sitting straight, his smile fixed. Little Jacky had been trapped with one hand reaching for a bribe off camera. 'A wild little bugger, even back then,' he said. 'Look at good little Sammie sitting up there as if butter wouldn't melt in his mouth. Why did you marry that mongrel?'

'That's enough of that subject. We do not discuss Sam.'

'Bugger your rules, May. When is the perverted bastard's appointment?'

'Stop this, Jack! And it's at two.'

A disintegrating rubber band held a collection of yellowing newspaper cuttings in an envelope. Jack opened the envelope and slipped the papers out, reading again an old tale he knew well. He lit a cigarette and spread the papers before him on the table. 'The world screwed me good. This is my bloody land.'

'It belongs to Sam and to me.' He laughed, and she added, 'We all have to make the best of what life hands out to us, or we rot. I learned that early. You have to decide what your priorities are, or you go down whingeing, blaming the world for your own mistakes. Put those photos away now. They always upset you, always get you started on Sam. You were fine until you started looking at them.'

'Why did you keep them, then?'

'I don't know. To read whenever I start to forget. I don't know. Why did I do what I did that day? If I could go back, Jack, I would go back, and undo every mistake I ever made, but I can't go back, and neither can you, so we have to keep on going forward.' She reached for the cuttings. He pushed them out of her reach. 'I don't ever want to forget what I did that day. Give them to me.'

'Burn them.'

'No. Give them to me, Jack,' she said.

He shook his head.

'You've been drinking today, and I know it.'

'You want to castrate me. Lead me around like a spayed bloody pup.'

'I am not going to live my life in fear of what you may do while outside of a pint of whisky, and the sooner you accept that, the better for all.'

He ripped the photograph of the toddlers in two. Placed his cigarette on the face of the twin who wore the smile. 'I hate that bastard. I hate his very name.'

'For God's sake. Will you ever grow up?'

Three weeks later the same yellowing newspaper cuttings, plus photographs were tossed to the kitchen table in Warran. Bronwyn stood back, dusting her hands, well pleased with herself. 'It's all the old stuff about you and Liza, Annie. The old man brought it from Narrawee. We can get some copies,' Bronwyn said.

Ann stood at the door watching David's eager hands searching, selecting, rejecting. 'Bubble, bubble, toil and trouble – ' she said, then she left the room, left them to the papers and the past.

They heard the car engine fire, heard the car roar away.

'I probably should have shown her first. I thought she'd be ... be interested,' Bronwyn said, but David was deep in the photographs.

'Look at her expression. She's looking out on a world filled with magic, Bron.'

'Yeah. From all accounts, it turned into a nightmare. I shouldn't have done it, David. At least I should have warned her. I thought she was over it. I thought she'd like to have some shots of when she was a kid. Mum never took any of her.'

David sat, reading and re-reading the old news. He could remember the case. As a youth he'd followed it for weeks in the papers. The child he had read of then, was now his wife. How had he forgotten the name? And his mother, how had she failed to associate the name? Distance? Liza Burton was the one they'd never found, thus hers was the predominant name.

He read each cutting, shuffling them into order before him, remembering the boy he had been when he first read of the missing children. His mother's comment, 'They've found one of the Burton girls – '

ANN ELIZABETH FOUND BURIED ALIVE IN CELLAR
FATHER TELLS REPORTERS 'I TRUSTED MY MOST PRECIOUS POSSESSION TO A PROTECTOR OF PERVERTS'
POSSIBLE SIGHTING OF LIZA AND EDWARD CROW IN SYDNEY
TINY ANN ELIZABETH STILL IN COMA

Ann Elizabeth Burton. Wife of David Taylor. It explained much.

David's mind was miles away when Bronwyn walked back to the room, placing Ann's watch on the window sill. 'She still hasn't got that catch fixed. She'll lose it one of these days.'

Without a word he took the watch and walked away.

'I'm going to nick up to the library and get some copies before I take them back, David.'

She followed him to the bedroom, watched him drag the briefcase from beneath the bed. With no second thought, he fitted the small key into the lock, and the case sprang open, revealing a strange nest of treasures. Small fabric scraps entangled in the key of a wind-up mouse. A handkerchief. Old envelopes. A stained dog collar. And pages, hundreds of pages, folded small.

'I've stirred up a bloody hornets' nest,' she said, and she left him to it.

He was still sitting amid the litter when she, and the scent of food, breezed in an hour later. 'Annie not back yet?'

'No.'

'I got some Chinese. Come and get it.'

'Come here,' he replied. She walked to the door, frowning at the bed covered in papers. 'It's unbelievable,' he said. 'They go back to the sixties. This one is from 1967.' Keeping up a running commentary, his hands continued their search. 'Here. Read it, Bron.' He was tossing the pages down now, one after the other.

Bronwyn leaned against the door jamb, shaking her head. 'You know if she sees you, she'll be hopping mad. She used to keep all her stuff in a golden syrup tin when we were kids. No-one considered touching it.'

David checked his watch, then quickly repacked the briefcase. He kicked it deep beneath the bed he shared with its keeper. 'She's probably gone up to see the old slug.'

In the kitchen, he poured two glasses of beer, and they drank, and they ate, their heads together, looking at aged photographs, reading old headlines. When the bottle was empty and the plastic containers bare, he took an old motel breakfast menu from his pocket and handed it to Bronwyn.

She blew a smoke ring at the ceiling, her eyes following it. 'That's her stuff, David.'

'Just this one. Read it for me Bron. Tell me I'm paranoid if you like.'

Bronwyn shrugged and she read the words aloud.

Blood red on the white on a summer night, drawn forth by a jokers lance

Black were the wings of the demon things, frenzied by the dance –

'I didn't know she wrote that sort of stuff. I like – ' She caught David's expression, and knew she'd said the wrong thing. 'But I've got rotten taste in literature. Ask Ben. I've read everything Chef-Marlet has ever written and I'm sweating on his next one.'

'I didn't ask for a critical appraisal. She wrote it the night we got back together. I found her at dawn sitting on the bathroom floor, scribbling on the back of the breakfast menu. She said she was making a shopping list.'

'So it's a bit ... Annie. You have to know her; you're married to her for Christ's sake! She's always been different. She couldn't talk for the first six years of my life. We all thought she was deaf and dumb. You know that, don't you?'

'I don't know anything about her, Bron. I learn more about her when she's asleep than when she's awake. She talks.'

'You know she even talked one night before she could talk. I know that sounds a bit wacky, and I've never told anyone else, but we used to share a double bed, and one night she disappeared, didn't come home. Showed up at dawn and ran off again with some milk. I was about seven, but I'll swear on a stack of Bibles she was talking in her sleep that night. I couldn't understand it all, and I was going in to wake Ben, when she stopped. A month or so later she spoke in church. "I don't want to," she said, as clear as day. Everyone nearly died of shock. Best church service I ever went to.'

'I suppose Ben would have been old enough to remember what went on at Narrawee,' David said thoughtfully. 'I might go up and have a word with him.'

'No-one knows what went on. That's the trouble. Ben remembers her coming home though.'

By nine-thirty, David was sitting in Ben's back room at the newsagent's. 'It's the business in Narrawee that I'm trying to get a handle on,' he said.

'I can't help you. I haven't got a clue what happened to her.'

'What do you know?'

'Mum was in hospital. Bronwyn had just been born. Dad was off on a binge somewhere and Mum sent a telegram to Narrawee. May arrived. Johnny was fourteen, I was about eleven. We stayed home to look after the cows and chooks, and May took both girls back with her.' Ben silenced, shrugged. David waited.

'Well, that's all I know. Mum came home with Bronwyn. She wanted the girls back. Dad was still missing. Sam kept making excuses. They couldn't get away at the moment. They'd be up next Friday. Then when Friday came, they'd be up the following Wednesday. He sent up some classy photographs of the girls.'

'Like this one?' David took the photograph of Ann from the envelope. He handed it to his brother-in-law.

'Yeah,' Ben said, his eyes darting to the door, to the window. 'That's the one Johnny took with him. Is he back?'

'No. No. Bronwyn found them down at the farm. There's other stuff too. She got some photocopies.'

'Johnny's probably dead. Dead six months after he left home, or he would have been back for Annie. For months after she came home from Narrawee, he wouldn't make a move without her, then he ups and goes, leaves her screaming on the road – but that's not what you're here for, is it?

'Johnny got into awful strife when Dad found out the girls were in Narrawee. I reckon he would have killed him if Ponsford hadn't turned up. Anyway, both girls were missing. It was all over the papers. It's a wonder you don't remember it.'

'I remember, but I had no idea that one of the kids was Ann.'

'Annie's always been pretty close-mouthed. There was a bloke, a worker missing too. They reckoned he'd taken the girls. Dad caught the bus down to Melbourne the next morning. He was too upset to drive. Then Sam found Annie and took her to hospital.

'Dad stayed down there for over a month. When he brought Annie home she wasn't the same. She couldn't speak ... didn't seem to hear. Screamed. Huddled in corners and screamed. Mum was scared of her, so Johnny took her over.

'She hadn't started school. It was a long walk, and Liza wouldn't go to school, but Annie was sort of born reading. Read anything she could. Read my readers when she was five. I started school late too. She could write a bit before it happened, and when she came home, Johnny got through to her with writing stuff down, then he sent away for sign language books.

'She took to it like a duck to water. I remember the day she made the sign for dog.' He patted his knee. 'She loved the dog – old Mickey. Johnny would show her a sign once and she'd remember it. This went on for ages, over a year. Johnny took off when Annie was almost eight.'

'No idea why he went?'

'No. That's what I could never work out. He saved her life when she was a baby, you know. She was born dead and Johnny got her breathing. He sort of adored her, I mean, who wouldn't. She was such a relief after Liza. Anyhow, where was I?'

'Johnny – '

'Yeah. Dad never believed that Annie was deaf. He'd hit her, try to make her talk. He'd creep up behind her, make noises. She'd have her head in a book, or anything else she could pick up. Anyhow, he'd come into the room and bash two tins together, just to see if Annie reacted. She never did. But he could make her react by showing her pictures from Narrawee, letters from Narrawee. He'd get her screaming. "If you can scream, you can talk," he'd say, and he'd keep it up for hours – and so would she.

'Johnny started fighting with Dad. He always got beaten, but he'd get in a good punch or two. He tried to keep Annie away from the house when Dad was in it. She was with him the day he and Old Fletch's son were poking around out at the old burial ground, down Dead Man's Lane. They found some bones that weren't Aboriginal.'

'It was in the papers. I was about the same age as the kids who found them. One of them died, didn't he?'

'Yeah. John Fletcher. Within a week, he was dead. Encephalitis. His mother, old Fletch's wife, was a bit mad. She hated Australia, and she came down to our place after the funeral, carried on like a nut, blaming Johnny for taking her boy near taboo land. Reckoned the blacks had pointed a bone at her boy for disturbing the graves of their ancestors. All the kids used to go out there in those days. Back in the sixties, nobody worried much about sacred ground. Anyway, she committed suicide that night. Jumped off the bridge with three flat irons tied to her belt. Poor old Fletch. He didn't drink before that. Hasn't come out of his bottle since.

'It wasn't long after, Dad was getting stuck into Annie, and Johnny just sort of quietly picked up the fire poker, and he swung it like a golf club, hit Dad over the head. We thought he was going to kill him. Mum pulled him off, but you know, that was the first and only time I ever saw Mum put anybody before Dad. Dad's on the floor, out to it, bleeding like a stuck pig, and Mum is packing up Johnny's stuff in his school bag. She gave him the money out of her egg-money jar and told him to run and not to stop running until he'd put a thousand miles between him and Mallawindy. And he did, eventually, with Annie screaming behind him.

'Ever noticed how Annie doesn't cry? From that day to this, I've never seen her cry, David. Not once. He'd belt her until she was bleeding, and she'd laugh at him.'

trust

~

Ann drove for hours that night, her mind travelling in circles that kept bringing her back to Uncle Sam. She'd seen him that one time at the open day, had met him and liked him, but when she and David married, it was in Sydney, with a celebrant and stranger witnesses. No church, no guests, and no Sam to give her away. No Malcolm either. David couldn't stand him.

She hadn't been back to Narrawee. May still wrote, still telephoned – if not so wearied by the tumbling thing within her, she might have driven down to see May tonight, but the thought of her own bed drew her back to Warran, to her own Narrawee.

David had owned the block in Mahoneys Lane since he was twenty-one. It was a twenty minute walk from the town centre, but only five from the river. Nob Hill, the locals called it. Her house sat well with its older neighbours.

She'd planned it on the old Narrawee house, built it in white brick. She'd copied the windows, the white steps to the front door, but instead of a cellar beneath the house, they had a two-car garage, with a large patio for a roof, and circular metal stairs leading up from the garden. They had five bedrooms, three up and two down, a large lounge upstairs and a kitchen/family room below. It was sparsely furnished. There had not been time yet to hunt for the items she wanted, so she did without. In her mind, it was always for after the baby. If there was a baby.

Time, with Ann's watch, had been missing for hours. As she drove down the deserted main street, and past the town clock, she noticed its hands drawn down in a scowl. Tonight the whole world was scowling at her. David would be scowling too. He didn't like it when she took off into the night, but there were times when the house became claustrophobic and she had to run.

Roger had been on her mind tonight for the first time in months. He'd bought her the watch, and it was too expensive to lose. She'd given back his ring, but he had her name engraved on the watch. He wouldn't take it back.

'Some you win, and some you lose, pretty lady,' he'd said, and slid the ring onto his smallest finger. He asked for no explanation, and she gave none, but for days after, that gold ring on the small finger brought back memories of Johnny, and she didn't know why.

She'd left Melbourne two weeks later. Packed up her flat and moved to Albury. It was closer to Warran, and David. It was in Albury that she picked up a line on Johnny.

'It's been driving me mad for days. Every time you come in here you remind me of someone,' the woman who worked in the milkbar said, then she took out a photograph of Johnny, a box on his shoulder. 'I dug it out, last night, and remembered his name. John Burton. I worked with him at the Shepparton cannery for a few months, back in the sixty-nine peach season.'

Ann had taken the photograph. Photograph of a boy. She always thought he was a man. 'Where did he go? Do you know – ?'

'He kept to himself. A bit of a loner, then when the peaches ended, all the casuals were put off. He said he'd be going home.'

But he didn't go home. Ann had the photograph copied and framed. It wasn't a good shot. Out of focus, indistinct, faded like her memory of him. David was taking his place, using up his space. Too tolerant David. She'd have to go home, take his baby home to bed. She patted her stomach, let her hand linger on the movement of a small foot as she yawned.

'Getting crowded in there, eh? Don't knock it, kid. It's safe.' Her position altered, she rubbed at her lower back. One more month. Just one more.

Dee Williams, her doctor's wife and neighbour, said she enjoyed being pregnant. Ann loathed it, loathed its restrictions; it stole her running, her freedom. Pregnant women only ever reminded her of her mother, and of the baby boy born dead on the floor. Her fault. If she hadn't gone out that night, there would have been another brother. She didn't want to breed, but the one within her didn't care. Since the fifth month, it had been doing well, but like its host tonight, it was tired of driving, its own small feet running, attempting to get out.

She parked her old Holden beside David's, and crept around the back of the house, too weary to search for her missing watch. It would be in her car, somewhere.

Ted Crow. Ted Crow. Annie's voice was always louder at night.

'Shut up,' she said. Light-headed with weariness, she boiled the jug and made a cup of tea, then she pulled a chair up to the table and sat.

Dark bird, guarding secrets.

'You in my head, and aerobics in my belly. What is left of me?' she asked, and she sipped her tea and craved a chocolate biscuit, but didn't have the energy to get up and get it.

Red fish lost mid dappled shadow ...

'Shut up.' The words meant nothing to her, but she'd have to write them down. Get them out of her head and on paper before she slept. Too often little Annie's voice startled her from sleep, words spoken, or not, she didn't know.

She found a chocolate biscuit and a writing pad, she took a pen from the shelf and sat again, biscuit in her left hand, pen in her right, left elbow on the table, supporting her chin while the words spilled to paper. Then the pad was pushed away. She slumped in her chair, head on her hands, too weary to shower and go to bed. Maybe she'd crawl into the spare bed and let David sleep.

'Where have you been to this hour, Ann?' He was at the passage door.

She sprang upright, snatched at the pad. 'My keeper has come for me.' He stepped forward, placing his hands on her shoulder. Her back to him, she lifted her arms, held them wide. 'Got the old straight-jacket ready?'

'What have you been doing?'

'Trying to pick up a few clients.' She patted her stomach. 'This put them off.'

'It never puts me off. What have you been writing tonight?' He reached for the writing pad.

'The memoirs of a pregnant cow,' she said, ripping the page out, crushing it in her hand.

'It sounds interesting.'

'It's not.'

'How can you see to write in the near dark of this room?' He flicked on the overhead light, picked up her watch from the windowsill and offered it. And she looked at his eyes, knowing, knowing what he'd done and hating him for it.

'You snooping swine,' she said.

'I didn't consider it snooping.' Her hand reached for Bronwyn's cigarettes. She took one out, lit it, daring him to comment. 'That's not good for the baby, and it's a stupid habit. You don't need it.'

'Habits are easy to make, and to break.' The legs of her chair protesting, she pushed back from the table.

He caught the hand that held the paper. 'I've probably read worse tonight, Ann. Give.'

'Take it. Take them all. Publish them. Tall tales and true.' She threw the paper at his face, tossed the watch with its small key after it.

He caught the watch, placed it again on the windowsill. 'You are my wife, Ann. Sit with me. Start trusting me.'

'Trust? You go through my personal things and then speak of trust.'

'Trust,' he replied. 'I trust you. Why can't you trust me?' He smoothed out the paper and stood beneath the light, frowning over the minute script.

You cannot see the dark bird, and yet I know him well,
Lost in dappled shadows, guarding secrets, hiding lies.
Scarlet swimmer, mid the black mists in the place where demons
    dwell,
Open your eyes.
Where came the faceless memory, disguised now by that name
It came in from the garden, to the place of little light,
One for sorrow, two for joy – Then the waiting time, the pain,
of too long night.

Annie E. Burton

'Annie Burton,' he said. 'You don't like me to call you Annie.'

'It's my pen-name. I'm going to bed.'

'Not yet. I want to talk. We don't communicate, Ann, not on anything other than a surface level. I'd like us to try to make a start tonight.'

'What do you want to know? I write. It was my job for years. The words come, I write them down.'

'I'm not particularly interested in how you do it, only why. You can start with the one written on our first night together. Don't deny it. I read it, and I remember you writing it. Blood and prancing demons with their lances. How am I supposed to feel? How could you crawl from my bed and write a thing like that?'

'A perfect night for it poor Roger might have said.'

'It was the happiest day of my life. I thought you were happy too.'

'I was. It's not about ... about you. You know I was happy, David.'

'But you are not happy now?'

'I am. You . . . you just want to own me, own all of me. Everything. You suffocate me.' She picked up the scrap of paper. 'This too. You want it all, David, and it's too much.' She stood, and he caught her wrist. 'Don't hold me. I want to go to bed.' His grasp remained firm. She sat again, stared at the cigarette burning away in the ashtray. 'Let me go, or I'll scream.'

'What is the poem about?'

'I don't know. Let me go.'

'I don't believe you.'

'Then we're wasting our time, because it's the truth. The words come from a part of my subconsciousness that I can't contact on a conscious level. Make sense?' He shook his head. 'No. It doesn't make any sense to me either. It never has. I'm tired, David. I'm eight months pregnant, and I want to go to bed.'

'We will go to bed later, and don't pull the pregnant bit with me. You were not concerned about being eight months pregnant when you ran out of here, nor were you concerned that I might have been worried sick about you. Talk to me, Ann. Start back at your beginning. Tell me about Narrawee.'

'Read all about it. You've got the cuttings.'

'I did, and I spoke to Ben too.'

'Ben couldn't tell you anything.' With her free hand she attempted to prise his fingers free.

'He told me what he knew.'

'Sharing my life with you is only a habit, David. It's living with someone rather than living alone. Let me go. You're suffocating me.'

'Sit with me. Talk to me.'

'You went behind my back to my family. You talked about me. You're threatening me, and I don't like it.'

'Do I look like a threat?'

'Yes. Yes, and a snooping bloody swine.'

'Part and parcel of being married, Ann, is the licence to let your tongue fly at times and know that your partner will understand and forgive. It's not the well-mannered game we play, with two parallel lines drawn through certain subjects that I must dance forever around, making sure I don't overstep a margin. I'm tired of the dance, Ann, tired of your secretive ways, tired of your desire to be free to come and go at will, and with no explanation. And that bloody briefcase. Every time I saw it, I wanted to know what was in it, but I respected your privacy. Well, tonight, to hell with privacy. I want a wife.'

'Keep your voice down. You'll wake Bronwyn.'

His voice grew louder. 'Then let's wake her. Get her out here. Who knows – perhaps together we might be able to sort you out. I can't do it alone, I know that much.'

'I don't need sorting out. I've handled it. For years, I've handled it. I just want people to leave me alone.'

'Handled what?'

'I don't know. Shut up.'

'Open up to me. Tell me what it is you're handling. Give me the truth for once, Ann.'

'You get the truth. You always have.'

'Maybe I do, but I want more of it. Tell me what happened in Narrawee.'

She laughed then, her eyes raised to his. 'Now you've discovered who you're married to, you want to hear all the dirt. You're just like everyone else, aren't you? Get your kicks from another's misery. The newspapers make a fortune out of people like you.'

'Talk to me, Ann, and stop trying to change the subject. What happened to you in Narrawee?'

'Good question. Very good question.' He waited, watching her, until slowly her eyes met his. 'I could fake an answer for you. Is that what you want?'

'Tell me the facts, as you remember them, Ann.'

'The facts. Preferably starting with the disappearance of Liza. That's what you want to hear about, isn't it? Everyone is interested in Liza.' Her words were bitter, and he made no reply. 'Get your pencil and paper ready, David. Use the back of Annie's poem. She won't mind – just as long as you don't destroy it. Write at the top, exclusive interview with the surviving Burton sister. Come on, write it down, David.'

'Stop your nonsense. I don't want to write it down.'

'I loathed Liza. I was jealous of her. That's number one fact. I can't remember what she looked like, but I know I loathed her, because Dad loved her, and because he loved her best, Mum had to. They gave Liza everything and I got her hand-me-downs. I didn't mind her old dresses and shoes but hand-me-down love stinks. It stinks.

'Number two fact. Ted Crow, the kidnapper. I know his name. I've always known it. I can give you a description of him, but I can't remember him. I'd underline that, because it may be very important. You should be writing it down. You could probably sell it to the newspapers for a fortune.

'Number three fact. I know I spent half my time in Narrawee, watching Liza, trying to keep her out of the cellar. The cellar had a flight of steep and narrow stairs, very old. These are all known facts, David. Number four fact – '

'It looks as if you might need your fingers to count on,' he said releasing her wrist. 'Stop fighting me. Just tell me what happened.'

'But that's the punchline. I don't know what happened. I honest to God do not know – and I don't want to know.' She rubbed her wrist, reddened by the struggle, and he took her hand, kissed the inside of her wrist.

'I'm sorry, my love. I didn't mean – '

'Like to hear my hypothesis, David? Like to hear what I've believed since I was sixteen? Want to know why I ran away from you, went to Melbourne that night?' He nodded, but remained silent. 'I think I'm a murderer, David. I got a picture of pushing Liza down the stairs. I think I killed her.'

Night silence. The clock ticking. The sound of breathing. His eyes watched her, worried now. 'The newspapers blamed Ted Crow.'

'When I think of Ted Crow, I think of freedom. I think of blue sky and flying free. When I think of Liza, I remember blood. I remember the stairs and the black.'

'Tell me, my love. Let it out.'

'I've let it out. Now I'm going to bed.'

'What about Crow? Why didn't he come forward if – ?'

'Maybe he took the body away, buried it. He must have done something to make me think of free, and why do I remember his name, but nothing else of that bloody Thursday? May blames him for taking Liza, but I think of him as ... as clouds, and I think of ... of, Push me Johnny, push me high, I'm a bird and I can fly, high up to the clear blue sky. I made Liza Burton die.'

'What woman in her right mind would leave two small girls in the care of a gardener? The paper said he'd only been working there for a few weeks.'

'Sam was in Queensland and she ran out of bread.'

'They said Sam found you.'

'He hired a car and drove home. It's about twenty hours down the Newell Highway.'

'Why didn't he fly back?'

'Why? Why? Why? Who knows why? Maybe there was a plane strike. Who knows anything? Why was I locked in the cellar? Who locked me in, David? Old Ted Crow? If he kidnapped Liza, or killed her, why didn't he kill me, kidnap me too, to cover up his crime? And if he locked me in, then why do I think of him as freedom? Stop asking me why. I've gone over this a million times, and there are no answers. It's mad, David, and it's been in my head since I was a kid. Night and day, day and night. Ask me to describe Ted Crow.'

He shrugged. 'Describe him, Ann.'

'Sandy hair, about forty, he spoke with an English accent. How could a six-year-old child remember that, but not the man? Ask me if he had a long nose? A bald head, and I don't know. Was he fat, skinny, tall, short? I don't know. Did he speak with a broad accent, or did he sound like Prince Charles? I don't know.'

There was nothing he could say. He sat there, staring at her, shaking his head. He'd asked for this, but it wasn't what he'd expected.

'Say something. Don't you look at me with your pity. I want your love, not your pity.'

'I'm ... I'm trying to take it in, understand. That's obviously why you don't like lifts, the underground trains.'

'I dare say it might be. Glad we managed to sort something out tonight.'

'You should have come to me that night, told me then.'

'I've told you now, and you hate me.'

'I love you. Keep talking. More might come to you.'

'There is no more. You've read what came later, so you know more about it than I. They think I climbed on the wardrobe, built a staircase of crates up to the window. I don't remember doing it. I spent weeks in hospital. That part is like a nightmare. White beds. Strangers' hands always touching me and I couldn't get away. Dad. Sam. Crow. The core of my brain is like a ball of crumpled facts that the air has been sucked from. It's shrivelled into a hard lump of black that I can't unravel. All I remember clearly of the hospital is a boy. He read me stories – like Johnny did. Fairytales. He gave me a magic place where I could get away from the black, and he somehow moved me from behind that lump of black, to a place beyond it. But the black is still in my head, David. It writes the poems. Not me.' She sat watching him shake his head. 'Interesting isn't it? Good bedtime story? Feeling sleepy yet? Want to sleep in my bed tonight, or have you got some hang-up about sleeping with a murderer?'

'Stop it, Ann. You've probably imagined pushing Liza, but even if it were true, you were only a baby. Do you remember pushing her?'

'I remember wanting to. I remember when I was four, wanting to smash her head open and see if her blue eyes worked the

278

same as my doll's.'

'I love you, whatever you've done, or think you've done, that can never change. Would you speak to a professional about this?'

'What do you think?'

'It would be better for you to get it all out in the open.'

'Better for my well-being, or yours? You could always put a padlock on your door.'

'Shut up, Ann.'

'You started this, David, so hear me out, and believe me. If I were to learn for a fact that I had murdered my own sister, I wouldn't be able to live with it. I wouldn't want to live with it – or want you to live with me. Stop your digging. Please. Stop watching me, and let me forget it again. You're making me feel trapped, and I'm a wild screaming animal when I'm trapped. I have to get away, and at the time I don't care if I leave half my life in that trap. I ran from it once, and I can do it again. If you value what we have here, then work at helping me to forget that day, because there won't be much left of your wife if she ever remembers. She did something so bloody terrible that day, that for seven years, little Annie Burton stopped speaking, hid from it.'

She took the page, smoothed, folded it. 'My hand wrote this. I know it. I watched it write. But my head doesn't write it, David. It pours straight from the tip of my pen. It's like it comes down a direct line from that black core of facts. I don't know what I've written half the time. I only know that it cleanses a place inside me, gives me breathing space.' She swallowed, held his eyes. 'But . . . but the words, the words, ''my husband, my husband, David,'' they're like a shield around me. They fill me up with blinding white light, and the dark place that has been inside my head for ever hasn't got a chance against it. My life here with you is a sanctuary like none I've ever known. Please God, David, please don't make me run from you again. I've got nothing without you. I am nothing without you.'

She reached out to him, and he opened his arms, and he took her, held her, rocked her.

'Shush, my love. It's all right. Shush. I'll be your shield, your sanctuary. I'll be whatever you need me to be. I'm on your side. Always. Always.'

'Only you,' she said, her face buried against his chest. 'Only you and Johnny ever made me safe.'

the mouse-wheel

~

December 1988

Amanda Elise Taylor brought May running from Narrawee. She brought Ellie out of Mallawindy. She tempted Malcolm from his typewriter, and Ben from his shop. She twisted Bronwyn around her tiny finger, while a year seemed to melt into a brief cluster of days, and Christmas of 1988 arrived.

Ben came with a teddy bear almost as tall as he. He handed it to Ann. 'Never can think what to buy you, Annie. Happy birthday for yesterday.' He laughed as she took the soft toy. 'You can give it to Mandy if you don't like it.'

'No-one ever gave me a teddy bear. I love it,' she said and she kissed its nose, and wished she knew how to kiss Ben.

His youth, like his hair, had been stolen in the past years. He was ageing, moving directly from freckle-faced youth to middle-aged man. Ann hadn't seen it happening. Too content in her own baby-scented world, she no longer looked outside. They were still good friends. Occasionally a hand sign from their childhood was utilised to explain a thought not easily put into words – but not today.

'Where's everyone? I thought they'd all be here.'

'Bronny and Nick are always late, and David's gone off to pick up the chickens. My heart isn't into cooking poor old chooks.' She sat the bear at the table, then walked to the stove and prodded her baked potatoes, checked her pudding, not yet at home with kitchen skills. She sat, took up her needle, and settled to sprinkle a bridal veil with seed pearls.

Ben watched her needle flying, making invisible knots. 'I don't know where you get the patience to do that sort of stuff, Annie.'

She turned to him, her hands still a moment. 'It's therapy, and a lucrative hobby, Ben. Something for my hands to do. They still want to talk – never took kindly to staying still, so I keep them busy,' she said. 'Anyway, who are you to speak of patience? You, with the patience to plant trees and watch them grow for twenty odd years? Any patience I have, you and your trees taught me.'

'They reckon my bridge will never work. That engineer bloke from Daree says it'll sag in the middle, could end up damming the river. He's a decent bloke though. He gave me a bit of a design – said not to tell anyone it came from him. He reckons the only way it's got a hope of working is if I fix a pole right through the centre of each tree, then put in stays angled up to the pole from each end. I'll have to reinforce the top end of the trunks on Bessy's side, and trim off a bit on our side – ' His face grew younger as he spoke, and his freckled hands drew pictures in the air. 'He reckons the stays will act as a sort of cantilever to hold the trees up in the middle, stop their sag. I've bought a heap of bolts and stuff, and some massive angle iron. We'll dig out a bit of clay on both banks so I can bed them in. It's just a case of finding the nerve to fell them, and getting it started. But I keep chickening out.'

'Do it, Ben. Anyway, what if it sags or falls into the river? It might flood Mum off her land.'

'Yeah.' He smiled, a gentle Ben smile that the years could never alter. 'More ways of killing a cat than choking it with cream, eh? I'll have to give it a go soon. Can you remember the day we planted those trees, Annie?' Ann nodded, and stitched on. 'You look happy lately. Happier than I've seen you looking for twenty years.'

She glanced up quickly, surprised by his words. 'I am, I think. I'm in a permanent state of high. I can almost see a future with Mandy.' They were silent for minutes. She broke the silence. 'I never wanted to have kids. I was scared Mandy would be born dead like Mum's last one. Now I can't remember a life without her. We want another one, or two, or three.'

'Ever think about Johnny these days?'

'Only always. I still dream about him. The weirdest dreams – .'

'You know I can remember the night you were born ... just like it was yesterday. I remember the gunshot and swimming the river in the dark. Johnny made me do it. He was an eight-year-old kid, and I was five. I thought he was so old, because Grandpa said he was big enough to carry a pocketknife. All I wanted was to be as big as him so I could carry a pocketknife. I wonder if he's married, if he's got kids, Annie?'

'I always dream of him as alone, wandering the sand dunes.'

'He could have died. Ever consider that?'

'No. No. He's not dead. I've contacted the registrar a couple of times. Anyhow, I'd know if he were dead. I'd feel the space in here.' She placed a hand on her breast. 'We'll see him again one day, Ben.'

'I used to think so once, but I've sort of gone past it. I used to think a lot of stuff once. Reckoned that I'd probably get married, have kids of my own. My future sort of doesn't go beyond felling my trees these days. It's like I've got to build it. I've got to.'

'Then get them down and get on with your future. You've got plenty of time for kids. You're younger than David.'

'I feel about ninety some days.' He shook his head and looked away to the sound of a car approaching. 'I don't think I'd ever try to raise a kid in Mallawindy.'

'Leave the hole.'

'I can't. I swore once that I'd never let him drive me out. Can't break a promise, Annie.'

'Bloody promises,' she said. 'We hog tie ourselves with promises. Who but we ever keep them? It's Johnny's fault. Remember, Ben. If he promised something, he'd do it. Remember when we thought all the wild red poppies that used to grow in the top paddock had died?'

Ben nodded. 'He searched until he found one for you. He built a chicken wire fence over it and covered the seed pods with a lolly bag. He made you a little garden full of poppies the next year.'

'Yeah. He promised me he'd come back, Ben. He promised that if I – .' Her hands signed tears, and Ben smiled.

'You weren't meant to take him literally, Annie. He made a lot of promises that day. He told Mum that if he ever set eyes on the old man again, he'd kill him. Do you remember that one?' The room had gone quiet. Only the potatoes sizzled in the oven. Only the clock ticked on the wall. 'That's why he's never come back. He can't, Annie. I think he's waiting for him to die.'

Ann stood, folded the tulle and placed it in a pillow slip. 'Get out of Mallawindy, Ben. Don't waste any more of your life.'

'It's my mouse hole, Annie. Dad built me a mouse-wheel in there. He taught my little feet to scuttle around in circles, and I've been scuttling the same circles so long, I'm worn in too deep to ever get out now.'

Malcolm Fletcher, also invited to dinner, arrived, preventing further talk of scuttling feet.

A second Christmas slipped by before Mandy's bald head sprouted its crop of curls. They were gold, as Liza's curls had been gold. Her Nanna's hair, Ann said. Never Liza's. Never.

Malcolm was captivated by the infant. He came each Friday,

frequently bringing Ellie along for the afternoon. Age had brought peace to Malcolm, now he watched that same peace seep into the eyes of the one he'd long ago claimed as his own.

'You've done well with her, Burton, but explain to me why you insist on using the common Mandy? Amanda has a regal ring to it. This one warrants a regal title. You'll agree of course, Mrs Burton.' His tone brooked no denial, and Ellie nodded, nodded, pleased at last to have another baby to hold.

'What's in a name, sir? A rose by any other name would smell as bad. I think she needs a new nappy,' Ann laughed.

Still sir. Always sir.

'I'll do it, love,' Ellie said. 'You should be toilet training her, Annie. All of you children were trained by two.' Ellie took the little girl's hand and walked with her to the bedroom. Ann was finally receiving Ellie's love, if by proxy. Mandy got many kisses and cuddles from Nanna.

'Liza was still wetting her pants when she was seven,' Ann said, passing a nappy.

'She was born with a weak bladder, love. It wasn't her fault. My word this one looks like her. Getting more like her every day too, aren't you, Nanna's darling.'

Without warning, Ann snatched back the nappy and finished the changing herself. She picked up her child, held her too tight. That's who Ellie was kissing, cuddling. Not Mandy, but the memory of Liza. 'She's nothing like Liza. She's a Taylor. She's David. He was blond as a kid. She's got his eyes, the shape of his face. She's not a bit like Liza.'

The subject effectively closed, the visit ended soon after, but when Ann and Mandy were alone again, Ann's ire was still escaping.

'You don't need second-hand love, my sweetheart. You've got enough without her leftovers. You're nothing like that vile, snivelling little pants-wetting bitch.'

'No bile bits,' Mandy commented.

Ann laughed. 'Mummy is naughty. She must learn to keep her mouth buttoned and not to let things slip in front of tiny parrots, mustn't she? But you're not like her, and I won't let them say you are.'

'Not bitta fings, Mummy?'

'No, my lovely. But I mustn't do that again. I mustn't. I mustn't. You need a Nanna, and you'll have one. Mummy will have to learn to keep her big mouth shut.'

two old men

~

Malcolm's snug little cottage, positioned directly across the road from the Burton house, had twin bulbous bay window eyes that followed Jack's every move. He had wind chimes too. Bells from hell, they dangled from wide eaves, taunting Jack in the dead of night, their distant jangling gnawing at his brain.

Thick as thieves were Ellie and Malcolm, drawn together by Jack's own grandchild. Nobody took Jack to see it, but he'd seen its photograph on his lounge room mantelpiece. 'Poor bloody Jack is nothing,' he snarled, sucking hate from his bottle. 'Take him nowhere, give him nothing,' he muttered on while the wind chimes played.

This was his lot in life, to be treated like shit, tormented by a world that would not give him his due. Too old to get work, or too unreliable, his annual income was eroded by inflation, and Ellie's money cancelled any hope of a government hand-out. She bought him a slab of beer on Fridays, which he drank on Saturdays, but she wouldn't buy him whisky.

He needed whisky and new clothes too, and a new car, but he needed to get to Narrawee to get them. Bloody May wouldn't let him have his whisky in Narrawee, and he needed that more than cars or clothes. Whisky dulled memory, bought him a misty peace.

Bloody bitch of a woman, too smart for her own good, and his. She wanted him dead. Wanted him out of her life. Poor bloody Jack Burton, backed into a corner and no way of getting out, backed into it by bloody Saint Sam. A bastard, too good to be true.

'Take a dive you saintly bastard,' he screamed. 'Buy yourself a boat and go overboard. Go for a tour of the inland and die of bloody thirst. Disappear off the face of the earth and let poor bloody Jack have his turn. I want to go home.'

The August winds were back, and the wind chimes raucous when Jack ran out of whisky and went prowling with a half brick. He tossed it through Malcolm's bay window, and considered tossing a gallon of petrol and a match through with it, but he held back from petrol. Burning brought back memories of another burning. He settled for ripping the wind chimes from their hook, stamping on them, then tossing them to the road.

The following afternoon he booked up some petrol to Ellie and drove himself to Warran and to the address he found in the telephone directory.

The house surprised him. It looked a bit like the old place. He drove backwards and forwards, cursing his father and Sam until he saw his grandchild run into the front yard, saw her chase and pick up a kitten. He parked his car and walked to the low fence to take a closer look.

It was Liza.

He looked at the hair and he wanted to breathe in its scent. He looked at the soft limbs and he wanted to hold them, feel them holding him. And the silly little mouth that had planted wet kisses on his cheek. He wanted it all back. He wanted it. The world had looked different when he had her to hold. He could have been different.

'Could-have-beens don't count any more, they just lie on the floor till they all blow away,' he said, his eyes misting as he stared at the child.

Narrawee was his. Liza should have been growing there. Should have been. Could have been. She would have been a second Ellie now, her beauty unspoiled by work, her gumption not knocked out of her by that bloody church.

'Oh, shit,' he moaned. 'Shit. How could a man have done what he's done? How can he keep on living, knowing what he's done? God, you bastard, help me. Somebody help me.'

'Hello man.' His grandchild walked towards him, the complaisant kitten looped over her shoulder.

'Hello yourself,' he said.

'Is you a bad man?'

'No. I'm just poor old Jack Burton,' he said.

'I dot a pussy cat.'

'You take him around the back. You go around the back to Mummy now, or pussy cat might get out on the road,' Jack said.

'I done go on a woad.'

'No. You mustn't go on the road. You go and find Mummy.'

She was close. Too close. Close enough to touch, and his hand rose, wanting to touch the golden curls. But he didn't touch. He backed away and returned to his car.

His wheels screamed away from the kerb, and he burned rubber back to the highway, burned off the last of his tread, then broke every road rule through the town.

He wanted fate to wipe him out, and when it didn't, he considered aiming the car at a telephone post or a tree. Get it finished, like his old man wanted it finished. 'Bloody hard old bastard,' he howled. 'Bloody old mongrel bastard. It's your fault. It's all your fault. You stole my bloody dreams.' The road home was a blur before his eyes, as he screamed out his hell, his hate, his hopelessness.

Malcolm Fletcher met him in the middle of the bridge. His big Ford refused to give way, so Jack faced him, front bumpers duelling. Malcolm had more weight behind him, and heavy duty tyres. Slowly Jack's Camira was forced back, pushed into the bridge, pushed off to the verge of the road. Malcolm waved his hand and drove off into town.

The Camira wasn't going anywhere. Jack had never lifted its bonnet; motors and greasy hands were for mechanics. The motor moaned and coughed until the battery died, and he climbed out of the car, looked at the damage. He'd never liked the Camira, so he kicked in its door, finishing what Malcolm had started. He walked back to the bridge, and kicked the bottom rail, stained by the car's paint. He kicked it until it broke away and fell to the water. He considering taking the big dive himself, but Ellie had insured his life years ago. She'd end up winning by his death.

'I'll shoot the cold bitch first. I'll take her with me. If I'm hanging on to her apron strings, she might bloody get a man through the pearly gates.'

He was limping when he walked into the kitchen and picked up his gun. 'Say your prayers, you praying bitch,' he said, the barrel against his wife's ear. 'Let Jesus know we're on our way to glory.'

'Bronwyn's been here, Jack. She took your cartridges out.' Ellie's newspaper was open at the crossword, a pencil in her hand. She watched him slide the drawer open, snatch up two cartridges and slip them into the gun. But the urge to die had left him. Fate. Snide bloody fate always foiled his plans. The trouble was, he didn't want to die. He wanted Narrawee. He wanted the grandchild to come to him, lift her little arms to him. He wanted a new start for poor bloody Jack, where someone would love him. He wanted his mother.

'What's a five letter word, ending with D, meaning harvest, love?'

'Yield, you ignorant halfwit.'

'Thanks, love. It fits in with eleven.'

'You wouldn't miss me if I were dead, would you?'

'Of course I would, Jack. Don't say silly things. Goodness me, I miss you every time you go away.'

'Miss me like you miss a bloody boil on your bum, you lying bitch.'

While she pencilled in the y-i-e-l, he walked back to the bridge where he sat and patiently waited for his neighbour. And he let him have it. Let him have both barrels in the radiator.

Ellie offered to pay for the damage, but this time Malcolm refused to settle for money. He rang the local cop, then Ellie used his phone to ring the NRMA. The cop and the mechanic arrived together and Jack's car limped off home to Narrawee, but only after Ellie put on her sunglasses.

Ben drove her to Warran the day after. 'Make her sell up, Annie,' he begged. 'Go and throw a match at the house. Burn her out. Don't let her go back.'

The glasses hid Ellie's eyes, but Ann could see beyond them. 'Can't the cops pick him up in Narrawee?'

'They don't want him. Fletch refused to take her cheque, but she gave it to the cop. It's an unwritten law at that bridge, Annie, that the bloke on the river side gives way to the bloke on the town side. We all do it. Fletch does it too, with anyone else. The old coot has had a running feud with the old man for twenty years, and everyone in town knows it.'

'He ruined your Dad's car. It sounded like death warmed up when he drove away. I hope it got him to Narrawee,' Ellie said, more relaxed today – even with her blackened eye. Happier today, more talkative.

'And for once in his life he was stone cold sober, Annie. Fletch was drunk as a lord. He belted into the old man with his walking stick.'

Ann laughed, but Ben wasn't laughing today.

'Jack is all right if people would just leave him alone – ' Ellie started.

'Don't give me that drivel, Mum. I'm sick of hearing it. Sick of the whole stupid farce.' Ben turned to Ann. 'And sick of seeing her like this, too.'

Ann had stopped smiling. Ellie was studying her fingernails and twisting the worn gold band on her finger. Almost worn through, dented now, but it wouldn't come off. The ring would have to wear off.

'Sell the farm, Mum. Buy a unit up here. Let us live out a few of our years as a normal family. Do you think I want Mandy to see you like ... like that?' She snatched the sunglasses. Ellie covered her eye with the hand that wore the dented ring.

'That's my father's land, love. And it's my life. Your Dad never means to hurt me, and I never ask any of you to worry about me.' She reclaimed her glasses.

'Have you any idea what our childhood did to all of us? The old cry, "Run for the river, loves." The old lie, "He doesn't mean it, loves." The old plea, "Don't drink any more, Jack. Please Jack, I'm sorry, Jack." For Christ's sake, Mum, what had you done to be sorry for? I never knew. Why do you stay with that maniac bastard?'

Mandy, momentarily forgotten by all, now nodded from her perch on Benjie's lap, 'Dat manat basad, Mummy.'

Ben laughed, he laughed until he cried. Then there was no more laughter, only silence, and the old clock wearing time away. Ann stood helplessly there. Her hands reached out, but they didn't know what to do. Should she hold him like she held Mandy, pat his back and whisper soothing words? He'd break in her arms.

Mandy knew what to do. She knew about the magic of baby kisses, and she kissed the freckled hand that hugged her to him. 'Das all bettered now, Unka Benny. Maddy tissed him all bettered. You hab a look at my pussy cat, Unka Benny. Nanna said her is going to get some babies, fwom her tummy.' Wriggling to the floor, Ben's finger held fast in her hand, she led him away.

Later, his tears locked underground, Ben returned to the kitchen door, Mandy in his arms. Ellie picked up her handbag. 'Are we ready to go then, love? The cows are waiting,' she said.

'You go your own way to hell for all I care, Mum. I give up

on you. This little one is worth ten of you,' Ben said softly. He kissed the golden curls, then placed Mandy down.

That night Ann spoke of many things. She spoke of Johnny and of the day he ran. She told David of her recurring dream of Johnny, of walking with him through a field of bones, a golden ring of light over his head. She told him of Ben's visit, and her voice trembled when she spoke of her brother's tears. 'Dad was down here, David. He told Mum that he saw Mandy playing out the front with the kitten. He'll come back one day when he's drunk, and he'll do something. He'll steal her from us. I want to take her and run. I want to hide her away, safe from him.'

'If you see him, call the police.'

'For looking at his granddaughter? They'd laugh at me.'

'Then laugh at yourself, Ann. What did he do apart from look?'

'I don't want him to be able to look at her. I don't want him to think she looks like Liza. She's mine. Mine and yours. He's polluted this place, David. He knows where she is, so she's not safe anymore.'

'She belongs to Ben and Bronny too, and old Fletch, and Nanna. They love her. They all love her. Would it be fair on them, fair to Mandy, to take her away from this safe little pool of love that surrounds her? No more smuggled chocolate frogs from Aunty Bronny. No more of Nanna's special baby eggs.'

'I never worked on fair principles, or what was right or wrong for others. I just know that it's right for me, for us. I'm not strong enough to protect the whole world, David. Just us. Let me protect us.'

'I love this place, the neighbourhood. I'm not prepared to pull up roots and head off into the unknown. Given time to consider, I don't believe you are either, Ann.'

'There's something on the wind, David. I can hear it. I can hear little Annie whispering in my brain. "Run. Run. Run."'

brief candle

~

December 1990

Heat was on its way, but this day personified the word fine, and Ann felt fine. Seated high on the patio, she was embroidering a tiny blue dress with deeper blue rosebuds, and nursing a secret she could barely contain. She should have been down there at David's side, pulling weeds in the sun, but on this day of days, she wasn't brave enough to move. Time, a mad whirr of a thing that never stood still for a second, had gone on a go-slow strike. She wanted today gone, and the next, then she'd scream her secret from the roof tops. But not yet. Too soon yet to raise a false hope.

'Mummy. Mummy. Daddy gived me a worm,' Mandy chuckled as she ran up the stairs and placed a fat worm in her mother's hand.

'Yucky,' Ann said, as all mothers must say 'yuck' when confronted by earthy surprises. 'Put him back in the garden, sweetheart. Worms make our garden grow.' She stitched on. The frock was almost finished, only the hem left to hand stitch. For that she would need to fit it. Mandy was growing fast, her frocks and tiny shoes outgrown in weeks. The red playsuit she was wearing today was already too small; still, this dress should fit through summer. The frock folded across her lap, she sat looking down at her family, and listening to the tinkle of Mandy's voice discussing the habits of worms.

'What work does him do, Daddy? Mummy said him do's good work.'

'That particular bloke is a special weed worm. His job is to make the weeds grow tall in our lawn. He does his job very well, doesn't he?'

'Does bees do some good work? an' butterflies? an – '

'Fingers away from bees. Bees sting.'

'But him do's some good work, Mummy said.'

'He makes honey. Special honey just for you, but he also stings tiny fingers if they try to stop him making his honey, so don't touch.'

'I love honey. Dat's a nice bee.' Minutes later the bee struck and further weeding was cut short. 'I don't like dat bee. I like just worms. I won't get him's honey, just some honey fwom da shop, Daddy.'

They had been too successful with her. Wanting her to grow brave and free, they'd allowed her to be free to explore her world. She swam like a fish, she climbed trees like a monkey and poked sticks at jumping spiders for the pleasure of watching them jump. Strong-willed and lion-hearted, Mandy was stalking bees again within minutes, her hands held behind her. David, never a sun lover had joined Ann in the shade.

'Mandy! Put Daddy's shovel down before you cut your toe off. Remember, Daddy told you about the bee, and you didn't listen.' They laughed, watched the shovel hastily leaned against the fence, wide eyes peering closely at a swollen finger. 'She learns from experience.'

'Perhaps one of the more wilful three-year-olds, do you think?'

'She's a Taylor,' David replied. 'We always get our own way in the end – although some things take longer than others,' he added meaningfully, planting a kiss on Ann's laughing mouth.

Mandy saw the kiss. 'Why did him tiss you for, Mummy?'

'Because you did what Daddy said. You made us happy. Come up here in the shade for a while – or put your hat on for Mummy.'

'I done want hats on.'

'Daddy wears a hat. Put your hat on and be just like Daddy.'

'In a minny.'

'So much waste in my life, David,' Ann said, sipping orange juice while waiting for the bee chaser to grow bored with her game. 'I could have had six babies by now.'

'You would have if it had been up to me. Anyhow, you still look sixteen – and a bit,' he tempered his statement.

'A big bit. By the time Mandy is twenty-one, I'll be almost fifty.'

'I feel ten years younger than I did ten years ago.'

'Mister Fletcher never changes. Mandy called him Papa the other day. He's always with Nanna, so she put two and two together in her own little head, and decided he was her Papa. You should have seen his expression. I thought he was going to howl.'

'He loves her, and you. If he was forty years younger, I'd be jealous.'

'He's been a father to me. He has a right to the name of Papa.'

'Mandy!' David jumped to his feet, ran for the fence, grasping the escape artist as she attempted a quick getaway. Tossed over his shoulder, he carried her up to the patio and seated her on her own small chair. 'Stay,' he said. 'Sit. Look at your sensible Tiddy having a rest in the shade.'

Tiddy was the magic word. The cat tolerated most treatment, but she wasn't in the mood for games. From the corner of a slitted eye, she watched Mandy approach and as a small hand grabbed, the cat rolled over, did a quick side step and scuttled for the staircase, Mandy in hot pursuit.

'Don't run down those steps, Ma – '

But a bare foot slipped, and tiny hands grasped at a railing too far away. She twisted, and in slow agonising motion, rolled over, and over, around and around to slam headfirst onto the concrete path below.

Ann reached her first. She picked her up, brushing the gravel grazed forehead with her fingertips as the world tilted, hushed. It was another time. Another place. The blood trickling from a nose. Blood on golden curls. The red bib. It belonged –

Not here. Not in this place. Never in this place.

She stood looking at the blood on curls, her hand drawing away.

'Get her in the car, Ann. She's not breathing.' David's voice cut a pathway through the swarm of hornets in her brain.

He drove to the hospital, the horn blasting while Ann breathed her own life into the soft mouth. They ran with the child into casualty.

Doctor Williams arrived minutes later in his golf clothes. He ushered Ann and David from the room. Stunned they stood in the long polished corridor, where nurses bustled and trolleys rattled and squealed. They heard no cry from the room with the swinging door.

Then he came out. The man with the green smock over golf clothes. He walked alone through the swinging door. 'I'm sorry,' he said.

Sorry? Silly little word. They ignored it, their interest centred on the swinging door.

'I'm sorry.' Hands held open, empty, useless to save or comfort the couple waiting at the door for their golden child to run to them. 'We lost her,' he said. 'We lost her,' his words repeated in an attempt to force the fact home.

They looked at him then, and there was silence. A deafening silence.

Shock waves started slowly, jarring, crushing heart and flesh and bone.

Searing heat of flame, greedy for oxygen, sucked air from

lungs. It burned them, dissolved tissue, depleted brain and limb of air to live.

Run ... I told you.

Mouth open, gasping in a vacuum where eyes no longer saw, for there was nothing left to see.

Swept away. All swept away.

Disintegrated by the blast.

Devastation.

All gone?

All gone.

Run! You would not heed me.

Disembodied hands, clutching, clawing, as sinews snapped. Nothing to hold them. Nothing to hold. Fend off the hands, shake them off like so much flotsam.

Too cold. Shivering, teeth chattering cold, while icy fingers scratched and gouged the flesh from her soul.

Run.

Nowhere to run.

Wasteland. All gone now.

All gone.

All gone.

How soon a fine world can decay.

The car was gone by the time the men reached the casualty entrance. Doctor Williams drove his neighbour home. Like one of the walking dead, David followed where he was led, and when his neighbour left, he sat, vacant eyes staring at a child's swing-set swinging lonely in the breeze.

Ann returned long after the sun had gone from the sky. Her hair was wild and windblown, her eyes heavy lidded, blood still stained her shirt. She refused to look at David. From the garden she had picked up the small blue frock she'd been embroidering. It was soiled. She placed it on the table and walked to the sink.

He couldn't look at her, look at the blood. His first words weren't easy. She didn't hear them anyhow.

'Come to me. I need to hold you, to cling to someone. Come to me, Ann.'

'Do you want a cup of tea?'

'No,' he said. 'Sit with me. Forget the tea. Reach out your hand to me, I'm dying, Ann.'

She ignored him. Didn't want to hear. She was functioning in a place outside of thinking. She placed two cups on the table, found sugar, milk, poured the tea, then seated herself on the opposite side of the table, out of his reach. He watched her stir her tea, watched her taste it, add more sugar. He saw her remove a pin from her lapel and place it in the tiny blue frock that lay between them on the table. Her gaze followed his to the frock. Again she took it in her hands.

'Put it away. Please put it away. Please change that shirt,' he said.

'She's growing like a weed. Three months younger than young Frances Williams and inches taller already.'

'Stop it, Ann. You can't hide from this. Mandy is dead. Put that dress away.' He took it from her hands, placed it over the back of a chair. Minutes passed while her eyes stared at the tiny frock. The only life in the house was a cat, meowing for food at the back door.

'Get it out of the house,' she said.

David walked to the phone, dialled. He spoke quietly, then returned to the kitchen, to sit again until he heard a tentative knock on the front door. The telephone began its ringing as he handed the cat to a work mate. Ann pulled the plug from the wall, cutting it off mid ring. Then all was silent, as it should be.

'Your mother always wanted us to have her baptised,' David said minutes later.

'I know of a good cure for warts too. Toss a dead cat over a convent fence at midnight. Let God's little helpers look after their altar boys. I'll look after my baby.'

'For God's sake, don't do this,' he moaned.

'Good old God just wiped out the only decent thing I ever did do. With one God almighty stroke of his pen, he wiped her name off the roll. The Lord giveth, the Lord taketh.' Again she sat in silence smoothing the frock. She smiled as she fitted three fingers into the tiny sleeve and buttoned the neck.

'Put it away,' he whispered.

There was too much pain in her. Something was going to give. Words were becoming hard to find. Her hands spelt 'Cremation,' then she forced that one word out.

He shook his head and stared at the blood-stained blouse.

'We let her live . . . free. We have to let her stay free.'

'No.'

'There will be no hole in the ground, not for my baby. No-one will . . . cover her with dirt, David.'

'Stop it, Ann. You're killing me.'

She glanced at him, then back to the small dress. She brushed at the dirt, shook the frock, brushed at the dirt.

'Put that dress away.'

'It blew across the lawn to meet me. She's out there, David.'

'Put it away, and take that shirt off.'

She stood, looked at her shirt, and she stripped it from her as she walked to the sink. She took up a box of matches and held a flame to the fabric of the tiny frock. The cotton caught, blazed. She dropped it to the sink, watched it turned to ash, as her hands, two graceful entities, began signing. 'Fly to her with north wind. Fly to cloud. Home to sunset. You be free now my beautiful. You be yesterday dust on the wind that blow in my eyes. Make me tear.'

The room had filled with smoke. The smoke alarm was chirping. It was better. She couldn't hear him, barely see him.

He slapped her. 'Scream, damn you. Cry for her, Ann. Cry,

and give me leave to cry with you.' He slapped her again, then his hands strong on her shoulders, he shook her like a puppy at play with his rag toy.

She looked at him, rubbed at her eyes, trying to clear them of smoke, of fog. 'I want to cry,' she said, then her hands signed. 'My heart cry too big.'

He watched her hands, but could not read them. He looked at his own hand, reddened by the slap, then at her white face, her reddened cheek. And he wept.

She had never seen his tears before. She watched the blue, blue eyes fill, overflow, trickle silently away. Her sigh, a series of sighs, she placed her arms around him, pressed her face to his. He had tears enough to spare, to share.

TAYLOR. Amanda Elise. Infant daughter of David and Ann.
She has left this world to explore eternity. Funeral private.

Bronwyn on Ann's left. David on her right, so close to the small white coffin. It was covered with flowers. Everyone sent flowers.

I baptise thee in the name of the father and of the son.
Dearly beloved, we are gathered here.
Ashes to ashes, dust to dust.

Everything got swept away with yesterday's dust, spilled milk, a trickle of golden syrup, even blood. And if the wind couldn't blow it away, you shovelled it up and dug it into the garden.

Sweet Mandy, just another little pawn in the big chess game of life. One wrong move and checkmate. Pack up all the bits and put them in a box.

David out of reach, weeping again. So many tears. So like another's tears.

You invented me too strong, little Annie. You shouldn't have been so happy in Narrawee. You should have shed a few tears on my blueprint. Everyone cries. Look at Ben. His eyes are raw jagged wounds, pumping tears straight from his heart.

She drew her eyelids down, safe from Ben's pain, and she moved back, deeper into the dark place.

Can't breathe in here, Annie. Can't reach ... have to ... get away.

Ben watched her attempt to stand. He saw her collapse at David's feet.

word colour

~

Noise had colour, substance. Strange, she thought. I have never noticed the shape of noise before. Head turning from side to side on the pillow, she dodged a ball of crumpled noise that bounced off the ceiling of the hospital ward.

It was the cleaning time. The nurses were there, bringing with them their business-like noise. They changed the sheets, tried to wash her, comb her hair, but they couldn't touch her. Nothing could touch her. She was away, locked safe behind the looking-glass. Their noise, splashing against the looking-glass, only made her image less clear. But in the night, when the shadows hid the light, and nurses hid in quiet corners, she travelled unseen down the long corridor of the years, seeking that book of the yesterday time, where each white page was filled with Annie's words. And she had time to read all the pages, and they made her free. Free, but with no place to go. Only the bed. Only the pill sleep. She liked the pill sleep. Sleep was beautiful.

The man with the ocean blue eyes came to her bed often. He tried to touch her. She couldn't let him touch her. Each touch, each cluster of his words hammered at her brain, trying to make her remember the other one who had worn his eyes. She was gone. Gone with all the other yesterdays. Gone into black.

'Mandy,' he said.

The word hung before her. Lump of death squeezed into grotesque form. It creaked and crackled and fell on her bed from a great distance. A falling star, defiled by blood.

Don't look. Don't think.

'Physically strong,' the other one said.

'Sedative.'

They were coming too fast now. She backed off as the words spilled to her pillow.

Drug, tending to sooth. It unravelled slowly, like the words in the fat man's little blue book that had her name on it. Her name, written beneath the other name, the John name that wasn't her Johnny. The John who found the bones, not powdery, not bleached like other bones. No teeth, like the other skulls. Then that John died, and her Johnny ran away, his golden ring twinkling in the sun.

'Ann, Ann, talk to me.' Again his words came at her. Dear impotent missiles, falling like chocolate-coated snowballs.

He loved me best – better than Melissa. And Johnny and May, they loved me best, and Mr Fletcher. Four people loved me best in all the world. I was someone. They thought I was someone, when I really wasn't anyone. Funny really. They loved a reflection.

I'm just a reflection, an opaque rejection. I won't pass inspection.

'Psychiatrist. Tuesday.'

All mental disorders must be trained to erupt on Tuesdays, Annie Blue Dress.

A chuckle bubbled up from her core. She thought of her father and the spiders in his briefcase and the soft, funny mouse curled there and she wanted to giggle at the grand joke he played on the world, but the giggle burst before it reached the surface.

The blue eyes saw the giggle. They came close, then she saw the slim silver light fall from his pocket.

Slowly.

Splat to her sheet.

Cold metal splat.

Torpedo shaped splat. It sat there, waiting to explode, to blast her from this place. But she didn't want to leave this place. Not any more. Out there was too hard. Little Annie didn't want her to leave again either. They were glued back together where they belonged. Friends again.

She could touch the torpedo though, if she wanted to. Just touch it. Her finger reached out. Touched. It rolled the metal. She watched the light move as the sheet moved. Her finger continued rolling it forward away from light, back again and into light. Away. Back.

'Paper.' David was already halfway through the door. 'Where will I find a writing pad?'

'It's unlikely that pen and paper will help, David. Whatever is preventing her speaking is not physical. You saw her with her old teacher. He tried communicating with the deaf signs. I've already let it continue too long. Had I been made aware of her past history earlier, I would have suggested moving her to a hospital where they have the facilities – as Dr James no doubt will suggest.'

'Ben said she did this when they sent her away to the deaf school. Just nothing, a closing down, the nuns said. She came out of it, and she will again. She showed interest in my pen, Pete. That is the first spontaneous action I've seen since the funeral.'

'It fell to her bed. She played with it. She also kicked a basin of water at one of the aides yesterday – '

'No doubt telling them, the only way she could, to keep their hands off. She hates hospitals. I should have kept her at home like Bronwyn wanted me to.' David walked away in search of a writing pad.

The silver torpedo was lost when Ann opened her eyes. It remained lost for most of the day because little Annie didn't want her to find it. But she found it. She found it, clipped to the writing pad, tucked beneath her pillow. All through the next night she held it, and at dawn when the world was silent, she placed its point on the blank white paper.

Little Annie wouldn't make it move.

But as the light grew stronger, so too did the fingers.

Deep mid the gums where the soft winds moaned, and sang their song
    to the dusk.
I picked the flower from the tallest reed, growing out of a charred
    black husk.
And neath the soil, I saw the worm sit waiting patiently.
His name was death and black his breath.
But he smiled at you, and me.

High on a hill was the black crow's nest. They stole the flier's name.
You heard their words, you dried their tears, you played their silly
    game.
But the play is done. The waiting's o'er. You've found the key that
    fits the door
Now lovingly go fit their shroud. And with each stitch, we'll laugh
    aloud.

Oh silent night, unholy night, when all was fear, when all was fright,
You gave them time. You played your part.
Now the play be done, let the living start.

Annie E. Burton. Dec. 1990

'She's in there. She's still functioning on some level.' David and Doctor Williams spoke quietly beside the bed. For the first time in over a week, some of the strain had left David's face.

'You say she's got a briefcase of similar – '

'I'll dig it out and bring it with me in the morning. The psychiatrist is due around nine, you said? I'll want to speak to him before he sees her.'

'He said nine.'

'I'll be here.'

Williams reached for the pad as David slid it beneath his wife's pillow. 'I'd like to keep it, show Dr James.'

'She won't destroy it. She's never destroyed them. Leave it with her, Pete.'

'Does she look more relaxed to you?' David and Matron Hogan were standing beside Ann's bed.

'Hard to say, Mr Taylor,' the big woman replied. 'She hasn't altered her position for hours. Doctor left instructions that she was not to be disturbed,' she added, noticing the visitor's hand reach for a wisp of hair curling across his wife's mouth. Her patient ignored the contact. 'Perhaps she is more relaxed.' Eyebrows raised, Matron watched his hand gently stroke the woman's cheek. Then dark eyes opened. Wild eyes. They locked onto the blue. Slowly David withdrew his hand.

Ann looked at the hand, and to her own, and to what it grasped. It was his pen. Silver. Gift from Mr Fletcher at Christmas. She offered it.

'Thank you, my love,' he said. She sighed, then slept again.

David refused to leave. He sat by the bed, catnapping in the hospital chair. Matron Hogan, with some telepathic perception of unrest in her hospital, wandered the corridors in her dressing-gown. Near dawn, she brought two cups of coffee and watched with David a while.

'Doctor James is very good. A down-to-earth man, and not at all the stereotype image we are inclined to imagine. He'll probably suggest moving your wife to the psychiatric hospital in Daree.'

And Ann's eyes opened. They sought, found David. 'No,' she said, and he sprang up from his chair, leaned across the bed.

'No, my love.'

'No.'

'You'll stay here, close to me. I promise you. I promise I won't leave you.'

'Promise.'

'I promise.'

'He locked the door,' she said. 'He locked the door. It was him.'

'But now it's open. No more locked doors. I won't let anyone lock you in. I promise.' His hand reached for her hand. Her finger touched, and he linked his with hers, kissed her fingers. Her free hand rose to his face, wiped at tears. She looked at her hand. Damp, tasted the salt on her tongue.

'No more tears, my David,' she said. 'No more tears.'

'No, my love,' he wept. 'No more. You're here. No more tears.' Her hand fell back to the bed, and her gaze returned to the ceiling. 'Ann. Stay with me. Ann.'

'Tired.'

'Stay with me. Stay with me. Talk to me.'

'Hold me. Make me stay.'

Weak but determined, the next morning Ann left the bed. By the following evening, her bag was packed. Had she been strong enough, she would have walked home, but she wasn't strong enough to walk further than the garden.

The nurses gave up trying to keep her indoors. Malcolm Fletcher came early and stayed late. Bronwyn came too, but she didn't stay long. No smoking in hospital wards. She played with her packet of cigarettes while stalking the room. 'I'll see you at home tomorrow, Annie,' she said, and she left, a cigarette in one hand, her lighter ready in the other.

'That's what I need, sir,' Ann told her old teacher when they were alone again.

'I will have no part in procuring that diabolical weed for you, child.'

'Something to hold,' she said. 'Bronny knows. Something to hold on to when the world gets too hard.'

He turned away, understanding her need for something to hold. 'Pop into bed. Sleep and get well, child.'

'Please, sir. If you won't, I'll walk to the cafe in my dressing-gown.'

She had never asked one thing of him, in all of the years he had known her, had never made one demand, accepting what he chose to give. He purchased the cigarettes and lighter, then running the gauntlet of Matron Hogan and her watchdogs, he smuggled them into the one who needed something to hold.

'God bless you, child,' he whispered and he waddled away.

Ann walked down to the sunroom, now in darkness, she slid the glass door wide and crept out to the garden where she wandered beneath the country stars until the black of night gave way to the blush of a pink dawn. The air was warm, it smelt of roses. She loved the country nights, loved to wander the silent world of shadows and scents and scuttling things while the world slept. But this night was like none before. Morning would come, a new and terrible morning.

She knew it all now. She shook her hair back and lit another cigarette. Smoke sucked into her lungs, she strived to fill her mind, herself with anything, anything that might still her memories.

Doctor Williams found her in the sunroom at 10 a.m. The psychiatrist was waiting. 'He's here to see you, Ann. Come along. I assure you he doesn't bite.' Taking her arm, he led her back to her room where he introduced her to the lanky stranger.

Her strength was still away. Williams left, and she walked to the window, unready yet for strangers. She offered the new doctor a cigarette, expecting to sidetrack him into a lecture, but he accepted, producing a lighter from his pocket.

'Have a seat, Mrs Taylor,' he nodded towards a chair.

'I thought you preferred your patients horizontal. Does it give the average headshrinker a feeling of power?'

'Feel free to lie down if you'd be more comfortable. I imagine you must be feeling weak after so long in bed?'

'I'll feel a lot better when you leave for your next appointment.'

'Yours is my only appointment today. I spent some time looking at the contents of your briefcase, Mrs Taylor – '

'Ah ah. David explained, of course, that I am the medium for a wandering spirit. You should see me when I'm possessed, Doctor James, I froth at the mouth, bite, snarl. He gets a weekly rabies shot.'

'I am free until two. Do you know any good psychiatrist jokes?'

She raised her eyebrows and flashed a wide plastic smile that she held for a moment, then allowed to slide.

'You're claustrophobic, I believe, Mrs Taylor?'

'All the more reason not to commit me. Lock a claustrophobic woman in a padded cell and she'll go mad.'

'At what age did you realise you had a problem?'

'What has that got to do with anything?' she asked.

'It is a topic I thought you may wish to explore.'

Her fear of locked doors and city lifts was restricting. Perhaps she may sidetrack him yet, and learn something constructive in the process. 'The city,' she said quickly. 'When I first moved to Melbourne, I noticed that lifts sucked the air from my lungs. I can't use underground trains either. Everything slows down. Goes to black – ' She sucked on the cigarette, noticed her hand shaking, and she despised its lack of control.

'Continue, Mrs Taylor. Explain black. Do you faint?'

'How do I know? Black is black is black and there is no more.' She turned her back.

'Do you remember the accident, Mrs Taylor?'

'Discuss that particular subject and I cut the appointment short.'

'Fine. Fine. We'll find another topic.'

She ground out the cigarette and snatched up her packet, spilling the remaining cigarettes to the floor, and she left them there. Her hands, legs, stomach shaking out of control, she walked to the door.

'I had quite a long talk to your husband. He was able to fill in much of your early life for me. You sign your writing Annie, yet David tells me you dislike him calling you Annie.'

'People who write bullshit should always use a pseudonym.'

'Writers usually remember what they've written. Explain this one.'

'I thought you were trained to interpret its Freudian significance.' She stood looking out into the passage, and he walked to her side, where he leaned against the door jamb, sucking on his own cigarette.

'Your husband mentioned your father to me, Mrs Taylor. He suggested he was – '

'Stark raving mad? I'll agree with that in part.'

'David also said you were subjected to physical abuse as a child.'

'Did you hear the one about the navy psychiatrist who wanted to be buried at sea, Doctor James? Half of his patients drowned attempting to dig his grave,' she said.

'You obviously don't wish to discuss your father. Is there perhaps a topic you would care to discuss? Books? Politics?' he asked, returning to his chair.

'Are you into gardening? The roses are beautiful this year. The scent of them at night is – .'

'I leave my garden to the gardener, and he doesn't like rose thorns.'

'The gardener,' she said, then she shook her head, wiping the palms of her hands across her face.

For minutes he waited, allowing the silence to grow while she stared into the passage. 'Did you know you are a sleep talker? Your husband told me that you speak frequently of Sam's roses.' Her chin lifted. She turned to face him. 'You also speak of a Ted Crow.'

'You should be talking to David. He obviously knows the night talker more intimately than I, due to the simple fact that being asleep is not conducive to social intercourse, with self or even with any extras you dig out of your subconscious.' Panic, anger, had taken control of her tongue, words too sharp, words uncensored began sliding from it. Backed into a corner by their joint scheming, their sharing of her secrets, unconsciously now, she backed inside, stood with her back to the wall.

He was speaking again. She didn't want to hear him, wouldn't hear him. So easy to go back. 'No,' she said, determined to hold on until this man had gone and she had time to think, to plan her next move. But what? Nothing. Live with it? Die of it? Why bother?

'They tell us that our writing, and our dreams put us in touch with our subconscious. Allow us to express pain, admit to fear, Mrs Taylor. David said you did not cry when your child died.'

'Leave that alone.'

'We are allowed to cry for help. Your child was killed in a freak accident – .'

'Shut up about my baby.'

'Do you remember the accident?'

'I was born an accident. My whole life has been one bloody series of accidents. I remember nothing. I have nothing. No little girl. Nothing. Shut up about that.'

'But you do remember your little girl?'

'I remember nothing. It wasn't my fault,' she said.

'No. It wasn't your fault,' he agreed.

'It was. Stop humouring me. It was my fault. Everything is my fault. I built that house. I planned it. I planned those bloody stairs. I wanted that house. Always. Do you know that's all I could remember once – that house and the date of Johnny's birthday. They were the only things I wouldn't let go. Even when I tried to let it disappear into the black, it wouldn't go. I couldn't forget Johnny, wouldn't forget him. Won't forget him. I ruined everything because I wouldn't play her game. But she kept everything stuffed in the golden syrup tin. The doll's eyes, and all the stuff she bought home from Aunty May's – '

She stopped as suddenly as she had started, her eyes wide, her mouth open. The doctor was watching her. She felt the rush of blood to her face. She turned her back, stood rocking from toe to heel, heel to toe. Rocking. 'Jesus,' she said, and she covered her face with her hand. 'Jesus.'

Sometimes there is no choice – only one way to go. Like the night with Mr Fletcher – a one-way street. She had to get out of here. Get this done and get away. Give him a little. Get rid of him. She coughed, swallowed, then she turned to him, flashed a smile.

'Give that man a pat on the back. He's cured me. So now I remember the accident.' The psychiatrist nodded, and she didn't like his silence. 'She fell down the stairs. She was chasing the cat. Wearing a red playsuit. I remember the blood on her golden curls.' Still he made no reply. She stared at him, then she yelled. 'Is this what you want? Am I crying yet? Am I bleeding?' He held her gaze, but remained silent. 'I was on the front patio, embroidering a little dress, and – ' Her hand went to her waist. She stepped towards him, her eyes wide. 'I was pregnant! I thought I was pregnant. I – '

'Had you miscarried, rest assured it would have been on your chart.'

She looked to the chart on her bed. He picked it up, offered it. She sat, took the chart, studied it. 'Psychiatrists must need hides like rhinoceroses. What gives you the right to pick at people's brains?'

'Your parents are still living, I believe.'

'I want David.'

'Tell me about your father, Mrs Taylor.'

'What do they call those old gods, half man, half bull?'

'It escapes me at the moment.'

'That's my father. And Mum was a mother earth. She grew babies, then lost them. She lost ... lost three. Linda Alice was Mandy's age. Poor Mum. She got stuck with me, couldn't lose me.

Tried hard enough when I was – . She had the longest, most beautiful hair. Gold, like a shower of sunshine, and she used to have trouble with doors – and bulls. Ran into a lot of them. I used to fall out of trees. Funny really. We never had any falls when Daddy was out of town. That's what love can do to you. We were both dizzy with love when he was around.'

'Your brothers and sisters, were they also subjected to abuse?'

'They cried a lot. He always stopped when they cried, but I wouldn't cry, so he wouldn't stop. Logical. I could scream, though. God, I could scream. And if you don't stop this I might let one go.'

'You never cried?'

'No. Not since I was eight. I used to laugh. Same, only different. Laughter hurt him, but tears only hurt me. Gave me a headache. Made my nose stuffy.'

'You were eight when you returned from Narrawee?'

Startled by his use of the word, she spoke on quickly, attempting to cover her reaction. 'I was six when I came home . . . home from Narrawee.'

'So you were six when Liza went missing.'

'If you say so.' The palm of her hand wiped across her top lip, her eyes sought escape. The door was open. She could leave when she wanted to. Get this over with first. Get it done and then go.

'Continue, Mrs Taylor.'

'I think I've finished.'

'Ted Crow worked at the property when you were there.'

'My David, my very dear traitor. My shield with big holes in it.' She looked at the doctor. 'What else did he tell you?'

'Not enough, Mrs Taylor. Tell me about Ted Crow.'

'Nothing to tell. I don't know him. I'm suffocating in here. There's no air.'

'The window is open.'

'It's not enough.'

'You have been to Narrawee recently.'

'Narrawee, the money tree, where May-the-magic-lady lived. The happy ever after lady. She could go measure, measure, measure, and snip, snip, snip, and then her foot would dance on the old treadle-machine and there they'd be, fourteen pair of little girls bloomers made from one fine old linen sheet. Liza used to wet her pants. It wasn't her fault. Poor Liza, nothing was her fault. Poke a kitten's eye out with a stick and it wasn't her fault, you know – '

'Tell me about May.'

'She had a purse full of green money, but the shops weren't open the day we got there so she cut up a sheet.'

'And – '

'And she . . . she bought me a doll with sleeping eyes and she didn't make me give it to Liza when she cried for it either. So Liza threw her doll in the incinerator, and because she didn't have one any more she thought . . . thought May would give in, and May wouldn't, because I was her pet, and Liza bit me. I've still got the scar – . I'm imploding. I'm going to die.'

'Did you cry when she bit you?'

'Tears, tears, tears. You've got tears on the brain, Doctor James. Hydrophobia, hydrocephalus, hide of elephant.'

'Tears are our safety valve.'

'Bull men grow stronger on tears and blood, but you weaken them with dry eyes. Johnny told me that. Weaken him, he said – .' She sucked air, rose, walked to the window, pushing it wide, drawing in deep breaths of the warm air. Too many breaths, too fast.

James waited for her to make the next move. He waited for five minutes and still she stood, looking out at the garden, breathing deeply. He walked to her side, took her arm and led her back to her chair, where he offered her a cigarette and waited ready with his lighter.

'Why do I believe that you want to speak to me, Mrs Taylor? Why do I believe that for many years you have been desperate to

315

speak of your memories – confused as they might be?' Her head was tossed in denial, but he continued. 'I was both pleased and surprised to learn today that I had caught up with one of the Burton sisters. I was in my final year of psychiatry at Melbourne University in 1967.'

She stared at him, her fists clenching and unclenching, her face grey. 'I don't want to know this. I don't ... leave it alone.'

But he spoke on. 'I actually saw you one day. I remember those dark eyes, the cloud of black curls against the white of the pillow.'

'One of the poking, prying doctors. And you're still at it. White coats and stethoscopes. No trees outside the window. Just clouds and – ' Blood was thundering in her ears, drowning out the sound of her words. She silenced.

Her eyes were black pits. Empty, and for the first time, Doctor James considered his next move. He'd spoken for an hour to David, who held back nothing. Both men had agreed that if Ann had been responsible for Liza's death, it was better faced than repressed.

He took a stiff and yellowing page from his notebook, glanced again at the words written there in red crayon. Ann snatched it from his hand, shredded it. He picked up the fragment with the hole, worn through by a small moistened finger.

'Was the word once written there, *die*, Mrs Taylor?'

'Stop this. I can't breathe. Stop this.'

'The window is open wide.'

'It's never enough. There is never enough – '

'No locks. No bars. There were bars on that cellar window, Mrs Taylor?'

'Apples.' Her voice was barely a whisper.

He leaned closer. 'The employee who disappeared with Liza was never found. Did you climb up to the window, watch him ride away? Did he take Liza with him?'

'I ate apples.'

'Apples?'

'They had apples growing on trees at Narrawee.'

'An orchard?'

'A huge tree. Near the old house. Aunty May said it grew from a seed, and they are the best apples in the whole world. I can climb up the top, get my own apples. But I don't climb in Narrawee. I might get holes in my pretty dresses. My name is Ann Elizabeth in Narrawee, and she doesn't have holes in her dresses, not like little Annie had in Liza's old dresses. They put the apples in the cellar to keep them fresh and cool, and if you go into the cellar you can get the biggest apples.

'I won't go in the cellar, but Liza does. He gives her apples, and I said, "Don't you go in that cellar, Liza. He's bad. I'll tell Aunty May".' But I can't tell Aunty May, because ... because ... because it's too late. He put his dirty thing in her and now she's dirty and I have to bury her pants – .'

She screamed then. 'Stop me. Stop me. Someone stuff up my mouth.' Her fist slammed into the window screen and the wire ripped away from the frame with the force of her blow.

The doctor was by her side. 'Let's get rid of it, if it's worrying you. I think there's supposed to be a snib here somewhere.' He reached across her, removing the screen from its frame, lifting it to the floor.

Her mouth open, she sucked in air, too much, too fast. He offered her a cigarette. She took it, walked back to the bed, and when she failed to light it, she swore at her trembling hands. He offered his lighter, waited until she was sucking in smoke.

'What else do you remember, Mrs Taylor?'

'Stop it. Please God, stop it. What good will it do now? What good will it do to wake it all up now? Will it get you a write-up in the psychiatrists' journal? Doctor James solves 24-year-old mystery.'

'You are my prime concern at the moment. Consider me the interested third-party. I followed the story after you were released, always hoping that one day I'd read that the mystery had been solved.'

317

'Then you just solved it. She's dead. You're famous.'

His own pulse quickened, but he hid his interest. His voice remained quiet, soothing. 'So, she died there, Mrs Taylor.'

'Yes.'

'You remember the details of her death?'

'Yes.'

'Can you speak about it?'

She covered her mouth with a hand, then quickly drew it away. 'You take some sort of oath, don't you? A doctor's oath of confidentiality.'

'Be assured that nothing you might say to me will go further than this room – if that is your desire.' He drew a chair towards her.

Her next words were long in coming. Her fingers combed her hair back from her face, then she said softly. 'Can we go back to the beginning; back where you came in?' She picked up the writing pad, looked at the words she'd written there.

'Start wherever you'd like to start. Stop if you begin to feel uncomfortable.'

Silent again, her fingers fiddled, her mouth worked, attempting to create the right words. She swallowed several times, then it came in a non-stoppable torrent. 'I know this will convince you that I am stark raving mad, and you are probably the last person in the world I should tell, but I don't write those poems. I might hold the pen, but I swear to you that I don't even know what I've written half the time. I fold them up and poke them away. Later when I pick one up, it's like ... like something from a book. Author unknown.'

'But you know the author, Mrs Taylor.'

'What is the educated opinion of dual personalities these days, Doctor James?'

'They make good movie shows. What age were you when you first started finding these poems?'

Perhaps she was relieved by his flippancy. She glanced at him, then away. 'Little Annie was writing poems before she could write. I am the interloper. Me. Aunty May created me in a looking-glass when Annie was already six years old. She took little Annie back to Narrawee and she brushed her hair with a golden brush, and made it into long sausage curls. She dressed her in a beautiful blue dress with a white lace collar then she showed her, her reflection in a looking-glass. I was born. Annie named me Annie Blue Dress.

'Annie Blue Dress was special in Narrawee. Aunty May was the boss, even the boss of Uncle Sam. She'd say jump. He'd say, how high. May liked Annie Blue Dress better than Liza. Little Annie was happy, content to move behind the mirror image Aunty May had created. She'd never been special to anyone except Johnny. Aunty May was such an important lady. What she said was the law. She had beautiful clothes and a big car and lots of money, yet she preferred the girl in the looking-glass to Liza, competition winner, Daddy's Shirley Temple. Annie Blue Dress was strong too. The only thing that can cut glass is a diamond. Aunty May said so.'

Doctor James waited for her to restart, but when no words came, he prompted. 'Can you continue?'

'I was a Narrawee thing. It had to be put away when Annie went back to Mallawindy. We lived together, Annie and me, in a half-real world. For years, we were locked in some place ... like ... like paralysed spiders in a hornet's nest.' She looked away from him to her hands. 'Then Dad killed our dog when we were thirteen and something happened inside our head.' She shook her head. 'This sounds crazy.'

'Not at all. Continue.'

'Little Annie sort of backed off the night Mickey died. She loved Dad because he learned her sign language, and he used to explain things to her, say poetry to her, and tell her things about the world. Everyone would run away from him when he went crazy, but little Annie never ran, and sometimes it paid off. When his mad bull was gone, then the other one would come out of his

319

eyes and want to talk, so she stayed, and she waited, and she talked to him with her hands, and he understood her.

'Mum couldn't understand the signing. It was alien. Devil worship. Annie was some demon, sent to try Mum. Anyway.' She swallowed, licked her lips. 'Anyway, the night Mickey died, something crazy happened. It was like ... like walking out of a dark room into light. Everything was bright. The moon was orange and the land was cold, white, and the stars, and the tin roof – . Everything was light.

'He had murdered my dog. He'd killed him, shot him with his gun and left him in the moonlight, lying there in a pool of black blood. I hated him that night. Hated him. Hated him, but Annie made excuses, like Mum. The dog was dead on his feet. He was half crippled. But he was my dog. My dog.' She slammed a fist into her breast. 'A few days later I discovered I could talk, so Annie wouldn't be outdone. She started talking too, but inside my bloody head.'

'Where is she now?'

'She's me. I'm just ... just her reflection. The façade she shows to the world.'

'You're the one speaking to me, so what is she doing?' he asked with a smile.

'She doesn't do. She talks, makes pictures, writes poems. But it feels different now. Somehow, it feels different.'

'Tell me how it feels different.'

'It's like I've been half blind. Now when she makes a picture, I can trace it to its end. I can see what she can see.'

'What can you see?'

'Anything I want to see. I can even see that last day. Liza's red overalls and her frilly white blouse. A bib shaped like a heart on the overalls. Metal buckles that Liza wouldn't even try to do up. I ... I tried to teach her. It was easy. I couldn't understand how it could be hard for someone bigger than me. She was nearly eleven months older, but every day I had to help her do up her shoes, do up her buckles, like Mum used to in Mallawindy. She'd grizzle, ''I can't do it,'' so Mum would do it for her. ''I can't reach the tap. I want a drink.'' Mum would jump up, get her a drink. Not for me though. Never for me. In Mallawindy, Liza had a grip on everything that should have been mine. Like the doll I won in a raffle when I was four. We both had tickets, but my ticket won. I had to walk up to the stage and take the doll from Mrs Norris.

'Dad ... he wanted me to give the ticket to Liza that night, let her go up to the stage and collect the prize. She was the pretty one, the important one. She was Miss Tiny Tot 1963. But I knew my ticket had won. It was number 48. I was four, and two times four is eight. Johnny said so. He said when we bought it that it was my lucky number. And it was. He took my hand and he walked me up to the stage, and Dad couldn't do a thing about it because the whole town was watching him. Mrs Norris gave me the doll. It was so beautiful.

'I only had it for two days. No-one was watching him at home. He made me give the doll to Liza, but all she wanted to do was strip it and bite its finger off. I snatched it from her, and he ... Dad, knocked its brains out on the wall so neither one of us could have it.' She stopped, looked at him. 'Its sleeping eyes were flip-flopping orbs. I kept them. I've still got them.'

They sat in silence while the ash grew long and grey on cigarettes and was flicked off into the ashtray.

'I used to believe I hated Liza enough to have smashed her head open, picked up her eyes, put them in my golden syrup tin too. Since I was sixteen, I've lived with the fear that I killed her, pushed her down the stairs.' She covered her mouth, with her hand, shook her head. 'I didn't kill her Doctor James. I did not kill her, and do you know, that is all I care about. I don't care that she's dead, but I didn't kill her.'

'But you know who did. Continue if you can.'

'Where do I start? Where can I start? My head is like a tornado, and I can't get out of its way any more. May went shopping. She left Liza and me with him. We were supposed to be watching television, but as soon as May left, he came in. "The black cat has had her kittens in the cellar," he said. Liza followed him out, but I stayed inside. I tried to stop her going into the cellar when we first got to Narrawee. I'd stand at the door yelling Liza, Liza, Liza, but she'd never take any notice of me. I wouldn't go in the cellar with him.

'Anyway, that day, I think I can hear a car coming. I have to get Liza out of the cellar or there is going to be trouble. I've seen them before in there ... with ... He does things to her now. He used to just get her to touch him, but now he ... he does his things. I know, but I don't want to know, so I don't know. I just stay away.'

She took a sharp short breath. 'They're in the cellar. He's – ' Her hands now sought for words, sought the right word. 'She's got her pants off. She's on his knee. He's ... his face is – .'

'Go past it, Mrs Taylor. Go past it.'

'Aunty May is going to catch you, this time, you bad man.'

Her face hidden by her hands, she sucked air through the fan of her fingers, rocking, rocking backwards and forwards on her chair. 'It's my fault. Always my fault. I should watch her better. I should – '

He took her hand. 'Go past it, Mrs Taylor.'

'I can't. I can't. I can't.'

'I have the picture, Mrs Taylor. You witnessed the rape of your sister. Try to go past it.' She looked at him with empty eyes. 'Can you speak of what you saw?'

'Saw. Saw. What I saw. She gets her overalls on, but two legs in one leg. Brainless. Can't even dress herself. Stupid. Greedy.' Ann's fingers were in her hair, massaging her scalp, her elbows covering her face. 'It gets mad then. It gets terrible. He's yelling, crazy. He picks up a piece of old pipe ... water pipe. He hits out. Swings it at – . He hits her. Hits her head. I can hear it. Hear the smash. Terrible. Smash. Apple on concrete smash. It's like ... it's gone mad. It was – . There's blood. Noise and blood. I – '

He interrupted. 'Have a sip of water for me, and take it very slowly.' He filled the glass, held it for her, and when she was done and the glass was back on the table, her words tumbled out, eager to be free.

'He picked her up. She flopped in his arms. He was – . My back is . . . at the wall . . . near the door. Stone wall. Cold through my dress. Cold.' Then her hands began signing, and James called time out.

'A couple of deep breaths for me, that's the girl,' he encouraged. She did as she was bid. 'Another one now and hold it in your lungs. That's the girl. Hold it while we count to ten.' He spoke on, of inconsequential things, until her breathing returned to near normal. 'I think we'll give that day a rest, Mrs Taylor. Tell me about Johnny. David said you still advertise for information.'

'I have to find him. He left . . . left when I was nearly eight. I searched. If I saw the name, Burton – If I saw a birth notice. Engagement notice . . . in the newspaper, I'd send a card. Some wrote back. Not Johnny. Never Johnny. I searched Melbourne . . . made a thousand phone calls. In Darwin, in Sydney. I still search. Never hear.'

'How will you handle returning to the house where your child died?'

'I don't know. I feel . . . like Dorothy and Toto, picked up and tossed out of all they knew as reality, into a new reality. I don't want it.'

'This is a very pleasant room, a pleasant view of the garden. Stay a while. Give yourself time to come to terms with Mandy's death.'

'If I go home in two days, or in two years, it won't alter the new reality. I'm not Dorothy. I can't go back to the old. Mandy is gone. She's not going to be there in two days or ten years.' He nodded. 'Can I go now?'

'I'll want to see you again.'

'You've got what you wanted. There is no more.'

'I believe there is. I believe you suffered an almost total amnesia at six, and your little Annie voice, her poems are segments of memory from a time you chose to forget, a time that you now remember in total. I'm in Albury on Thursday. Could you – '

'Later.'

He flipped through the pages of a small diary. 'Christmas, then I have a conference. I'll be away for two weeks in January. I'd like to see you before I leave.'

'I just want to – . I need time to – . Later.'

'February, February the second. How does that sound?'

'Like six weeks.' She shrugged. 'Mum believes that God created the whole world in six days, Doctor James. Dad used to tell her that if he'd stuck around for six weeks he would have blown the whole bloody thing up again. But I like the look of the second, of the second, 1991. Almost a mirror image.' She stood and began checking empty drawers.

'Do you think it might be wise to wait long enough to have your pregnancy confirmed? Also, the authorities should be informed regarding Liza's death. You don't know where . . . where he took her?'

She shrugged. 'He buried her. I watched him. He buried her in the rose garden. She's somewhere near the middle. Under a rose. I think it was the Peace Rose. He dug it out, then planted it on top of her. There should be the remains of the water pipe down there too. He hammered it in with the back of his shovel, and I wondered if it was going through her heart. I didn't care. She was gone, and I didn't care. I must have been a delightful kid.'

'How did you evade him?'

She shook her head.

'Would you be prepared to give the police a statement? We could get an officer to come here, speak to you while you're waiting for that pregnancy to be confirmed. The gardener was in his forties. I dare say he may still be living.'

She turned back to the window. 'English,' she said. 'Sandy hair, about forty.'

He frowned, looked again at his diary.

the telephones

~

The day was almost over when Ann escaped the hospital. She knew she had to tell David of the pregnancy, but there was no joy in this telling. A child so wanted, a planned brother or sister for Mandy, had now become a painful link between the now and that better time.

'Mum called just before I left the office,' David spoke before her own words were ready. 'Dad had another stroke this morning. He's very low. They don't expect him to survive.'

'You'll have to go to him.' Then her words came, cold, lonely words. 'They did a pregnancy test this morning, David. It was positive.' His eyes filled. He slowed the car, glanced at her. 'Watch the road,' she said.

He parked in the garage, and they walked to the back door, and into the family room, once a place of a chuckling child. But it was empty now. The house was empty. Silent. It smelt empty. Ann couldn't settle. No dishes to wash, no toys to pick up. She walked upstairs to the bathroom and stood beneath a hot shower, washing the hospital from her, out of her hair, filling the room with fog. It offered no place to hide. There could be no more hiding now. She had set the wheels in motion, and they would keep turning until they reached the end.

Quickly she slipped into her dressing-gown and hurried back to his side. He was all there was. She found him stripping off his tie, his business shirt, and her hands reached out to him.

'You've been living in this place, David. You stood and faced it all, while I ran. I thought my lack of tears made me strong, but you are the strong one. I'm nothing without you.' He took her hands, gathering her into his arms. 'What have I given back, David? Look what I've done to your life.'

'You gave to me too much content. Shared with me my greatest sorrow, bore me a child who was perfection, and will bear me another.'

'I don't want to have it, David.'

'We will make it different this time, my love. We were too brave, too certain of our happiness.' He kissed her as they stood beside the bed, and she clung to him, his kiss kindling life in limbs too long dead. 'You're exhausted. For a moment I wasn't thinking. For the first time since – . I wasn't thinking, Ann.'

'Don't think any more,' she said, holding his face to her own. 'Take the thinking all away.'

Bronwyn had been to the house. She'd moved little dresses from wardrobes, taken away tiny shoes and dolls and prams. Too thorough, there was nothing left to show that Mandy had lived, but while David was at work, Ann found the photographs hidden away in the wardrobe. Golden curls, soft baby limbs and a smile that broke her heart. She had lived. And she would not be hidden away.

Christmas songs on the radio. Christmas everywhere. Ann faced each dawn of each new day, determined just to make it through to night. She placed the photographs back in the lounge room, returned the fretting cat to the laundry, and she waited for the telephone to ring.

So much to say, if she knew where to begin. But not now, not yet. Let the wheels turn slowly. Let them find Liza, then she would tell him. He didn't need more on his mind. His father was moving closer towards death hundreds of miles away across the ocean. She had to be strong. Keep it inside. She had to prove to him she was strong enough or he wouldn't go if that call came from New Zealand to fly.

And it did.

'Your mother said they don't expect him to make it through the night. You are going to him, David.'

'You come with me.'

'I can't. Not yet.'

'And I can't leave you alone. We'll go together, Ann.'

'He's your father. Go, or you'll never forgive yourself, or me.'

'Come with me.'

'Don't make me into a ball and chain around your neck. I've got a doctor living next door. I've got Ben, I've got Fletch, I've got Bronny. Anyhow, I can't go, even if I wanted to. I've already booked you through, left your return open, and you've got the last seat on tonight's plane to Sydney.'

'Ring Bronny and ask her to stay with you.'

'I will. Just hurry. The plane leaves in half an hour. I've packed your bag. Check it's all there before the taxi gets here.'

It tooted its horn minutes later, and Ann walked David to the gate. 'Ring Bronny straight away,' he said. 'I'll call you in the morning. You've got Mum's number. Call her. Tell her what time my plane gets in so she can pick me up at the airport.' Then he was in the taxi, waving from the taxi window, and too far away now to call more instructions.

Her arm fell to her side. She could feel his physical energy pulling away, her strength, her resolve, going with him. She stood on the footpath watching the taxi until it turned the corner, became lost to her view. Still she stood on, mentally travelling the bitumen road with the taxi, seeing it in her mind's eye turn onto the highway. She counted seconds, saw it drive into the airport gate, and she waited, too fearful to return to the house looming empty there.

'I'll be fine,' she whispered, 'I will be fine.' Slowly she walked back through the gate. She stopped beside a rose, her hand reaching to touch a weighty bloom, and a late bee settled on her wrist. 'Mandy,' she moaned. 'Mandy,' and she ran.

The chicken, she'd been cooking with care when her mother-in-law rang, was now black. She pulled off a drumstick and offered it to the cat who came to rub at her leg.

'You're just a selfish ball of fluff who doesn't know any better. You eat and sleep just the same. You don't know the old world has ended. Even your feeder has flown away. I can't function rationally for ten minutes. How can I live for a day?'

She turned away, switched on the radio, stood twisting the selector up and down the band. Christmas songs. ' – just like the ones we used to know, where the tree tops glisten and children listen, to hear – ' Again she twisted the dial. 'Talk to me, radio. Or you, Annie. Say something. Anything. Someone, talk to me. I can't stand this. I have to get out of here.'

The cat, bored with the conversation, walked away, stepping daintily over a dress-making pin in its pathway. Ann pounced on the pin. 'Careless fool of a woman,' she scolded, then a shiver travelling the length of her spine, she let the pin drop back to the floor. 'Doesn't matter any more, old pin. You can all come out and live on the floor. She's gone. Move your relatives out too. Tell them there's a whole world outside the sewing room for you to populate.'

She stood staring at the pin. Glittering pin, black bead head. Black onyx ring, worn on the smallest finger, sized for a much slimmer hand – .

'Stop it. Stop it,' she yelled. 'Ring Bronny. Or Ben. Yes. Call Ben.' She started towards the telephone in the hall, but stopped at the door. 'How can I ring Ben? His eyes will break me. Soft moss on a ring-barked gum tree. Green, oozing moisture. How can I ever see him again? I'll drown in your eyes, Benjie Burton.

'Jesus! Don't let me do this. Please God, don't let me do this.

Let's ... let's ring up the Mallawindy pub, Annie. Tell Jack Burton the cops are digging for Fool's gold in Narrawee. I wonder how Sam's taking it?' She laughed then. She stood at the table and laughed. She laughed because she couldn't cry. She laughed until her stomach cramped and she became afraid, and ran for the lifeline of telephone.

'Be there,' she prayed. 'Be there, my strong Bronny. I need you now.'

'Hello?' a male answered.

'Nick. Is Bronny there please?'

'I'll get her.'

Ann sucked air.

'That you, Annie?'

'David had to go. I'm losing it. Can you come? Quick.' It tumbled out. The bare untarnished truth. She gasped air as she leaned against the wall, her heartbeat slowing to a steady thump, thump, thump.

'See you in five, Annie. Stay on the phone and talk to Nick until I get there. He wants to ask you how David went about buying those shares.'

Just a ploy, Bronny's ploy, but she talked shares to Nick until Bronwyn walked in her back door.

They spoke that night of many things, and of Narrawee. 'I think they are digging down there, Annie. Did you see tonight's news? Police told reporters today they had received information on the disappearance of a seven-year-old girl who went missing in 1967. It's got to be Liza.'

'I sent them there. Told them where to look.' The truth. Clean. Cleansing.

'You remembered?'

'I think I did, but I've gone past the stage of knowing what's real, and what's not any more. If they find her, I'll tell you a fine story.'

'Tell me tonight.'

'Tomorrow. I'm pregnant, Bron. That's real. I knew before Mandy died. I was going to scream it from the roof tops. Now it's too late. I don't want it.' The truth.

'I know this sounds like the usual platitude, but things will look better in time.'

'Not in this house. I see her everywhere. I see her shadow on every wall, but the rooms echo with emptiness when I walk into them.'

'I love this place. It's the nearest thing to a home I know.'

'I thought I was building my own safe fortress. It turned into a nightmare too.'

'You look exhausted. Go to bed.'

'I'll sleep better once I know David is with his father.'

'Is he going to phone when he gets in?'

'No. He'll go straight to the hospital. He'll phone in the morning.'

'Then it's not much use sitting up is it? I'll climb into bed with you. You can kick me if you dream, and I'll wake you up. That's my best offer.'

The telephone woke them at 7 a.m. David's distant voice sounded so near. 'He's gone, my love,' he said.

'You saw him?'

'I've been with him all night. I stayed with him. He died before daybreak. I told him about the baby. He couldn't talk, but I felt him squeeze my hand. He knew I was there. I think I'll be able to get a seat out in the morning.'

'When is the funeral?'

'At ten – tomorrow morning. It's what Dad wanted. Fast. No frills.'

'How is your Mum coping?'

'She's strong. She says . . . says he's gone to look after Mandy. I tried to book on a flight tonight, but they are booked out.'

'Don't worry about me. Stay with your Mum for Christmas. It will be hard on her.'

'I'll leave straight after the funeral. Don't go near Mallawindy.'

'Why should I?'

'Promise me. I've got a bad feeling. God, I wish you were with me.'

'I'll be here when you come, David. I promise.'

'Okay my love. I'll probably see you late tomorrow.'

'There's a plane to Daree tomorrow night. It leaves Sydney at about six. I could drive down to Daree and meet you?'

'No. It's too far.'

'It's something to do, David – '

'I'll look at a timetable. I'll call you tomorrow before I leave.'

At seven-thirty that night, the phone moved the sisters away from the television. Bronwyn picked it up, then called to her sister. 'STD. It's some cop, Annie. They want to speak to you.'

Minutes later, Ann placed the phone down. Her hand was shaking.

'They've found her. Found Liza,' she said. 'It was no dream, Bronny. Now it starts, and it won't end until it's ended.'

the priest

~

He stood at the window in the departure lounge, staring out at the plane that brought him down from Brisbane, and he wondered how they'd made it this far. It looked like a well-travelled Ford, the best of its life gone.

Planes and airports. He'd seen enough of them today to last a lifetime. The small plane that had flown him out from the island had left at dawn. They were held up in Sydney, and now again in Melbourne. He wasn't destined to reach Perth. He yawned, flexed his shoulder muscles.

He didn't like planes, particularly these big birds, but he did as he was told. He'd never been to Perth, didn't care if he went there or not, either. His life spent safe within his books, the outside world had long taken on an irrelevance.

There was much noise, much movement, the airport was packed. Christmas travellers milled, arms filled with brightly wrapped parcels, flowers. People flying home for Christmas.

Christ's birth.

Take the child out of Christmas, and what did that leave? he thought. Nothing much. It was not a priestly thought, and he smiled a wry smile.

The plane had been due to take off half an hour ago. They'd

boarded, taxied out to the runway then aborted, off loaded the passengers to wait again. Maybe they'd noticed the bald tyres too. He turned from the window, walked through the crowd to the long corridor.

He wanted a coffee. There must be a kiosk down there somewhere.

Too tall, a strikingly handsome priest in his black suit, the band of white at his throat, unsuitable attire for a day that promised heat, but the uniform suited him well.

'What a waste, eh.' The speaker, a middle-aged blonde, stared blatantly as he walked by.

Again the strange half smile touched his lips.

What a waste: Perhaps his life had been wasted. Many would have considered it so. No fame, no bank account. He'd served his church without ambition, content to bury self beneath the black mantle of anonymity. He had done no harm, and about as much good, but he was fed, and he was clothed, he had his books – what more was there?

The kiosk was busy. He stood back, eyeing a slice of fruit cake, plastic wrapped, then his eyes were drawn to a newspaper, the headlines black.

His expression altered. He stepped forward, reaching for a paper, and as he read the crease deepened in his brow.

'Coffee,' he said, and continued reading. When the plastic cup was placed before him, the woman had to ask twice before receiving a response.

'And the paper, Father.'

'Thank you, yes.' Still scanning the front page, he returned to the departure lounge, turned to page two. He saw the name, the town. One heel as a pivot, he turned, picked up his hand luggage and walked briskly away.

People. Too many people. He pushed through the crush to a row of telephones, all in use. He found sufficient cash, waited, foot tapping until a phone became free, and he dialled the operator.

'I want the number please of a Mrs Taylor, Warran. NSW.'

'Street name, and number.'

'I'm sorry. I don't know the street. Possibly Mrs A E Taylor.'

'There are seven listings for Taylor in Warran. There is D for David. An E for Edward. A K for Keith – .'

'Seven. Thank you. Thank you,' and the priest placed the phone down.

He looked up at the flapping flight information. The Perth flight still showed 'Delayed'.

In Mahoneys Lane they watched the television and ate their breakfast, then Bronwyn left for work. 'I'll pop home at lunchtime, Annie. If you need me, call,' she said.

'I'm fine, Bron,' Ann lied.

She made more coffee when she was alone, and she drank it while watching the television reporter repeat for the umpteenth time. 'The skeletal remains of seven-year-old Liza Burton were found here late yesterday. Police are treating the death as a homicide – '

Of May, there was no sign. She was probably at the Toorak flat. The wife of the Narrawee manager was having her say though. Her one day of fame in a lifetime of none, and she was making the most of it. 'We've managed the property for Mr and Mrs Burton for over twenty years. Never in all of my born days did I – '

The phone rang, and Ann ran to answer, expecting it to be David.

'Mrs Taylor. Mrs Ann Taylor.'

'Speaking.'

'This is Greg Mathers from the *Daree Gazette*. I was wondering if I could – '

She broke the connection and stepped away, the realisation of what might be to come, hitting her for the first time. Slowly she returned to the television, the screen still filled with the face of the woman. 'No. I never saw the man – Edward Crow. Of course May and Sam often employed casuals, but whatever possessed her to leave those two – '

Ann hit the off switch.

At nine, she dialled her mother-in-law's number in New Zealand. There was no answer. New Zealand was hours ahead. The funeral should be over. She called Sydney Airport, asked the time of flights coming in from New Zealand, but could glean no information on passengers on incoming flights. He was probably halfway home; hadn't had a chance to call, and while she kept the phone off the hook, he couldn't call. She hung up and another news man rang.

Her neighbour knocked at the door at nine. She brought the newspaper with her.

TWENTY-FOUR YEAR OLD MYSTERY SOLVED. SKELETAL REMAINS OF CHILD FOUND ON PROPERTY WEST OF MELBOURNE, the headlines screamed.

Police acting on information given to them by the sister of the missing child.

'They've all but plastered your address on page two,' Dee Williams said. 'Peter just called me. He said they've been ringing the hospital, looking for information.'

'Hospital?'

'They've got onto Mandy's death. It's all over the second page. Double tragedy. The bloody-minded sods.'

Ann borrowed a cigarette, she made coffee and filled ten minutes speaking of the weather. Then the phone rang and Dee left, taking her cigarettes with her, but leaving the paper.

The phone rang three times in the next five minutes, and she couldn't let it ring. Like a merry-go-round, and she a child riding it, she had to cling in here, ride it till it stilled, or fall off, fall on her face. She answered calls, waiting for the one call she wanted. She filled the jug again and plugged it in, not wanting any more coffee. It was something to do. Just something to do with her hands.

She put on a load of washing and the phone drew her from the laundry.

'David?' But it was just another reporter. 'Find some other bones to pick, and get off this line. I'm expecting an important call,' she yelled.

ANN TAYLOR SCREAMS AT REPORTER

'Cool it,' she warned herself. 'Cool it. Give them no more grist for their mill. Just ride it out until he comes home.'

The priest stood beside the hire car, his head down, his hands clasped across his brow as he studied the city map. He didn't know Melbourne – hadn't set foot on the mainland in sixteen years, but the car was an automatic, and all he had to do was find Sydney Road. Somehow.

He sucked a breath deep into his lungs, took a handkerchief from his pocket and wiped his brow, one finger tracking roads on the map. He found Pentridge prison.

'I should have finished it back then. I'd be out now. Twenty years in the bluestone college instead of in the prison I built for myself.'

He'd cancelled his ticket and booked a hire car, and it had all taken time. They'd fill his seat to Perth soon enough, but his luggage would do the round trip. Fate, or God had grounded his plane, kept him in Melbourne this day. Fate, God, or the devil.

The hire car was small for one of his size. He tucked his frame in, adjusted the seat, and glanced again at the road map, his hand combing back his thick black hair.

'That poor little girl,' he said. In his mind, he had never allowed her to grow – perhaps he had never expected her to grow. He shook his head and started the motor.

For years he had put away emotion, denied it. He had travelled where he was posted, unquestioning; hiding from self and from memories, and rejoicing in the non feeling, but emotion was threatening to sink him now. There were people he should have called, and he knew it, and he didn't care. Raw, gut-wrenching emotion had stripped him of reason, reduced reason to the basic instincts of a homing pigeon.

'*Twenty-four year old mystery solved. Skeletal remains of child found on property west of Melbourne.*

He read it all.

'*Police, acting on information, given to them by the sister of the missing child, early this morning discovered the remains on a property, five kilometres north of –* '

Double tragedy for the Taylor family, who two weeks ago lost their only child in a freak accident. An employee at the Warran Hospital told reporters, Mrs Taylor, who suffered a partial amnesia after the death of her sister, has now regained her memory of that day.

The priest looked at the sky, not so bright as it had appeared to be half an hour ago. 'God works in mysterious ways, love, his wonders to perform.' His voice a mimic, but cynical – as the one he mimicked had never been.

'I was sent here today, Mum. A last minute addition. I didn't want to come, but I came. I did as I was bid. You trained me well, didn't you?' Again he mimicked the female voice. 'Never question God's judgment, love.'

He tossed his hand luggage to the rear seat, tossed the paper with it. The car had followed the traffic onto the freeway when the priest's collar came off and was tossed with the paper to the back seat. He pulled at the fabric at his throat, loosened it, and out of the priest came an ordinary man.

'It only takes seven hours if you plant your foot, and the bloody coppers are taking a day off,' the priest said, his voice a perfect mimic of Jack Burton's. He could do Jimmy Cagney too, and John

Wayne. He could do his grandfather. 'Nothing ventured, nothing gained, lad.'

The entertainer priest. The one who took his duties with a wry smile. This was definitely one priest who had missed his calling.

'I've got to get to her before the world gets in and finally breaks her,' he said, and he took his father's advice and planted his foot. His large hands sure on the wheel, Johnny Burton was off and flying like the homing pigeon.

Bronwyn walked home at one for a quick lunch, and she didn't want to leave. Ann was cracking. Reporters had been trying to get to her all morning, they'd even pursued Bronwyn when they saw her open the gate. She told them to piss off, but Liza Burton was big news, and if that wasn't bad enough, they were asking questions about Mandy's freak death. That was what was getting to Annie, and Bronwyn knew it.

She heard the knocking at the front door as she prepared to leave. 'Bastards,' she said.

'Little pig, little pig, let me in. Oh, no, not by the hair of my chinny chin chin, will I let you in,' Ann said. 'I thought it would be three lines on page ten, Bron. I didn't know. I went out to put some washing on the line and a camera flashed over Dixon's fence. They want to eat me alive, chew me up and spit out the bits on the front page.'

'I'll pull the outside blinds before I go, Annie. Just stay put. Turn the television up loud and ignore them.'

'I don't want noise. I want silence.'

'David hasn't rung?'

'No. I can't get his mother. I can't take the phone off the hook. I want to run, Bronny. I want to run so far, but I'm trapped here like the little pig while they blow down my house of straw.' She was pale, her hands were trembling.

Bronwyn looked at her watch. She had to go. She worked in a one-woman office and she was the woman.

'I'll get Dee Williams to come in.'

'She's been here and I don't want her. I don't want anyone. I'm fine. You go, Bronny. David will ring soon. I'll be fine when he rings. He's all right, isn't he? He hasn't had an accident or anything, has he? There haven't been any plane crashes?'

'Stop that, Annie. He's fine. As you say, he's probably halfway home.'

The phone rang again and Ann sprang up to answer it. 'Go to hell,' she said.

'Take a couple of Aspros, and have a glass of wine. Put a video on.'

'Have you got a spare packet of cigarettes?'

'It's no good for the baby.'

'I'm no good for the baby if I'm in a mad house, Bron. Please don't nag me.'

'I'll ring Fletch. See if he can come down.'

'He's not home. I tried him. I tried Ben's house. Nobody is home.' Bronwyn handed her a packet of cigarettes, watched her hand shake as she removed one, lit it. It wasn't Annie. It wasn't the one she'd known these last years. Her eyes were black voids, empty as they had been on the night she ran off for Melbourne.

'Go Bron. You're late.'

'I'll close up at five-thirty. On the dot, Annie.'

The hire car had flown freeway, highway, and narrow bitumen strip, making light work of the trip. Locked in, air-conditioner on, Johnny had been unaware of the scorching heat of the day until he wound the window down to look for old landmarks.

Red hot wind swept his hair back from his brow, and at first glance he was Jack, but he was a younger, stronger Jack. His hands on the wheel made it miniature. His arms, bare now to the elbow, showed heavier bones, thicker wrists. His shoe on the accelerator was two sizes larger. The Vevers were made of stronger stuff, and though Ellie had donated no feature, she was at Johnny's core.

For the past hour, he had been talking aloud. It stopped his thinking in this halfway place, between here and where he must be. Mile upon mile of road he had covered.

'Miles,' he said. 'Why am I thinking in miles again?'

He knew the answer.

He was in the land he'd travelled with his grandfather, when he'd asked the all child's question. 'How many more miles, Grandpa?' Every muscle was tensed, as in vain he attempted to push the car faster with his will alone. He had to get there.

He'd broken every speed limit. Lunchtime had come and gone, his only stop in Albury, to buy petrol, coffee and use the roadhouse toilets, but he was almost there.

'I can smell it,' he said. 'It's coming for me, drawing me in.' He squinted one eye against the sun, glancing at a sprawling weatherboard farmhouse as it flashed by. 'That's the old Thomas place. I'm less than twenty miles out of Mallawindy. Smell the earth. Smell that river. Just follow the tree line, and you follow the river home, lad,' he said, and he thought of the old man who'd died between the main course and sweets that night. He'd tried to save him too. Back then, he'd tried to save the world, tried to save a confused little girl, tried to kill his father, but Ellie wouldn't let him.

'Failure,' he said, then he mimicked his mother's voice. '"Johnny is going to be a priest when he grows up." Maybe that's why I did it, so I wouldn't be a failure in your eyes – or was it just a good place to hide, Mum?'

He eased his wallet from his pocket, then from it he took a small foil-wrapped parcel. With one hand he unwrapped it, exposing a ring. And the sun, beating in through the window caught the shoulder diamonds, flashing red and blue fire in his eye. The car swerved into the gravel, his wallet slid to the floor, but he gripped the ring as he pulled on the wheel, over-corrected, almost lost control. He was tiring fast, unaccustomed to a day of driving, and to this dry heat.

'Concentrate,' he warned. 'Concentrate. You are no good to her dead.' He glanced quickly at the ring, then he forced it for safety onto his smallest finger. It felt odd there, unclean. 'But we can't lose it now, little Annie.'

A large ring, expensive, heavy gold band, twelve diamonds, and the square black stone. He'd almost sold it in those early years. The inscription stopped him. How could he have explained it? 'Bent bastard,' he said, and he sounded like his father.

The road ahead appeared to be sinking too early into twilight. The wind was growing stronger too. He sniffed the air. Smoke on the wind. The scent of burning eucalypt.

'They've got a forest fire up there somewhere,' he said. His foot went down, and the small car again picked up speed. He sighted Watson's property on his left. He was five miles out of Mallawindy.

'A brief stop?' He shook his head. He had to get to little Annie, the rest could wait. Forty minutes should have him in Warran.

Push me Johnny, push me high. I'm a bird and I can fly. High up to the clear blue sky. I made Liza Burton – .

'I'm in Sydney, Ann. The plane to Daree leaves around five, and it connects with the bus. I should be home before nine.'

'I'll pick you up in Daree, David.'

'Just be home for me when I get there, my love. I just want to know that you're there, and you're safe, and you are waiting for me. Is Bronny with you?'

'She had to go to work. She'll be here around five-thirty.'

'Good. How have you been?'

'I've been ... watching television all day.'

'You sound – '

'Have you . . . have you seen a paper?'

'I just landed.'

'They've found Liza. Found her . . . body, David.'

There was a long silence. 'Are you . . . '

'I'm okay. Don't worry about me. Put the phone down and catch that plane and come home to me.' And the line was cut.

'I'm fine,' she said to the empty phone. But she lied. Her heartbeat was wild, her head was crawling, and her brain wouldn't turn off. She wasn't sitting down watching television, she'd been walking the house for hours, running to telephones. They wouldn't let her sit still, and when she tried to rest, her bones kept running on the spot.

Have to think of the baby, she told herself, but when she sat, the phone rang again. She wouldn't answer it. She didn't have to any more. David was in Sydney. He was coming home.

And she didn't answer it the next time it rang.

Four more hours, and he'd be home. Just four more hours. She let it ring, ring, ring. And it kept it up until she screamed at it, because four hours was too long, and Bronny wouldn't finish work until five-thirty, and it took her twenty minutes to walk home, and she was alone, with vultures parked outside her front gate, aiming their cameras at her every time she walked to a window.

The blinds were pulled, the curtains drawn to shut them out, shut the world out, but they locked Ann in.

Shouldn't have started it. What did I expect, Annie? Not this. Not this.

The phone continued. Maybe it was Bronny. Maybe it was Ben. It rang out, and commenced once more. And she couldn't take any more. She snatched it off the hook.

Another stranger's voice.

'I am attempting to contact Ann Taylor, formerly Ann Burton – .'

'Leave me alone,' she screamed and disconnected. Then before it could ring again, she pulled the plug from the wall, and she walked again, walked the passage, walked the rooms, walked. A caged rat, with no way out.

Far better to get in the car, drive to Daree than this. Far better.

They were leaning on the door-bell again. She stood in the passage, rubbing her eyes, her brow. The ringing continued. Insistent knocking followed. She stood, rubbing, rubbing her eyes, her hands covering her face. Cold face. Cold hands. With the windows closed, and the house airless, she had turned on the air-conditioner. The family room was cold as a freezer, and the chill was seeping down the passage.

She walked to the family room. Sat, shivered. At least the noise of the air-conditioner was a constant. She stood, walked again. She lit a cigarette then stubbed it out, and she walked, and the door-bell rang.

She sat again and looked at the wall. It was moving, closing in, as another wall had once closed in on her. Shadowed wall. Black. The black was coming, and she was cold, shivering cold. No strength to fight it any more.

Hold on. Hold on, Annie Blue Dress.

Footsteps on concrete. Walking away, like in that other place.

May's footsteps walking away. 'One more dark and one more light and I'll be back. I promise you, sweetheart. Just be brave for me. One more dark, and one more light.'

She'd waited for the footsteps to return. Waited. Waited. She'd been a good girl. Aunty May's good girl.

Dark coming again soon. Footsteps coming down the side.

'Trip-trap. Trip-trap. Trip-trap. Who's that walking over my bridge? Only me, just little Billy Goat gruff. I'm going to eat you all up, said the ogre.'

Ogres with their cameras, gobbling up lives. Parasitic life forms, their survival dependent on another's misery.

Coming to get me. Coming to get me.

It would all come out now.

'And why did Ted Crow kill Liza, and not you, Mrs Taylor?'

'Good question. A very good question.' Her brain could find no logical answer. She needed Malcolm's devious head to write the new scenario. He'd be good at it, but he wasn't home to write it.

'We have to get the murderer to bury the body while the child looks on, sir, and then we have to find a reason why the murderer didn't kill the sister, and bury her too, sir.'

'It defies logic, Burton.'

It defies logic.

The police had called. They had asked no questions, but they were coming tomorrow. They wanted her to help draw up an identikit photo of poor much maligned Ted Crow.

She laughed. Laughed loud, laughed long.

'He had black wings and a long sharp beak,' she said, and she laughed again.

Give it up. Give in. Put it in the too hard basket, and – escape. Escape to that other place, that better place.

Hold on, Annie Blue Dress. It has begun, and we will find an end together.

Rat-a tat-tat. Tat-tat.

Rhythm in the knock.

And again. Rat-a-tat-tat. Tat-tat.

She walked to the rear passage, looked through to the opaque glass of the back door, through which she could see the shape of the one knocking. Tall as her father. Broad as her father. Dark shape.

Where was Jack Burton hiding? Were they pursuing him too? Or had he come to help them get her? Where was Ellie? Where was Ben? Where had Malcolm gone today?

Is the world out there still turning for them?

David. Poor David of the laughing eyes and smiling, asking mouth. I will be gone before you get here. Don't hurry home. Nothing to come home to. Going, going, gone.

Rat-a-tat-tat. Tat-tat-tat, and a voice.

'Annie.'

A stranger's voice, speaking Annie's name.

'Annie? Annie, love?'

A stranger's voice? Oh no, never, never, never a stranger.

Ann lifted her head. She stood, listening, shivering.

'Annie, it's me. I know you're in there, love.'

And she heard. And she tried to accept the words, but her mind rejected them. This was all part of the game. This was all a part of the lie. Let go of the lie. Let it slip away. But her bones that would not lie down, were walking her to the opaque door.

'It's me, love. Johnny. Open the door.'

Johnny.

Little name, lost too long. All gone away. Silly lonely little word, it was picked up by the north wind, tossed around the wide eaves to howl at the chimney, and be carried away like so much thistle down in a storm.

But a tiny echo of the name puffed itself out with its own importance.

'I'm here. I'll look after you, love. It's Johnny.'

The voice was breaking, and her hand reached out. It grasped the door knob, and slowly, so slowly the door was opened. And he was there.

He was there.

He was.

Coal black eyes wide, she stood, afraid to move, to breathe, afraid action may make him unreal.

His tears had started. No more room for words. He reached out to the trembling rod of cold sprung steel, forced too long in rigid bend, then the steel rod snapped and Ann screamed his name.

'Johnny.'

It was the primal scream of her childhood, the howl of a wounded thing that wouldn't die. And the tears came. Hot, scalding tears. A flood of tears locked away for too many years, they burst like water from a fractured main and they mixed together with her brother's as they clung there, clung in the doorway, clung until the world became a blurred distant thing, until it went away, far, far away, but she and Johnny had never needed the world.

johnny is home

~

They were braver later. There was a pulling back, a realisation of years past, and of the others he had left behind. They spoke, they side tracked, and they wept. Ann made tomato sandwiches, and they ate them together. They always liked tomato sandwiches. They drank tea, and he still took two sugars, and too much milk, and she always took two sugars and too much milk, because he did.

'Never weaned,' he said, and they laughed and they looked at each other's red eyes, red noses and they wept again, and he held her and the ring on his smallest finger caught in her hair.

'Why did you keep it?' He shook his head, and she said, 'I went back to the sand dunes, just before Mandy died. We built sand castles there, Johnny.'

'You remember that day, love. Fletch – John Fletcher.'

She nodded. 'Everything. Everything now. Why did you keep it?'

He took the ring off, handed it to her. He watched her turn it in her hand, peer at the inscription. 'It's all I had, love. I was going to come back, when I was ... was big enough. I stayed close to you for that first year, but I never felt quite big enough. I let you down, love. I let everyone down.'

She shook her head and handed back the ring, and he tossed it disdainfully to the table as he yawned, exhausted by emotion, and by his day, and his drive. 'We knew we'd found something strange when we dug him up that day. The Aborigines always buried their dead in a seated position, knees up, chin down, and their skulls had teeth, but the bones we dug up were buried in a flat grave. Burnt. There wasn't much left except the skull and a leg bone. I knew as soon as I saw that ring in your hand. I knew what we'd found.

'You were barely communicating. "I find," you signed. "Grow on grass. I know nothing." I looked in your golden syrup tin that night, and it was all there, love. The big black bird who the beautiful stepmother had placed a spell on. The one about the cellar. It was all there.'

'He loved Liza. He loved her, Johnny.'

Lightning split the sky, lit the room. All the blinds were open now, the windows open.

'How much have you told the police?'

'Where Liza was buried. I – '

'Tell them. Show them your little poems.'

She looked at his eyes, and her tears started again. She shook her head, and tried to dry her eyes, but tears oozed and trickled faster than she could wipe them away.

They stared at each other, and he wept with her, then he held her a while and they tried to laugh at their tears. It was all too new, this weeping. New for both. They didn't do it very well yet.

She drew away, tried to laugh off her tears, but howled again. 'Wine,' she said. 'Bronny said to drink wine. Wine always makes me happy. Do you drink?'

He nodded, watched her take a cask of riesling from the refrigerator, watched her pour.

'Little Bron. How did she grow?'

'She's my rock, Johnny. I don't know who she gets it from.'

'And Mum?'

'She's got her cows. She's ... I don't know how she is, or

who she is. I don't know her, Johnny. I don't know if there is anyone in her to know.' She silenced, took a tissue from the box and blew her nose. 'Did she know?'

Johnny shook his head. 'I don't think so, love.'

'You didn't tell her?'

'No. She was . . . child-like. Towards the end I got to think she was younger than I. I couldn't hurt her, Annie. I couldn't ever hurt her. She made me leave. I was fifteen, half out of my brain. He was my father. What could I do? Kill him. I tried, but I couldn't do it to her. She married him in the church.' His voice was bitter, and he picked up his glass of wine, drank it down like medicine and poured another.

'I never saw you as a priest. I thought I'd found you once in a used car yard.'

'I might have made a better fist of selling cars. I sold just about everything else there for a few years. I went up to Brisbane after that first year, worked all day and went to school at night. It didn't leave me too much time to think.'

'Mum will be pleased. Doesn't that buy her a seat in heaven? A son given to God.'

'I'm not a priest's bootlace. Never was. It was atonement for my sins, a hole I crawled into. I had nothing, Annie love. Nothing.' He emptied the glass, then pushed it away. 'It doesn't make me happy,' he said. 'I stay away from it, love. What's he doing these days?'

'Spends half his life in Narrawee, comes home and drinks. Mum has a ball when he's away. Goes to cards, plays bingo, then she tiptoes around him when he comes home. Nothing has changed. May still writes, *Sam is looking forward to seeing you at the end of the month*. And Dad picks up his briefcase and leaves.' Ann's hands played with the wine glass, she turned it in circles, turning, turning. She drank, then looked at her brother. 'I saw Sam a few years ago, Johnny. He's a good man. He's a really good man. He doesn't drink.'

Johnny shook his head. 'I opened his briefcase the same day I looked in your golden syrup tin. In for a penny, in for a pound, I thought. I opened it with one of Mum's bent hairpins. Any proof I needed was in his case, love.'

Minutes passed, he yawned again. Weariness was overtaking him. 'It has to come out. For you, and for me, it has to come out. My whole life has been a lie.'

'I hated Sam when I was tiny. I hated him, Johnny.'

'Dad nearly killed me for letting you and Liza go there. "You let them go to that filthy bastard," he said.' Johnny silenced, yawned again. 'I should have known better. Sam always smiled too much. His eyes were cruel. They followed you. He liked to touch, but his hands were always damp – .' Ann filled her wine glass, picked up Johnny's, but he shook his head, and stood, stretched his limbs.

'I've been up since four.'

'Do you want to crash out for an hour?'

'A strong coffee will do the trick. I'll wait until Bronwyn gets here, then I'll ... I'll go ... go home.'

She looked at him, shook her head. He couldn't go home. Bad could only be made worse. It had to stop here. He had to stay here tonight.

'At least make yourself comfortable.' She pointed to the big recliner. 'It's David's private property, but the bus doesn't get here until after eight.'

Johnny looked at the big chair, then he tested it. Almost big enough. He lifted the footrest, pushed back, and swung his feet up. 'What happened to Mr Fletcher, the old school teacher?'

'He's still in Mallawindy. He's a ... a – ' She tried to say friend, but he was more than a friend. 'He made me go to school.'

His eyes were closed against the glare from the window. 'He was old when I was a kid.'

'He's reached that era of non-ageing. Looks the same as he did ten years ago. He weighs a tonne, drinks like a fish – ' She spoke on about the old man, pleased to think of him. She spoke of his house, and his on-going feud with Jack Burton. The wine had gone to her head, loosened her tongue, and it had dried her tears, but by the time the jug had boiled and the mug of coffee was made, she knew most of her words had fallen on sleeping ears.

She picked up the onyx ring, and stood near the window, looking at the inscription, still clear, unworn.

'Sam and May 1953'.

On tiptoe, she walked to the bench, took up her handbag and dropped the ring into it. Car keys, sunglasses, the drapes pulled slowly, afraid the noise may wake the sleeper, but he didn't move. She slipped her shoes from her feet, and crept to his side.

'Sleep on, my Johnny. Sleep long,' she whispered, and she was out the back door, closing it carefully behind her.

After five-thirty. She may be in time to catch Bronwyn before she left the office.

Her head held high, she walked around to the garage while cameras flashed, and she flashed the smile she saved for cameras. She waved a hand to videos. A little drunk, but ready now to write the end.

'Mrs Taylor, Mrs Taylor. Have you got a moment?'

'Tomorrow,' she said, and again she flashed her smile.

'Is it true that the death of your daughter – '

'Tomorrow.'

Tomorrow the world would be safe. She would make it safe.

Ellie sat at her kitchen table, staring vacantly at the wall. 'Hello, loves. I wondered if you'd come down when you heard,' she greeted Ann and Bronwyn. 'Bessy's been with me all day, but she had to go home and fix tea.'

'Where is Dad?' Ann said.

'Probably at the hotel, love.'

Bronwyn walked to the gun, still propped against the wall

behind the old wireless that never sang. She defused it, tossing the twin cartridges into a drawer, then she kissed her mother and told her that Johnny was asleep in Ann's family room.

Ann stood watching. Dark head, and fading gold, together. The young fresh face, and the old. Together. Arms around each other. She turned from them, walked to the stove, placed wood in it, filled the kettle, while Ellie wept her few expected tears.

Unreal tears, they soon dried, and she was cutting cake. Ellie's response to any given situation was a reflection of Jack's. He was not here to offer her guidelines. She placed slabs of fruit cake on a plate, then pointed with her knife to the photograph of Liza. 'That poor little girl,' she said.

Ann followed the knife's point to the photograph. Unreal too. Over-painted chocolate box thing. But at least in this place un-reality was the norm, so Ann slipped into unreal. She ate fruit cake, drank tea, spoke of the bushfires, and the forecast of rain. 'I might pop up and tell Ben that Johnny is home.'

'Ben's gone, love. I thought he would have called you?'

'Gone? Where?'

'Away.' Storm clouds moved, lightning flashed, thunder rolled.

'What do you mean, away?'

'Cape York. And he said that when he got there, he was going to get on a boat and row to China.'

'Because of . . . because they found Liza?'

'Oh, no love. It was before we even heard about that. It was after he cut down his trees.'

'We didn't notice they were down. Did they reach?' Both girls were on their feet and looking out the window. They could see the space, but not the bridge.

'He cut them down three days ago. Bob Dooley and Bessy's Mick were pulling on a rope from the other side of the river, and the trees fell exactly where Benjie wanted them to fall. Him and the others moved them together with young Mick's tractor, then they set up some pole things in the middle and hammered a few planks on.' Ellie looked down to her folded hands. She blinked a while at the condition of her chipped nails.

'He was so happy, like a little boy again, running backwards and forwards across his bridge, the heels of his boots making a real racket. He had half the town down here when it was finally finished. They were all helping to build a bit of a rough ramp up to Bessy's side while Ben hammered on the steps he'd made for our side.

'When he told me to try it out, loves, he looked so proud. He was standing on Bessy's side, just looking so proud of himself. So I walked across to him. Your Dad came down too. He was being ... like he always is with Benjie – .' She looked down at the table, swept some crumbs into her palm. 'He said, "A drum of petrol should neaten it up okay." Benjie knew he didn't mean it, because he just laughed at your Dad. "I've done what I set out to do, which is more than you ever did you useless old b-a-s-t-a-r-d," he said.

'Benjie never swore, and when I spoke to him about it, he said, "There comes a time when a mouse has to know when it's time to jump off the wheel, Mum." That's the last time I saw him. Dooley came down late last night and gave me the keys to Ben's place – and his message about Cape York and going to China.'

Bronwyn and Ann had listened this far in silence. Now Bronwyn sat and placed her head on her folded arms, and she laughed, her hair in the saucer of her tea cup. She laughed until Ann joined with her.

They fried eggs later, and made toast against the red hot embers and they laughed. They made fresh tea, and giggled, trying to control twitching lips, but a word or a glance set them off anew. Ben had broken free. He'd gone off to row a boat to China, and they laughed at the visual image of him pulling on the oars, riding the waves across the ocean. Away, far far away from bloody Mallawindy.

Ellie smiled quizzically, watched them eat egg, almost choke on egg, and her green eyes didn't understand their laughter. She shook her head at them. Surely this was not the time and place for joviality, not with little Liza dead; still, she'd been dead a long time, and Jack wasn't around to see her, and their laughter was infectious. Ben, rowing to China. Goodness me. He'd never leave his land. He was his grandfather's blood. Her blood. Of course he'd come back to his cows.

Ellie had a fine big laugh when she let it loose.

They washed the dishes, scraped egg yolk from the forks. Wiped the old table down with a cloth, then sat again.

'Your Dad is taking it very hard – about Liza.'

'Poor old Dad. As usual, giving comfort where he can – to self,' Ann said.

'What about you, Mum?'

Ellie had no reply. For minutes she sat twisting the thin gold remnant of wedding band, still trapped there by a knuckle. Ann watched her, willing the ring to snap, to fall to the floor, through a gap in the floor, to be gone forever into the earth.

And Ellie twisted, and she twisted, then she cried out as the slim circle split, and the ring was over her knuckle and tinkling to the floor.

'It's bad luck,' she said. 'It's broken – ' She sprang to her feet, her eyes starting their old familiar ooze. The trembling mouth, the bowed head. She cried so well over nothing, but she'd had a lot of practice. Tears glistening on soft fabric, gathered and draped by the years. Threads hanging loose where puckered lips were stitched in place. Her eyelids, heavy drooping cowls, folded into the concertina pleating of cheek and weathered jowls.

Bronwyn found the thing on the floor. She handed it back as she glanced up at the old clock, ticking its life away on the mantelpiece. 'Jesus! Where did the time go? I promised Nick I'd let him know what I'm doing tonight. Stick it on with a bit of Bandaid, Mum, then get your good dress on. We've got to go. Johnny is waiting to see you.'

'I can't go, love. Give Nick a call from Bessy's place. Use Ben's bridge.' A Bandaid found, peeled, taped around her finger.

Bronwyn looked at Ann, shrugged. 'I'd better ring him, Annie. I'll nick over and use old Fletch's phone. And you'd better be dressed when I get back, Mum. We're not taking no for an answer. Put your hair up, and put a bit of make-up on too. I'll be back in ten minutes.'

Ann sat at the table, her fingers tapping wood. She tapped until Ellie found something to say. 'I'll take it down to the jewellers, get them to add a bit of gold. It was too tight anyway.'

'I like the Bandaid, Mum. It's a real statement.'

'You come out with some silly things sometimes, love. Smell that rain coming. It will put the fires out, but the wheat farmers won't be too pleased with it. Mr Watson has a bumper crop, too. I was talking to him in town yesterday.'

'Nothing comes when you want it, does it? We've got no control over fate and the weather. Are you going to change your frock, Mum?'

'No, love. I can't go tonight.'

Ann sighed. She stood and walked to her parents' room. Years had passed since she'd been in there. It still smelt the same. She looked in his wardrobe, touched a white shirt, hanging on its wooden hanger. A child again, she sniffed at the scent of aged timber, good solid timber, then she turned to Ellie's smaller, cheaper wardrobe. Many frocks, all stitched by Ann's own hands, hung there. A black suit. A grey suit. A soft green floral frock, made for Ellie's last birthday. Sunday frock. It looked well with her green eyes and her fading sunshine hair. She slid it from its hanger, then searched the wardrobe floor for shoes. She picked up the handbag from the door knob.

'Come on, Mum. I want you out of here tonight. We'll pick Bronny up at Mr Fletcher's,' she said, but Ellie had turned the television on, not wanting to miss her show.

'I just want to see what happened to Carolyn's baby. It was born right at the end of last week's show.'

'It's just fiction. You've got your own drama right here, and if you don't move very fast, you might have even more.'

Ellie glanced at her, but remained in front of the television. Ann walked through to the kitchen, found a plastic bag, folded the frock into it, placed it on the kitchen table. She returned to the lounge room, looking briefly at the large photograph of Liza, posed, over-painted, and below it, to a photograph of Mandy. No comparison, apart from the curls. People never looked further than the surface. People saw what they wanted to see, expected to see. She turned on her heel and re-entered her parents' room.

Jack's briefcase had lived out its life on top of the wardrobe. She could reach it easily now. She took it down, tried her own small key in the lock, and it turned. Her hand beneath the lid touched hair, touched proof. She smiled as Ellie came to the door.

'Annie! What in heaven's name are you doing with that open?'

'Just feeding the mice,' she said. 'You should have trapped them twenty odd years ago, Mum.' Ellie stared at her. She didn't understand. Ann closed the case with a snap, and took it with her to the kitchen where she picked up the plastic bag then walked out to her car as headlights became visible on the river road.

Ellie was behind her. 'You can't take that! Take it back at once, Annie. That's your dad's. You can't touch that.'

'Get in that car. Please Mum. Johnny is planning to come up here. We can't let him come here and you know it. Please Mum. That might be him.'

'It's Jeff Rowan, the young policeman,' Ellie said. 'He's been backwards and forwards all day.' She walked back to the house. Ann followed her, placing her keys in her handbag.

From the kitchen window they watched the car halt, disgorge Jack. They heard the clink of bottles.

'I hope he hasn't been on the whisky,' Ellie said.

'One day you might realise that you have made an art form out of stupidity.' Two sets of eyes locked on the doorway where Jack would make his final entrance.

He could always be relied on to make a good entrance, unstable but effective. The step up to the kitchen floor forced a decision to lift his feet, so he leaned against the door jamb, half in and half out, his eyes blinking into the light.

'The whole bloody town is swarming with newspaper men, thanks to you, and everyone of them bought me a drink. Paid me to talk to them. They want to put me on national television tomorrow night.'

'As Bronwyn was saying, play your cards right and you could make your fortune out of this.'

Jack walked to the table, sagged down to a chair. He looked old tonight. The years were eroding his good looks, absorbing them. Or am I seeing him as old because I have seen the young Jack Burton today, the strong Jack Burton. Head to one side, Ann studied her father, while her hands massaged her temples. She saw the white scar half circling his wrist, and she smiled. 'Any more tea in the pot, Mum?'

Ellie passed her the pot.

'Any more tea in the pot, Mum?' he mimicked. 'You sit there and pour your bloody tea, and accuse me with your mad bloody eyes.'

'I never accused you. Never once. I blamed myself. Easier to blame yourself,' she said, adding sugar to her tea, stirring, tasting, adding more. His eyes followed her movements, while from the lounge room, canned television laughter came on cue. 'They want me to help draw up an identikit photo of Ted Crow. They'll probably want Sam and May to help with it.'

He tossed the dregs of a tea cup in her face. She didn't flinch, didn't wipe the tea away; she let it drip to the table, her eyes holding his. 'Get out,' he snarled. 'Get to buggery out of my sight, you mud-raking bitch.'

Ellie took her arm, urged her to rise. 'It's better if you go, Annie.'

Ann shook off Ellie's touch. Too little, too late had come from that hand. Then she sighed, patted the hand, looked at its Bandaid and at its age. Forgive it. Forgive this hand that never touched. Forgive it. Johnny has come home and the old world is winding down to a halt.

Tomorrow. Everything will be okay tomorrow.

'It's my birthday today. No-one has said happy birthday yet,' she said.

'H – .' Ellie began, but she closed her mouth, turned away.

'Remember my third birthday, Dad. The ginger kitten. Johnny brought it home for me and you had to wring its neck a week later because Liza poked its eye out with a stick.'

Jack was on his feet, and Ellie ran to him. 'Don't let her upset you, Jack.'

He pushed her from him. 'What do you care? When did you ever care how bloody upset I was? When did you ever see anything that didn't have four bloody legs and a tail?'

Ellie backed towards the door, ready to run. Jack poured a measure of whisky into a glass, tossed it down, poured more, his eyes on Ann.

'Don't drink any more, love. You come up here, Annie, and you always cause trouble. You always did. Why can't you be like the others?'

'Because I'm not like the others, am I Dad?' Ann turned to her father, watched him drink. 'Johnny came home.'

'So you worked it out between you. I should have known. What are you doing for an encore? What's the plan for tomorrow?'

'That it be over.'

'It's never bloody over. It's only just started, you stupid bitch. Every newspaper man in Australia is going to be dogging my heels.'

'Just tell them about Ted Crow. Old Mr Crow.'

'That's what you told the coppers?'

'What else?' Ann glanced at Ellie who had backed out to the verandah. There were things she wanted to say, that tonight she must say. 'Go over to Bessy's, Mum. Tell her about Johnny. I'll pick you up there. Ask her if she'd like to come down too.' Ellie remained where she was. Ann turned to Jack, shrugged. 'Do you want to know the main question I keep asking myself? It's May. How does she tame you?'

'She makes me look at the world through rose-tinted glasses,' he said, and he laughed, and refilled his glass, drank again, and Ellie's voice came from the verandah.

'I saw that on the television a while back. They say they're working miracles these days with tinted lenses.'

Ann looked at her watch. 'David will be home soon.' She stood, eased the sweat-soaked fabric of her skirt away from her legs.

'You go then, love. Tell Johnny I'll see him tomorrow. I'll get Bessy to drive me down. Oh, and don't you go driving off with all those things in your car.'

'You are a caricature he sketched on a blank sheet of paper. I've known you for thirty years, but I don't know you. Your son has been missing for twenty-two years. Ask yourself why? Ask Dad, why? Or do you already know why?'

'Leave her out of this, you bitch.'

'Were you able to keep it from her, or is that why she made Johnny run, why she wanted to get rid of me?'

'She knows bloody nothing. Leave her alone.'

Ann reached across the table for her handbag and the car keys it contained. She turned her back to Jack.

'She's got your briefcase in her car, love,' Ellie said.

It was done too easily. It was done too fast. Jack's hand snaked out, and the floor rushed up to meet Ann.

A thump. Mind-stealing pain as her eyebrow slammed into the corner of a timber upright. Impact of elbow, of hip on bare board.

And embarrassment. Common everyday variety embarrassment of lifted skirt, of lost shoe, of being caught off guard.

Slowly she gained her knees. Heaviness leaned on her. Easier to stay on her knees, wait for the room to still. Ellie was gone. Jack stood alone in the kitchen. Old king of the beasts. Half god, half bull. Her left hand went to her temple where blood oozed hot and sticky. With one eye, she measured the distance to the moving doorway, but she needed both eyes. She wiped at the blood, partially cleared her vision, then one hand gripping the wall for support, she stood.

'You used to stare at a poor bloody man with your crazy eyes.' His voice was high, in defence. 'I won't say a word, Daddy. I promise Daddy.' He drank now from the bottle, his face turned to the photograph of Liza, his blemished treasure.

Ann leaned there, watching him. He drank again, then threw the bottle at Liza's portrait, shattered it. Glass and whisky sprayed to the floor, and the photograph fluttered free to settle at Ann's feet. She picked it up, swaying as she looked at it.

Daddy went to Narrawee to get his Liza and get me,
But he found her in the cellar, playing with the dirty fella.
'Shut up you bitch.'
When he tried to kill him dead, he got Liza's head instead.
So he put his golden treasure with the flowers to bloom forever.
'Shut up, you bitch. Shut up.'
Scraped the blood all off the floor. Locked his Annie with the door.

Her head throbbed with blood and words. They both wanted out, but her heart was beating out just one word. 'Danger. Danger. Danger.' Her hand went to the cluster of cells in her womb. 'Danger,' the womb guarding the cells warned.

In silence, she looked at him. Looked at his eyes. Once the bad was out, and all used up, his eyes would grow as soft as velvet. He was God then, safe. New cells didn't understand that child cells had once loved him, that a child had sometimes sat with him in this kitchen for hours. Much of what she'd learned, prior to Malcolm, had come from him.

He'd made her read the Wheetie packets at breakfast. He'd made her read the newspaper at tea. He'd made her read May's letters.

She had to let the bad out. Let it all out tonight, and then she could ask him why it took so long. She had to ask him. Just watch him, she soothed the cells. Just read him, but be ever ready to run. She removed her second shoe.

'It was my fault, Dad. I should have told May. I knew it was wrong. I should have told May.'

The bus had arrived at Warran at 8.20. At 8.25, when David entered his back door, he found somebody sleeping in his chair. No introduction was necessary. It had taken the men fifty seconds to decide where Ann had gone. Another fifty and they were in the car, heading out the Mallawindy road.

Now they were almost there.

The sky to the west and the north was a blood red ocean, its waves tipped with liquid fire.

'Nowhere else on God's earth can he paint such a scene of destruction, David.'

'Storm clouds, and smoke from the fire. I could see the fire when I was driving through.'

'A fitting welcome home,' Johnny said, and the car sped on, the night growing dark too quickly as the sky to the west faded into purple.

Dark night when they turned onto the river road. No fear of a speeding ticket here. They bounced over corrugations, rattled the boards on the old bridge, then they were at the wooden gate, through the gate, Johnny left swinging wide, and on again, bouncing, bumping down the rutted track.

Ann's car was parked in the yard. David had hoped it wouldn't be there. His heart thumped in his breast. He braked, and was out, while hot tyres breathed an audible sigh of relief.

Her car doors were locked. He was trying the rear passenger side when the house, previously well lit, disappeared into the night. Afraid now, he turned to Johnny. 'Turn the lights back on, John. Leave them on high beam,' he said.

The yard was deserted. Two drowsy hens with ruffled feathers, eyed the men with suspicion.

So this was it. So this was the day of reckoning. Johnny Burton placed his feet on home soil. Slowly he stood and faced the river, smelt the water. He looked at the shape of the willow two hundred yards away. Crickets chirped, bull frogs courted, their chorus echoing along the banks of the river. The building, dark against the overgrown shrubbery took his breath away.

'Has it been twenty-two years, or was it just yesterday I left?' he said, and he walked purposely towards the house.

But time is a strange and variable commodity. It can't be bought, nor trapped, nor borrowed. Only the telephone company can sell time. Bronwyn placed five dollars on Malcolm's hall-table to pay for her time.

Conversation can be worth five dollars, but kind minutes fly too soon, and as she looked at her watch in the half light of the lounge room, she noticed the time.

Malcolm was in his study, its bay window wall gave an unrestricted view of the Burton property in daylight hours. He sat over his typewriter, a puffed-up toad tormenting a fly. His pursed lips moist, his breathing fast, his interest was centred on the window. He repelled Bronwyn as always. Only by exercising inordinate willpower while in his presence did she manage to keep up the pretence of respect for this bloat of man. She did it for Annie's sake, but it wasn't easy.

'How is your sister bearing up?'

'She was bad this afternoon, but tonight she's on a high. Maybe a false high. Johnny coming home has sort of pushed this Liza thing underground, I think. I've left the money on the table for the call, Fletch.'

'I am not a pauper, Burton,' he replied, not allowing his gaze to stray from the window.

'Can you see something out there?' she asked, peering at the dark mirror and the reflected image of the toad.

'There has been some considerable movement of traffic across the road. I noticed a police car a while back. There is another car there now, and the house lights are out. A wire come down, do you think?' He rolled back on his chair, and with effort, stood, took up his walking stick. Bronwyn followed him outside.

They heard the voice as they watched a truck trundle by on its way to no place.

'That sounds like David. What is he doing here? And where the hell is Annie?' Bronwyn's voice overrode the distant call, and Malcolm prodded her into silence with his walking stick, but a night bird was calling to its flighty mate; words had no chance against the sounds of the bush. A noisy place, the river's bend in the dead of night.

'Silence!' the old headmaster bawled and forest things stilled. They heard the voice again. Bronwyn ran, leaving the fat man to make his own way across the road.

run for the river

~

Ann had snatched up the old gun when she saw David's Ford; she knew Johnny would be with him. She killed the lights at the main as she ran down the passage, then she swung left, and ran around the side of the house to the river. Dark. Black as pitch.

Sensing the moisture beneath her bare feet, she lifted the heavy gun, tossed it like a javelin, and she heard the satisfying splash. Giant fish splash. And it was gone. Easy.

'You crazy bitch of a bloody girl.' He wasn't far behind her.

It was yesterday. She was running from him again. It was all her yesterdays, but she had to get across to tomorrow. Her left eye was closing, halving her vision, but she didn't need to see. Smell the river, smell the mud, smell the chickens. She ran along the river until her fingers found the chicken-wire fence; they followed it down, down to the shallows where it was only a token, and easy to climb.

Up to her knees in water, the sucking squish of mud to her ankles, it was memory, everything was memory. Smell of cows. Smell of wood-smoke. Over the fence she clambered, finding toe holds, hand holds, unchanged in all the years she'd been away, then she turned and followed the wire back to the bank, back to the main fowl pen and to the cave of darkness behind it.

It smelt of yesterday too, of old dung and feathers. She rested there, and he came to stand only metres away.

'That was my father's gun. It was worth money, you mad bitch.'

'It was my father's too, and now it's not worth anything.' She listened. They were calling again, voices from two directions.

'Burton! Burton!'

'Ann. Where are you?'

And Bronny's voice, concerned. 'Annie! Are you out there? Go back inside. Go back to the light.'

The distant house was now ablaze with electricity, but it had no hope against this night. Then lightning lit the land, and Ann backed deeper into the shadow of the fowl pen.

'Annie? Annie, love? Ann – ' Johnny's words lost anew as the heavens rolled, gathering power for a mighty thunderclap that shook the land. So close. So close tonight.

'He always hated my guts,' Jack said. 'Going to dob me into the cops back then. Get rid of me. Always too smart for his own bloody good. He saw me washing out the car boot the day I got back. "What did you have in there, Dad," he said. "A bloody mongrel dog," I said, and I spoke no lie.'

'It should have ended in Narrawee,' Ann whispered. 'Why bring the body up here?'

'Where better to hide the perverted bastard's bones than in the Abo's bone yard? I burnt him. I stripped my brother and fried him so Jesus Christ wouldn't recognise him.

'I knocked out every bloody tooth in his head and chucked them in the river. No-one would have looked for him out there – anyway he wasn't missing, was he?'

'It should have ended in Narrawee, Dad.'

'Should have beens don't count for much now, do they?' he said. 'The depraved bastard needed a bigger hole than we could cover up.' He sighed, and a hand reached for his pocket, felt for cigarette, lighter. 'I searched for his bloody ring. I searched the boot. I sifted the sand for hours, looking for it.'

'It was growing on a reed, like a black and gold flower,' she said softly. 'I picked it up to give to you, but my pocket was sewn up. Then Johnny saw it.'

'Ann. Ann.'

'Burton. Where are you child?'

'Annie. Annie, love.'

She wanted to go to David, wanted Johnny, wanted the sanity of the fat old man, and the rock of Bronny, but she was leaning against the rough timber of a fowl house, hiding from them, hiding with him.

Her legs were trembling; her knees were urging her to slide her back down the wall and sit on the cool earth, hide in the dark place of unknowing again, be the child again and make the world go away. She breathed deeply, rubbed her heel in the dust, trying to rub out the world, make them all go away, and give her time. David had come home too early. Johnny had not slept long. Their coming altered everything, confused everything.

Too weary for more words, her hands moved, made the easy words. Not easy for Ellie. Was she afraid of what she might see on those moving hands? Poor Ellie – a little golden girl turned into a wooden puppet by this man. Or had she turned herself into a puppet so she didn't have to know?

She sucked on air, moist now with rain, sucked deep, striving to draw strength from her roots, buried deep in this land. Warmth trickled over her eye. She wiped at it, felt the sticky blood, as his cigarette lighter flared, died, only feet away.

'Too long?' she signed. He didn't see her hands. 'It took too long,' she said. 'You promised me. May promised me that she'd come back. She promised me there would be one dark, and when it got light, she'd unlock the door. I waited through the dark and it got light, but she didn't come back. I waited all day.'

'A bloody man's world is ending and you want to talk broken promises.'

'Why didn't she open the door, Dad?'

'Bloody Jesus Christ,' he moaned as thunder rolled across the sky, circling Mallawindy, hemming it in. Hemming him in. No escape now. They were all out there, baying like a pack of dogs for his blood. Newspaper men everywhere. The game was up.

May knew this would happen one day. Only three months back she'd been at it again. 'Make the decision, Jack. We can't go on like this. Make the decision, and come home to me. Give me a husband I can be proud to have at my side.' But he was as determined as she. He'd let it go on, and on, and on. Maybe he got to like the game – liked the two sides of poor bloody Jack – the man his mother had planned for him to be, and the bastard his father had created.

And Ellie. He'd loved her once. Fell in love with a shower of golden sunshine, and a dream. But her hair had turned to straw, and the dream became a nightmare.

'I want to go home,' he said. 'I'm too old to fight, to old to play bloody games. I just want to go home.'

'One dark and one light, she said – then I fell and the dark came back.'

'Shit,' he said. 'Shut up about it. Shut up.'

Voices, more distant. A cow lowing. Truck on the road.

'Tell me, Dad.'

'Tell you more bloody lies.'

'Tell me the truth. All I want is the truth.'

'Everything took time. He was booked on the plane to Brisbane on the Wednesday and we had him loaded in the boot of my bloody car. We were running scared, running blind, making crazy plans as we went. He had to go to Brisbane, May said. It was our only chance. Get the bastard to Brisbane, then decide what came next.' His voice was low, beaten. He sucked on his cigarette, and it lit his features. She stared at the glow of a partial face, then his hand was at his side, the glow hidden behind his palm. 'I followed her car to the Toorak flat. She locked it in the garage, and we drove into the city, parked the bastard in a Collins Street carpark. May bought a wig at Myers and I got the moustache from a theatrical supplier. I put them on while she drove me to the airport. I pulled out the old actor, put him on stage again, and he had to give the performance of his bloody life.' Again he sucked on his cigarette. 'I stepped into that role, born for it, and by the Jesus, I made my brother into a better man.'

'Shush,' she warned, and he lowered his voice.

'I sneezed all the way to Brisbane, the mo tickling my nose. May drove my car to Daree.' Jack sucked on his cigarette, and Ann saw his mouth, his nose, in the orange glow. 'Shit,' he said. 'Shit.' He was back with his memories now, reliving that day as he had every day since Liza and Sam died, died in the cellar, died together.

'I hired a '65 Falcon Fairmont in Brisbane, booked Sam into his hotel, then headed back to Daree, my foot planted to the floor. We switched cars on the highway. May drove back to Toorak, and I took the perverted bastard to Mallawindy, out to Dead Man's Lane and burnt him. And I rejoiced in his burning. I danced in his smoke and watched him fry, and I rejoiced – that dirty defiling bastard.'

'Shush.'

'She was just a bloody loving little baby.'

'A greedy baby. You made her greedy. ''The old black cat had her kittens in the cellar, lass. Come down with Uncle Sam and see them. Uncle Sam has got a big bag of lollies for his special girl. Come into the cellar, lass, and I'll give you the biggest apple in the box. Who's going to come for a ride on the horse with Uncle Sam?'' '

369

'I knew what he was when he was bloody sixteen. I caught the bastard molesting young Barbara Dean, and I nearly killed him for it. "Don't tell," he said. "Don't tell, Dad." Snivelling bastard. Then the old man belted me, for hurting his boy. And I didn't say one bloody word. That's loyalty for you. And where did it get me? I curse myself every day of my life, for my misguided bloody loyalty. I could have become the old man's white-haired boy that day. Could have got the lot.'

'It doesn't work that way, Dad. Was I your white-haired girl when I told tales on Liza?' He made no reply, and she turned away, watching the wild display in the northern sky, and she waited, waited for the thunder clap to die. 'Why did May go along with it?'

'Why wouldn't she? He couldn't make it with a woman. Never could. She only married the bastard because she couldn't have me. She told me that on her wedding day. "But you'll be my brother, Jack, and we'll all live together in Camelot," she said. That's what she always called the old place. Her Camelot. A nineteen-year-old kid, tying herself to that piece of shit, and I couldn't stop her.'

Ann could hear his tears, and they still hurt her. Why? Love? He made it into a four-letter words. She breathed deeply, trying to get under the hurt, trying to hate him, then she sighed. 'I ate his apples that day, Dad, and I only ate the biggest ones. I measured them with my hands, and I ate them with the juice running down my chin. I found his bag of lollies and ate them for free. I counted minutes. I made up poems, then I built a staircase out of packing cases and I looked out the window, but May didn't come. I thought the night was coming back – that she'd forgotten me.'

'It was one thing to want the paedophile bastard dead, another one to do it. She was out of her mind when she left me in Daree, and she had to get the hire car back to Toorak and hide it. I thought she'd crack.' He sighed. 'But she didn't crack. She still had the sense to call in at the bakers for a bloody loaf of bread! It wasn't until she opened the cellar and you weren't there waiting for her that our plan went to hell. She panicked, called the cops, and sent me a telegram. '*Both girls missing. Sam in Brisbane.*' I didn't know what she was up to. I rang her from bloody Bessy's, but the cops were with her. She was bawling, saying, ''I have to contact Sam.''

'She was two steps ahead of me, but I caught on when she gave me the phone number. Then I sat on that phone for two hours, leaving my own bloody messages for Sam. I made sure I drove the poor bitches on reception stark raving mad before I slotted in a quick call from Gentleman Sam. Said he was calling from Goondiwindi. He picked up his messages. Told them to tell May when she rang back that he'd left for home and to send his bill and luggage to Narrawee.

'We'd formed this half baked plan to let Sam go missing in Brisbane. The flight record would prove that he'd flown up on the Wednesday, and I'd be in Mallawindy when the telegram came on Thursday. But it worked out better.'

'Better for you. It was two days. I was in that cellar for two days.'

'I knew you'd be in there. I got the bus down Friday morning and picked up the hire car at Toorak. It had the miles on the clock. Sam had been in Brisbane all right, and the poor bastard had driven day and night to get home too. He still had his hotel key. It was perfect. All I had to do for a few months was be in two places at once, and there were a lot of pubs in Melbourne where poor broken hearted Jack was wiping himself out while Sam played coppers' helper in his wig and mo. They kept asking, why he didn't fly back. He said Goondiwindi was half way home – .' Jack cut his sentence short. The voices were closer now. Too close.

'She's probably run for Ben's bridge. I'll go over to Bessy's.' Bronny ran by only metres away.

'I'll check my house.' Fletcher's voice. 'She may be over there.'

'We didn't plan for it to go on forever,' Jack kept his voice low. 'We were going to wait for a few years and send Sam to Central Australia, let him die in the desert. Then I took off when young Linda died, and May got used to having Sam around. Jack was dead, she said. Drowned, the poor bastard, gone for fish food. It might have been all right too – if not for your mother. She wouldn't let it alone. The coppers kept calling, asking bloody questions, so Jack came back to Chook-Shit County, and it was so bloody good to be able to hold his head up again, he wouldn't give it up. That kid is still down there, in Narrawee, little Barbara Dean, grown old now, but every time she looks at Sam, my gut turns to water.' He cried then, and his body shook with his tears.

'Shush,' she said. 'Shush.' Her hand reached out, but she drew it back.

'People don't forget. She won't ever forget. I won't wear that perverted bastard's name to my grave.'

'Shush, Dad.'

'That land belongs to Jack. It's been his for twenty-four bloody years and the poor God-forsaken bastard couldn't have it.'

'They'll hear you.'

'What's it matter? What's the bloody use of anything now?' he said, but his voice had lowered. 'What are you doing hiding here, anyway? Get out there and bay for my blood with the rest of the bastards.'

'I'm not hiding. Not any more.'

'You used to look at me with those bloody big eyes. Kill me with those bloody eyes. Why didn't you talk to me? I had enough guilt to carry around without that.'

'Everything got mixed up in the dark. The Ted Crow story. The bird was a man, but he wasn't a man. ''Red herring'', she said. ''We need a red herring, just in case.'' And May saw the crow in the garden. ''Old Ted Crow,'' she said. ''He's our red herring, Jack. He rode off into the forest on his motor bike.'''

'She drummed it into you. Sandy hair, about forty, came from

England. On a working holiday. He locked you in the cellar and took Liza for a ride.'

'Ann!'

'Annie.'

Her tears were trickling now, child tears, woman tears, all one and the same. So many tears. Too many. Where was all the water coming from?

'Sam was dead. I knew he was dead, but he wasn't dead, because he came to the hospital, so it must have been you who was dead, but you came to the hospital too. I didn't know what was dream and what was real. I didn't know what was sleep and what was wake, so I pushed it all away – pushed it back into the cellar where it belonged and waited for the dark to be over, but it wouldn't be over, because the dark had crept into my head.'

'Annie.'

'Burton.'

She sniffed, wiped at her eyes with her wrist. Rain was coming, thundering across the paddocks. Lightning was splitting the black sky.

'I went there that day to bot a few quid to get me home. I didn't know they'd taken you and Liza down there. You tried to keep me away from the bloody cellar, but I opened it and I caught the bastard at her. He hid behind her. He lifted her up as I swung at him. He hid behind that little girl, used her as a bloody shield. I didn't mean to hit her. I wouldn't have hurt her for all the world. He killed her. He killed her.'

Guilt is the brick wall that halts all progress, Annie Blue Dress.

She sighed too deeply, then she lied. She gave him absolution. 'It wasn't your fault, Dad. It wasn't your fault.'

Torchlight in the distance, scanning the land. Another was

coming from Bessy's side. Ann took a sliding step backwards as the first large raindrops hit. Thunder shook the world and the earth trembled beneath her feet. Black night. Black as the cellar. Only the glow of his cigarette. Intermittent orange glow. Highlighting, distorting his features, as he sucked the last from the weed before the rain killed it.

Our kaleidoscope man, Annie Blue Dress.

May screaming out her years of hate, cursing her husband's name. Sam tossing the lantern, trying to hide in the dark. Flickering light. Flickering madness. Too much fear. And screaming. Screaming that slowly died.

Uncle Sam was a very bad man, and a very bad man was he.

He cried for his May, but he couldn't get away, and he died with a 1,2,3.

I promise, Daddy, I won't ever say a word. I'm your good girl, Daddy.

He loved me best that day, Annie Blue Dress. Liza was dead, so he had to love me best in all the world. He held me, and he kissed me, and he cried. He knew he could trust me. Take him home. Let him go to May, wear his rose-tinted glasses. He's a good man when he's Sam. Let him be good, Annie Blue Dress.

'Annie, for Christ's sake answer me. I'm getting wet.'

'Ann. We're all here.' David's voice, strange against the pounding rain.

'Burton. Burton.' Her old knight in his tarnished armour was waddling in to do battle for his child, his comic-book silhouette looming large against the headlights of the Ford, where raindrops slanted down.

They were all here for her, for the one they knew as her reality. Not one for him. No-one ever for Jack Burton. Except May. Except little Annie.

Take him home, Annie Blue Dress. The storm is moving on.

'Go. Run along the river. Go, Dad, and never, never, never come back here.'

His hand, that smelt of soap and cigarette, touched her shoulder. Timid thing. Timid touch. She touched the hand with her own, just briefly, then she stepped away from it. 'Jack Burton has to die tonight. He took his gun, and ran into the forest. He was struck by lightning. He drowned, Dad. He's got to be dead.'

'It's too late, you loyal little fool,' he said. 'It's too bloody late now.'

'Only if we let it be too late. Run, Dad. Go out to Dead Man's Lane and I'll find you there. I promise you. I promise I'll get you home to Narrawee. Run, Dad. Run. Run. Run.'

epilogue

~

Mallawindy: Named for a man who cut his canoe from the giant river gums and buried his dead in the sand dunes.

Mallawindy: Too far north of Melbourne, too far west of Sydney, too far off the beaten track to ever grow.

The river cut its course around the town, attempting to bypass it as it hurried on to the shade of the gum forests, hurried on to where the air was thick with bees, and the scent of eucalypt and honey strong. Only there it slowed its pace and took the time to glance behind.

Did it turn to find a simple pathway through this land, or was it an obstreperous thing in the dreamtime, fighting the will of the gods who charted its course? Old motives were long forgotten, for once having turned to face the gold dust of a newly risen day, the river lost its way, drunk on eucalypt and silence.

It weaved, it coiled, it narrowed between tall clay banks. It turned back on itself, but a river cannot dally long, time sent it on its way, leaving in its wake a broken silver ring, that wed it forever to Mallawindy.

Mallawindy: A small scar on the sunburnt skin of the land.

At the edge of town, set well back from the highway, a mud brick farmhouse stood taller than its neighbours. Its chimney leaned to the west, as if paying homage to the setting sun, and the sun given its due, did not shine too hard upon the painted roof. But on the last Sunday in September, bedlam reigned beneath it. A tiny infant's wail. And laughter. Too much laughter, and too many voices.

They had all come home for Ellie's birthday, and the house too small, carpets too new, rooms built to suit another era, did not suit them. It wasn't home. Not quite. They didn't feel at home with the ornate ceilings and the curtained windows, the papered walls and the odour of flowering vines.

In the late afternoon they wandered down to the clumsy construction they called Ben's Bridge, and like a herd of cows, strung out at milking time, they ambled across it in twos and threes.

'It's quite safe, loves. I use it twice a day,' Ellie said.

'Not too safe if we meet Bessy's bull in the middle,' Bronwyn replied, and laughter welled, echoed.

The river carried sound.

Ann crossed over slowly, carefully, the new child held close to her breast – too close. David walked behind her, watching each step she took across the uneven planks. He'd wanted to drive around. Be safe. Stay safe. Perhaps one day, this fear will pass, he thought, but it was only a fleeting thought.

Ben brought up the rear with Malcolm, who waddled over rough ground, his walking stick prodding. Shy Ben, quiet Ben. He hadn't rowed his boat to China, but he had seen Brisbane before he saw a newspaper – and if Brisbane was an example of the seething world outside of Mallawindy, then others could have it.

The film he'd bought for his trip north, was a thirty-six. He'd only taken twenty-eight, and twelve of those today. Eight of the tiny boy who had Annie's eyes, and her mop of black hair. Benjamin John, already named, Little Ben.

Camera at the ready, Ben waited until the Burtons were spread across his bridge, then before Malcolm could place his considerable weight upon it, he called to them.

'Okay. Hold it there.' He lined them up in his viewfinder, calling instructions, and they did as they were bid; they posed for Ben.

The priest who came home, had packed his vows and black suit away. Johnny Burton, the man with the shared secret, his hands, big hands, capable hands, were coloured by hard labour and red soil. One rested on Ellie's shoulder.

'In him I have the best of Jack,' Ellie told the mourners at the memorial service. 'Jack will never be dead while Johnny is alive,' she said to May, who came alone that day.

She and Sam had moved permanently back to Narrawee, but poor Sam was down with the flu. He had sent his condolences and a fine card. *'He's at peace at last, Ellie. Be happy for him. Love as always, Samuel.'*

'Move in, Bron. I'm cutting half of you off,' Ben yelled, and Bronwyn leaned to the side, waving her cigarette as she blew a perfect smoke ring at the photographer.

'Pull the blanket back a bit, Annie. I can't see his face.'

Ann loosened her grasp, released a tiny hand, a tiny face, as she flashed a smile she saved for the camera. Ben would never see that she feared his bridge, and wanted her small burden safe on the other side. Hadn't she helped him plant his trees? Hadn't she helped him watch them grow?

And the camera clicked.

It trapped the Burtons, trapped the river, trapped the forest, and the day.

Such a fine day. The sun was setting behind them, the old Burton house waiting, eager for their noise to come and fill the empty rooms.

Oh, Lord, such peace in this land tonight.